FANTASIES

My Favourite Mistake by Stephanie Bond

When Denise Cooke married Redford DeMoss in a chapel in Vegas, she knew it was a mistake. So, despite an *incredible* honeymoon, she filed for divorce. Little did she realise that Redford would turn out to be her true Valentine…

&

Valentine Vendetta by Sharon Kendrick

Fran was out for revenge against devastatingly attractive Sam Lockhart – the man who'd broken her best friend's heart. But as Fran worked with Sam on his charity ball, Fran's new Valentine wish was to have Sam all to herself!

Read one novel then flip the book and read the other.

And don't miss our romantic, hot tips for your own Valentine's Evening!

Stephanie Bond was seven years deep into a systems engineering career and pursuing an MBA at night when an instructor remarked that she had a flair for writing and suggested that she submit to academic journals. But Stephanie, a voracious reader, was only interested in writing fiction – more specifically, romantic fiction. Upon completing her master's degree, she started writing a romance novel in her spare time. Two years later in 1995 she sold her first book, a romantic comedy. In 1997, with ten sales under her belt to two publishers, Stephanie left her corporate job to write full-time. Stephanie lives in Atlanta, Georgia.

Valentine
FANTASIES

STEPHANIE BOND &
SHARON KENDRICK

*M&B™ and M&B™ with the Rose Device
are trademarks of the publisher.*

*First published in Great Britain 2006
by Harlequin Mills & Boon Limited, Eton House,
18-24 Paradise Road, Richmond, Surrey TW9 1SR*

VALENTINE FANTASIES © by Harlequin Books SA 2006

My Favourite Mistake and *Valentine Vendetta* were first published
by Harlequin Mills & Boon Limited in separate, single volumes.

My Favourite Mistake © Stephanie Bond 2005
Valentine Vendetta © Sharon Kendrick 1999

ISBN 0 263 84981 3

109-0206

*Printed and bound in Spain
by Litografia Rosés S.A., Barcelona*

MY FAVOURITE MISTAKE

STEPHANIE BOND

This book is dedicated to the memory of
Cheryl Ann Porter, a sister Mills & Boon writer
who could light up the room with her smile
and leave your ribs aching from laughing.
You will be missed, Cheryl.

1

"THIS IS A MISTAKE," I said, suddenly panicked by the horde of women pushing at me from all sides. In the minutes just prior to Filene's Basement "running of the brides," the crowd was getting hostile, all elbows and bared teeth.

Next to me, my friend Cindy turned her head and scowled. "Denise Cooke, you can't back out now—I'm counting on you!" The normally demure Cindy Hamilton shoved a woman standing next to her to make room to reach into her shoulder bag. "Here, put on this headband so we can spot each other once we get in there."

I sighed and reached for the neon pink headband. It wasn't as if I could look more ridiculous—I was already freezing and humiliated standing there in my yoga leotard (the Web-site-recommended uniform for trying on bridal gowns in the aisles). February in New York did not lend itself to leotards—I was numb from my V-neck down. "This is a lot of trouble for a discounted wedding gown when you're not even engaged," I grumbled.

"This was your idea, Miss Penny Pincher," Cindy reminded me.

That was true. I was helping Cindy with her Positive Thinking 101 class, and her assignment was to prepare for an event with the idea being that it would then become a self-fulfilling prophecy. Since Cindy wanted to be married more than anything else in the world, she'd decided to buy a wedding gown. Cheapskate that I am (an investment broker-slash-financial planner, actually), I had suggested Filene's biannual bridal event for a good deal.

So here we were at seven-thirty on a cold Saturday morning, poised with oh, about eight or nine hundred other freezing leotard-clad women, waiting for the doors of Filene's to be hurled open. There were a few identifiable teams with members wearing identical hats or T-shirts. Like me, they were friends who had been commandeered to grab as many dresses as possible from the clearance racks, thereby increasing the odds of the bride-to-be getting a gown she wanted.

"Remember," Cindy said, her eyes as serious as an NFL coach dispensing plays, "strapless or spaghetti straps, with a princess waistline—white is my first choice, but I'm willing to go as far left as light taupe. I need a size ten, but I can work with a twelve."

I nodded curtly. "Got it."

"If you find a gown that might work, put it on so no one can grab it out of your hands."

I swallowed and nodded again, suddenly apprehensive.

"And who knows," Cindy added with a grin. "You might find a dress that you'll want to keep for yourself."

I frowned. "Barry and I haven't even talked about getting married."

"Good grief, you've been dating for two years—he's going to propose someday, and then you'll already have a dress. It's *practical*."

I started to say it was presumptuous, then remembered why Cindy was there and clamped my mouth shut. Barry was…great, but I couldn't see myself getting married…again.

Like every time I remembered my last-minute and short-lived Las Vegas marriage to Sergeant Redford DeMoss, I got a sick feeling in my stomach. My first marriage was one of those events in my life that I wanted to expunge from my memory, like a stupid teenage stunt…except I hadn't been a stupid teenager—I had been a stupid adult. In the three years since my marriage to and subsequent annulment from Redford, I had managed to block the incident from my mind for the most part. But since two of my best friends, Jacki and Kenzie, had recently gotten married and my last single friend, Cindy, seemed hell-bent on doing the same, the memories of my incredible wedding night had been popping into my head at the strangest moments—I couldn't seem to outrun them.

Someone behind me stepped on my heel, scraping it raw. I winced, not sure how I was going to outrun this dogged bunch, either.

"They're opening the doors," Cindy announced excitedly.

A cheer rose from the crowd and everyone lurched forward collectively. The two security guards unlocking the doors looked as frightened as I felt. When the doors were flung open, self-preservation kicked in—I had to match the pace of the crowd or be trampled. I squeezed through the double doors and ran for the escalator, my heart pounding in my chest. The escalator was instantly jammed, and everyone still clambered upward, some screaming as if we were all vying for front row seats at a rock concert. At the top of the escalator, we spilled onto the second floor where several freestanding racks bulged with pouf dresses. I had no idea where Cindy was and I hesitated, not sure where to begin.

Women stampeded by me in a blur and began yanking dresses by the armfuls from the rack. It was a locust swarm. I realized I was going to miss out if I didn't move quickly. Cindy's order of "strapless or spaghetti straps" vanished in the wake of the disappearing gowns. I grabbed whatever I could get my hands on, draping the gowns over my shoulders until I could barely see or hear past the mounds of rustling fabric.

Within one minute, the racks had been picked clean. As if on cue, everyone began trying on dresses where they stood, stripping to their underwear and in some cases, even further, heedless of the male salesclerks and security guards milling about. Keeping an eye out for a neon pink head-band, I sorted through my spoils like a lion pro-tecting its kill.

I had managed to snare a white satin gown with cap sleeves, size fourteen; an off-white long-sleeved lacy number with a straight skirt, size twenty; a pinkish Gibson-girl design with bishop sleeves, size twelve; a dark beige high-neck gown with an embroidered bodice, size four; and a creamy halter-style gown with a pearl-studded skirt, size ten. My shoulders fell in disappointment—I had struck out for Cindy.

Although…the halter-style gown was actually quite nice. I peered at the designer label and my eye-brows shot up—*really* nice. Then I peered at the price tag and my eyebrows practically flew off my head—a $2000 gown reduced to $249? Cindy would be crazy not to buy this dress, even if it wasn't ex-actly what she was looking for. While juggling the other gowns, I stepped into the halter dress and twisted to zip it up in the back, then smoothed a hand over the skirt, reveling in the nubby texture of the seed pearls. Longing welled in my heart, surprising me, because I was the most no-nonsense person I knew—a dress couldn't possibly have any power over me.

"That's perfect on you," said a salesclerk next to me.

"Oh, I'm helping a friend of mine," I replied quickly.

"Pity," the woman said, nodding toward a mir-rored column a few feet away.

I glanced around, looking for Cindy in the frenzied mob, then reasoned I might as well walk past the mirror on my way to find her. I moseyed over and stopped dead in my tracks.

Even over the leotard the dress was dazzling, and for a few seconds, I *felt* dazzling—my makeup-free face and dark blond, disheveled ponytail notwithstanding. For my quickie Vegas wedding, I'd worn a "What Happens Here, Stays Here" T-shirt, which in hindsight, had been a big red flag to my state of mind. I'd told myself a hundred times that it wouldn't have mattered if Redford and I had been married in a lavish church ceremony with all the trimmings; but now, looking at myself in the mirror wearing this glorious gown, I had to admit that the right wardrobe would have lent a touch of sophistication to the surreal occasion.

If I ever married again, I would wear this dress… or something like it.

"Do you have any size sixteens?" a girl yelled in my face. "I need a size sixteen!"

I shook my head, then realized that all around me, women were bartering unwanted gowns, some hoisting signs heralding their size. I relinquished the size four to a peanut-sized woman, and during the hand-off, the rest of my bounty was ripped from my arms by circling gown-vultures. I was still reeling when Cindy skidded to a stop in front of me.

"There you are!" she shrieked over the melee. "I found my dress!"

Indeed, over her leotard she wore a sweet, strapless white satin gown with a princess waistline. Laughing like a child, she twirled, sending the full skirt billowing around her.

"It's perfect," I agreed. The dress *was* perfect for Cindy's cherubic beauty, but I felt a pang of sadness as I glanced down at the halter dress I wore…it would have to be sacrificed to the vortex of bargain-hunting brides, which had, if anything, increased in intensity as latecomers descended on the leftovers and another round of frantic stealing and swapping ensued.

Cindy stopped twirling and stared at me. "Wow, that dress looks awesome on you."

I flushed. "I was just trying it on…for you. It was the closest thing I could find."

Cindy's blue eyes bugged. "You should keep it, Denise. If Barry got a look at you in that dress, he'd fall on his knees and beg you to marry him."

I laughed. "Right." Barry had never been on his knees in my presence—to propose or do anything else—but I had to admit, I was tempted.

A flushed, middle-aged woman stopped and looked me up and down. "Are you going to keep that dress?" Without waiting for an answer, she proceeded to pick up the fabric of the skirt to scrutinize the pearls.

A proprietary feeling came over and I firmly removed her hand from my—er, *the* dress. "I haven't decided."

The woman glared at my bare left hand. "My daughter Sylvie already has a wedding date."

I frowned. "So?"

"So," the woman snapped, "what good will that dress do you hanging in your closet?"

She was testy, but she had a very good point, especially considering the fact that I'd been lamenting only yesterday how small my closet was. Still, what business was it of hers if the dress hung in my cramped closet until it dry-rotted? (A distinct possibility.)

Cindy stepped up and crossed her arms. "My friend is going to get married again someday." Cindy still harbored lingering guilt over my impromptu marriage—she blamed herself for getting the flu and leaving me to spend Christmas and New Year's Eve in Las Vegas by myself. Otherwise, I might not have fallen under Redford's illicit spell.

"Again? Someday?" The lady snorted and her body language clearly said that women who didn't get it right the first time around didn't deserve a production the second time around. Another good point. I *had* blown it the first time I'd walked down the aisle—well, okay, to be morbidly honest I hadn't "walked down the aisle." I was married in a chapel drive-through, which, in my defense, had seemed the most economical route at the time.

My groom, who I barely knew, was a gorgeous officer on leave. And the spontaneous marriage had been prompted by intense physical chemistry (Redford was rather spectacularly endowed), and perhaps a bit of misplaced patriotism that I had mistaken for love. It was one of the oldest clichés in the book—an observation which, I realized ruefully, was also a cliché. The biggest mistake of my life was redundant. Ridiculously, tears pooled in my eyes.

Cindy gaped at me. I never cried…*ever.*

"There, there," the older woman said, and actually patted my arm. "You'll feel better once you take off that dress."

Cindy drew herself up. "Keep moving, lady—the dress is ours."

The woman huffed and stalked away, head pivoting, presumably looking for other women she could provoke to tears.

Mortified, I blinked like mad to rid my eyes of the moisture. "I don't know…what happened."

"Never mind," Cindy said in her best-friend voice. "Let's go pay for our dresses."

I shook my head. "I can't buy a wedding dress, Cindy."

"Of course you can…everyone knows you have a fortune squirreled away from clipped coupons and rebates."

I had a reputation among my friends for being, shall I say, "thrifty." "I don't mean I can't afford it. I mean I…I don't think I'll ever get married…again." But if that were true, why hadn't I simply handed over the dress to the pushy woman?

Cindy shrugged. "Fine. If you still feel that way

in six months, sell the dress on eBay. Knowing you, you'll probably make money on it."

I bit my lower lip. Cindy was right—even if I took the dress home, no one was going to stick a gun to my head and make me get married. Barry seemed to be as leery of walking down the aisle as I was. Although if one day Barry got the urge…

I almost laughed out loud—Barry wasn't the "urge getting" kind of guy. He was just as methodical and nonsensical as I was, which explained how we had contentedly dated off and on for the past two years without the drama that most couples endure. I was lucky. Luck-*eee.*

"It's a great deal," Cindy urged in a singsongy voice.

I looked at the price tag and wavered at the sight of the red slash through the original price of $2000 and replaced with the hastily-scrawled $249. I loved red slashes. It's a great deal. And I probably *could* turn around and sell the dress on eBay for a profit. In fact, I might make enough to surprise Barry with plane tickets for a vacation. He'd been wanting to go to Vegas, and I'd been resistant, for reasons that now seem childish…

As childish as me standing here obsessing about buying a gown simply because it resurrected too many memories…? Memories a wedding dress might exorcise…?

"Okay," I said impulsively. "I'll take it."

Cindy clapped her hands, then stopped, as if she

were afraid that her celebrating would change my mind, and herded me toward the checkout counter.

Only later, when a gushing salesclerk handed me the gown, bagged and paid for, was I seized by a sudden, unnerving thought:

What if Cindy's "self-fulfilling prophecy" experiment rubbed off on *me?*

2

THE WHOLE "self-fulfilling prophecy" thing was still nagging at me when I got home and I realized I would have to get rid of something in order to make room for my impulsive purchase. Buyer's remorse struck me hard and I cursed my weakness for a good buy. To punish myself, I laid out the brown suede fringed coat I had splurged on last spring but rarely wore, plus a pair of rivet-studded jeans and a white embroidered shirt that had seemed exotic in the store, but smacked of a costume when I stood before the full-length mirror in my bathroom. I had never worked up the nerve to wear the outfit. As much as I loved the pieces, it seemed unlikely that the urban Western look was going to come back in style any-time soon, and if it did, I obviously couldn't carry it off. But my friend Kenzie could, and since she now lived part-time on a farm in upstate New York, she would probably find a way to wear them and look smashing.

Looking for other things that Kenzie might wear, I unearthed a sweater with running horses on it that

Redford had given me and, after a moment of sentimental indecision, added it to the giveaway bag, as well. Then I hung the wedding gown in the front of the closet because it was the only place the skirt could hang unimpeded by bulging shoe racks.

The phone rang, and I snatched up the handset, wondering who it could be on Saturday afternoon. (I was too cheap to pay for caller ID on my landline phone.) "Hello."

"Hey," Barry said, his voice low and casual. "What are you doing?"

I dropped onto my queen-size bed whose headboard still smelled faintly of woodsmoke two years after the fire sale at which I'd bought it. "Just cleaning out my closet."

"I have good news," he said in a way that made me think that if I'd said, "I just bought a wedding gown," he wouldn't even have noticed.

I worked my mouth from side to side. "What?"

"I just passed Ellen in the hall—you really bowled her over at lunch yesterday."

I sat up, interested. Barry was a producer for one of New York City's local TV stations, and Ellen Brant was the station manager. Barry had referred her to me for financial advice on her divorce. Over lunch I had listened while she had told me the entire sordid story about her cheating husband, while she downed four eighteen-dollar martinis. "But he was a rich sonofabitch," she'd slurred. "And now I have an effing—" (I'm paraphrasing) "—boatload of money to invest."

When she'd told me the amount of money she was talking about, it was more like an effing *yacht*-load (although at the end of the evening she hadn't made a move to pay the slightly obscene bar bill). Grey Goose vodka had bowled her over. I honestly didn't think she'd remember my name...or even my sex, for that matter.

I wet my lips carefully, trying to keep my excitement at bay. "Do you think she'll open an account at Trayser Brothers?"

"I'm almost sure of it. You're still coming to the honors dinner tonight, aren't you?"

"Of course I am. I wouldn't miss seeing you get your award."

"I might not win," he chided.

I *pshawed,* supportive girlfriend that I was.

"Ellen will be there. I'll try to pull her aside and feel her out," he promised.

I was flattered—Barry had never been keenly interested in my profession, but then most people were vaguely suspicious of investment-types, as if we hoarded all the moneymaking secrets for ourselves, while collectively laughing at everyone who trusted us. (Not true—I was currently poor and working toward precisely what I advised all my clients to do: buy your apartment sooner rather than later.) But, Ellen's boatload of money notwithstanding, I felt obligated to point out the potential pitfalls of advising my boyfriend's boss on financial matters. "Barry, you know I appreciate the referral, but..."

"But what?"

"Well, Ellen *is* your boss. I don't want this to be a conflict of interest for you."

He gave a little laugh. "Gee, Denise, it's not as if you and I are married."

Ouch. I glanced at the wedding gown, barely contained by the closet, and my face flamed. "I know, but we're…involved."

"Trust me—it won't be an issue. In fact, Ellen will be indebted to me for introducing her to you. This could turn out great for both of us."

"Okay," I said cheerfully, pushing aside my reservations.

So help me, dollar signs were dancing behind my eyelids. I could picture the look on old Mr. Trayser's face when I announced in the Monday morning staff meeting that I'd just landed an eight-figure account. "Partner" didn't seem as far-fetched as it had last week…or at least an office with a window.

"What's the dress code for this evening?"

He made a rueful noise. "Dressy. And Ellen is a bit of a clotheshorse. I'm not saying it'll make a difference…"

"But it might," I finished, my cheeks warming when I remembered the woman's critical glance over my aged navy suit and serviceable pumps yesterday. I wasn't exactly famous for my style—my *most* trendy clothes were season-old steals from designer outlets. I was more of an off-the-rack kind of girl, and I didn't relish running up my credit card for a one-night outfit. But drastic times called for plastic measures. "I'll find something nice," I promised.

"I know you'll make me look good."

I blinked—Barry considered me a reflection on him? That was serious couple-stuff…wasn't it? I straightened with pride at his compliment.

"I'll pick you up at seven."

"Great," I said. "Oh, and thanks…Barry…for the recommendation." We had never quite graduated to pet names and as tempted as I was to say "sweetie" or "hon," I decided that while he was hooking me up with a revenue stream with his boss, this might not be the best time to start getting gushy.

"Anything for you," he said, then hung up.

I smiled, but when I disconnected the phone, panic immediately set in—I had two pimples from last week's peanut M&M's binge, and my nails were a wreck. It would be next to impossible to get a manicure at the last minute on Saturday.

I jumped up and whirled into action. After a shower, I dialed the cell phone of my friend Kenzie Mansfield Long, who was the most stylish person I knew; although I wasn't sure if she'd have service in the rural area of the state where she lived on weekends.

"Hello?" she sang into the receiver.

"Hi, it's Denise. I was taking a chance on reaching you—you have service now?"

"A tower just went up on the next ridge. Jar Hollow officially has cellular service."

"Did Sam arrange that just for you?" I asked with

a laugh. Her doting veterinarian husband was doing everything in his power to make country living more bearable for his city-bred wife, à la Lisa in *Green Acres*.

"The service isn't just for me," Kenzie protested. "It's for the entire town. And it helps me and Sam to stay in touch when we're apart during the week."

At the mischievous note in my friend's voice, I had the feeling that phone sex supplemented the couple's seemingly insatiable lust for each other. Kenzie's— or should I say *Sam's*—homemade dildo cast from the real, um, *thing* was infamous among our circle of friends. After seeing it, I could barely make eye contact with the man. In fact, it was that darn dildo that had resurrected my fantasies of Redford. He had been an amazing specimen of virility and, um...dimension.

Okay, the man was hung like a stallion...not that I'd ever seen a stallion's penis, but word on the street was that the equine species was gifted in that department. The fact that Redford's family in Kentucky was in the horse business had burned the association even deeper into my depraved brain.

No, I wasn't jealous of Kenzie's relationship with Sam...most of the time. I had known great, mind-blowing lust with Redford, but our relationship had burned out as quickly as a cheap candle. Barry, on the other hand, was no dynamo in bed, but he had staying power in other areas.

His IRA account was a whopper.

"How was the 'running of the brides'?" Kenzie

asked, breaking into my strange musings. "Did Cindy find a gown?"

"Yes," I said, then decided to 'fess up before Cindy told on me. "And I, um, bought a gown, too."

There was silence on the other end, then, "Barry *proposed?*"

"No," I said quickly, feeling like an idiot. "But I thought, you know, if ever....well...the dress was dirt cheap," I finished lamely.

"Ah," Kenzie said. "A bargain—now I understand. Well, one of these days, Barry is bound to come around. Valentine's Day is just around the corner, you know."

"Subject change. I called because I have a style emergency." I explained about the honors dinner and my desire to wow Ellen Brant and her pocketbook with my stunning sense of fashion. "Any suggestions?"

"You could wear your wedding gown," Kenzie said, then cracked up laughing.

"I'm hanging up."

"I'm *kidding.* Gee, lighten up." Then she snapped her fingers. "I saw the cutest striped dress in the window of Benderlee's, and I remember thinking it would look smashing on you."

"Will it smash the credit line on my VISA card?"

"Probably, but think of it as an investment." She laughed. "Knowing you, you'll think of a way to write the dress off on your taxes as a business expense."

"Ha, ha."

"I'm not kidding— I can't believe how much Sam

and I are getting back on our taxes this year, thanks to you. If you ever decide to go into tax preparation, I want to invest."

I laughed. "Thanks."

"And go to Nordstrom's for shoes. Ask for Lito, tell him I sent you."

My shoulders fell. "Okay."

"And tell me you're not going to wear your hair in a ponytail."

I squinted. "I'm not going to wear my hair in a ponytail?"

"For goodness' sake, Denise, loosen up. Your ponytail is so tight, it's a wonder you don't have an aneurysm."

My friends were good at reminding me that I was a tight ass. And a tight*wad*. "I'm loose," I argued, rolling my shoulders in my best imitation of a "groove"—until my neck popped painfully. I grimaced—was it possible to break your own neck?

"Wear your hair down and buy a pair of chandelier earrings."

"You think?"

"I was under the impression that you called for my advice."

"I did."

"You want this woman's business, don't you?"

"Yes."

"Then you gotta do what you gotta do."

I sighed. "You're right."

"So…Barry set you up to do business with his

boss," she said in a singsongy tone. "Maybe it's a good thing you bought that wedding gown. It sounds like he's thinking long-term."

I glanced at the dress I had so foolishly purchased and gave a nervous little laugh. "Or maybe he's trying to suck up to his boss."

"Hmm. Sounds like someone needs to take a lesson from Cindy in positive thinking."

I thanked Kenzie for her help, then hung up with a cleansing exhale. Kenzie was right—I should be grateful for the opportunity that Barry had made for me, instead of questioning his motives. I was letting my frustration with our lackluster sex life color other aspects of our relationship. It was embarrassing, really—I was an intelligent woman. I had proof that elements other than sex were more important to a successful long-term, um…association. Financial compatibility, for instance. Sex waned over time. But dividend reinvestment stock plans were forever.

A sudden thought prompted me to pick up the phone and order two plane tickets to Las Vegas for a long weekend as a Valentine's Day surprise for Barry. When I hung up, I heaved a sigh, feeling much better. Then I slanted a frown toward my bedroom.

I was suffering from a bad case of the all-overs, and the culprit was taking up too much room in my closet. I was already letting that ridiculous wedding gown interfere with our relationship, and for no good reason. Barry needn't ever know what I'd done. To-morrow I'd put that sucker on eBay and be rid of it for good.

Er—the dress, not Barry.

3

KENZIE WAS RIGHT—the dress in Benderlee's window looked better on me than the average frock, so I bought it despite the breathtaking price. And Lito at Nordstrom's had hooked me up with a pair of shoes with an equally stunning price tag. If I wore them every day for the rest of my life, I might get my money's worth out of them. Throwing caution to the wind, I had also bought a chic gray wool coat. I left my hair long and loose, which made me feel a little unkempt, but I have to admit I was feeling rather spiffy when Barry arrived. I opened the door with a coy smile.

He looked polished and professional in a navy suit, striped tie, not a pale blond hair out of place. "Ready to go?" he asked, then pointed to his watch. "Traffic is a nightmare."

My smile slipped. "I…yes."

"Good, because I'd hate to be late."

Barry wasn't the most attentive man I'd ever known, but tonight he seemed unusually preoccupied. Then I realized he was probably more anxious about the award for which he'd been nominated than he wanted to let on. Indeed, on the drive to the hotel, he checked his watch at least a hundred times, his expression pinched. And he seemed to be coming down with a cold since he sneezed several times. To see my normally calm, collected boyfriend so fidgety moved me. I reached over to squeeze his hand. "Relax. I hope you have a thank-you speech prepared."

He smiled sheepishly. "I made a few notes...just in case."

I instantly forgave him for not noticing how fabulous I looked. Besides, I reminded myself, I had dressed for Ellen Brant, and as luck would have it, we were seated at her table for the awards ceremony. In fact, by some bizarre shuffling of bodies and chairs, she wound up sitting between us. The woman was so cosmopolitan, even in my new clothes I felt gauche. I raised my finger for a nervous nibble on my nail, and tasted the bitter tang of fresh nail polish...a do-it-myself manicure was the best I could manage under the circumstances.

"Denise, your dress is divine," she murmured over her martini glass.

"Thank you," I said, taking my finger out of my mouth and sitting up straighter.

"She's smart *and* fashionable," Ellen said to Barry for my benefit. "I like this girl."

"She's dependable, too," Barry said. "And loyal."

I managed to conceal my surprise at his bizarre statement. Until I realized that to Ellen, recently betrayed by her husband, loyalty was essential. So on cue, I nodded like a puppy dog.

Ellen pursed her collagen-plumped lips. "Denise, why don't you call me next week and we'll go over the paperwork for that investment account."

"Okay," I said in a voice that belied my excitement. If Ellen opened an account at Trayser Brothers, I'd be able to pay off my outfit *and* buy my apartment. Plus a new bed that didn't reek of woodsmoke. A closet organization system. Caller ID.

I could scarcely eat I was so wound up. I tried to contribute to the conversation, but Ellen and Barry were soon absorbed in television-speak, and I thought it best not to intrude. Barry was, after all, hoping for a promotion, and Ellen would drive that decision. Instead, I chatted with other people seated at the table, spurred to a higher degree of socialization than usual by the open bar. Happily, the evening was topped off by a slightly tipsy Ellen presenting Barry with the award for excellence in producing that was acknowledged in the industry as a precursor to the Emmy.

For his part, Barry was the most excited I'd ever seen him—which was no compliment to me, I realized suddenly. But I postponed an untimely (and uncomfortable) analysis of our love life by clapping wildly. I told myself it was okay that he didn't name me personally in his thank-you speech, a fact that he seemed truly distressed over later when we were in the car.

"I forgot my notes and I went completely blank," he said in the semi-darkness, his hands on the steering wheel at the ten and two positions—he was a fastidious driver. "I'm sorry, Denise. You're the one who's had to put up with my long hours and my traveling."

"It's fine," I murmured. "I'm just so proud of you. And I know Ellen is impressed."

He made a dismissive noise, but was clearly pleased. Then he winced. "Oh, by the way, Ellen asked me tonight to be in L.A. Monday morning."

My good mood wedged in my throat. His travel to the West Coast had become more frequent in the past couple of months—in the wee hours of the morning, I wondered if something other than work drew him there. After all, if I wasn't thrilled with our sex life, he probably wasn't, either. "How long will you be gone?"

"Two weeks, maybe three."

"That's almost a month," I said, hating the way I sounded—horny.

"No, it isn't," he said with a practicality that did not put me at ease.

"You'll miss Valentine's Day."

He looked apologetic. "I'm sorry, Denise. Right now I have to focus on this promotion. I'll make it up to you, I promise."

"Want to spend the night?" I asked, not caring that I was being transparent.

He looked over at me and laughed. "Sure."

I smiled all the way home, determined that tonight

Barry and I would have great, boisterous sex. I might even pull out some of the tricks that Redford had taught me that I'd never shared with anyone else. I had shaved my legs to get ready for the dinner, so nothing was holding me back.

Unfortunately, we drove straight into a traffic jam in midtown that left us in gridlock. After thirty minutes had passed with no movement, I began to dwell on Barry's comment that I was dependable...and loyal. He made me sound like a cocker spaniel.

I studied his profile, noting how preoccupied he was, and realized abruptly that we had fallen into a serious rut. No wonder we'd never talked about marriage—we rarely saw each other and we rarely had sex.

For all intents and purposes, we were *already* married.

Feeling rebellious, I ran my fingers through my loose hair and whispered, "We could have sex right here."

Barry looked over at me with a shocked expression, then laughed nervously and gestured to the cars around his silver Lexus. "Are you crazy? We'd be arrested for indecent exposure. A stunt like that would mean my job, Denise."

I pulled back, humiliated at my own behavior. He was right, of course. The network's top female anchor had gone out drinking one night and performed a topless dance at a bar where at least one handheld video camera had been rolling, and everyone had been put on notice. Barry couldn't jeopardize his job just because I was feeling neglected. So we listened to National Public Radio and chatted about the evening.

"You seemed to be having a good time talking to everyone," Barry said. "Everyone thought you were great. Everyone loves you, Denise."

Something in his voice made me turn my head to look at him in the semi-darkness. He'd spoken with a sort of wistfulness when he'd said "everyone loves you," as if everyone else saw something he didn't. I waited for clarification, but Barry simply scanned the traffic, tapping his finger on the steering wheel to a jazzy song floating from the speakers.

I was imagining things. Barry loved me. He hadn't changed—I had. More specifically, that stupid wedding dress had made me paranoid.

And reflective.

Because the wedding dress had made me confront the possibility of marrying Barry…was it something I wanted? And if not, then what was the purpose of our being together? Companionship? An occasional sexual release? Were we merely a pit stop for each other on the way to…something else? I was suddenly seized by the feeling that I was looking at someone I'd known for years. Yet…did I really know him?

In hindsight, I'd known little about Redford when I'd married him—beyond his sexual prowess. A sudden stab of desire struck my midsection, but I closed my eyes against it.

During those few days with Redford in Las Vegas, I had been a different person, wanton and hedonistic…a bona fide nymphomaniac. I don't know what had come over me…okay, admittedly, *Redford* had come over me a few times, but I digress. My parents—especially my mother—would be appalled if they knew how I had behaved during that time, and my girlfriends would be shocked. I could scarcely think of it myself without being overcome with shame—nice girls didn't do the things I'd done with Redford. Especially after knowing the man for mere hours.

At the time, I'd thought that Redford DeMoss, with his chiseled good looks, military manners and tantric sex sessions was the most exotic creature I'd ever encountered. I'd only dated city boys who were competitive and frenzied. Redford's easy confidence and sexual aura had literally knocked me off my feet. Only later, after I'd returned to New York, did I admit to myself that everything that came out of his sensual mouth—words about down-home cookin', home-grown lovin' and small-town livin'—came straight out of a country song. He'd been playing a part—hell, we both had. It was a love-at-first-sight fantasy. We'd had no business getting married.

"Denise?"

I blinked myself back to the present and stared at Barry, who was staring at me. "Huh?"

He frowned and rubbed one of his eyes. "I asked if I left any of my allergy medicine at your place. If not, maybe we should backtrack to my apartment."

While I had been winding down memory lane, the traffic had begun to unravel. I was suddenly eager to get home—to my cozy apartment, not to Barry's sterile condo. "You left your toiletry bag at my place when you came back from L.A. Are your allergies acting up?"

"Yeah," he said, nodding toward my new coat. "I think it's the wool."

"Oh. Sorry."

"No problem," he said. "By the way, I noticed your new outfit. Good job."

"Thank you," I said, unsure whether or not he'd just paid me a compliment.

He squinted in my direction. "Did you cut your hair?"

"Um, no…I left it down."

"Oh. It looks…mussed. It's a different look for you."

I laughed. "I guess you'll feel like you're making love to a different woman tonight."

"Yeah." Except *he* didn't laugh.

While I pondered my state of mind and general mental health, Barry's cell phone rang—a crisis at the station—and he remained on the call through parking the car near my apartment, the walk thereto, and the walk therein, rubbing his watery eyes intermittently. Still talking, he headed for the bathroom, presumably in search of his allergy medicine. I scooped up the mail that had been pushed through the door slot and tossed it on the end table, then went to the kitchen to fix coffee for endurance (I was still feeling optimistic).

Listening to the distant murmur of Barry's voice,

I watched the coffee drip and gave myself a stern pep talk (no fantasizing about other men—i.e., Redford—while making love this time), and, to my credit, I'd managed to work up a pretty good lust by the time I carried a tray with two cups of coffee to the bedroom.

Not that it mattered. Barry lay sprawled across the bed, fully dressed except for his shoes, his cell phone closed in his limp hand. His toiletry bag lay open next to him—the allergy medicine had apparently kicked in rather quickly. I retraced my steps to the living room and drowned my disappointment in my coffee, which was a mistake, since it left me wide awake.

I found a grainy old movie on television and settled back with a cushion across my stomach. But my mind, as it is wont to do in the wee hours, spun into isolated corners of my psyche, stirring up depressing questions. Was Barry *the one,* or was I simply pinning all my expectations on him and our sexual friendship? Was my soul mate still out there somewhere, waiting for me to materialize? And the most depressing question of all: What if Redford DeMoss had been my one true love?

I brought the cushion to my face and exhaled into it. I knew I had hit rock-bottom lonely when I started thinking about Redford. He was a brief, distant episode in my life...a mistake. The speedy annulment only spared us both more grief and circumvented the inevitable split when he returned from the Gulf. And for me, it helped to gloss over the humiliation of having married someone like Redford. We were such polar opposites, and a quickie marriage in Las Vegas was so, *so* unlike me. At hearing the news, my friends had been, in a word, stunned. No—*flabbergasted* would be a more apt description. And my sweet, loving parents who lived in Florida…well, I'd never quite gotten around to telling them.

Similarly, there had never been a good time to tell Barry.

My face burned just thinking about it…and Redford. He had been insatiable in bed, with the endurance of a marathoner. I cast a glance toward the bedroom where the sound of Barry's soft snores escaped, and felt a pang of guilt. It wasn't fair to him that I compared the two of them in that regard. Redford had been on leave from the Gulf—he probably would've humped a picket fence. Although if we hadn't bumped into each other, he would've had no problem finding another willing partner. A compelling figure in his dress blues, Redford had oozed sex appeal—in and out of uniform. I closed my eyes, recalling my first memory of him.

I had been standing in line to check in to the Paradisio hotel in Vegas, fretting over Cindy's late arrival, when a tall, lone officer had walked in. He must have drawn all the energy from the room, because I remember suddenly having trouble breathing. The manager had offered him expedited service to circumvent the long line, but Redford had refused

special treatment. I couldn't take my eyes off him—
his broad shoulders had filled the uniform jacket, his
posture proud, but his expression relaxed and
friendly. My body had vibrated as if I'd been
strummed, every cell had strained toward him. He'd
caught me looking and winked. Mortified at my un-
characteristic behavior, I'd looked away. But later, we
had found each other again.

And again…and again…and again…

I gave myself a shake to dispel my destructive
train of thought. Great sex did not a relationship
make—as evidenced by my short-lived marriage.

Forcing my mind elsewhere, I picked up my mail
from the end table, hoping the caffeine would wear
off soon.

There were lots of credit card offers, which I immediately ripped into small pieces, just as I advised
my clients to do. There was an appointment reminder
from my OB/GYN for a few weeks from now—
yippee. There were bills, of course, and several use-
less catalogs. There was a thank-you note from Kenzie and Sam for a gift I'd sent for their log cabin in
upstate New York. A postcard from my folks from
their seniors' tour in England—they were having a
good time, although Dad missed cold beer. And there
was a long manila envelope—I squinted—from the
Internal Revenue Service?

I studied the address: Mr. and Mrs. Redford De-
Moss. My heart lurched crazily, followed by relief.
This was obviously some sort of mistake. Redford

and I had filed taxes once because our abbreviated marriage had spanned the end of a calendar year. I had filled out the forms myself because I'd wanted to make sure they were done properly (and economically).

Still, my hands were unsteady as I tore open the envelope, and slid out the letter written on heavy bonded paper. I skimmed the words, barely seeing the print. I was familiar with the form letter—in my line of work as a financial planner, I'd seen this same letter dozens of times, only not directed toward *me*.

Redford and I, it seemed, were being audited.

4

FOR AN HOUR I WAS NUMB. Alternately I stared at and reread the IRS letter commanding me and Redford to appear ten days hence, bearing proof that the joint return we'd filed three years ago was accurate as it pertained to a couple of items—primarily our income and the deductions we'd taken.

Or rather, the deductions *I* had taken. It had been the time frame when I was getting my financial planning business off the ground and, admittedly, I had taken some rather aggressive deductions regarding a home office. I chewed one home-manicured fingernail to the quick, then began to gnaw on a second. The fact that I was being audited by the IRS would not be perceived as a plus by my employer, or among my clients and potential clients. Ellen Brant, for instance, wouldn't take kindly to the news. Barry—

My heart skipped a beat or two or three. Oh, God, *what* was I going to tell Barry about Redford?

Barry, there's a tiny detail about my past I keep forgetting to mention...

Barry, you're not going to believe this...

Barry, want to hear something funny?

Nausea rolled in my stomach. I couldn't tell him about my annulled marriage *now*—he'd think I was only telling him because I had to.

Which was true, but still...

No, I'd have to be careful to keep this audit business under wraps. I paced and hummed to keep the panic at bay, my mind racing for a way out of the mess I'd landed in.

Suddenly I brightened: Barry would be in L.A. for two, maybe three weeks. By the time he returned to New York, the situation with Redford would be put to bed—er, put to *rest*.

If I were very, very careful, I'd come out of this situation unscathed.

I rubbed my roiling stomach. As if the secrecy and the possibility of being slapped with a fine or a penalty wasn't enough to give me a bleeding ulcer, there was the thought of being reunited with Redford.

Would he come to Manhattan? Then I scoffed—of course he'd come if he were Stateside. Under order of the IRS, he *had* to come. Probably with a new, young wife in tow, and maybe even a kidlet or two. They'd make it a family vacation—see the Met, the Statue of Liberty, the ex-wife.

Although, in truth, I wasn't really his ex-wife because the annulment meant I'd never *been* his wife. The potential complications swirled in my head, overridden by one gut-clenching question—had Redford thought about me since our annulment?

Annulment. Our marriage had been such an egregious mistake, it had to be indelibly erased. I eased onto the edge of a straight-back chair, remembering how overwhelmed I'd felt when I'd filed those papers. When I'd first arrived back in New York, I had still been awash with my lust for Redford, wistful and optimistic and certain we'd be able to work through any obstacles to be together. He would visit me in New York when he had leave from the Gulf and when he returned to his station in North Carolina. Then I would join him on his family horse farm in Kentucky when he retired from the Marine Corps in a couple of years. With his vision and my financial know-how, we'd grow the business exponentially. He'd made everything seem so…possible. I had been buoyed by the light of adventure in his eyes and blinded by the promises in his lovemaking.

But doubts about our relationship had set in almost immediately. I'd felt isolated and alone. He had warned me it might be weeks before he could call me or e-mail, and since none of my girlfriends had been with me in Vegas, I had no one to reassure me that I hadn't imagined my and Redford's feelings toward each other. Indeed, when I'd announced I'd gotten married, they all thought I was joking—sensible, down-to-earth Denise would never marry a virtual stranger in Vegas. Had I gone completely mad?

I didn't even *like* horses.

When I started thinking about how little I knew about Redford and how much longer he would be in the Marines, my doubts had snowballed. His comment about not being able to communicate with me had seemed lame. But it was the article that appeared in the newspaper a few days later that had pushed me over the edge: G.I.'s Desperate To Say "I Do."

I would never forget that headline. The story went on to describe how soldiers on leave from the Middle East conflict were driven to marry the first willing girl they met because they were afraid they wouldn't come home, and eager to have someone waiting for them if they did. Not surprising, the story went on to say, the divorce and annulment rates for those speedy marriages were astronomical. The women were portrayed as desperate in their own right—caught up in their desire to attach themselves to an alpha male out of social loyalty and the pursuit of cinematic romanticism.

Cinematic romanticism. According to the article, I wasn't in love with Redford—I was in love with the *idea* of Redford. Which explained why I would have fallen for someone who was so polar opposite to me, so radically different from the "type" of guy I usually dated…and so quickly. Over the next few days, I had come to the conclusion that it all had been a big, honking mistake. As soon as I'd gotten my period (thank you, God), I'd settled on an annulment.

Through the Internet I'd found a Vegas attorney to file the petition for a civil annulment. He'd had a greasy demeanor that made me feel soiled, but he seemed to be experienced in dissolving quickie marriages. He'd filed the petition on the grounds that "before entering into the marriage, the plaintiff and defendant did not know each other's likes and dislikes, each other's desires to have or not have children and each other's desires as to state of residency."

All true, except for the part about having children. Redford had expressed a desire for little ones, girls in particular. But I had assuaged my guilt by the fact that we hadn't discussed when or how many.

The attorney warned me that Redford could contest the annulment, and I have to admit that a small part of me had hoped he would. But upon returning to his unit, he must have come to some of the same conclusions because the papers were returned promptly, with his signature scrawled across the bottom, making it official: Redford and I had never been man and wife. Kenzie, Cindy and Jacki pledged their secrecy, and I pledged to drive Redford from my mind. They had kept their pledge. I had been somewhat more lax.

Sometimes a month would go by without me thinking of him. And then something out of the blue would trigger a repressed memory and I would spend a sweat-soaked night reliving the amazing ways Redford had turned my body inside out...the ways he had stroked and plied me to pleasure heights I hadn't known existed. Then whispered that he loved me and had taken me higher still.

During those long, lonely hours, regrets would hit me hard. I'd close my eyes against the dark and fantasize about still having Redford in my bed, with his strong arms and legs wrapped around me, his warm sex inside of me, his sigh in my ear. And I would entertain what-ifs…

The mornings after those tortuous nights I would drag my sleep-ravaged body out of my cold bed and promise myself it would be the last time I would lose sleep over Redford DeMoss. I attributed my recent and more frequent recollections of him to all the weddings and bridal talk among my friends—I had consoled myself that the wayward thoughts would recede when the excitement passed.

But now I wondered crazily if I had somehow willed this IRS audit through all the kinetic vibes about Redford that I had sent out into the universe. Cindy's theory about a self-fulfilling prophecy taunted me…

I don't remember falling asleep. One minute I was stewing in troubling memories, and the next, Barry was shaking me awake and sunshine streamed in the windows.

"Why did you sleep on the couch?" he asked, his eyebrows knitted.

"I was watching a movie," I mumbled, pointing to the TV, which was still on. I felt thoroughly miserable, still wearing my expensive (and now crumpled) dress, my face gummy with old makeup, my mouth furry and hot. At the crackle of the IRS letter beneath my hip, panic struck me anew.

Thankfully, Barry didn't notice the letter. He

reached toward me and pushed my hair out of my eyes, gazing at me with concern. "Are you all right?"

"Sure," I lied.

"Are *we* all right?" he asked, surprising me.

But it was just the gentle reminder I needed to bring me back to the present. Barry was here and he cared. My heart squeezed and I nodded. "Of course we are."

He smiled, seemingly relieved. "You know I love you."

I blinked. Barry and I had professed our affection for each other before, but he wasn't particularly verbal about his feelings. "I know," I murmured, feeling guilty that only last night I had questioned his loyalty to me.

"Good," he said. "I'm sorry about zonking out on you last night. I guess I was more tired than I realized, and the allergy medication took care of the rest."

"That's okay."

"So," he said, his voice suddenly sultry, "how about letting me make it up to you tonight—meet me at Millweed's at seven?"

My eyes widened. "A girl can't say no to Millweed's."

He winked and kissed my ear. "My thoughts exactly. I need to take off." He stood and pulled on the jacket he'd been wearing last night, then picked up his toiletry bag and moved toward the door. "Do you have any big plans today?"

Track down my ex-husband. I swallowed and considered telling Barry about the letter that was burning into my thigh. But I didn't want to break the romantic mood or raise any red flags. Besides, who knew if I would even be able to locate Redford? If he were still overseas, the audit would be a moot point. It seemed silly to bring up the subject in the event it amounted to nothing.

"No big plans," I said breezily.

"Okay, see you later."

My heart moved guiltily. "Wait," I called, and sprang up from the couch, heedless of where the letter might fall. I ran over to the door to stretch up and give Barry a full-body hug. "See you later."

He grinned, then angled his head. "You have something stuck to your butt." Before I could react, he reached around and peeled the letter from my backside.

I snatched it out of his hand and manufactured a laugh. "It's nothing," I said, crumpling the letter. "Junk mail," I added for convincing detail. Then I shooed him out the door and closed it more forcefully than I intended.

Sighing in relief, I leaned against the door and smoothed out the letter, just in case its meaning was somehow less ominous in the light of day.

I scanned the words addressed to Mr. and Mrs. Redford DeMoss and worked my mouth from side to side. No—just as ominous. A slow drip of panic started to raise the acid level in my stomach. How could I prepare myself for speaking to Redford again?

Assuming I could track him down, would he be angry? Belligerent? Aloof? Sarcastic? Disinterested?

Mrs. Redford DeMoss. Denise DeMoss. Redford had said it sounded like a movie star's name, and that I was as beautiful as one...

I set aside the letter long enough to take a shower. But as soon as I closed my eyes to allow the warm water to run over my face and shoulders, memories of Redford came flooding back. Everything about the man had been big—his body, his laugh, his spirit. He had made me feel special and protected and desirable. His lovemaking had awakened a dark, daring side of me that I hadn't known I possessed. He had been a generous lover—slow, thorough and innovative. I was pretty sure that a few of the things we had done were illegal in some states.

With a start, I realized my body had started to respond to the erotic memories. Feeling sentimental and keenly frustrated from my lack of sex, I slid my hands down my stomach to lather the curls at the juncture of my thighs, thrilling from the warmth of the water and the slick pressure of my soapy fingers. Redford had adored making love in the shower, had kissed and suckled and caressed me until I nearly drowned. He had an amazing way of prepping my body with his fingers, readying me for his entry until I thought I would die from wanting him inside me. My own fingers weren't as strong and firm, but they found the essence of my pleasure ably enough, and strangely, even though there were some details about

Redford that had faded in my mind, when I closed my eyes and sent my mind and body back in time, I could conjure up his presence in two breaths.

I leaned into the tiled wall and he leaned into me, the shower spray bouncing off his broad, muscled shoulders, his dark hair slicked back from his tanned face, his sensuous mouth nuzzling my shoulder, the soapy water mingling on our skin. He seemed to derive pleasure from mine, pleased that he could excite me, murmuring encouragement and throaty laughs when I was close to climaxing.

"I want to hear you, Denise…tell me how good it feels…"

I'd never been with anyone who was so…*conversational* during sex. The novelty of it—and the naughtiness—had pushed my level of sensitivity higher than I'd thought possible. "Um…oh…Redford…it feels wonderful…feels like…I'm going to…explode."

And I did, convulsing as the warm water pulsed over me, losing myself in the exquisite torture of a powerful orgasm that weakened my knees. I slid down the wall and sat on the shower floor, shuddering, recovering slowly under the cooling spray. As always, the inevitable guilt set in.

I told myself that I had fantasized about Redford this time only because Barry had left me in a state of unfulfilled arousal. And Redford was uppermost in my mind only because of the IRS letter. I was a sensible woman—everyone said so. What possible good could come of rehashing the past?

I turned off the shower, stepped out and pulled on a robe, giving myself a mental shake. But my traitorous feet took me into the bedroom to stand in front of the trunk at the foot of my bed, and I relented with a sigh. My heart was clicking as I raised the lid and moved aside family photo albums, high school and college yearbooks, and a box of cards and letters I'd collected over the years, my fingers keen to find a secret cache.

At the bottom of the trunk in a corner sat a Punch cigar box—the brand that Redford had smoked. I'd never before dated a man who smoked cigars; I remembered finding it so male and strangely attractive. Over the past couple of years I had felt comforted by the fact that I couldn't conjure up a picture of Redford in my mind—it convinced me that what I'd felt for him was a mirage. But when I touched the smooth surface of the box, I could clearly see him smiling and smoking a cigar by the pool at the Las Vegas hotel where we'd stayed.

Thick, dark hair with sun-lightened streaks, bronzed skin, laughing black eyes, sharp cheekbones...and a Tom Cruise smile that made me want to sprawl on the nearest horizontal surface in hopes he would trip and fall on me.

He had fallen on me quite a lot—that detail was burned into my memory.

My hand shook as I removed the cigar box, untouched since I'd left it there just over three years ago. When I lifted the lid, my breath caught in my throat and I felt as if I was being pulled backward through a time tunnel.

The gray velvet box holding my wedding ring sat on top. I used two hands to open it and at the sight of the wide gold filigree band, I was overcome with bittersweet memories...

"Do you like it?" Redford had asked while we were standing in the most garish jewelry store in the western hemisphere. Among the flashing lights and salesmen with bullhorns, I'd been doubtful we could find anything simple. But Redford had pulled one of the salesmen aside and cajoled the man into showing him the estate jewelry that Redford was sure was being held in the back for special customers. Sure enough, the man had disappeared, then returned with a tray of exquisite rings. I had fallen in love with the filigree band on sight...much like I had with Redford.

As I gazed at the ring, bittersweet pangs struck my chest. I was mistaken about being in love with Redford, but I was still in love with the gorgeous wedding band. He had paid an enormous sum for it— we'd argued over the cost, but Redford had parted with his money during our time together as if there were no tomorrow. And according to the newspaper article, that had been Redford's frame of mind exactly.

I had sent the ring to the attorney to include with the annulment papers that were served to Redford, but Redford had returned the ring with the signed papers with no explanation. The attorney had ad-

vised me to sell the ring to offset the fees of the annulment, but I couldn't bring myself to do it at the
time…or since.

I bit my lip and snapped the ring box closed, then
set it aside to riffle through the remaining contents
of the cigar box: a coaster from the hotel bar, a
matchbook from the place he'd taken me dancing,
the key to our room at the Paradisio hotel, ticket
stubs to shows, a party horn, postcards, our marriage
license, the annulment papers, and our wedding pictures.

I knew women who had hired no fewer than three
photographers on the day of their wedding to circumvent a no-show, faulty equipment, or a drunk cam-
eraman. Other women had white satin albums
trimmed with ribbon and lace, crammed with studio-
quality photos of them in their designer gown, a
glowing groom, twelve bridesmaids, twelve grooms-
men, three flower girls and a ring bearer. Other
women had 5x7s, 8x10s and 16x20s of the special
day. I had three blurry Polaroid pictures.

The first showed the two of us smiling at the
camera through the driver's-side window of Redford's rental car. In the second picture, I wore a
paper veil and held a small bouquet of silk flowers.
We were exchanging vows—Redford's mouth was
open slightly, caught midword. His voice came
floating back to me, a deep, throaty drawl that had
wrapped around me and stroked me like a big, vibrating hand…silken sandpaper. A shiver skated

over my shoulders—apparently memory cells existed in every part of one's body.

The third picture showed us kissing as man and wife. Unbidden, my mouth tingled and the elusive elements of his kiss came back to me—the way his eyes darkened as he inched closer, the possessive feel of his mouth against mine, the promise of his tongue...

With effort, I forced myself back to the present and to the photo in my hand. We were covered in confetti the witness had tossed on us through the open window. Redford was wearing a black sweatshirt. I couldn't tell from the photo, but remembered that I'd been wearing a T-shirt with no bra, my hair messy and hanging around my shoulders, not a speck of makeup. Natural, hedonistic...what had I been thinking?

In hindsight, I hadn't been thinking—at least not beyond the next orgasm. Redford had been the first man to tap in to my sexuality and I'd been blinded by lust. I had mistaken enthusiasm for love.

I did have a fourth picture, although not of our wedding. I carefully withdrew the framed 5x7 from the box, drinking in the sight of First Sergeant De-Moss in his dress uniform, achingly handsome in his official U.S. Marine Corps photo. He had given it to me somewhat sheepishly at the airport, and I had clutched it all the way back to New York. I ran my finger over his face, my heart full over my naiveté at the time.

The phone rang and I picked up the handset on the nightstand, happy for a diversion from the troubling thoughts on the continuous loop in my head. "Hello?"

"Hey, it's Kenzie."

I smiled into the phone. "Hey, yourself."

"So, did you wow the boss lady last night?"

"The dress was a hit. Thanks again for your help."

"Did you get the account?"

"I'll find out more this week, but I'm hopeful."

"You'll have to call me in Jar Hollow to let me know how it goes."

"You're not coming back to the city this week?"

"No, that's another reason I called— Oh, wait, Sam just walked in and I need to, um…give him a message. Can I call you back?"

"Sure," I said, then hung up with a smirk. A message—right. Good grief, the two of them were like teenagers. But I wasn't jealous…really I wasn't.

I tried not to imagine the acrobatics going on in Jar Hollow while I stared at Redford's picture and waited for Kenzie to call me back. The phone rang again less than two minutes later—of course, if the stories were true, she and Sam had had time for a quickie. I picked up the phone and sighed dramatically. "*Please* stop dangling your sex in front of me."

Dead silence sounded on the line.

My chest blipped with panic. "Hello?"

A deep, rumbling laugh rolled out. "Well, that's what I call picking up where we left off."

I swallowed. "Who…who is this?" But I would have recognized that orgasmic voice anywhere.

5

LAUGHTER BOOMED over the phone again. "It's Redford, Denise—your ex-husband. Who did you think it was?"

I was instantly nervous, hearing his voice when my body still vibrated from his memory-induced orgasm. "Um...someone else."

"Sounds like a pretty interesting conversation," he said, his smooth Southern voice infused with amusement. "If this is a bad time, I can call back."

"No," I blurted, my cheeks flaming. "I can talk now."

"Good," he said easily. "Listen, I got a letter from the IRS yesterday—looks like the government wants a little more of my time."

"I received the same letter," I said, regaining a modicum of composure. "You're out of the Marines?"

"Retired for almost six months now."

"Where do you live?"

"In Kentucky. Versailles, to be exact. This is where the girls are."

So he had children—the girls he'd wanted. I don't know why the news surprised me, but my disappointment was acute. And then I realized that Redford having a family certainly made things easier for me—I could shake my stubborn fantasies once and for all.

"That's nice," I managed.

"And you're still living in the same place?"

In other words, my life hadn't changed a bit. My chin went up. "I'll be buying my apartment soon."

"Great. So, do you live alone?"

I frowned. "Yes."

"No kidding? I thought you'd be remarried by now."

"Um, no, I'm not married." I stared at my closet door—plastic covering the wedding gown stuck out from under the door, mocking me.

"Not married? Don't tell me I ruined you for other men," he teased.

Had he always been so cocky? My mouth tightened. "Not at all."

"Darn. And here I was hoping that you still carried my picture around."

I glanced down at the framed picture still in my hand and dropped it back into the cigar box as if it were on fire. "Sorry to disappoint."

He cleared his throat, as if he realized he'd overstepped his bounds. "Well, Denise, what do you know about this audit?"

"No more than what the letter said."

"Three years seems like a long time to have lapsed to be audited." He sounded concerned.

"No," I assured him. "Considering the backlog at the IRS, I'd say three years is about right."

"Are you still a financial planner?"

"Yes. I work for a brokerage firm now."

"Congratulations. Does that give us an advantage? I mean, do you deal with the IRS often?"

"Only as an advisor to my clients regarding payment of fees or penalties."

At the sudden silence on the other end, I realized my response wasn't exactly comforting, and since the audit was most likely a result of my creative accounting, I felt as if I owed him a little reassurance.

"Redford, chances are this will be a routine interview. They'll probably just want to ask us a few questions, see a few receipts, that sort of thing."

He gave a little laugh. "I don't even know where my tax records are—in storage somewhere."

"I kept everything," I said.

"Everything?" he asked, his voice suspiciously nostalgic.

I glanced at the cigar box containing souvenirs of my time with Redford and closed the lid. "All the tax records," I corrected. "I'll bring them to the interview."

"Great. I guess I'd better start making travel plans."

"The interview is a week from Tuesday," I offered.

"Yeah, but I'm interested in buying a stud horse in upstate New York. I was thinking I could come up early and maybe kill two birds with one stone."

So Redford had entered the family business. Another area where we were opposites—the closest I'd ever gotten to a horse was walking next to a carriage in Central Park, and one of the beasts had nipped a hole in my favorite sweater.

"And I've never been to New York City," he continued, "so I thought I'd try to squeeze in some sightseeing since I might never get the chance again. How would you feel about being a tour guide?"

"Fine," I said, then wet my lips. "Are you coming alone?"

"Yes."

My shoulders dropped an inch in relief. I don't know why, but I didn't relish the thought of meeting his new wife. "When would you arrive?"

"Whenever you can fit me in," he said, and God help me, my mind leapt to a time when I had "fit him in" anytime I could.

"How about Friday?" he asked.

"I'll ch-check my schedule, but that should be okay."

"Great," he said, his genial tone making it obvious that our conversation wasn't affecting him at all. "And if you could recommend a place to stay while I'm there, I'd appreciate it."

"I'll look into it," I promised. "How can I reach you?"

He recited a phone number, which I jotted down.

"Although you never know who might pick up around here," he warned with a laugh.

On cue, I heard a shriek of childish laughter and the patter of little feet in the background.

"If you leave a message and you don't hear back from me within a few hours, just call again."

"Sure," I said, my heart dragging. "I'll talk to you soon."

"Okay. Listen, Denise…"

My heartbeat picked up. "Yes?"

"It's great to hear your voice again. I've thought about you a lot over the years and…"

And? I swallowed, waiting.

"And…I'm glad to know you're okay."

I closed my eyes before murmuring, "Same here."

We said goodbye and I disconnected the call on an exhale, feeling wobbly and acknowledging the sudden urge to eat a party-size bag of peanut M&M's. I settled for a cup of nonfat, sugar-free vanilla yogurt with a little cocoa sprinkled over the top (not the same, no matter how much the weight-loss gurus try to convince you otherwise) and tucked myself into a chair with my legs beneath me.

So I was going to see Redford again. I lay my head back on the chair and released a sigh that ended in a moan. Just speaking to him on the phone had left me feeling fuzzy, as if he had brushed his naked body against mine. How pathetic was I that the mere sound of his voice could rattle me after all this time? Especially when Redford had obviously found someone else to brush up against.

I wasn't naïve enough to think that Redford hadn't taken other lovers after our annulment. But because our sexual relationship had been so radical and so… *incomparable* for me, deep down I guess I'd hoped it had been for him, too. That he hadn't played the "kiss you all under" game with anyone else, or that no other woman had left teeth marks in his shoulder.

I laughed at myself. I hadn't really expected Redford to be pining for me, had I?

I mindlessly spooned yogurt into my mouth, sucking on the spoon (which even Freud would have deemed too obvious for analysis), while my thoughts coiled into themselves in confusion. I was scraping the bottom of the container with an eye toward licking the foil lid when the phone rang again.

My pulse jumped—maybe Redford had forgotten to tell me something. I idly wondered if he had kept my phone number and address somewhere, or if he'd simply looked me up through directory assistance. I padded to the bedroom where I'd left the handset and pushed the connect button. "Hello?"

"Hey," Kenzie said. "I called back, but the line was busy."

I wavered, wondering if I should tell anyone about my impending reunion with Redford. But I needed to tell someone, so I spilled my guts.

Kenzie was quiet for a few seconds, then said, "Damn. He's the one with the huge schlong, right?"

I rolled my eyes. "Do we have to go there?"

"Are you prepared to see this man again?"

"Sure," I said, trying to sound casual. "It's no big deal."

"I don't know, Denise. You were really weird when you came back from Las Vegas. Kind of... zombie-like."

A changed woman, like Eve after eating from the Tree of Knowledge. I swallowed hard. "I'll be fine."

"If you say so," she said, but sounded doubtful.

"Subject change. So you were saying that you're not coming back to the city this week."

"Right. I, um, haven't been feeling very well, and I think I'll take it easy here for the next couple of weeks."

"Flu bug?" I asked, flopping onto my bed.

"Actually...it's morning sickness."

A few seconds passed before her words sank in, then I sat straight up. "You're pregnant?"

She laughed. "So it would seem."

"Omigod...congratulations!" Disbelief rolled over me in waves. The fact that one of us was going to be a mother made me feel so...old.

"Thanks, Denise. Sam and I both are thrilled, of course."

"As you should be," I said, feeling myself going misty. "When are you due? Do you know what you're having? Do you have a name picked out?"

Kenzie laughed again. "August, no, and no. Lots of decisions to make between now and then. Oh, there's the other line. Talk to you later in the week?"

"Sure." I congratulated her again on the baby, then hung up, unsettled by Kenzie's declaration, yet knowing it was inevitable that we all move on with our lives. At least, it seemed as if everyone *else* was moving forward. Even Redford had moved on. His phone call proved that *I*, on the other hand, was pathetically mired in the past, more so than I would have thought possible.

With new resolve, I removed the wedding gown from my closet and lifted the plastic. I would need a good photo in order to list the dress on eBay and get top dollar. With trepidation, I undressed, then stepped into the gown and shimmied the satiny dress over my hips. The cool fabric glided over my skin like a caress. I fastened the halter around the nape of my neck, then reached around to pull up the zipper that ended just below my shoulder blades. Minus the leotard, the dress fit even better. I couldn't resist a peek into the full-length mirror sitting in the corner of my cramped bedroom, and at the sight of myself in the ethereal gown, I nearly lost my nerve.

I imagined looking down at the end of the aisle and seeing my groom standing there, his eyes shining with love and desire at the sight of me in this gorgeous gown. Later he would remove the dress with kisses and caresses, his hands and breath so hurried that the gown would have barely fallen to the floor before we were buried inside each other.

I blinked, realizing my arms were covered with goose bumps, and my nipples were budded. I wanted to keep this dress, but doing so would be wasteful and foolish. Just having it in my closet was making me silly and soft. And horny.

So I made myself step away from the mirror and, with relative detachment, set up my digital camera and tripod. I set the timer and posed for three shots in a bridal stance. Then I removed the dress and carefully replaced the plastic with a bittersweet pang. Some woman out there would both appreciate and be able to use the dress, and that gave me a bit of solace.

I pulled up the digital photos, selected the best one and cropped out my head and other extraneous background details. Then I logged on to eBay and listed my impulsive purchase in an eight-day auction, ending next Monday evening. I wanted to be done with the auction before I had to turn my attention to the audit.

> Exquisite designer wedding gown, NWT (new with tags), size ten, creamy white, halter-style dress with pearl-studded skirt and short train, will make any bride feel like a princess on her special day.

I sighed while transferring the details from the tags to the screen. My heart hung low in my chest, but I knew that getting rid of the dress would help to clear my head of past and future marriage fantasies. No wonder Barry wouldn't commit. I was probably giving off "rewind" vibes.

A fact that I repeated to myself over and over as I dressed for our dinner that evening. Since I'd had precious little to eat since the yogurt, my stomach was howling for food. And I had a headache from playing my conversation with Redford over and over in my head. But when I walked up to Barry, who was sitting at the bar in the hushed atmosphere of the posh restaurant, I forced myself to tamp down all thoughts of Redford and the past. Barry was kind, successful, ambitious and…here…in New York…where my life was. One could not underestimate the necessity of proximity to keep a relationship alive.

Barry stood and smiled back, but his eyes reflected something else—regret? Fear? Guilt? He brushed a quick kiss on my mouth and hurriedly threw back the rest of his drink.

Something was wrong…I could sense it. It was obvious from his stiff body language as we followed the hostess to a premium table, as he held out my chair, as he claimed his own seat and snapped the linen napkin over his lap. He didn't seem to want to make eye contact, and he was pulling on his ear—a sure sign that something was on his mind. Tiny alarms sounded in my head as I sipped from my water glass, and my mind started tossing out scenarios to explain his nervous behavior. He'd been offered a job in L.A. Ellen had changed her mind about doing business with Trayser Brothers. Then the truth spanked me:

Barry was going to dump me.

Of course—it made perfect sense. A classy restaurant on a Sunday evening… Break the news in public, then start the week with a clean slate as a single man. Leave town for a few weeks and things would be smoothed over by the time he returned. He'd asked me to meet him to avoid the awkwardness of taking me home afterward, had taken his toiletry bag home to avoid a trip back to my place. I swallowed a mouthful of water with my disappointment, my appetite gone. This was what I got for fantasizing about another man who wasn't even around, while ignoring a perfectly good guy who was right under my nose.

Moving and speaking awkwardly, Barry ordered a pricey bottle of shiraz. I perused the menu, seeing nothing, and watched him under my lashes, my nerves jumping. When the wine arrived and Barry lifted his glass to mine, he made eye contact for the first time.

"To a great friendship," he said, wetting his lips.

Sadness bled through me and I clinked my glass against his, wondering if he would make me wait until the end of the meal to do the deed. But after he drank from his glass, his eyes changed, and I steeled myself for his brush-off.

He reached across the table and clasped my hand. "Denise, we've been together for a while now…long enough, I think."

I nodded, determined to make it easy for him, easy for me.

"Will you marry me, Denise?"

A full ten seconds passed before his words registered. I squinted at him, confused. "Pardon me?"

He grinned. "You're going to make this hard, aren't you?" He swung out of his seat and got down on one knee in front of my chair. A stir sounded around us as other diners turned to stare. He reached into his jacket pocket and removed a black velvet ring box, then opened it to reveal a diamond the size of a peanut M&M. "Denise Cooke, will you marry me?"

My jaw was slack, which I knew wasn't a particularly attractive expression for me, but I couldn't help it. "Stunned" wasn't the right word—I was positively staggered. I felt the eyes of strangers on me, the air heavy with anticipation. Unwittingly, the setting of my first proposal rose in my mind—the bar, the paper clip Redford had bent into a band as a temporary engagement ring until, he'd said, he could retrieve his grandmother's diamond. In retrospect, it all seemed so childish.

I stared at the rock Barry offered me, overwhelmed by his gesture. "It's huge," I murmured.

"It's one of those new laboratory-made diamonds. About one-fourth the cost of a regular diamond."

I tried not to feel deflated. "Oh."

"I knew you'd approve, as frugal as you are."

I nodded. "Of course."

"So," he said, his voice high and tight as he gave a slight nod to the people staring at us. "What do you say, Denise?"

My insides were like hash. I felt like an idiot—I was sure he was trying to break up with me, and the man had been trying to propose! He wanted to *marry* me. It was my second chance to get it right.

I looked into Barry's shining eyes and my heart welled. I knew *this* man's likes and dislikes—that he wanted to have children...someday, and that we would always live in a big city, pursuing our big-city careers. There was no mistake that Barry and I were perfectly suited to one another. I took a deep breath and said, "Yes, Barry...I'll marry you."

6

CINDY AND JACKI stared at my left hand in the middle of the café table, then at me, their lunch salads forgotten.

"Oh, my God," Cindy said. "Barry proposed!"

I nodded. "Last night."

"It's a freaking boulder," Jacki said, her eyes bugged. "He must have spent a fortune."

I decided not to let them in on the "laboratory created" part. They might try to convince me it wasn't romantic to scrimp on an engagement ring. In truth, I appreciated the fact that Barry was saving money for other things, like our wedding, our honeymoon, disability insurance.

Cindy's eyes grew moist. "And this on top of Kenzie's baby news. I'm just so happy."

I squeezed her hand, sending up a little prayer that she'd find a good man soon.

"Have you told Kenzie?" Jacki asked me.

"Not yet," I said, wondering what Kenzie would say, then wondering why I thought she'd be anything but happy for me. "I'm going to call her later."

Jacki raised her water glass. "To the happy couple."

I clinked my glass to theirs in appreciation.

"Well, that's three down, one to go." Jacki winked at Cindy. "You're next."

Cindy smiled wistfully. "I hope so."

"How's the class going?"

"So far, so good. There's a really cute guy in the class who's been talking to me. And I found my *dream* wedding dress Saturday." Then she turned to me, her eyes and mouth rounded. "Oh, Denise—it worked! You buying a wedding gown turned into a self-fulfilling prophecy!"

"Huh?" Jacki said.

I squirmed as Cindy relayed the "running of the brides" stint and how I'd wound up with a gown.

"Did you know Barry was going to propose?" Jacki asked.

I shook my head. "No idea. Evidenced by the fact that yesterday afternoon, I listed the gown on eBay."

Cindy's face fell. "You didn't."

I sighed. "I did. And the reserve price I set has already been met."

Jacki lifted an eyebrow. "Knowing you, the reserve price was more than you paid for it."

"Well, yeah, but it's a great dress. If I'd have known that Barry was going to propose…"

"So cancel the auction," Cindy said.

I frowned. "After bidding starts, I can't." Since I made spending money by selling odds and ends on eBay, I wasn't willing to risk being banned from the online auction house.

"Don't look so glum," Cindy said. "You'll find another dress."

I picked at the fruit on my plate. "It's not just the dress," I said carefully, acknowledging the dread that had kept me awake all night.

"What?" they asked in unison, leaning forward.

"I, um, never quite got around to telling Barry that I was married before."

Jacki's eyebrows shot up. "Really? It never came up?"

I shook my head. "I thought about telling him lots of times, but I was afraid he'd think I was—I don't know—hinting or something."

Jacki pursed her mouth. "Last night might have been a good time to say something."

"He had to leave for L.A. earlier than he expected," I said. "We barely had time to finish dinner." My excuse sounded lame even to my ears. I groaned and dropped my fork onto my plate. "What am I going to do?"

"Call him today and tell him," Jacki said emphatically.

"Yeah, Denise," Cindy said. "Your marriage to Redmon—"

"Redford."

"—only lasted two weeks."

"Six," I corrected.

"Still," she argued. "You had the marriage annulled. That means it never happened."

I smirked. "Only it *did* happen."

Cindy scoffed. "It's not as if you have this secret long-term relationship in your history, or as if your ex-husband is going to show up on your doorstep."

I grimaced. "Well, actually…"

They lunged forward again. "What?"

I told them about the audit letter and the phone call from Redford, my sense of panic increasing as their jaws dropped lower.

"Your ex-husband is coming here?" Jacki asked. "The really hot one with the big Johnson?"

I frowned. "He's not my ex-husband. He's my… non-husband. And I'm afraid if I tell Barry now, he'll think there's unfinished business between me and Redford."

Jacki angled her head. "Is there?"

"No!" I said quickly. "Of course not. Redford has a family."

"He remarried?"

"Yes," I said, then squinted. "Well, he didn't say so exactly, but he mentioned children…girls."

"Marriage and children aren't mutually exclusive," Cindy pointed out.

"Is he still in the Marine Corps?" Jacki asked.

"Retired a few months ago. He joined his family horse business in Kentucky."

"Oh, that's so romantic," Cindy said. "He's a cowboy! Does he wear a hat?"

"I have no idea. He has his life, and I have mine. When this audit is over, we'll never see each other again."

"What about this audit?" Jacki asked. "Are you in trouble?"

"I don't think so. I called the field office this morning to confirm our appointment and from all appearances, it seems pretty routine." At least I hoped so.

"You'd better be careful," Jacki said, pointing her fork at me. "The IRS can ruin your life."

"My cousin Joey had to go to jail for six months," Cindy declared.

I frowned. "That's kind of extreme...did he not even bother to file?"

"Oh, he filed, but a fast-talking tax preparer found all these so-called 'deductions' that saved him a ton of money. Next thing you know, my cousin's being audited and the tax preparer has skipped town. Joey winds up in the clink, with a record for fraud. He lost his job and his wife left him. Sad."

I felt myself go pale. Trayser Brothers would fire me on the spot if I was charged with tax fraud. "I d-don't expect anything like that to happen. But still, I'd like to keep this quiet," I said sheepishly. "My clients might misunderstand."

"Does Barry know?" Jacki asked.

I shook my head.

"So you don't plan to tell Barry about the audit, about Redford, or that you were married?"

"Technically, she *wasn't* married," Cindy argued.

"Not according to the IRS," Jacki murmured, then gave me a probing look before turning back to her salad.

I studied a crouton, feeling guilty and miserable.

"When does the cowboy arrive?" Cindy asked, changing the subject with a sledgehammer.

"Friday."

"The audit is Friday?"

My cheeks warmed. "Um, no, the audit isn't until next Tuesday, but Redford wants to do some sightseeing."

Jacki looked up. "You're taking the man sightseeing?"

My defenses reared. "Just like I've taken dozens of friends sightseeing who've come to the city. And he wants to go look at a stud for sale upstate."

Jacki's mouth jumped at the corners. "And you *always* take visitors stud-shopping."

I frowned. "I'm not going with him, for goodness' sake. I don't even *like* horses."

Jacki nodded, but gave me that look again. "So when does Barry get back in town?"

"He'll be in L.A. for two weeks, maybe three."

"But that's perfect!" Cindy cut in. "Barry never has to know that Redford was even here."

"My thoughts exactly," I said, feeling better. "This whole mistake with Redford will be tied up before Barry gets back."

Jacki nodded thoughtfully. "A good plan," she

conceded, then gave me a sly smile. "As long as you don't repeat your mistake."

I swallowed hard. "No chance of that happening…none at all."

WHEN I GOT HOME from work that evening, I tried to push aside thoughts of calling Redford to firm up his schedule. Procrastinating, I checked my auction on eBay.

When the page loaded, I felt a tiny bit relieved to see that the auction stood at only one bid. True, the bidder had met my reserve price of $275, but maybe I'd attracted a no-pay bidder. Normally, of course, I would report a no-pay bidder, but in this case, I'd be willing to let it slide in order to keep the gown.

Then I zeroed in on the bidder's user ID: SYLVIESMOM. My mouth pinched involuntarily—the woman at Filene's who had tried to pry the gown off my body had said her daughter's name was Sylvie. Could it possibly be the same woman? I looked up the bidder's profile and saw the zip code was within Manhattan…it seemed too much of a co-incidence to be anyone but her.

And call me warped, but I was *not* going to let that woman have my dress, especially when now I could use it myself. I was even more concerned when I saw by the high number next to her user ID that she was a veteran buyer—drat! Then in a moment of blessed revelation, I realized I could simply have a friend, i.e. Cindy, bid on the gown and win the auction, with no one the wiser that no money had changed hands. What I had in mind wasn't ethical if the intent was to run up the price artificially. But this was an emergency, and I had no intention of taking any money from Sylvie's mom. I'd only be out the percentage of the sale I would owe the auction house.

By golly, I was going to win back my dress.

I called Cindy, but before I could tell her what I had in mind, she blurted, "He called!"

"Who called?"

"The guy from my Positive Thinking class! He wants to meet for a drink Friday night."

"That's great!" I said and my heart welled for her. She deserved a terrific guy.

"Maybe buying the wedding dress will work for me, too," she said, laughing.

I cleared my throat. "Speaking of the wedding dress, I have a favor to ask."

"What?"

I told her my plan to get my dress back, and she was hesitant until I told her who the bidder was.

"Ooh! That woman can't possibly have your dress. What do I have to do?"

I gave her the auction number. "Log on and bid three hundred dollars. No! Three hundred and *five* dollars. And thirty-three cents." Bidding in odd amounts could give a bidder an advantage.

"Okay," she said. "I'll call you back when I'm finished." Because she wasn't an auction/e-mail hound like me, Cindy had one phone line between her phone and computer.

I watched the auction screen on my computer, hitting the reload button every few seconds until Cindy's user ID, WANTSAMAN, popped up as the high bidder at $280. No matter what amount a bidder enters, eBay will only increment the bid by enough to win the auction. Since the minimum incremental bid at this price point was five dollars, SYLVIESMOM must have bid exactly $275, ergo Cindy's bid automatically adjusting to $280. Aha! With such a tentative initial bid, maybe the woman wasn't that serious about the dress…maybe we would scare her off.

Cindy called back. "Did it work?"

"For now. I'll keep you posted."

"So I forgot to ask you—are your parents excited about your engagement?"

I bit my lip. "I haven't told them yet."

"What? Why not?"

Good question. Even though they were in England, I could have called their cell phone. My mother, Gayle, put X's on the calendar to count down the days of my "fertile years." She liked Barry, and would be beyond ecstatic to learn of our engagement. My dad, Harrison, and Barry had never really clicked. But talking to my dad was like talking to a portly bronze statue. Still, he'd be happy if I were happy.

"They're out of the country. I'll call them…soon."

Cindy sighed. "If I were getting married, my parents would throw a parade."

I laughed. "Maybe this guy from your Positive Thinking class is *the one*."

"Maybe. Meanwhile, let me know if you see a bachelor go on the block on eBay."

"Deal. Talk soon." I said goodbye and hung up, dreading the call to Redford with every fiber of my being. But neither did I want to wait too long and disrupt his family's evening. Chastising myself for the ridiculous butterflies in my stomach, I dialed the number he'd given me and exhaled slowly while it rang.

The phone was picked up, then after much wallowing, a child's voice came on the line. "Heh-wo?"

One of his girls, apparently. "Hello, is your daddy there?"

"Who is dis?"

"Um, this is…a friend…Denise."

"Deece?" the little girl repeated. A man's voice sounded in the background, then more wallowing of the phone ensued.

"Hello?"

My pulse picked up at the sound of his voice—touchably close. "Redford?"

"Denise?"

"Is this a bad time?"

He gave a little laugh. "No. Sorry about that…Janie just learned how to answer the phone."

"No problem." For some reason, I felt weird talking about his children. I cleared my throat. "Did you make flight arrangements?"

"Yes, I'm flying into LaGuardia Friday around noon. Does that work for you?"

From Friday to Tuesday—five days. The last time we'd been together for that amount of time, we'd gotten into a lot of trouble. Of course things had changed drastically…

"Sure, that'll be fine. I called this morning to confirm our appointment at the IRS office Tuesday morning."

"Thanks. What do I need to bring?"

"Maybe your tax forms for the previous year and the following year, just to be safe."

"Will do."

I gave him the name and number of a hotel in my neighborhood. "I thought we could sightsee on Saturday."

"Sounds good."

"I have to work Friday, but I could take my lunch hour to meet you at the airport…if you want."

"That's not necessary," he said. "But I'd like it very much."

My midsection tingled. He'd like very much to see me, or he'd like very much not to navigate the trip into the city alone? "Will I know you?" I asked, and was astounded to hear how breathless I sounded.

"If you ever did," he said, and his words vibrated in the air with sudden intensity.

I swallowed hard. "I'll be wearing—"

"I'll know you," he cut in.

His words struck me as intimate, and my

tongue seemed to adhere to the roof of my mouth. "M-maybe we should exchange cell-phone numbers in case we don't connect outside baggage claim."

"Don't have one," he said cheerfully. "See you Friday."

"Okay," I murmured, then slowly disconnected the call, Redford's voice still reverberating in my head. Why was my skin on fire? My heart crushing against my breastbone? I didn't want to go back to the place I'd been when I was with Redford; to the darker side of myself, when nothing had mattered but being in his arms. My sense of reason had simply fled. It was almost frightening to think back to how bendable I'd been to his wishes, how easily I had trusted him with my future. Was I truly prepared to see Redford again? Would it be cleansing...or climactic?

To assuage my pounding guilt, I picked up the phone and dialed Barry's cell phone, but got his voice mail.

"Hey, it's me," I said. "Just missing you and wanted to hear your voice." I worked my mouth from side to side and considered leaving a blubbery admission about Redford then and there, but decided that was cowardly. Instead I said, "Call me when you can," and pushed the disconnect button.

I stared at my laboratory-engineered diamond ring until my eyes watered. There were so many reasons not to repeat my mistake of falling for Redford. For one, he was unavailable. For two, *I* was unavailable.

We were both unavailable. No mistake about it.

7

Friday
Days left on eBay auction: 4
Bidding on wedding dress up to: $875
Winning bidder: SYLVIESMOM

BY FRIDAY, I still hadn't gotten used to having the engagement ring on my finger. As I waited on the sidewalk outside LaGuardia baggage claim for Redford to emerge, I adjusted the lump beneath my glove to either side, then back to the middle, expending nervous energy. I had barely slept last night, so I was sporting a rather Goth look from the circles beneath my eyes. My stomach held only coffee. And while I stood there telling my silly self to calm down, the biggest mistake of my life strode outside in the cold February sunshine, and the temperature leapt at least two degrees.

My vision blurred, then cleared. Either I was having a stroke, or seeing Redford again was affecting the blood flow to my brain. I remembered him being a handsome guy, but in the three years since I'd seen him, he'd matured into a mountain of a full-grown

man, filled out and hardened. Of course, the black
Western hat *was* a little imposing, but no less so than
the long tan suede duster he wore—a full three cows'
worth.

I swallowed hard at the transformation from military officer to horseman. Cindy was right: Redford
was a cowboy.

He turned in my direction and his gaze latched on
to me. A grin spread over his face revealing white
teeth and high dimples. God, I'd forgotten about the
dimples…and the impact of his luminous dark eyes.
He walked toward me, and I was instantly conscious
of my prim ponytail and gray wool coat—a far cry
from the mussed hair and denim jacket uniform I'd
worn during our brief time together. He'd certainly
never seen me in a skirt (although he had seen me in
far less). I was surprised he even recognized me…
and alarmingly thrilled.

My heart was thudding like crazy when he
stopped in front of me, the tails of his open coat
swirling around him. Testosterone wafted off him
like invisible tethers, tugging at me from all sides.
Under the influence of his bronze, virile stare I managed a smile.

"Hello, Redford."

"Hello, Denise," he said, his voice guttural, but
smooth. Then he reached up with his be-ringed left
hand to remove his hat.

The gesture was so chivalrous, my toes curled. It
was just the kind of thing that he had done before to

make me feel so feminine and yielding. Beneath the hat, his thick brown hair was a bit longer than the military cut he'd sported when I'd known him. I was startled to see flashes of silver at his temples, a few lines around his amazing eyes. No doubt his experiences in the Gulf had matured him beyond his thirty-eight years. I had offered to meet Redford at the airport because he'd never been to the city. But I suddenly felt foolish because this man had been in places that would make the streets of Manhattan seem like a playground. A pang of gratitude struck me for the sacrifice he'd made, and I felt spoiled for the freedoms I had enjoyed while he'd been overseas. I had the sudden, crazy urge to give myself to him…just like before.

"You look well," I said, my voice unsteady.

"You look beautiful," he said, then leaned forward and dropped a kiss next to my mouth.

The feel of his lips on my skin was startlingly familiar, and I fought the instinct to turn toward his kiss, to meet his lips. I couldn't discern if the contact lasted longer than necessary, or if I was simply processing things in slow-motion. Even after he pulled away, I could feel the weight of his kiss lingering on my skin. When I'd known him before, Redford had elicited a strong visceral response in me, uncommon to *me,* but obviously not uncommon to him, judging from the women around us who literally seemed to lose direction when they saw him.

Everyone in Manhattan was familiar with the Naked Cowboy in Times Square—a scantily-clad guitar-playing tourist novelty—but Redford was the real deal with his khaki shirt tucked into loose, faded jeans, held on to narrow hips with a wide black leather belt. His black roper boots would have received a shine this morning from the horsehair brush his grandfather had given him, I thought as details came flooding back. And the bronze of his skin wasn't the sprayed-on version that many men in New York sported. The fact that I knew what *this* cowboy looked like naked gave me a boost of female satisfaction…and the dangerous stirrings of temptation. Redford clasped my gloved hand and my ring bit into my skin, a not-so-gentle reminder that I had no business being tempted.

"God, it's great to see you, Denise."

I didn't trust my voice…or any other part of my body at the moment, because everything was either tingling, swelling, or vibrating. From the left side of my brain, a rational thought found its way through the mush: *Lack of self-control is precisely how you wound up married to a virtual stranger in the first place.* I conjured up a casual smile that belied my quaking insides. "It's nice to see you, too."

His amazing smile diminished, and I felt a little indignant. Had he expected me to throw myself into his arms and tell him that I'd fantasized about his lovemaking for the better part of three years? The words watered on my tongue before I swallowed them, disgusted with myself. Two minutes into our reunion and I was already unglued.

I averted my glance and was pulled back to the present by the noise of the traffic and jostling pedestrians. It occurred to me that standing outside the airport was a very public place to be seen with a handsome man that my boyfriend had no knowledge of. While the likelihood of someone seeing us was remote, it could happen, considering how much Barry and his colleagues traveled. Panic crushed me for a few seconds while I looked from face to face, expecting any second for someone to recognize me. I cast around for a good reason to get moving. "Hungry?" I asked.

Redford grinned. "Always."

I chose not to read anything into his words. "Okay, let's drop your luggage off at the hotel, then we'll grab a bite to eat."

We joined the line at the taxi stand and I shifted from foot to foot, aware of his eyes on me, trying to think of something to say. The next five days stretched before me like an emotional obstacle course.

"You look different," I said, then gave a nervous little laugh. "I don't know why, but I almost expected to see you in your uniform."

He shrugged. "I just traded one hat for another, I guess. You look different, too."

A warm blush crawled over my cheeks. "You didn't seem to have any trouble recognizing me."

"Oh, you still stand out in a crowd," he said, making me more uncomfortable. "You just seem…more buttoned-up."

His teasing tone needled me. "Just more mature, I suppose," I said.

He made a face. "That's too bad."

I bit my tongue, mostly because I didn't know how to respond. I hadn't expected to be so overwhelmed with resurrected feelings. It was surreal—I knew him, but I didn't know him. We'd been married…then not.

"So you still don't own a car?" he asked, gesturing to the taxi stand.

"More trouble and expense than it's worth," I assured him, knowing how bizarre not owning a vehicle seemed to people who lived in less dense areas. "Besides, I either walk or take public transportation everywhere."

He looked me up and down and a smile lit his black eyes. "So that's how you've managed to stay in such great shape."

My thighs pinged, but I reminded myself that his wife probably wouldn't be thrilled knowing that he was complimenting his ex. Then a disturbing thought hit me—was Redford a ladies' man? Was he thinking that this IRS audit was the chance to reunite with an old flame and stoke the fire a little? I looked at Redford with dismay—had he changed so much? Then another possibility struck me—maybe he hadn't changed at all…maybe I had simply misjudged him when I'd known him.

"Are you okay?" he asked, placing his hat back on his head.

"Fine," I said, resolved that I wouldn't let Redford's powerful sexuality entice me into making another mistake. I stepped up in the taxi line, relieved to see we were next. "Did you make reservations at the hotel I suggested?" I asked, back to a safer topic.

He nodded and stepped off the curb, then walked around to the back of the taxi. Brushing off the cabbie's offer of help, he deposited his leather duffel bag in the trunk himself and closed the lid. "But would you mind if I run a quick errand first?"

Bewildered, I shrugged. "No, of course not."

He handed the cabbie a piece of paper, then held the door open for me to slide in the back seat first. I scooted as close to the opposite door as my bulky coat would allow, but when Redford climbed in, his big body touched mine from knee to shoulder. I decided that pulling away would seem prudish considering our former relationship, so I stared out the window as we drove away and racked my brain for something conversational to say.

"The drive in will at least give you a great view of the city," I offered.

"If I could take my eyes off *you*."

I jerked my head around and, indeed, he appeared to be studying me, his dark eyes earnest beneath the brim of his hat.

The left side of my body was on fire. "What's the errand you need to run?"

"Just a little business transaction," he said easily.

In my purse, my cell phone rang. I pulled it out and glanced at the screen—Barry. My stomach dipped. We'd been playing phone tag for days. I inadvertently glanced at Redford, feeling panicky.

"Don't let me keep you from something important," he said.

The cabbie turned around to verify something on the piece of paper Redford had given him. When Redford leaned forward, I hit the connect button and put the phone to my ear. "Hello?"

"Hi," Barry said. "Did I catch you at a bad time?"

Redford put his hand on my knee, leveraging himself to lean farther forward. I inhaled sharply and my panty hose-clad leg burned beneath his large hand.

"Um, no," I said into the phone. "I was just on my way to…lunch. How are things in L.A.?"

"It's crazy here," he said. "We're working 'round the clock to get a couple of local stations transitioned to our network in time for sweeps. Sorry I haven't been able to call."

"That's okay," I murmured.

"But I spoke to Ellen, and she said you had a good meeting."

I frowned, my first thought being that he'd had time to talk to Ellen, but not to me, then gave myself a mental shake—he had probably talked to her numerous times about work. "I thought it went well," I said. "She took the paperwork with her, so I don't have the account yet, but I think it will happen."

"That's great news."

"Yeah. I owe you big-time."

Barry gave an evocative little laugh. "When I get back, I'll collect."

The juxtaposition of Redford's warm hand on my knee and Barry's voice in my ear sent waves of guilt over me, and I had the crazy urge to blurt a confession right then and there…which, I realized a split-second later, would be disastrous. So I simply took a deep breath and said, "Okay," somewhat woodenly.

"Who are you going to lunch with?" Barry asked over a yawn.

Redford leaned back in the seat and settled next to me with a sexy smile.

I turned my head slightly away from Redford and held the mouthpiece close. "Um…no one you'd know."

"A client?"

Well, I was going to be advising Redford during the tax audit, so indirectly, he *was* a client of mine…sort of. "Yes," I said, peeling my gaze from Redford's long, thick, tanned fingers.

"Then I guess I'd better let you go," Barry said. "Do you have any big plans this weekend?"

"Not really," I squeaked. "I'll be in and out."

I glanced at Redford and he raised his eyebrows suggestively. Heat flooded my face and I was dimly aware of Barry saying something.

"I'm sorry, what was that?"

"I said have fun. I'll talk to you soon."

"Okay." I wondered nervously if being engaged

obligated me to a new, more gushy sign-off. "Bye...
you." I winced, my words sounding awkward and
ridiculous even to me.

"Bye," Barry said, suppressing another yawn.

I disconnected the call and slid the phone back into
my bag, as jumpy as a pussy caught between two toms.

"Bad news?" Redford asked.

I turned toward him, struck anew by the sheer
maleness of him. "Hmm? Oh...no."

"You're frowning," he offered. "Is my being here
an inconvenience?"

I averted my gaze. "No, of course not."

"You're fibbing," he said. "You probably thought
you'd never see me again, and then you get hit with
this audit out of the blue. Pretty crazy, huh?"

I looked back and nodded. "It's bizarre."

Then Redford picked up my gloved left hand and
looked at me hard. "Have you thought that maybe it
could be fate?"

8

I WAS STRUCK SPEECHLESS by Redford's question. Fate? Cindy, with all her romantic ideas about happily ever after, believed in fate. But the concept was too elusive for my linear brain to wrap itself around. Still, for a fleeting second when I looked into Redford's earnest eyes, heaven help me, I wanted to believe that fate had brought us back together. Then I came to my senses and withdrew my hand, emitting a little laugh.

"Redford, somehow I doubt that fate and the IRS are in cahoots. I'd say it's more like mathematical odds." And perhaps my questionable deductions, which I wasn't keen to discuss just yet.

Then he pursed his mouth and nodded. "You're probably right."

When he turned his head to glance out the window, I fought a faint sense of disappointment that he so readily accepted my pragmatic response. Troubled, I studied his profile and was privy to Redford's awestruck expression by the sudden and populous skyline that seemed to stretch into infinity. "It's colossal," he breathed.

My heart swelled with the same pride that I suspect all New Yorkers experience when visitors get their first look at the giant landscape.

"Flying in was dramatic," Redford said, his voice full of wonder. "But seeing it from this perspective, it's almost unbelievable."

I nodded, smiling. "New York is enormous, but everyone finds their little corner and settles in. And after a while you forget how big it is."

He leaned closer to the window to peer up at the towering buildings. A few blocks later, the cab turned down a side street, into a part of the city I'd never traveled. Several turns later, we were definitely off the beaten path, in a retail area that seemed to be dominated by car dealerships and repair shops. The cabbie turned in to a new-car dealership, then turned his head and asked, "This okay?"

"This is fine," Redford assured him, opening the door.

I frowned, confused. "Shall I hold the cab and wait for you?"

Redford shook his head and extended his hand. "That won't be necessary. We're driving out of here."

I put my hand in his, and even the nubby yarn of my glove wasn't enough to dull the zing of touching him. "You're buying a car?"

"A truck," he corrected, then closed the door. Again he waved off the cabbie's help with his bag and paid the bill, adding a tip large enough to disturb me. Redford shook the cabbie's hand, then gave a friendly wave as the car pulled away. The driver waved back, clearly puzzled. I squelched a smile, thinking the cabbie would no doubt tell his wife that evening about the Southerner who handled his own bag, overtipped, shook his hand and waved goodbye.

"Redford," I murmured. "You tipped that man a hundred percent."

Redford shrugged good-naturedly. "It's only money."

I stood flat-footed as shock waves rolled over me. *It's only money?* Redford personified my nightmare client. I had, of course, noticed his tendency to be loose with money during the time we'd been in Vegas, but I'd rationalized that it was *Vegas.* Even I had gotten caught up in the partying, freewheeling atmosphere. I'd lost thirty-five dollars on slots the first day…oh, and I'd wound up married. But in hindsight, Redford had been happy to let me take care of our taxes—was he a financial train wreck?

While I pondered that disconcerting line of thought, Redford smiled and shouldered his leather duffel bag, then headed toward the sales office. I trailed behind, more than a little uncomfortable. I'd never purchased a car before, but I'd heard enough horror stories from friends to know that it would be easy to be taken for a ride, so to speak.

And, sure enough, the salesman had seen Redford coming. He came over and the men shook hands as if they knew each other. By the time I caught up to them, the salesman was moving toward an area where gigantic pickup trucks were parked. Redford introduced me to "Jim," who was handsome in a slick kind of way, and I nodded politely.

"Ah, so this is the little woman," Jim said in a sales-y voice.

I opened my mouth to object, but Redford suddenly squeezed me close with a one-armed hug and laughed. "That's right." After a few seconds of utter confusion, I realized that Redford was working the salesman by pretending we were married in preparation for the good cop/bad cop negotiating blitz. I brightened—I could negotiate a bargain. I lived for chances to be bad cop.

"I believe this is what you asked for," Jim said, patting the hood of a gigantic red pickup with an extra-large cab that looked as if it could tow a house.

While Redford walked around the truck, nodding his approval, I sneaked a glance at the sticker price and nearly swallowed my tongue. Not only could the truck *tow* a house, it cost almost as much as one. I opened my mouth to start my bad cop monologue and Redford said, "I'll take it."

"Great," Jim said, beaming.

Since my mouth was already open, I gaped in horror. Sticker price? He was going to pay sticker price?

"Um, *honey,*" I said demurely, squeezing Redford's arm and, God help me, not hating it, "maybe we should discuss this."

Redford's eyebrows raised slightly and he seemed amused. "Discuss what, *sweetie?*"

I shot daggers at him behind the salesman's back. "The price," I said between clenched teeth.

But he only laughed and patted my hand. "Like I said, it's only money."

I felt faint, both from the teasing interplay and his irreverence. The financial demon in me reared her frugal head. "But, *honey,* remember we might have an unexpected expense coming up next week."

"*Sweetie,* you worry too much," he chided, his dark eyes half-serious. "I'll take care of everything."

His voice was so level, so calming that I actually believed him. I was breaking one of the cardinal rules I gave to my female clients: Don't assume your boy-friend/husband/significant other knows more about money than you do. With a jolt I remembered just how susceptible I was to Redford's charm. It was his money, after all—he had the right to spend it anyway he pleased.

Yet I didn't want Redford to be in arrears with the IRS. If my creative accounting was the root cause of any fines, I would offer to pay for everything, of course...although if it were more than a nominal amount, I wouldn't be able to...unless Ellen Brant opened an account at Trayser Brothers.

Thinking of Ellen made me think of Barry and all that I was keeping from him. Guilt washed over me anew—I was engaged to Barry, yet hadn't hesitated to pretend to be Redford's wife for the sake of saving a few bucks.

And the ease with which Redford and I had fallen into calling each other pet names was even more unsettling. Redford had often called me "sweetie" when we were together. Adrenaline rushed through my veins—I felt like I had stepped into quicksand, and was already up to my manhandled knees.

"Right this way," Jim said, his voice triumphant with a new sale. Then he turned to me and said, "Denise, you're exactly how Redford described you."

I blinked. "Pardon me?"

"Jim and I served together in Iraq," Redford said, his expression somewhat sheepish.

"He talked about you nonstop," Jim said, grinning.

I was shot through with shock and some other sensation that was unidentifiable—pleasure? Satisfaction? Dismay?

"Jim," Redford cut in, clapping the man on the back, "you wouldn't want me to start telling stories on *you* now, would you?"

Jim laughed outright. "No. I guess we all pulled a few stupid stunts while we were away from home, didn't we?" They shared a belly laugh as they walked to the sales office.

I stayed in the showroom to allow Redford to sign the paperwork and to allow myself time to absorb what Jim had said. Redford had talked about me to his buddies? Nonstop? Why had that declaration shaken me so? Because I had assumed that Redford had returned to his unit and lamented the big mistake he'd made by marrying a virtual stranger in Vegas, that's why. Of course, maybe he had chalked it up to one of the "stupid stunts" that Jim had mentioned.

Confused, I dropped into a chair, and pulled out my cell phone. I considered called Kenzie, but she had reacted strangely when I'd told her that Barry had proposed, and even more so when I'd told her about Redford's visit. In truth, we'd had quite a spat about mistakes I'd made and mistakes she was afraid I would make again. Until her hormones leveled out, I was prepared to keep my distance. Instead, I dialed Cindy.

She answered on the first ring. "Hello?" Her voice lilted with hope, and I hated to disappoint her that it was just me calling and not the guy from her Positive Thinking class.

"Hey, it's Denise."

"Hi! I'm having lunch with Jacki, and the suspense is killing us! Have you seen Redford? Does he look the same?"

I touched my hand to my temple. "Yes, I've seen him, and he looks…the same."

Cindy covered the mouthpiece and I could hear her say, "She's seen him and he looks the same!" then came back. "Wait—Jacki wants to listen, too. Okay, go ahead. You were saying he looks the same?"

"Maybe a tad better," I admitted, thinking of the black hat.

"Does he still have the Washington Monument in his pants?" Jacki asked dryly.

"I'm hanging up."

"No, wait!" Cindy shouted. "Jacki was kidding. What was it like when you saw each other again? Did you see fireworks?"

Jacki scoffed. "Enough with the fantasy, Cindy."

"Wait a minute," Cindy said in a huff. "Jacki, aren't you the woman who found Mr. Right based on the pair of *shoes* he was wearing? You have a *season pass* to fantasyland."

I rolled my eyes at their banter. "Hello? Can you two argue on your own airtime?"

"Denise, did you see each other across a crowded room?" Cindy persisted. "Did the world stop?"

"Oh, brother," Jacki muttered.

But I had to admit that those strange tingling sensations mounted in my chest again. "It was a little awkward, I suppose." I sighed. "I...I don't know why I called."

"Are you in love with him again?" Cindy asked dreamily.

"Of course she isn't," Jacki retorted, then added, "Are you, Denise?"

"Of course I'm not," I assured her. "I guess I'm just feeling a little out of sorts."

"That's because he was your first love," Cindy declared.

Jacki scoffed. "Does your first love happen to be wearing a ring?"

"Yes."

"What a coincidence, both of you wearing rings."

"I got it, Jacki," I said wryly. "Don't worry, nothing is going to happen."

"Where is he now?" Cindy asked.

"Buying a new pickup truck."

They gasped. "Just like that? He got off the plane and is buying a new truck?"

"And he paid sticker price," I added miserably.

They gasped again.

"Denise, I know that full retail is painful for you to watch," Jacki said gently, "but it's more proof that the marriage would've never worked." She sighed. "I know you've never quite gotten over Redford, but this audit is the best thing that could have happened. The more time you spend with Redford, the more you'll realize that getting an annulment was the right thing to do. Besides, he's married…and you have Barry now."

My shoulders fell in relief. "You're right. Of course, you're right. I knew you two would make me feel better."

"How's the bidding on the dress?" Cindy asked.

I frowned. "When I checked this morning, SYLVIESMOM was winning. Will you log on and bid again when you have time?"

"Absolutely," Cindy said. "You *will* wear that dress when you walk down the aisle!"

I smiled into the phone. "Thanks, girls. I'll call you soon. Cindy, have fun tonight on your date."

I disconnected the call and spent the next few

minutes practicing deep breathing and relaxation techniques.

I will not make the same mistake twice. I will not make the same mistake twice.

A few minutes later, I was feeling slightly more in control. But when the office door opened and Redford came out grinning and, from one evocative finger, dangling the keys to his new ride, my Zen fled.

"Ready to go?" he asked.

I nodded, trying to banish wicked, wicked thoughts from my mind. I followed him toward the monster truck, trotting to keep up with his long stride. He opened the passenger-side door for me and before I knew what was happening, he'd put his hands on my waist to lift me onto the tan leather seat. I gasped and instinctively put my hands on his shoulders. Our bodies connected like a plug and socket—instant voltage. My gaze locked with his; my breath frozen in my chest.

Redford seemed to be having trouble breathing as well, attested by the long, uneven white puffs in the frigid air of the cab. His hands tightened around my waist as he settled me into the seat. The leather must have been cold, but I couldn't feel anything except the warmth radiating from his body. My knees hit him chest level, my coat and skirt rucked up past my knees several inches to expose my thighs. I had a vision of another time when Redford had set me on a table for the purpose of devouring me. From the slightly hooded look in his eyes, I wondered if he were remembering, too.

I gulped air and gave a little cough, releasing his shoulders and squirming against his hands. He let go of my waist and stepped back, but gave my legs a lingering glance before closing the door. I exhaled noisily and counted to five. Considering our history, it was natural for us to experience a little awkward attraction…wasn't it? But we were adults…we could deal with it.

By the time I'd righted my clothing, he had tossed his duffel bag into the back seat of the cab and climbed into the driver's seat, where he began making adjustments to accommodate his long legs. If our brush with flirtation had affected him, he had dismissed it easily enough.

"I hope you don't mind navigating," he said, placing his hat on the seat between us. "It might take me a few hours to get my bearings."

"I don't mind," I said, still shaken.

"So, what do you think about my truck?"

"It's…red."

"Red is the color of DeMoss Stables."

I nodded. "Ah. And it's…big. I've never seen a pickup with a back seat."

"It's called a quad-cab."

"Oh."

His brows knitted. "You don't like it?"

I laughed and gestured vaguely at the dashboard that looked big enough to belong to an aircraft. "Redford, it's your truck. But you barely glanced at it before you bought it. Do you always make such rash decisions?"

His jaw tensed and, too late, I realized that in light of our past, my question seemed at once unnecessary *and* judgmental.

"Apparently so," he said quietly, then turned the key in the ignition, bringing the engine to life. He turned his dark eyes in my direction. "But then I usually know what I want when I see it."

The moisture evaporated from my mouth. I couldn't seem to drag my gaze from his. I was mired in confusion, tongue-tied. Was he referring to me? To our marriage? Did I want to know?

"Better buckle up," he said breezily.

Glad to have something to keep my hands occupied, I tugged on the buckle. But the strap was stuck from never being used.

"Here, let me," he said, and leaned across the seat, brushing past me to grab the strap, trapping me between the seat and his big body. His face was mere inches from mine, the scent of strong, musky soap tickling my nose. I squirmed, which, to my dismay, resulted in rubbing my chest against his. My cheeks burned as if we were naked, instead of wearing heavy coats. Just having him in proximity was wreaking havoc with my self-control.

A lazy smile lifted Redford's mouth as he pulled the belt over my shoulder and clicked it home next to my thigh. "I wouldn't want anything bad to happen to you on my watch."

I gave him a watery smile of thanks and prayed that he couldn't tell how much he was getting to me.

I wasn't in the business of feeding the ego of married men. A glance at the gold band on his left hand was enough to boost my resolve.

He turned on the heater, fastened his own seat belt, then goosed the engine a couple of times before pulling out of the lot. "Which way?"

I looked around to get oriented, then pointed right. I waited until he had pulled into traffic before asking, "Redford, what was that all about back there?"

"What do you mean?"

I wet my lips. "Allowing that guy to think we were…married."

He studied the road, then made a rueful noise. "Jim and I knew each other when I returned from my leave in Las Vegas three years ago." He shrugged. "Maybe it was wrong, but since you were with me, it just seemed easier to pretend than to explain that you and I were no longer…together." He looked over at me. "I'm sorry if it embarrassed you."

Considering I hadn't told Barry or my parents the complete truth either, I wasn't exactly in a position to judge. "No, it's…okay." Antsy, I glanced at my watch.

"Am I making you late?" he asked.

"No. I told my boss I'd be taking an extended lunch," (actually, I had told him I was on the trail of a big account), "but I'll need to get back soon."

"Do you still have time to eat?"

I wasn't the slightest bit hungry, but with some alarm I realized I wasn't yet ready to leave Redford's company. We had so much to discuss, yet so many things I didn't want to talk about. The audit. His family. My engagement. I guess deep down I knew that talking about those things would put an end to the flirtation that I was enjoying on some very base level.

Plus, I realized in astonishment, it would also put an end to the impossible fantasy I had been harboring in the recesses of my mind: that someday Redford would come for me.

The thought hit me so hard, I blinked back sudden moisture. I had discovered something about myself that I didn't want to know. What part of myself had I been withholding from friends and potential lovers since I had returned from Vegas three years ago? What part of myself had I given to Redford…and would I ever get it back?

"Earth to Denise."

I looked over at him. "What?"

His smile was gentle. "I asked if you still have time to eat."

My throat constricted. "Yes, I have time to eat."

The sooner we got things out on the table, the better.

The times we had made love on a table notwithstanding, of course.

"Good," he said. "Afterward I'll drop you off at your office."

"No," I said quickly, then gave a little laugh. "That's not necessary—my office is close to the restaurant I had in mind." A lie, but I couldn't risk anyone seeing me being dropped off by a good-looking stranger driving a red monster truck. I wouldn't want word getting back to Barry. My fiancé. The guy who was available and loved my mind. The guy with whom I had so much in common.

Redford winked and slanted a sexy smile in my direction. "Whatever the lady wants."

I feigned fascination with a passing landmark to cover my traitorous internal reaction. Blast that devilish smile of his! As the interior of the truck warmed I exhaled slowly, settling into the leather seat, forcing myself to relax one muscle at a time. I wasn't going to think about the days stretching before us— I was going to deal with Redford one hour at a time.

But it's over a hundred hours until he leaves, my mind whispered.

I was in big trouble.

9

"TABLE FOR TWO?" the hostess of Rutabaga's asked me, although she could barely take her eyes off Redford.

"Yes," I said, slightly irked. The man was like a tranquilizer dart.

She checked a seating chart and smiled past my shoulder at Redford. "It'll be just a few moments."

I smirked and stepped back into the knot of people who were also waiting for a table. Redford had removed his hat and was studying the dark, oaky decor, although not as closely as he was being studied by every female in the place...me included.

To say that Redford stood out was an understatement—with his stark good looks, brawny build and Western-flavored clothing, he looked as if he'd just walked off a movie set. My mind flashed to the movie *Crocodile Dundee,* where a bushman visits Manhattan for the first time. Like the character in the movie, Redford seemed oblivious to the attention he attracted.

"Looks like a nice place," he offered. "Do you eat here often?"

"Sometimes," I lied.

Actually, I'd chosen the eatery for its proximity to Redford's hotel, its carnivorous menu, its tucked away location and its high, dark booths…not that I expected to see anyone I knew. For as long as I'd lived in New York, I could count the times I had actually run in to someone I knew—unless it was a regular haunt—on one hand.

"Denise! Fancy meeting you here!"

I froze, then turned to see Sam Long, Kenzie's veterinarian husband, walking toward me holding a carryout bag. Sam taught at a clinic in the city three days a week to be close to Kenzie, who was holed up in Jar Hollow this week with morning sickness.

I managed a smile. "Hi, Sam."

He gave me a quick hug. "Hey, congratulations on your engagement—Kenzie's been talking about it all week."

I felt Redford's gaze snap to me and I sensed him inch closer. For reasons I couldn't fathom, I found myself wishing that Sam hadn't said anything, although the subject was bound to come up sooner or later. And considering the inappropriate feelings that Redford had resurrected in me, sooner was better.

"Thanks, Sam," I murmured. "Congratulations to you on the baby."

A grin split his face. "Amazing, huh? I'm still trying to get used to the idea of being a father. I guess this is a big week for all of us." He looked around. "Is Barry with you?"

"Er, no," I squeaked.

"Traveling again? Well, he doesn't deserve you," Sam said cheerfully. "But then I married up, too."

Sam and Barry had never really hit it off, which had concerned me a little simply because I was so close to Kenzie and wanted us all to get along. But Kenzie had assured me that Sam was shy and didn't normally warm up to people right away.

Redford cleared his throat, and Sam looked back and forth between us, clearly puzzled.

I inhaled deeply. "Sam Long, meet Redford De-Moss. Sam is married to one of my best friends, Kenzie, and Redford is…an old friend."

Realization dawned on Sam's face. "Oh, right, Kenzie said something about your ex coming to town, some kind of tax business, right? Nice to meet you," he said to Redford.

Redford extended his hand. "Same here."

"You're from Kentucky?"

"That's right."

"Know anything about horses?"

Redford smiled and his stance eased. "A fair bit. You?"

I watched in amazement as the two men fell into conversation like old buddies, throwing around horse terminology, each visibly excited to find a kindred spirit. Sam had specialized in equine research and lived on a farm in upstate New York where he ran a small-town veterinary practice.

"I'm heading up to Valla Farms Sunday to check out a teaser stud," Redford said.

"That's only about thirty miles from my place," Sam said. "I'd be happy to go along and look him over for you."

"I'd be much obliged," Redford said.

"Denise, are you riding up, too?" Sam asked. "I know Kenzie would be thrilled to see you."

I shook my head. "I wasn't planning to—"

"Come with me," Redford said, his voice husky... challenging.

I swung my gaze up to meet his and saw something had clouded his eyes—disappointment? Determination? I was thoroughly confused. And intrigued.

"Unless you have other plans," he added mildly.

Sam gave a little laugh. "I would consider it a personal favor, Denise. Kenzie could use some company."

Redford lifted one eyebrow in question, and I wavered. In the nearly one year since Kenzie had commuted to Jar Hollow on the weekends, I had never visited her home there. My excuse had always been that I didn't have a car. But since Redford was going to be stopping there, it seemed ridiculous for me not to go. Besides, it might help to smooth things over with Kenzie.

I gave a cautious little shrug. "Okay."

"Great," Sam said. "I'll let Kenzie know." He gave Redford directions, then extended his hand again. "Nice to meet you, man. I think it's great that the two of you can put the past behind you and still be friends."

Redford shook Sam's hand and nodded. "See you Sunday."

"Your table is ready," the nearly giddy hostess announced to Redford.

With my tongue in my cheek, I followed her to a booth. Redford walked just behind me, his hand hovering at my waist. He helped me out of my coat, casting a lingering glance at my engagement ring when I removed my gloves to stuff them in the pockets. Then he removed his own coat and hat and hung them on a nearby rack. I watched him, guiltily stealing a glance at the way his jeans hugged his lean hips from behind, the way the muscles in his back played beneath his shirt. The man could turn the most simple movements into sexy athleticism.

I realized my mouth was watering, and not from the aroma of steak in the air. I pinched my thigh to derail my wayward thoughts and had conjured up a casual smile by the time he returned to slide into the booth, sitting opposite me. A waitress showed up to take our drinks order, then left us alone in an awkward, tense silence.

"Your friend's husband seems like a nice guy," Redford offered.

"He is," I agreed.

"And you're engaged to be married."

I blinked, then lifted my chin. "As a matter of fact, I am."

He reached over and picked up my left hand to study the engagement ring Barry had given me. The callused tips of his fingers brushed my sensitive palm, sending waves of awareness shooting up my arm. It was all I could do not to pull my hand back.

He rubbed his thumb over the large stone. "Wow. Impressive."

With some effort, I found my voice. "Thank you."

"It looks flawless. And it's much bigger than the one I would have given you," he said, nodding.

His grandmother's ring. He had promised to get it from his family safe and bring it with him on his next leave. I flushed, feeling shallow, and pulled my tingling hand from his. Self-consciously, I put my left hand in my lap and fingered the hem of my napkin.

He picked up the menu. "So, how long have you been engaged?" His voice was tinged with…anger? Impossible.

I picked up my menu. "Not long."

"Did I hear Sam say a week?"

I frowned. "Why the inquisition, Redford?"

He shrugged, still perusing the menu. "Because when I asked you on the phone if you'd gotten remarried, you said you hadn't."

I raised my eyebrows. "I haven't."

"And that you live alone."

"I do. Redford, if I didn't know better, I'd say you were…irritated that I've moved on with my life."

He glanced up at me, his mouth set in a straight line.

"B-but that would be ridiculous," I stammered. "B-because you're married with a family."

"Excuse me?" He dropped his menu.

"Well, aren't you?"

"No! What on earth gave you that idea?"

I dropped my menu. "Because you said…on the

phone…that you were in Versailles…because your girls were there."

His face crumpled in laughter. "I meant my nieces." His eyes twinkled. "And my mares."

My pulse raced wildly. I was at a loss for words, until my gaze rested on his left hand. I pointed at the irrefutable evidence. "What about your wedding ring?"

He looked down. "Oh. That."

"Yeah…*that*."

He slid it off his finger and pushed it across the table toward me. "It's the one you gave me, Denise."

I stared at the plain gold band as if it were booby-trapped. My mind reeled. "You kept your ring?" *Didn't you?* my conscience whispered.

"I put it in storage and just never got around to doing anything with it. I thought you might want it back to, you know, melt down into a nugget or something."

"A nugget?"

"Isn't that the fashionable thing to do with wedding rings once the marriage is over? Make a nugget pendant out of the ring?"

I shook my head. "I have no idea."

"Some of my Marine buddies who were married more than once just kept adding to theirs." He laughed. "One guy's nugget got so big, he had a belt buckle made out of it."

I pursed my mouth. "Impressive." And it reinforced the information reported in the newspaper article that had prompted me to file for the annulment—soldiers liked to get married.

He sobered and cleared his throat. "You can take it. Sell it if you like."

Glinting under the light of the pendant fixture that hung over the table, the plain band of gold looked new. The large circumference of the ring reminded me of how difficult it had been to find a band to fit Redford's thick finger...the man had large hands. Hands that knew how to do indescribable things to me. With great effort, I brought my mind back to the present.

"You sent *my* ring back with the annulment papers," I murmured.

"I figured you could sell it to help pay the legal fees."

I pressed my lips together and nodded, unable to admit that I had kept the ring...and not just because I'd forgotten about it.

He picked up his ring and extended it toward me. "Do you want it?"

I swallowed and shook my head.

He nodded matter-of-factly, then tucked the ring into his shirt pocket, where it pushed against the polished cotton. The rounded neck of a snowy white T-shirt peeked just above the top button of his khaki-colored shirt...under his jeans he would be wearing equally white boxer shorts. The elastic waistband would ride just below a tiny mole on his left hip. My mind seemed determined to delay processing Redford's bombshell of a revelation.

"So," I said slowly, "you're...not...married?"

He held my gaze. "Nope. But you're engaged."

"Right."

His dark eyes were unreadable, his expression still. My emotions ran the gamut from nervous to miffed to flattered to worried. I'd agreed to spend time with Redford because I'd thought he was married and it seemed…safe. Now, I wasn't so sure.

The waitress came to leave our drinks—water for me, sweet iced tea for Redford—and to take our orders. My stomach was in such turmoil, I couldn't conceive of eating, but I ordered soup to appear normal. Conversely, Redford ordered a porterhouse steak, baked potato, mixed vegetables and a chef's salad with extra cheese.

When the waitress left, he rested his elbows on the table. "So…who's the lucky guy?"

I took a drink of water from my glass. "His name is Barry Copeland. He's a television producer."

He nodded. "Sounds exciting. How long have you known him?"

"A couple of years."

He gave a little smile. "I guess that's the proper amount of time to know someone before you get married."

I nodded. "I…suppose so."

"Have you set a date for the wedding?"

"No."

"Are you going to do it up right this time with a fancy dress and lots of attendants?"

I squirmed, thinking about that darned dress hanging in my closet. "We haven't discussed it, really."

"I heard you tell Sam that your boyfriend was out of town."

"That's right. He's in L.A. for a few days."

He pressed his lips together. "He doesn't know that I'm here, does he?"

I shifted in my seat and tried to look indignant. "What makes you think that?"

"Because no man in his right mind would leave town while his fiancée plays hostess to her ex-husband."

"Redford, you're not my ex-husband," I said lightly.

"Oh, right—the annulment." He leaned back in the booth and pulled on his chin. "A signed piece of paper that says nothing happened between us doesn't make it so. I was there, Denise…something happened."

Beneath the table, I had frayed the end of the napkin with my frantic picking. "That was a long time ago, Redford. I was…different."

His dark eyebrows lifted. "Different? Different how?"

A flush climbed my throat and heated my face inch by inch. I realized that I needed to be blunt for my own salvation. I leaned forward for the sake of discretion and chose my words carefully. "People sometimes do strange things when they're in a place where they don't know anyone. I'm not the woman that you knew in Las Vegas…that was…temporary."

His eyes narrowed slightly. "Temporary?"

I nodded. "A...phase."

He pursed his mouth and leaned forward until our faces were mere inches apart. "You're telling me," he said, his voice low and husky, "that the amazingly sexy, sensual woman I knew and married in Las Vegas no longer exists?"

His words stroked my skin like the blade of a knife—raising gooseflesh and promising peril if I made a wrong move. His eyes were dark and teasing...tempting. Challenging me to be that woman again—the one who'd given him full power over her body and done things she'd only read about, the one who'd fallen under his spell so completely that she'd thrown caution to the wind and married a man with whom she had nothing in common. Only one answer made sense, but I wavered, lured by the promise in his eyes that we could pick up where we'd left off. Five days of pure carnal bliss.

I opened my mouth and the words stalled on my tongue. I moistened my dry lips. "Redford..."

The tip of his tongue appeared to wet his lips. "Yes?"

"Here's your food," the waitress announced.

I sat back and watched awkwardly while she deposited various plates and bowls in front of us. I felt light-headed from the pressure of the decision at hand.

When she left, Redford was still staring at me. "You were saying, Denise?"

I inhaled deeply, then exhaled. "I was saying that you're right, Redford. That woman doesn't exist."

The light went out of his eyes, but he smiled none-theless. "Okay. You don't have to worry—I'll be-have myself." He picked up his fork and knife. "Are we still on for sightseeing tomorrow?"

I nodded slowly, relieved that Redford had ac-cepted my explanation without question. Maybe we could be friends after all…. And we still had to get through the audit on Tuesday. "You'll be okay by yourself tonight?"

His eyebrows shot up, then an amused smile curved his mouth. "I'll manage."

My cheeks flamed. "I didn't mean—"

"Relax, Denise. I didn't expect you to entertain me every minute that I'm here. Jim's coming by tonight and we're going to get a drink, maybe find a cigar bar."

Go out on the town, find a couple of girls? To which he had every right, I told myself. "You still smoke?"

He nodded, then grinned. "I'm afraid you'll find me pretty much the way I was when you knew me before."

My thighs tingled. He was mocking my assertion that I was different now. I carefully picked up my soup spoon. "So I'll come by your hotel in the morn-ing, say around ten?"

"I'll be ready," he said, all pleasant politeness.

I watched as he dove into his food with the enthu-siasm I remembered—the enthusiasm with which he approached everything in life, including sex. Once upon a time, he had tackled my body with animalistic energy. It had changed my life…for a few precious days. He'd just let me know that he was willing to take me to that place again, where nothing mattered except how good we made each other feel.

I focused on spooning some type of soup into my mouth, but my hand was shaking. I just hoped that Redford wouldn't notice.

10

WORK FRIDAY afternoon was a blur. I spent most of it staring at my computer screen, (I received a quick e-mail from Barry who said he'd call later), and communicating with Ellen Brant's voice mail (saying I was looking forward to hearing from her and finalizing the paperwork for her investment account). Ellen's assistant finally called me back and asked if we could meet Tuesday afternoon. I couldn't imagine the audit taking all day, so I agreed. I should have felt happy, but honestly, I felt lousy that I was taking advantage of an opportunity that Barry had arranged, yet I was keeping so much from him. I typed a chatty, understanding e-mail reply to Barry, then looked up laboratory diamonds on the Internet, telling myself I needed to be familiar with the emerging industry if an investment opportunity presented itself.

The technology was fascinating—a machine compressed carbon under extreme pressure to form a diamond, in two days replicating the same process that took nature thousands of years to achieve, except the "laboratory" diamond was flawless. (So Redford had been right.) Diamond mine owners were concerned about the competition, but seemed sure that most customers would prefer "real" diamonds, citing that eternal love was best represented by a naturally formed stone. Creators of the engineered diamonds, however, argued that love was best represented by a flawless stone.

I bit my lip, frowned and logged off.

On the walk home, I found myself looking at my surroundings as Redford might: leaning my head back to gaze at the buildings, taking time to notice the street vendors, even splurging on a bouquet of Gerber daisies, which were scandalously expensive this time of year. I resisted, however, buying a bag of peanut M&M's. If I had the willpower to turn down Redford's offer of a sexual escapade, I could resist anything.

When I arrived home, the tickets to Las Vegas that I'd ordered for me and Barry were in the mail—a reminder that I had made the right decision concerning Redford. I found a vase for the flowers and nuked a wedge of low-fat lasagna—my scant lunch had left me starving. While I ate, I booted up my laptop to check my wedding-dress auction, then frantically dialed Cindy.

"SYLVIESMOM is winning!" I said. "You have to bid higher!"

"How high do you want me to go?"

"It doesn't matter, because there won't be a transaction. Just keep bidding!"

"Okay."

I looked at my watch. "Wait a minute—aren't you supposed to be having a drink with the guy from your class?"

She sighed. "He called and asked for a rain check. He said something had come up. Personally, I think he got a better offer."

"That's not possible," I murmured, furious with the jerk. "Want to come over?"

"Thanks, but I told my neighbor I'd help her paint her bathroom. You're not entertaining Redford tonight?"

"No," I said, too quickly.

She picked up on it. "Did something happen after we talked?"

"No," I said, then swallowed. "Well...yes. I found out that Redford's not married."

"Really?"

"No wife, no kids."

"*Omigod*—maybe he's still in love with you!"

I emitted a strangled laugh. "Cindy, that's ridiculous. If he were in love with me, don't you think he would've gotten in touch with me before now?"

"Maybe he was afraid you'd reject him."

I laughed again. "Trust me—Redford is afraid of nothing."

"So, if he's not in love with you, what does it matter if he's available?" Then she gasped. "You're not still in love with him, are you?"

"No!" I snapped. "I...well, it just makes me uncomfortable, spending so much time with him now that I know."

"Are you afraid of him?"

"God, no. Redford would never hurt me."

"Then what? You don't trust him?"

"No, of course I trust him. Redford is the most honorable man I know."

"Ah…you don't trust yourself."

"No— I…" I stopped and took a deep breath. "I feel guilty gallivanting around with a single man behind Barry's back."

"Denise, going to the Empire State Building isn't gallivanting. Besides, it's just one day."

"Two days—I'm going stud-shopping with Redford on Sunday."

"Come again?"

"We ran into Sam today, and the horse farm is close to his place, so I'm riding up with Redford to see Kenzie."

"Sounds logical to me."

I chewed on my lip, then exhaled. "You're right. It's completely logical. I'm making too big a deal out of this, aren't I?"

"Yes."

"Thank you. Have fun painting. Oh, and don't forget to raise your bid!"

"I will!"

I hung up, digesting Cindy's sensible words, then alternated between compulsively checking my dress auction and picking up the phone to call Barry and rat on myself. Instead, I dialed my mother's cell phone, expecting to leave a message, astounded when she actually answered.

"Hello?"

"Hi, Mom. It's Denise."

"Denise, what a nice surprise. Is anyone dead, dear?"

I frowned. "Uh…no."

"Oh, I thought you might be calling with bad news. I had a premonition this morning that I was going to hear bad news today. Didn't I, Harrison?"

I could picture my dad nodding. This wasn't going well. "Actually, Mom, I called to tell you that…Barry and I are engaged."

My mother shrieked and covered the mouthpiece. "Harrison—our daughter is getting married!" She came back on the line. "Oh, Denise, we're so happy for you! Aren't we happy for her, Harrison?"

"We're happy for you, sweetheart," my father shouted in the background.

"Have you set a date?" my mother asked.

"No—"

"Oh, you'll have to get a dress! Oh, won't that be fun!"

Thinking of the gown hanging in my closet, I massaged my temple. "Yes. How's your trip?"

"Horrible," my mother declared, then launched into a diatribe about how miserable the weather had been. "*Noah* never saw such rain. I've been wet through and through since the minute we arrived."

I had made appropriate sympathetic noises, then told her to call me when they returned to the States and gave them my love. She was shouting, "My daughter's getting married!" to her friends before she even disconnected the call.

I felt like crap.

What would my mother think of me if she knew that I'd already been married once?

Not *married,* I chided—my marriage to Redford had been *annulled.* Obliterated. Expunged. It didn't exist.

Which wouldn't be so hard to believe if Redford DeMoss wasn't so very, very real. And so very, very sexy. I closed my eyes and remembered the way he had leaned across the table, baiting me with those amazing eyes to let down my guard, to let him in— literally—again. Even now, a tug on my midsection, a warming of my thighs betrayed my answer to Redford. I wanted him so badly it hurt. If only everything I held dear—everything I wanted to be—wasn't at stake. If I gave in to my desires this time, it could be a mistake I'd never recover from.

Desperate for a distraction from my relentless thoughts of Redford who was at this moment with his buddy Jim and probably picking up women with a mere eye-twitch, I turned to the most un-sexy chore I could think of: I delved into the depths of my archived files and pulled out our tax records.

What I found was not comforting. Although I had receipts for most of the home office deductions I'd taken, the expenses themselves were a stretch—and significant. The U.S. tax code at the time was such that as a couple, we actually paid more taxes than if we had been two single people filing. I'd filled out the forms a few days before the annulment had been finalized and, in hindsight, had not been in the best frame of mind. My marriage had been a big mistake—being penalized by the government had only added salt to my wounds. I'd felt entitled to…fudge a little on the return. Now I just felt like eating fudge.

Damn, I wished I'd bought that bag of peanut M&M's.

Even worse than my questionable deductions, I'd dragged Redford into this mess. And I would be humiliated when the tax agent dressed me down for taking advantage of the government, then levied fines and penalties—maybe even criminal charges. Somehow I couldn't bear the thought of looking inept in front of him. Being dragged off in leg irons didn't hold much appeal, either.

Buried near the financial papers from the time we'd been married, I found pamphlets and books on Thoroughbreds and the Marine Corps and logistics— Redford's field of expertise in the Corps. I'd bought them at a bookstore at the Las Vegas airport to learn more about my new husband and his life—what I thought would become my life. The books were dogeared. As I flipped through, I found myself absorbed once again, as I had been three years ago, and settled against the headboard of my bed.

Logistics, I realized, had prepared Redford to run just about any kind of organization. It was good training for the Thoroughbred business he loved, which, I learned from yet another book, required managerial knowledge of every aspect of the business—from hiring good people, to buying quality stock, to overseeing the intricacies of breeding. And I do mean intricacies. Those chapters I read twice, alternately wide-eyed and wincing. Yikes. (But I still wanted to see a stallion's penis.)

Around 10:30 p.m. the phone rang. I tore myself away from my reading long enough to pick up the handset, expecting to hear Barry's voice on the other end. I couldn't wait to tell him about the tickets to Vegas.

"Hello?"

"Hi, Denise. It's Redford."

My throat closed. In the background I could hear bar noise—music, muffled voices.

"Did I catch you at a bad time?"

I guiltily set aside the book on Thoroughbreds. "Just reading. Are you and Jim having a good time?"

"Oh, yeah, sure, it's great to catch up." He cleared his throat. "Denise…I just wanted to call and say…"

"Yes?" My breath caught in my throat. Curled up in bed with the voice of a sexy guy in my ear.… Heaven help me, I felt as if I were sixteen again. My breasts grew taut beneath my thin nightshirt.

"I just wanted to say that it was great to see you again, and…well, good night."

"Good night," I murmured. "I'll see you in the morning, Redford."

"You don't know how good that sounds," he said, his voice low and earnest. "Good night, Denise."

I hung up the phone, lay my head back and groaned. Shivers skated over my skin and heat radiated from the juncture of my thighs. I was in a bad place if Redford was able to turn me on with a few innocent words.

I smoothed a hand over my stomach, then under the elastic band of my panties, closing in on the center of my pleasure. Releasing myself was insurance, I told myself. It would help me to resist the barrage of sexual cues that Redford emitted naturally...

I closed my eyes and his face came into my mind, his eyes hooded and his jaw clenched in restraint. He was above me, inside of me, thrusting cautiously at first, until I could accommodate the amazing length of him fully. Then I took over the rhythm, lifting my hips to meet him thrust for thrust. A warm hum droned deep inside me, flowing over my stomach and down to my knees. The pleasure was singular and intense. I reached under my nightshirt to stroke a budded nipple. Redford loved it when I touched myself. I groaned and strained harder against the pressure in my nest. The vibration inside intensified, like a chant of many voices, rising to the pinnacle note. The bed beneath me seemed to fall away in pieces as I shot into space, crying out his name. "Redford...Redford...ohhhhh...oohhhh...."

I lay still for a few seconds, imbedded in my mattress, marinating in the pleasurable pulsing of recovery and the languid angles of my limbs. It was the last time, I promised myself—the last time I would fantasize about being with another man...about being with Redford. I couldn't continue to condition my body to respond to him physically...his memory had become a sexual habit, I realized...one I had to break if I were ever to get on with my life.

The more my mind swirled, the more alert I became. Other worries began to infringe: the IRS audit, Ellen Brant's business, deceiving Barry and my parents, the wedding dress I was trying to win back. I tried to relax, to tell myself that I needed to be refreshed and emotionally tough to get through the next few days. Yet as I stared at the ceiling, adrenaline coursing through my veins, I knew that tonight I would get about as much sleep as I used to when Redford had been in bed with me—little to none.

11

Saturday
Days left on eBay auction: 3
Bidding on wedding dress up to: $1029
Winning bidder: SYLVIESMOM

THE NEXT MORNING, dead tired and running fifteen minutes late, I trotted into the lobby of the hotel where Redford was staying. That darned SYLVIES-MOM seemed determined to get my dress!

Redford was leaning against a stalwart wood column, dressed in jeans and a navy blue sweatshirt, holding his duster coat over his arm and his black hat against his thigh. I bit back a groan—the man was gorgeous. My stomach quickened, the memory of last night's self-gratification fresh.

He grinned as I approached, then squinted. "Hey, there. Are you feeling okay?"

So much for concealing my dark circles. I nodded and fingered back a lock of hair that had fallen out from under my wool hat. "Fine. Sorry I'm late."

"No problem," he said, nodding toward a picture

window with a particularly nice view. "I was just en-joying the scenery."

As were the people around him, I noted wryly—several women behind the reservations desk ogled him openly. I frowned, knowing that I'd probably worn that same pathetic look on my face around Redford.

"Ready to go?" I asked.

"Wherever you want to take me," he said, swing-ing into his coat and planting his hat on his head.

I refused to acknowledge the spike in my pulse, resolute to be the pleasant but distant tour guide. We would be so busy today, there would be no time for intimate eye contact or waxing nostalgic about our few days in Vegas. I walked two steps in front of him, pumping my arms as fast as my bulky coat would allow. I had dressed for minimum exposure and sex appeal today: loose jeans, turtleneck, chunky sweater, Merrill loafers, unflattering hat.

"I like your hat," he said, easily catching up with me with his long stride and holding open the door that led outside.

"Thanks," I murmured, bracing myself against the cold blast of February air. "I thought we'd go to the Statue of Liberty first."

"Sounds great."

"Is there anything special you'd like to see today?"

He made a rueful noise. "Ground Zero."

I stopped, my heart in my throat as I looked up at him. Of course he'd want to see the World Trade

Center site—the remnants of the event that had pre-cipitated the U.S. re-involvement in the Gulf, where he'd spend the better part of two years, witnessing war and its aftermath.

Beneath the brim of his hat, his eyes were grave, his expression solemn. "I think it's probably neces-sary that I see it."

I nodded, blinking away sudden moisture, then re-sumed walking. "Of course," I said when I found my voice. "In fact, you'll get your first view from the ferry on the way to Liberty Island."

"Do you want me to drive?" he asked, hooking his thumb toward the hotel parking garage.

"I thought we'd take the subway."

"Great. I always wanted to ride the New York subway."

I smiled. "It'll be packed because it's Saturday, but that's part of the charm."

"If you say so," he said cheerfully.

I picked up the pace, heading toward the near-est station. "Did you have a good time last night with Jim?"

"Oh, sure," he said. "Drank a few brews. Talked about the Corps. Oh, and he gave me tickets to *42nd Street* for tonight. Want to go? We could have an early dinner."

I balked.

"Never mind," he said quickly. "You've probably seen it a dozen times."

"Actually...no." It was one of those classic Broadway shows that I just hadn't gotten around to seeing, in favor of more trendy fare. "I'd like to go."

He grinned. "Good. I really didn't want to have to ask Jim to go to a Broadway show with me."

I laughed. "Did he retire from the Corps, as well?"

"No, he's a reservist. Was called up to serve a few months, and we wound up in the same place for a while."

During the time Redford had returned from Vegas, a newly married man. I wet my lips that were already chapped from the cold, and descended stairs into the subway station.

"How has it been for you? Retirement, I mean. And…re-entry."

He smiled. "Back into civilian life, you mean? I'm adjusting. In peace time, being a career military man probably isn't so different from having a corporate job. I had regular office hours with people reporting to me and people I was accountable to. Wartime is a different animal. But it was satisfying to know that I could help my country, my fellow soldiers, my men."

"When did you come back to the States?" I asked. "Weren't you stationed in North Carolina?"

"Right. Cherry Point. But when I came back from the Gulf a year and half ago, they sent me to Albany to finish my service until retirement."

I swallowed hard. "Albany…New York?"

"Yeah. There's a Marine Logistics Base in Albany."

I averted my gaze and concentrated on buying

tickets for the train, but Redford quickly stepped up to pay. Standing behind him, waves of anguish and shock washed over me. If I'd known he'd been so close for so long…

I gave myself a mental shake. What? What would I have done? Called him up to see if we could rekindle the flame? Obviously he'd had the chance to contact me and hadn't. And why would he? I'd made it clear that we had no future together. A fact that was still true…

I chose my words carefully. "And you didn't make it to Manhattan all the time you lived in Albany?"

"Nope," he said, turning to hand me a ticket. "I was working on a special project and had very little free time. And, to be honest, the city didn't have much appeal to me at the time."

Ouch. I'd asked for that. I walked through the turnstile and found a place to stand on the platform, Redford following close behind. "We're going south to Battery Park," I said woodenly. "We'll get the ferry from there to Liberty Island."

Redford seemed fascinated by the crush of people around us…and cautious. When one of a trio of guys horsing around banged into me, Redford pulled me toward him protectively, admonishing the men.

"Watch your step."

The biggest of the three squinted at Redford, instantly belligerent. "Why don't you make me, *cowboy?*"

Alarm gripped me. "Redford—"

"Look here, son," Redford said with a smile to the man who looked to be about the same age. "Neither one of us want trouble."

The man leaned forward, thrusting his face close to Redford's. "Maybe I do—*unnnhhhh.*"

Before the thug could finish his sentence, Redford's hand had snaked out to grab the man by the neck, his thumb pressed into the man's Adam's apple. The guy emitted feeble, hissing sounds as his two cronies backed away. My heart beat wildly.

"Now I'm going to ask you again," Redford said mildly, neither his voice nor his body betraying the least amount of strain. "Watch your step. Okay, friend?" He released the troublemaker with a slight shove backward. The man grabbed his throat, gasping for air and hacking uncontrollably before disappearing into the crowd.

Oblivious to the admiring stares directed his way, Redford glanced toward the approaching train. "Is this one ours?"

"Um, yes." My eyes were still wide as the train slowed and stopped.

"You okay?"

"Redford," I said as I crowded onto the train. "That man—thank you for standing up for me, but…"

He stepped in behind me and reached up to grab a strap, effectively encircling me with his body. He raised an eyebrow. "But?"

I sighed, resisting the urge to sink against his big

body. "But you have to be careful in Manhattan. What if that guy had had a knife, or a gun? Which he probably did, by the way."

Redford seemed unfazed. "He's just a petty punk, Denise. Besides, I've been shot at lots of times."

When the train took off, my heart was still clicking in amazement and—I must admit—pride. And God help me, Redford's calm command of the situation ignited a sensual fire in me. Here was a man who would sacrifice his life for a noble cause…or for *me*.

You gotta love a man like that.

Not that I *loved* Redford. I was being hypothetical.

The train lurched forward, slamming me into Redford's chest. He steadied me with his free hand, emitting a little laugh. I looked around for a pole to grab on to, but the nearest one was filled with hands.

"Hook a finger through my belt loop," he offered.

I didn't *want* to look at his belt loop area, but after that invitation, how could I not? I lowered my gaze along the opening in his coat to take in his belt loops—and lower still, where I hadn't dared to look before. The substantial bulge I remembered was still there. (Redford, as a man's tailor would say, dressed "left.") Ignoring the stab of desire that hit me unexpectedly, I glibly hooked my pinkie through a belt loop and looked elsewhere. "Thanks."

"No, thank *you*," he said, his eyes dancing.

The ensuing flush kept me warm until we arrived at Battery Park. We made our way along the waterfront to purchase ferry tickets, then bought a cup of strong coffee and watched a woman juggle frying pans until the ferry arrived. Crowds were light because the weather was brisk. But it was a beautiful, clear, sunny day. As the ferry took off across the water, I felt as if I were in a romantic movie, standing at the rail next to a big, handsome guy, the wind blowing in my face. It would have been perfect if we had been in love. Those pesky regrets threatened to break through my careful resolve.

As we passed southern Manhattan, I pointed to the skyline and tried to explain where the twin towers had once stood. "Almost twice as tall as any building you see there."

He stared hard. "I can envision it from all the pictures I've seen." Then he pivoted his head to look at me. "You love living in the city, don't you?"

I nodded.

"Could you ever see yourself living anywhere else?"

I squirmed, remembering that once I'd naively thought I could live in Kentucky on a horse farm. I tried to make light of his question. "Well, my parents are always hinting that I move closer to them in Florida, but I've resisted."

"They're still in Fort Myers?"

I nodded, surprised that he remembered. "Are your parents still in good health?"

He smiled wide. "Oh, yeah. My mom is as sassy as ever, my dad just happy to have me back in the business. He's pushing me to expand the stables in a big way."

"I thought you were retired," I teased.

He laughed. "DeMoss men don't retire…we die in a full sweat."

I had seen Redford in a full sweat, and it *was* to die for. "A-aren't your siblings still involved in the business?"

"Both my brothers and both my sisters, and they're good. So good that I don't feel very useful most of the time."

His brothers were older, I remembered, his sisters younger. "Which one has the little girls?" I asked, although I felt as if I was prying.

"My brothers are both single," he said. "One of my sisters is married now—Sarah. She's the one with the little girls—Janie and Maggie."

I resisted the urge to ask more questions about his family. I didn't need to know. With a start, I wondered how much—if anything—they knew about me. "Do they know why you're up here?"

He nodded, but said nothing, which made me even more uncomfortable. Had Redford, like me, neglected to mention to his family that he'd gotten married in a quickie ceremony in Vegas? And if he had mentioned it, what must they think of me? My behavior must have seemed even more unwholesome to people who undoubtedly held very traditional values—not unlike my folks. My face burned.

"Oh, wow," he breathed as the Statue of Liberty came into full view.

I turned to take in the view I never tired of, no

matter how many visiting friends and relatives I brought on this trip. Newly renovated, Lady Liberty was spectacular in the morning sun—her copper robe in green and blue patinas that shimmered in the light, giving the illusion of moving cloth.

"Did you bring a camera?" I asked.

He shook his head. "I have a photographic memory." He swung his head toward me and gave me one of those intense looks. "I remember *every*thing."

My tongue adhered to the roof of my mouth. How was it possible to get turned on through a thousand layers of clothing? I maintained a frozen smile while we docked and disembarked. We bought tickets for the "insider's view," and were assigned to a park ranger for our guided tour. I hadn't visited the monument since it had been refurbished—the lighting had been enhanced and a new video system installed. But most of the time, I looked at Redford.

He listened intently as the guide explained the Statue's symbolism, history, construction, and restoration. He even asked a couple of questions. I marveled at how content I was doing something so mundane with Redford, but his sincere interest in small details made the outing more interesting to me, too.

The tour culminated in a walk out onto the statue's narrow observation deck, sixteen stories up, around the calf of Lady Liberty. From there we had a breathtaking view of New York City and the Harbor. I had a breathtaking view of Redford, too. The wind tousling his hat-flattened hair, his profile sharp and strong, his shoulders mountainous. The sheer strength that emanated from him was…inspiring. He looked over at me and winked, and I glanced away lest he think I was staring at him.

But the moment left me with a bad feeling in my stomach, as if I could be…might be…falling under his spell again. But that, I knew in my heart of hearts, would be the ruin of me. The one thing that kept me from turning around to run was the knowledge that Redford wouldn't entice me to cheat on Barry. As long as I kept my head, I'd be fine.

I repeated the mantra to myself all afternoon as we traipsed from one tourist destination to another. We ate hot dogs on the steps of the Metropolitan Museum, and Redford bought souvenirs for his nieces. We strolled through Central Park, and talked about current events and music. He asked about my job, and where I lived. The mood was light and conversational until we visited Ground Zero.

I had been to the World Trade Center site many times, but not recently…and not with anyone who seemed as connected to the site as Redford. He removed his hat as we stared over the sixteen-acre crater, bustling with construction activity in the distance, but almost silent where we stood with others who came to pay their respects. The heavy gratelike fence that surrounded the site might have been impersonal, except that portions of the fence had been turned into makeshift memorials—pictures, flowers, stuffed animals, and other items commemorating loved ones.

The temperature seemed even colder here, the wind more bitter, wailing mournfully around us.

We didn't speak. As I watched emotions play over Redford's face, my chest and throat grew tight. When he reached down to clasp my gloved hand, I didn't mind—it seemed like a moment to be touching another person. When we left the site, he still clasped my hand, and it struck me that anyone passing by would have mistaken us for a couple. And since I was engaged to another man, that didn't seem quite right.

I broke our handclasp to glance at my watch. "I guess I'd better be heading home to change. If you can find your way back to the hotel, I can cut through here to my apartment."

He nodded. "I'd like to walk to your place to pick you up, if that would be okay."

He looked so…accommodating, it would be rude to say no, I decided. Besides, it wasn't as if I was going to show him my bedroom or anything crazy like that.

"Sure." We made plans to meet in an hour and I gave him directions to my building. I felt his gaze on me as I walked away, but told myself he was only concerned about my safety, which was why he'd offered to come by.

Of course I worried all the way home. What would he think of my place? And did I really want to be able to remember Redford standing in my living room?

By the time I arrived at my apartment, I was sweating under my bulky clothes. I booted up my computer and shed the layers, then sat down to check my auction. WANTSAMAN was winning with a bid of—*gulp*—$1375! I bit my lip, feeling a little guilty for stringing along SYLVIESMOM. Then I remembered the way the woman had tried to tear the dress off my back and frowned. She'd live.

The phone rang and I raced for it, hoping it was Barry. "Hello?"

"It's Kenzie. So you're finally coming to see me, huh?"

One side of my mouth slid back. "Only if you're in a better mood."

She sighed. "I'm sorry about the other day, but this thing with your ex is really weird—I'm worried about you."

I bit my lip. "Why?"

"Because, when you came back from Vegas, it was like you'd joined a cult or something. And I'm afraid you're still hung up on this guy. I'm kind of glad he's married."

"I'm not still hung up on him, and he's not married."

"Oh. Dear. Now I'm really worried."

"Don't be, Kenzie. I'm fine, really."

"Sam says Redford is a nice guy…kind of rugged?" she said, her voice questioning.

"I…guess so."

"Well, I'll be interested to meet him, but I'm more excited that you're coming up. I've already cleared out the guest room to make room for the nursery—I can't wait to tell you my ideas."

"That's nice. But do you think you and Sam can behave yourselves long enough to have company?"

Kenzie laughed. "We don't have sex twenty-four hours a day, Denise."

"That's not what I've heard."

"My hormones are so crazy I haven't felt like having sex for two days now."

"Okay, that's approaching too much information. I'll see you tomorrow."

"Will you have your cell with you?"

"Yeah, I'll call when we get close."

We said goodbye and I hung up, Kenzie's words still playing in my mind. *"When you came back from Vegas, it was like you'd joined a cult."* I frowned. What a strange analogy, but in some way fitting for what I had experienced with Redford in that short time span in Vegas. I had lost myself, turned my mind and body over to him. And I had been so heartbroken after the annulment that months had passed before I could draw a painless breath.

I pushed the disturbing thoughts from my mind while I straightened my apartment. Then I took a shower, telling myself that my raised vital signs did not mean that I was anticipating Redford's arrival.

I was in a quandary about what to wear. Chances were, Redford would be wearing jeans or chinos and maybe a dress shirt. I didn't want to appear too dressy, but I wanted to look nice. Not for Redford, but for…anyone.

Yes, I wanted to look nice not for Redford, but for perfect strangers.

I settled on a plain V-neck black dress and strappy sandals, with my standard low ponytail and simple jewelry.

I paused to study my engagement ring, and guilt consumed me. On impulse, I picked up the phone and dialed Barry's cell phone. To my surprise, he answered. It was a sign, I decided.

"Hi," I said. "Did I catch you at a bad time?"

"Just trying to wade through a month's worth of Nielsen ratings."

I pictured him on the other end rubbing his eyes. Working like a dog, while I entertained my ex. "I talked to my mom yesterday and told her about the engagement. She's thrilled. Dad, too."

"That's great," he said. "I haven't told my folks yet, haven't had a chance to call and have a conversation."

I closed my eyes. "I miss you."

"Me, too," he said. "Are you doing something fun tonight?"

"Um, maybe," I said, fingering my ring. "You?"

He laughed. "Hardly." His phone made a clicking noise. "I'm sorry, Denise, I need to get this. Can I call you tomorrow?"

I would be on the road with Redford tomorrow. "I...might be out."

"Okay, then I'll catch up with you Monday."

Then I'd tell him about the tickets to Vegas. "Sure. Bye…Barry."

"Bye."

I hung up the phone, fighting an unreasonable spike of frustration with Barry because he hadn't taken the time to reassure me that he adored me and that we were good together. When I glanced at my sparkling diamond again, though, I felt horrible. The ring spoke volumes. Hadn't he taken the time to get to know me over two years? Hadn't he gotten to know my parents and my friends? Hadn't he taken an interest in my career and hooked me up to do business with his *boss,* no less? And hadn't he gone to the trouble of buying me a fabulous ring and proposing in public? And while he wasn't a dynamo in bed, he was at least *there* in body and spirit. Redford had been living a couple of hours away for over a year and hadn't bothered to look me up.

A knock on my door sounded and I inhaled deeply. Maybe an evening at a Broadway show would convince me once and for all how different Redford and I really were: city girl, country boy. I smoothed a hand down my sleeve, hoping I wasn't overdressed, then swung open the door.

And hung on to the knob to keep from falling.

Redford stood there, hatless, looking like a million dollars in a black suit, white shirt, and black dress shoes. A taupe-colored wool scarf that looked remarkably like cashmere was draped casually around his neck. His dark hair was neatly combed, still slightly damp, his square jaw clean-shaven. In a word, he was…mouthwatering. (Or was that two words?)

"You look beautiful," he said.

I finally found my voice. "You look…great…too."

His grin was the perfect accessory. "Do I pass?"

"Um…yes."

"Good. I wouldn't want you to be embarrassed to be seen with me."

I swallowed. "No chance of that." I gestured behind me. "Just let me get my coat."

And my resolve, I thought as he followed me inside.

12

REDFORD STEPPED INSIDE my apartment and closed
the door behind him. "Nice place," he said, nodding.

I tried to picture the eclectic furniture and scarred
wood floors from his perspective. "It's old," I said
with a little smile. "But it's solid and the neighbors
aren't psychopaths." I pointed. "Living room here,
kitchen there, study there, bathroom there, bedroom…there. It's small. Everything in New York is
small." I was babbling.

"It's nice," he repeated, running his hand along a
built-in wooden bookshelf. "Good bones, lots of
character. Did you say you were going to buy it?"

I nodded. "Someday." As soon as Ellen Brant
opened her account and my commission check was cut.

"So you and your fiancé are going to live here?"

I blinked. "Well…I don't know." The truth was, I
hadn't even thought about it. Barry and I had lived
separately—and contentedly—for so long, I just assumed… Frankly, I don't know what I assumed.

He accepted my ambiguous answer and studied
the framed photographs on the bookshelf. "These
must be your parents."

I nodded. "In front of their home in Florida."

"You look like your mother."

I warmed because I thought my mother was beautiful. "Thank you."

"Who are these people?" he asked, gesturing to other frames.

"My girlfriends," I said. "There's Jacki and her husband Ted. There's Cindy." I smiled. "She's single, but determined to meet Mr. Right. And this is Kenzie, Sam's wife."

"I'll meet her tomorrow."

"Right," I said slowly, thinking ahead to the long drive. "I thought I'd bring our tax files and we could discuss the audit."

He looked uncomfortable, then recovered. "Sure."

But his reaction made me think that he was dreading the audit more than he let on. No doubt he was worried about the potential cash outlay…as was I. Not to mention the exposure of my tax-cheating ways.

"And this must be your boyfriend?"

My head jerked around to look at the small frame of Barry, his corporate head shot. "Fiancé. And, yes, that's….him."

"Nice-looking fellow."

Thanking him seemed weird, so I just smiled and headed toward the closet to get my coat.

"Does he smoke cigars?"

"Hmm?" I pulled out my coat, turned my head and froze. The Punch cigar box of keepsakes from our wedding sat on the shelf. Redford tapped it with his finger. I didn't want him to know what a sentimental fool I was. "No!" I practically shouted, and he jerked back his hand.

"I'm sorry, I didn't mean to pry."

I felt ridiculous. "No, it's okay, really. I…" My voice petered out and I stood there, stewing in my deceit. I wondered idly if I was losing my mind. Some people say it's always the quiet ones that will fool a person, and I decided that was me. On the surface, I was a nice, thrifty, hardworking good girl. But deep down, I was naughty.

I had begun the train of thought half in jest, but by the end, the revelation that I wasn't a very good person struck me hard…was it possible that the hedonistic, hypersexual, irresponsible way I'd behaved with Redford in Vegas was the true Denise Cooke, and the rest of this was just an act?

"Are you okay?" Redford asked, taking my coat and holding it behind me. "You look like something hurts."

I pressed my lips together, then shook my head. "Just hungry, I suppose."

"I can fix that. Ready to go?"

I nodded and followed him outside into the cold and down the sidewalk, in the direction of a more well-traveled street in order to catch a cab.

"Nice neighborhood," he said.

"Yes. It'll be beautiful in the spring." I dug my gloved hands deeper into my pockets. "Everything really comes alive."

"Sorry I'll miss it," he said with a wistful note in his voice.

I looked over at him. "I'll bet Kentucky is beautiful in the spring, too."

"Oh, sure—nothing like it."

"Is the grass really blue?"

He laughed. "Sometimes. Actually, bluegrass is a type of grass that has a dark cast to it. When it's tall and blowing in the fields, it looks blue."

When we got to the curb, he surprised me by hailing a cab like a pro. I slid inside, saying, "There are lots of good places to eat close to the theater. We shouldn't have a problem—"

"I made reservations," he cut in.

"Oh…that's nice."

"The concierge at the hotel recommended a place called Millweed's."

The place where Barry had proposed. My throat constricted. "Yes, I've…heard of it."

"Is that okay with you?"

"It's great," I said cheerfully. In fact, what better place to be reminded of Barry?

The restaurant hadn't changed much in the six days since I'd been there, except for the addition of a piano player. As luck would have it, we were seated at the same table where Barry and I had been seated. I wasn't surprised—in fact, I rather expected it. When the same waiter appeared, a strange sense of déjà vu enveloped me. It was as if some otherworldly power was forcing me to compare the two men—one I had a life with, the other I had a lust with.

"Okay, I get it," I murmured to myself.

"Pardon me?" Redford said, one eyebrow raised.

"I said I think I'll get a glass of wine."

"How about a bottle?"

"Even better."

The waiter was staring at me. "Weren't you...?"

He remembered me. I shifted in my seat and tried to look clueless. He glanced at Redford and back to me and cleared his throat. "Never mind."

Redford looked at me and I shrugged. After surveying the wine menu, he ordered a bottle of something I'd never heard of that seemed to impress the waiter. I was accustomed to Redford in his hat and boots, drinking a long-neck beer. I was comfortable with the *aw-shucks* version. This refined side of Redford disarmed me. The man sitting across from me would have looked at home at the head of any corporate boardroom.

And was so achingly handsome that he would be welcome in any woman's *bed*room.

"Does your ring need to be sized?" Redford asked.

I blinked. "Pardon me?"

He pointed to my left hand. "You keep twisting your ring."

I looked down to see that he was right. "Um, maybe I do need to get it cut down a bit."

"Size six, right?"

I nodded, surprised that he remembered, although

anything he did at this point shouldn't have surprised me. I clenched my hands together in my lap, grateful when the waiter reappeared to present the bottle of wine to Redford. He glanced at the label and nodded, then the waiter uncorked the bottle and poured a half-inch into his glass. I watched, mesmerized, as Redford held up his glass to look at the brilliantly berry-hued wine. Then he swirled the liquid slightly and inhaled the aroma before taking a sip and nodding to the waiter. "Very good."

The waiter filled my glass, then Redford's glass, and took our orders—steak for Redford, trout for me. When we were left alone, I felt trapped. I wanted to stare at Redford, to drink him in, yet I didn't dare. To avoid eye contact, I sipped my wine…heartily. Whether Redford picked up on my discomfort or was feeling uneasy himself, I wasn't sure, but he seemed content to listen to the pianist and empty his own glass. Gradually, I relaxed, even closing my eyes.

"Would you like to dance?" Redford asked.

My eyes popped open. "Dance?"

"You know—stand close and move our feet at the same time, more or less."

I gave a little laugh. "I…don't know."

"Come on," he said, standing and extending his hand. "I don't get dressed up that often."

I stared at his hand and in one split second, I recalled the magic that those long, blunt fingers had worked on my body. Of its own accord, my hand went into his and I felt myself being pulled to my feet. I followed Redford the short distance to the tiny, dimly-lit dance floor next to the piano and told myself it was safe for us to touch in front of so many people.

He pulled me close in a slow, smooth waltz—my right hand in his left, near his shoulder, his other hand firmly on my lower back. My left hand I laid loosely on his shoulder, keeping my engagement ring in sight. Redford moved with remarkable grace and natural athleticism. Beneath my hand, I felt the muscles move in his shoulder, felt the heat radiate from his body. He had taken me dancing in Vegas, I recalled, and had held me so close we had breathed the same air. I looked up into his face, my heart buoyed crazily by the glimmer in his dark eyes.

Wordlessly, we found a rhythm and our bodies moved in tandem. My breasts brushed the wall of his chest and I closed my eyes against the thrill that zinged through my body. And to shut out the glimmer of my ring.

Our bodies merged as close as public decency laws would allow. I put my cheek against his shoulder and drew the clean, minty scent of him into my lungs. He put his chin next to my temple and I imagined that he pressed his lips against my skin. *What-ifs* revolved in my head while my body responded to distant memories…sexual familiarity.

Suddenly I became aware of the hardening of

his sex against my stomach. He retreated from me slightly, but knowing how I affected him made me feel heady. I followed him and brushed against the length of his erection with the slightest twist of my body. I felt his jaw clench and he emitted a low groan.

"Don't start something you don't intend to finish."

Tiny hairs raised on the back of my neck, and I shivered. Being in Redford's arms intercepted all rational signals to my brain. Feeling like a tease, I stepped back and inhaled deeply. A glance at our table showed our food had been delivered, topped with warming covers. "We should eat—we don't want to be late for the show."

He nodded curtly, visibly straining—willing away his hard-on, no doubt. I tried to help by walking back to the table slowly and in front of him. When we arrived at the table, he held out my chair. I sat, still tingling from our encounter. After scooting my chair in, he leaned down and murmured, "That was close."

A thought I repeated to myself throughout our dinner and the show; but as the evening progressed, it was harder and harder to remember why being close to Redford was so treacherous. Our seats for *42nd Street* were spectacular and the show itself was amazing—quintessential Broadway. Coupled with the fact that people around us stared at Redford. "Is he a movie star?" someone behind us whispered. And all I could think was how much I enjoyed his company. He laughed and applauded throughout the show, occasionally looking over to wink or smile. When the show was over, heaven help me, I didn't want to go home.

As we walked through the lobby, I cleared my throat. "Redford, I was thinking...since we didn't make it to the Empire State Building today, what would you think about going...now?"

"Is it open late?"

"Until midnight. The city is beautiful at night."

He grinned. "Sounds great. I'll get our coats."

I stood there watching him walk away, and my insides welled with anticipation...and trepidation. This reunion with Redford wasn't going as I'd planned. Instead of remembering all the logical reasons I had for ending the marriage, I was remembering all the titillating reasons why I'd said, "I do" in the first place.

"Denise? Oh, it *is* you."

At the sound of my name, I turned...and froze. Barry's boss Ellen Brant was coming toward me, all smiles.

13

AS ELLEN WALKED toward me, I slid my gaze across the room toward Redford, who was handing the clerk our coat-check tickets. A sweat broke out along my hairline, but I managed a smile for Ellen and the older woman next to her. "Hi, Ellen. Did you enjoy the show?"

She gave a dismissive wave. "I've seen *42nd Street* a dozen times, but Mother can't get enough of it."

She introduced me to her mother. I nodded politely, eager to disappear. "It was nice to meet you—"

"Denise is newly engaged to one of the station's producers," Ellen told her mother. "I believe you've met Barry Copeland?"

Her mother nodded. "I met Barry at the station once. He's a handsome young man. Congratulations on your engagement."

I smiled, near panic. "Thank you."

"I'm looking forward to getting together Tuesday afternoon," Ellen said with a little society laugh. "I've got to get my ex-husband's money working for me as soon as possible."

I tried to chuckle, but it sounded more like a hiccup. "You'll feel good about working with Trayser Brothers."

"I feel good about working with *you,* Denise," Ellen said magnanimously. "A person can't trust their money to just anyone these days."

"How true. I don't mean to be short, but—"

"Here you go," Redford said, holding my coat behind me.

Dead silence fell around us. I gave him a tight smile and slid my arms inside, my heart thudding in my ears. I dreaded lifting my gaze; when I did, as expected, Ellen's mother was frowning quizzically at Redford, and Ellen's penciled eyebrows had climbed high on her forehead.

My mind swirled. If I introduced them, word would get back to Barry. If I didn't, word would *definitely* get back to Barry, and on top of that, Ellen would probably write me off for being rude. I cleared my throat.

"This is Ellen Brant, the general manager of a local television network, and her mother. Ladies, this is, um…um…"

"Her neighbor," Redford cut in and his voice had taken on a…*feminine* edge?

I swung my gaze to him, baffled.

He reached forward and shook the women's hands with two fingers, his wrist as limp as a dishrag. "How do you do? *Love* those earrings."

"Thank you," Ellen said, rearranging her face

from suspicion into a knowing smile. "Did you enjoy the show?"

"Oh, did I! It gets better *every* time," he said, clasping his hands together, a wistful expression on his face.

My mind could not comprehend what I was seeing and hearing. Redford DeMoss, career military man and the most heterosexual man I'd ever met, pretending to be...*gay?* I was stupefied.

"Well, it was nice meeting you," Ellen said to Redford. "Denise, I'll see you Tuesday afternoon." Then she leaned forward and sighed near my ear. "All the best-looking men are gay, aren't they?"

I nodded and made sympathetic noises and wished them well. Only when they had disappeared from sight could I bring myself to look at Redford, who wore an innocent expression.

"*What* was that?" I asked, crossing my arms.

"What?"

"That bad impression of Steven Cojocaru."

"Who?"

"A TV personality. He's...flamboyant."

Redford shrugged. "Just trying to help you out of a spot. You said the woman worked for a television station. I assume she knows your boyfriend?"

"Fiancé," I corrected. "Ellen is his boss."

He lifted his hands. "So...you're welcome."

My face burned when I realized why he'd done what he'd done. So word wouldn't get back to Barry that I was out with another man—another *straight* man. "Thank you, Redford."

He pressed his lips together. "I just hope he deserves you."

I couldn't speak. Deserve *me?* I was doing things behind Barry's back. *He* deserved someone better than me. I glanced down and rubbed a finger over my engagement ring.

Redford sighed heavily. "But if you tell anyone what I did, I'll have to kill you."

I looked up and laughed, shaking my head. "All gay men don't act that over-the-top."

He shrugged. "I know, but I improvised. It worked, didn't it?"

I pursed my mouth, then nodded.

He looked at me, then fingered a lock of my hair that had come loose from my ponytail, leaving a tingling trail across my skin. "You promised me a night view from the top of the Empire State Building."

I exhaled and smiled. "Yes, I did."

The Empire State Building was always a crowded attraction, but at this time of the day there were fewer children. And at this time of the year, people stayed on the observatory for less time, so the lines moved quickly. When we stepped out onto the observatory, I shivered in my coat—the air temperature at this height was breathtaking. Redford saw my reaction and put his arm around me. I didn't object—I couldn't imagine any mischief unfolding in the frigid air and blustery wind.

Redford was immediately riveted to the unending view—lights twinkling and moving across the city like Christmas tree decorations, buildings glowing as if they were atop a Lite-Brite board. I pointed out landmarks as we walked all around the platform—the George Washington Bridge, the Chrysler Building, Times Square, the Reuters Building, the Woolworth Building.

"It's like being on top of the world," Redford said.

I nodded, then broached a subject that had been eating at me. "Redford, are you...seeing someone special back in Kentucky?"

He shook his head then looked back to the view. "No."

I wet my parched lips. "Are women scarce in Kentucky?"

He laughed. "Not at all."

Which meant he looked...as any normal red-blooded single man would do. I injected a teasing note into my voice. "I would think that you could have just about any woman you wanted."

His laugh was self-deprecating, but he didn't offer a comment. For my part, I wished I hadn't asked. Redford's love life was none of my business...anymore.

A bitter gust of wind blasted us, and my teeth began to chatter. Redford pulled me in front of him and shielded me with his big body, rubbing my arms briskly with his hands. Suddenly his hands slowed and a few seconds later, he lowered his arms and crossed them over my chest. I felt his chest rise and fall with a sigh. I closed my eyes and eased my head back against him, then raised my hands to cover his.

He hugged me closer against him, uttering a low moan that reverberated through my body.

"Denise," he whispered against my temple. "I—"

I didn't let him finish. I lifted my mouth to his for a desperate, jarring, upside-down kiss. His lips were warm and firm, his tongue strong and determined. I sighed into his mouth and strained against the awkward angle. He broke the kiss long enough to turn me in his arms, and I met him again, willingly.

My mouth remembered his—every texture, every flavor. Our teeth clicked and our tongues danced, sending white-hot desire shooting through me. I pushed my hands into his hair and kneaded the back of his neck, pulling his mouth closer, deeper. His arms tightened around me and even through my coat, I could feel his urgent desire for me. My body leapt in response, also remembering that magic wand of his. The way his face contorted with pleasure when he thrust deep into me…heaven…

I pressed my body against his erection and he groaned. His hands slid down my back and underneath me, pulling me against him. I gave in to the thrill of him and thrust my hands through the opening in his coat to wrap my arms around his warm back, pulling him closer. I lowered my hand to stroke the thick knob of his shaft through his clothing, and he sucked in a sharp breath.

The sound of persistent throat-clearing reached my ears—and apparently Redford's. We lifted our heads to see a security guard standing a few feet away trying to look as if he hadn't noticed us. I realized other people around us were doing their best to ignore us, and I flushed with embarrassment. Making out in public—was I sixteen years old?

"Let's go," I murmured, my ragged breath coming out in white puffs.

Redford tried to take my hand, but I pulled it back and stuffed it deep into my coat pocket. His mouth tightened, but he didn't press me. Our walk back to the elevator bay and the ride down were quiet. I assumed his mind was as chaotic as mine…or perhaps not since he didn't have as much at stake. For Redford, a weekend fling would simply be a pleasurable reunion. For me, it would be going back to a place where my body overrode my mind, and I couldn't live the rest of my life that way. I had a good, logical life waiting for me, with Barry…a man whose ring I wore, whose proposal I'd accepted mere days ago. What kind of woman was I that I could be tempted into an affair so soon after taking a man's ring?

That kind of woman…carnal…reckless…rash.

No! I would not barter my long-term happiness for short-term gratification.

When we exited the building, the wind had kicked up, howling around us, sending litter twirling in the streets and making it nearly impossible to talk. I wanted the wind to pick me up and twirl me into next week. My eBay auction would be over, the IRS audit would be over and I'd have Ellen Brant's business. My life would be back to normal…better than normal because I would be a content engaged woman with a fat bonus in the bank, and a wedding dress in my closet.

And Redford would be a memory.

His dress shoes sounded against the sidewalk with military precision, the wind whipping the legs of his slacks. At the curb Redford hailed a cab and we slid inside. I huddled against the door inside my coat, Redford staring out the window, occasionally pulling on his chin. A couple of times, he started to say something, but changed his mind. When the cabbie neared my building, I leaned forward. "Let me out at the next corner, please."

"We'll both get out," Redford said.

"You can go on to your hotel."

"I'll walk to the hotel," he said in a voice that brooked no argument.

I alighted from the cab, steeled for the argument I knew was imminent. When Redford paid the cabbie, he turned to look at me and jammed his hands on his hips. "Denise—"

"I'm sorry, Redford," I said, my voice clipped. "I made a mistake kissing you back there."

He was quiet for a few seconds. "Are you saying you don't have feelings for me?"

His question startled me in its directness. For a few seconds, I was flustered, then irritated. "Redford, how can you ask me that? I'm *engaged* to another man."

"A few minutes ago, you weren't thinking about your boyfriend."

"Fiancé."

"Whatever." He stepped closer to me and tipped my chin up with his hand, forcing me to look at him. His eyes glittered in the shadow of a streetlight. "Denise, I was on the receiving end of that kiss. Do you have feelings for me?" His Adam's apple bobbed. "Did you ever?"

A lump formed in my throat and my tongue felt swollen in my mouth. "Redford, my feelings…" I swallowed and tried again. "The feelings that we… that I…had for you…when we first met." I gestured vaguely. "I was caught up in you…in your sexuality…in your openness. I confused my physical attraction for you with…love." I exhaled and brushed the hair out of my eyes. "So…yes, I'm still attracted to you…obviously. But…" I pressed my lips together.

He dropped his hand and gave a little laugh. "So I'm only good for meaningless sex."

"I didn't say that."

"It's okay, Denise." His shoulders lifted in a shrug, then he put his hands in his slacks pockets. "That's not such a bad thing for a man to hear." A sardonic smile came over his mouth. "I had a wonderful time with you today…and tonight. And if it makes you feel better, I promise to keep my open sexuality under wraps tomorrow."

I shook my head. "Redford, I don't think I should go upstate with you."

He cocked one eyebrow. "Oh, come on, I'm not *that* irresistible. Besides, I thought we were going to go over our tax files." He gave me a teasing grin. "That should pretty much kill any inclination to... make a mistake...shouldn't it?"

Standing there with his hands in his pockets and the wind ruffling his hair, he looked boyish and completely harmless. Like a rejected prom date, content to be friends. I sighed. Kenzie would be disappointed if I didn't go. And Redford and I did need to talk about our taxes. And it seemed that we *had* cleared the air of our inappropriate attraction. "Okay. What time should I be ready?"

He smiled. "I'll pick you up at eight. Bring some riding clothes."

He was striding away before his words sunk in. *Riding clothes?* He couldn't possibly mean *horse* riding clothes...although, was there another kind? "I don't like horses!" I yelled after him, but he only threw up his hand dismissively.

"I...don't...like...*horses!*" I shouted at the top of my lungs, but the wind whisked my words away.

I frowned and walked inside my apartment muttering, "I don't like horses."

14

Sunday
Days left on eBay auction: 2
Bidding on wedding dress up to: $1653
Winning bidder: SYLVIESMOM

WHEN I OPENED THE DOOR Sunday morning, Redford stood silhouetted in the early morning sunshine wearing faded jeans, a blue work shirt, a tan corduroy jacket and, of course, the hat.

So much for not being irresistible.

He gestured at my wool skirt and sweater. "Those don't look like riding clothes."

I set my jaw against an internal reaction to his outrageous sexiness, then crossed my arms. "I…don't… like…horses. You and Sam are going to look at your stud. Kenzie and I…aren't." I turned around and he followed me inside.

"Horses are the most beautiful animals that God created—well, aside from women."

I gave him a bland smile.

"At least wear some sensible shoes."

I looked down at my suede clogs. "These are sensible."

He clapped his hands together. "Okay. Ready to go?"

"I just need to get a bag of clothes I'm taking to Kenzie. Oh, and would you mind helping me with the box of tax papers sitting outside the bedroom door?"

I went into my bedroom to pick up my purse and the bag. When I checked inside the bag, I remembered with a start that I'd included the sweater Redford had given me when we'd first met. I entertained thoughts of keeping it, then told myself that getting rid of the sweater was for the best. I needed to get rid of all my Vegas keepsakes. I wasn't sure what I would do with my lovely wedding band, but eBay was always an option. The thought of selling it online gave me a queasy feeling, but it was the logical thing to do. Considering I was marrying someone else, that is.

At the sound of footsteps behind me, I turned to see Redford standing in the doorway, holding the box of papers and staring at something off to the right. I followed his line of vision and my pulse blipped. Last night I had removed my wedding gown from the closet and hung it from the mirror on my dressing table, both to get it out of the way and as an extra reminder of where my head should be.

"Wow," he said. "Nice dress. You'll be a beautiful bride, Denise."

I shifted uncomfortably. "Thanks."

His gaze was level and earnest. "I'm glad to see you plan to do it right this time."

I looked away. I had thought the same thing myself, but hearing it from Redford was unsettling.

"We have a long drive ahead of us," he said quietly. "We'd better get going. I'm parked illegally."

"Right."

We walked outside and he put the box in the back seat of the monster truck. "Wait and I'll help you up," he said across the expansive hood.

"I can do it," I said, remembering the full-body slide the last time he'd "helped" me. I grabbed a hand strap and after a couple of bounces, vaulted myself into the seat, landing with less than gymnastic precision. I closed the door with a solid bang, then fastened my seat belt and exhaled, exhausted.

Redford climbed inside, grinning, and put his hat on the seat between us. "You're getting the hang of it."

The words were on the tip of my tongue to point out that sling-shotting myself into a gargantuan truck was not likely to be a skill that I would use again, but I realized he was only making conversation. I was being too sensitive…too vulnerable. And the day had just begun.

He started the engine and maneuvered the vehicle out of its spot and down the narrow side street, watching both mirrors to make sure he didn't clip something or somebody.

"Do you really need this big of a truck?" I asked.

"Yeah, to pull horse trailers. The double cab is a

luxury, though. It's nice to have room for extra supplies or extra people."

I laughed. "I can't believe how much it cost."

"Jim gave me a great deal—we worked it out over the phone."

So he hadn't paid full sticker price. "Oh. Good."

"It's nice to have a comfortable vehicle for a long trip."

"It's comfortable," I agreed, feeling cradled in the leather seat. "Will you be on the road a lot?"

"Quite a bit during the sales season, twice a year."

I smiled. "You'd think you'd have a cell phone."

He pursed his mouth. "No. Don't see much need for one. Have you had breakfast?"

I shook my head. "I'm not hungry, but coffee sounds good."

"I was thinking the same thing."

He pulled up to a drive-through and got two steaming cups to go. Before pulling back out on the street, he reached under the seat and withdrew an atlas. "Do you want to navigate?"

I sipped from my cup and murmured with pleasure as the warm liquid slid down my throat. "Sure."

"Care if I turn on some music?"

"No. That would be nice."

He found a country music station—which I didn't even know existed within the vicinity of the city— and turned it to a pleasing volume. Soon we were on our way to the interstate and I looked around, suddenly struck by the surreal scene: I was in a truck with my ex on a horse-buying road trip, listening to country music. He sat behind the wheel, completely at ease. And why not? This was his life. And this would have been my life if I'd stayed married to Redford.

"You okay?" he asked, shifting in his seat. The muscles in his legs rippled beneath the fabric of his jeans, diverting my attention…and my concentration. "Are you warm enough?"

Was I ever. I nodded, then looked out the window, taking in the passing landscape. I'd never been north of the city, so all the road signs and landmarks were alien to me. I smiled, thinking about Kenzie making this fateful trip to see Sam Long under the guise of doing an article on the small-town hero. Kenzie was even more of a city girl than I was, and had been hoodwinked into taking her boss's dog with her. But the trip had changed the trajectory of her life.

I glanced at Redford under my lashes and thought about how my life had changed when I'd met him. Within a few hours, my entire persona had seemed to change—I had turned into a lust-crazed creature with no regard for the ramifications of my actions.

Good God. In hindsight, I had morphed into a man.

I turned my attention back to the scenery racing by, and Redford seemed content to do the same. On the one hand, I was glad not to talk, but on the other, I was disturbed, frankly, over how comfortable we were not talking.

I was a mess.

Fairly quickly, Manhattan fell away behind us and the traffic thinned. An hour into the projected four-hour drive, we were traveling on a two-lane road lined with frost-encrusted trees and sudden small towns. Redford occasionally leaned forward to glance at the sky, his brow furrowed.

"Is something wrong?" I asked.

"It's clouding up," he said. "The forecast said snow tomorrow, so let's hope it holds off."

"Right," I said with a little laugh. "I would hate to get snowed in."

"I could think of worse things," he said, slanting a smile in my direction.

My breasts tingled. "Redford," I chided.

"I just meant we'd have a good excuse to miss the IRS audit," he said, trying to sound indignant. "What did you think I meant?"

I gave him a stern frown. "Never mind. But that reminds me—" I turned around to lift the lid from the box containing our tax papers. "I had a chance to go over the forms, and there are a few things we should talk about before the interview."

He sipped from his coffee cup, then winced. "Do we have to?"

"Yes."

His mouth tightened. "Okay, but I should warn you that my expertise is in logistics, not numbers." Then he grinned. "Luckily, you're great with numbers. I'm not worried. We'll probably walk out of there with a refund."

I squirmed. "I suspect they'll ask a lot of questions about the deductions I took on my home-office expenses."

He shrugged. "So, you'll just explain, that's all."

I swallowed hard. His confidence in me made me feel even worse. "Still, I'd like to go over everything so we go in looking united."

"You mean like a team?"

"Sort of." I rummaged around in the box and removed the form, which was several pages thick.

"That's our form?" he asked. "I don't remember it being that thick."

"You didn't read it before you signed it?"

"No…I trusted you."

Which certainly didn't make me feel better, considering we'd been flagged for an audit. "Okay, let's start with the numbers and how I came up with them." I switched to professional mode, launching into a discussion of the form, attached schedules, and supporting documents—which, between his complicated pay schedule and overseas status, were considerable. To his credit, his eyes didn't glaze over. But halfway through the file, and an hour later, he broke in with a little laugh.

"Gee, Denise, no wonder you wanted out of the marriage. You probably couldn't face dealing with the tax forms every year."

I couldn't think of an answer, so I didn't give him one. And just like that, I felt the mood in the cab of the truck change.

"I'm so sorry, Denise."

I turned to look at him. "For what?"

His expression was pained. "For...proposing. You barely knew me. I was on my way back to the Gulf, not sure when I'd return. It was crazy. To be honest, I was relieved when I got those annulment papers."

I had assumed as much, but hearing it was like a kick in the stomach. "There's no need to apologize, Redford. It takes two people to make that kind of mistake."

"Yeah, but you were the one smart enough to try to remedy the situation. Thanks to you, we were both able to resume our lives without any fallout. I'm grateful, Denise."

My throat constricted suddenly...and I wasn't sure why. It was exactly what I'd been hoping Redford would say someday: that he hadn't felt abandoned or angry when I'd filed for an annulment; that it was the right thing to do under the circumstances. I should have felt relieved...so why didn't I?

"There's a convenience store up ahead," he said. "By my estimation, we're halfway there. Want to stretch our legs?"

I nodded, grateful for a break. From both the confines of the truck, and our discussion.

Redford pulled up next to the gas pump—I couldn't imagine how much gasoline it took to keep the monster truck running. When I alighted, I noticed the sky was indeed growing cloudy and gray, which wasn't uncommon for February, but unsettling none-theless. I glanced at my watch and decided to wait until we were closer to call Kenzie, especially since I couldn't get a signal on my phone here.

After I exited the ladies' room, I pulled a bottle of water from a wall cooler and walked up to the counter where Redford had engaged the rotund clerk in a conversation about—as near as I could tell—fishing lures. The man could befriend anyone.

"I'll get that," Redford said, taking my water. I acquiesced, knowing it wouldn't do any good to argue, then walked outside to get as much fresh air as possible before we set off again.

I dragged the cool air into my lungs slowly, mulling over Redford's "gratitude" to me for having our marriage annulled. His admission, coupled with the knowledge that he had lived so close to me after he returned to the States, was—I had to concede—bruising my ego.

My chest ached with unexpected grief, and tears gathered on my lashes. (I never cried...*ever.*) My ego was more than bruised. To be honest, I was crushed. Which was incredibly foolish and selfish of me, considering I was the one who had ended the marriage, and I was the one who was engaged to marry again.

"Ready to hit the road?" Redford called behind me.

I blinked like mad to dissipate the tears—thankful that I could blame runny eyes and a red nose on the weather, if necessary. But when I turned, the sight of Redford standing there looking so impossibly masculine in his jeans and boots and black hat was sobering enough to evaporate any tears—along with all the moisture in my mouth. Defeated, I headed back to the truck and hurdled into my seat.

"You okay?" Redford asked when he fastened his seat belt.

"I wish you would stop asking me that," I snapped.

He blinked, then a little smile came over his face. "I know what you want."

I closed my eyes, at my wits' end with his innuendos and worse, with my Pavlovian responses. "Redford—" I stopped when I opened my eyes and saw what he had in his hand. A bag of peanut M&M's.

"These used to be your favorite."

I sighed. "They still are."

"Good." He handed me the candy, then pulled two bottles of water from the small plastic bag.

"You didn't want a snack?" I asked, tearing open the candy.

"I was hoping you'd share."

"No way," I said, laughing.

"Take them all," he said as he started the engine. "The more you have in your mouth, the less you can talk about taxes."

I stuck my tongue out at him and he laughed as he pulled the truck back onto the road. Despite his teasing, he ate a few pieces of the candy, and I was struck again by the alternate ease and discomfort I felt when I was with Redford. It was like being on a roller coaster…in the first car with nothing to hold on to…except Redford himself.

"Back to the taxes," I said when the last piece had been washed down.

"Please, no," he begged. "Tell me about your friends, Kenzie and Sam."

A legitimate question…and an interesting story. "Kenzie works for *Personality* magazine. Sam was on the cover one month for the 'small-town hero' issue. He's a veterinarian, and a part-time fireman in Jar Hollow, and he saved a lot of people in a nursing-home fire."

He pursed his mouth, nodding.

"Anyway, they met when he went to the city to have his photo taken. Then she went to his place to do a follow-up article…and then there was the cover curse."

"Cover curse?"

"It's a long story, but basically Kenzie went to stay on his farm for a while and got into all kinds of predicaments, including almost burning down his clinic."

"Yikes."

"But Sam fell in love with her anyway."

"That's a helluva guy."

"So, long story short, Sam teaches in the city a few days a week, and she works from their home up here a few days a week, so they're together as much as possible." I smirked. "I have to warn you, though— Sam and Kenzie are shmoops."

"Is that some kind of northern religion?"

I laughed. "No. I mean, they smooch and look at each other like teenagers. And Kenzie talks about how much they—" I stopped and cleared my throat as Redford fought a smile. "Anyway, the girls and I call them shmoops."

"Okay, well I'll try not to notice if their clothes start flying off."

"Now, back to the taxes…"

He groaned. "Why don't we save that for the drive home this evening?"

"I won't be able to read in the dark!"

His white teeth flashed in a wide grin. "I know."

I sighed. "Okay, there isn't much left anyway. For the most part, I…I just need to make sure that Tuesday morning we go in there—"

"United," he finished. "Got it. They will see one united couple, by golly. We'll be so united, they'll think we're still married."

"Well," I murmured, settling back in my seat, "we don't have to take it that far."

I tried to call Kenzie several times on my cell phone, but couldn't get a signal, and then when I did, my battery was dead. But Sam's directions were good and, after passing through the adorably quaint town of Jar Hollow, (I saw some of the businesses that Kenzie had mentioned to me—the Cut and Curl, Jamison Hardware Store), and driving up a steep hill, we pulled into a clearing that gave way to a plateau with a picturesque view that would be stunning in the spring. I could see why Kenzie would have been enchanted.

From her description, I recognized a smaller log building, which would be the clinic, to the right of where we sat; and the larger building, the log home that Sam had built himself, to the left. It was spectacular.

"Nice," Redford murmured. He nodded toward the two vehicles—Sam's truck and Kenzie's car. "Looks like they're home."

I opened the door and climbed down. "They probably heard us pull up."

Redford put on his hat and together we walked to the front of the cabin. The picture-perfect landscaping was undoubtedly Kenzie's handiwork. I rang the doorbell and from inside, a horrific noise erupted— like a dog pound on the night of a full moon.

"That would be their pets," I explained.

"Good watchdogs," Redford said.

When a few seconds passed and no one came to the door, I said, "Maybe they're at the clinic."

"Or maybe they're…you know." Redford's eyebrows wagged suggestively.

I smirked. "I forgot to tell you that Kenzie's pregnant."

He laughed. "Big surprise."

"I mean, she said that lately she hasn't been in the mood to…you know."

The door suddenly swung open with Sam telling the dogs to be quiet. He looked flushed and his hair was ruffled. "Hi, Denise, hi, Redford. Welcome to our home." He laughed. "Our noisy home."

I said hello and the men shook hands. Tingling with embarrassment, I stepped inside the beautifully decorated log cabin. From the looks of Sam, we had definitely arrived in the middle of...something.

Kenzie appeared from a hall, barefoot and running. "Denise! It's so good to see you!"

We hugged. "You, too...new mama. Er, I tried to call, but my battery died."

"Oh, that's okay, we were just...cleaning. So that's Redford?" she whispered in my ear. "Yowsa. He looks like that and he has a big—"

"Kenzie—" I cut in, my voice a warning. "I'm an engaged woman."

"Don't worry," she said out of the corner of her mouth. "I won't say anything...suggestive. And Sam and I will be on our best behavior all afternoon."

"Good," I said. "By the way...your blouse is on backward."

"Great news, Kenzie," Sam said from the doorway. "Redford has a double-cab pickup—there's room for you and Denise to ride along."

Kenzie clapped her hands, then looked at me. "Oh, Denise, is that okay? I thought we'd stay here, but there's a pony at Valla Farms that Sam and I want to look at."

I stared at her. Kenzie Mansfield used to be the most cosmopolitan woman I knew and now she stood barefoot and pregnant in a log cabin, talking about ponies? What had happened to the woman I knew?

She'd fallen in love with a man and lost herself.

"I don't like horses," I murmured.

"Are you up for it?" Redford asked, his eyebrows raised in question. He held his hat in his hands and— Good grief, he was so…appealing.

"Come on," Kenzie urged in my ear. "It'll be fun." Then she winked. "Besides, horses can be kind of sexy."

Great. Just…great.

15

"RELAX," REDFORD URGED.

Easier said than done, considering I was astride a mammoth creature capable of tossing me off like a rag doll and trampling me beneath its razor-sharp hooves. Worse, Redford sat behind me on the beast, thigh to thigh, his arms loosely around mine, demonstrating the proper position for holding the reins.

I could barely breathe, but I murmured, "I'm relaxed," over my shoulder.

"Your back is a ramrod, and your arms are like rebar."

"I don't know what that is."

"Trust me, it's stiff."

His sexy voice rumbling in my ear wasn't helping matters. Plus I felt like an idiot wannabe, wearing my riveted jeans, embroidered shirt, horse sweater, and suede fringe jacket. Kenzie had loaned me a pair of her Doc Martens—they were snug, but had weathered the random piles of horse poo that littered the stable floor. However, there was no piece of equipment that could stem the pungent odor of horseflesh…ugh—it was an acquired smell, at best.

But the owners of Valla Farms had been accommodating…while they prepared the stud that Redford was interested in, he had asked to saddle one of their trail horses to help me, he said, to get over my fear of horses. I had been reluctant (a slight understatement), until I started feeling like a sissy as Kenzie and Sam had pleaded with me to give it a try. I had acquiesced, frankly, to get it over with.

Now, as I was being jolted around on the saddle atop "Reggie," I was regretting my weakness. Sissies got the last laugh—they lived longer.

"The horse can sense your fear," Redford said into my ear. "Loosen up—try to get in synch with the animal, to anticipate its movement. It's not unlike making love."

I jerked my head around. "You're not helping."

He chuckled in my ear. "Okay, I'll be quiet."

As we walked in a circle, I tried to do what Redford said, to loosen my muscles and my joints, to sway with the horse, not against it.

"That's good," he murmured.

"I feel like I could fall off."

"Use your thighs and knees to hang on."

His unspoken words "not unlike making love" hung in the air.

"Besides, I'm not going to let you fall."

But when I pressed my knees into Reggie, he startled and picked up speed.

"What did I do?" I cried.

"Maintain even pressure with your knees—when you squeeze, he thinks you want him to speed up."

Not unlike making love. With Redford's chest pressed up against my back and being cocooned in his arms, my imagination—and memory—didn't have far to leap to make the connection.

"By the way, I like your sweater," he said. "Looks familiar."

I decided not to answer. Explaining that I'd been on the verge of giving it away seemed too complicated. But knowing that he remembered the sweater put a warm feeling in my stomach…and lower.

I forced myself to concentrate on the efficiency of the horse's movements, and Redford's. Soon I was rocking rhythmically in the saddle, pleased to be getting the hang of it…until I became aware of something else entirely. Where the saddle rose up in front of me, it was applying pressure to my womanly regions… And the more relaxed I became, the more the pressure hit…*home.* Panicked, I glanced from side to side. Was this normal?

"That's it," Redford murmured in my ear. "Now you're getting the hang of it."

Indeed. It was like dancing—my shoulders flowing, my hips rocking. I was at the perfect angle to be stroked by the hard leather saddle with every stride, and I could feel myself growing warm and moist. Being sandwiched between Redford's muscular body and the powerful horse was one of the most erotic things I'd ever experienced. With a start, I realized that if I didn't stop, the inevitable would happen. And if I had an orgasm right here and now, I'd have to throw myself under the horse to be trampled because I'd never be able to face Redford or my friends—or anyone—again.

"I'm ready to stop," I said suddenly.

Something in my voice must have convinced him not to argue because he said, "Okay. Gently pull back on the reins, and say, 'whoa.'"

I did, and to my amazement, the horse stopped.

"See, not so hard," Redford said, sliding down first. Then he talked me through dismounting properly, and quickly, so the horse wouldn't move. When my second foot landed—in squishy poo—I felt a little unsteady, not to mention light-headed, from using dormant muscles and from my secret little sensual experience. Redford steadied me with his hand and gave me a wink. "You're a natural."

Despite the cold, my cheeks felt warm from his praise. I was exhilarated, flush with accomplishment…and heightened physical awareness. "Liar. But thank you, Redford. It was…fun."

"Good," he said, his dark eyes sincere. "I'm glad I could introduce you to a new experience."

I realized that every time I was with Redford, he introduced me to new things—things I wouldn't have done on my own—and wound up liking. I couldn't look away from his gaze, and felt a new, sizzling connection with him. My sensitized areas tingled and I was at a loss for words.

A man entered the stable yard and told Redford they were ready in the broodmare barn. (From my reading, I knew that was a place where the girl horses stayed until they were ready to…you know.) Redford handed off the horse we'd been riding to the man and the four of us walked to the long, narrow building the man indicated.

There the scent of horseflesh was overpowering. The barn was lined on both sides with unbelievably nice stables, each door adorned with a brass plate with the occupant's name on it. The horses themselves weren't visible, but we could hear them moving around and occasionally neighing.

A man who identified himself as the foreman shook our hands and welcomed us to Valla Farms. "Mr. DeMoss, I understand you're here to find a teaser stud to take back to Kentucky."

"That's right," Redford said with a nod.

"We have a horse I think you're going to like. His name is Henry—he's part draft horse."

"Sounds good," Redford said. "I'd like to see him in action."

"I'll bring him in now, sir."

The foreman moved away from us and I asked Redford, "The stud isn't a Thoroughbred?"

"No. I'm looking for a teaser stud, not a stallion. Thoroughbreds don't make good teasers—they're too high-strung."

I frowned. "What's a 'teaser' stud?"

He nodded toward the big gray horse being led in. "You'll see."

"Henry" was neighing—squealing really, lifting his big head as if he were calling out to the horses in the stalls. The foreman checked a clipboard, then pointed to the first stall. The man leading Henry opened the stall door, then stood back as Henry stuck his head in.

Blam! I jumped as the mare delivered a swift kick with her rear hoof that zoomed past Henry's head and landed against the stall door. Henry seemed to take the reaction in stride as he backed away and waited patiently as the handler closed the door, moved down two stalls and opened another one. Again Henry stuck his head in, sniffing the air, emitting a low squeal. The mare inside, after a bit of stamping and shuffling, lifted her tail and urinated. A bit gross from my perspective, but Henry seemed satisfied and retreated. The foreman made notes on his clipboard and directed the handler where to take him next.

Henry made his way down the stable row, sticking his head in and dodging powerful kicks when necessary, or neighing and rearing his head when a mare backed up to him and flipped her tail.

I wasn't an expert, but I took a wild guess that tail-flipping was a signal that she wouldn't mind being mounted. Except instead of obliging, Henry would whinny and back out, moving on to the next mare.

"A teaser stud," Redford said in my ear, "gets the

mare excited so when the high-strung and high-dollar Thoroughbred stallion struts in, she'll be ready."

The analogy wasn't lost on me. A hot flush bloomed on my chest and scalded my neck. Since Redford's arrival Friday, I'd been in a near-constant state of arousal. He was intimating that he was getting me worked up, and Barry would get the benefit. Knowing that Redford knew he was getting to me only made me more uncomfortable…and more aroused. I couldn't look at him, didn't trust my reaction. But I realized with dismay that the sex life of animals and the sex life of humans was more alike than different—both were complicated.

By the end of the exercise, Henry was…stirred up, giving me my first look at a stallion's penis. (I could strike that item from my life list.) I was duly impressed…and a little fearful for the mares. Henry must have known he wasn't getting any action today, though, because he lost his erection as soon as the last stable door closed. Redford asked the foreman more questions about the stud while he patted down the horse. Sam also looked the horse over, checking teeth, eyes and hooves, and removing a stethoscope to listen to the horse's organs.

It was hard for me to take my eyes off Redford, though. Seeing him in his natural environment was mesmerizing. He was a big man, could hold his own against a behemoth like Henry when he started to prance around. While still talking, Redford grabbed the lead rope and settled the horse down within seconds.

"He's something," Kenzie whispered.

I turned to look at her. "The horse?"

"No, not the horse, silly—Redford."

"Um...yes, Redford knows his way around horses."

Kenzie angled her head. "He seems to know his way around you, too. Are you sure there's no unfinished business between the two of you?"

I looked at her, my throat and chest tight. "I'm engaged, Kenzie."

She narrowed her eyes. "But you're not married yet. If you still have feelings for this man, Denise, you'd better find closure now rather than later, when so many lives will be upended."

Her dialogue was cut short by the appearance of Sam. "Kenzie, are you ready to look at that pony?"

"Oh, yes! Let's go."

Redford was shaking hands with the foreman when we walked up, making plans to talk again after he returned to Kentucky. I felt a sad little pang thinking about him leaving, but reminded myself that I, too, would soon be swept back into my regular life.

The four of us followed the handler to a barn, where he handed off Henry, then were led to another building that he called the birthing barn. Inside were more stalls, equally as fancy as in the broodmare barn. He led us to one on the end and opened the stall door. Inside, a brown mother and her leggy gray foal stood nuzzling.

Kenzie fell in love instantly. "Oh, isn't it the most precious thing you've ever seen?"

Sam agreed, but seemed more interested in checking out the foal's physique.

"This here is Henry's foal," the handler said.

I looked at Redford. "So he does get to...um..."

Redford laughed, his eyes merry, then he leaned down. "Eventually you have to let the teaser stud go all the way, or he loses interest altogether."

My skin burned. Was his remark a veiled threat... or a promise? Was Redford implying that this was my last chance? His expression looked innocent enough, but I knew Redford well enough to know that there wasn't anything innocent about him.

Kenzie and Sam arranged to come back to get the foal, and Kenzie chattered about it nonstop as we started back to their house. How she wanted their baby to grow up around horses and to have his or her own pony. Sitting in the back seat with her, I nodded, pretending to listen. But I was actually still pondering her earlier warning—if I had unresolved feelings for Redford, I should explore them now, while Redford was here and before I married Barry.

Throughout the day, the skies had grown increasingly leaden, the temperature increasingly colder. And within a few minutes of getting on the road, we encountered freezing rain.

"I was afraid this was going to happen," Redford said, shifting into a lower gear.

"Don't worry—we have plenty of room for the two of you to spend the night," Kenzie piped up.

The panic must have been apparent on my face because she quickly added, "The apartment over the clinic has two beds."

Which made the atmosphere in the cab of the truck less awkward, for sure.

She gave me an apologetic smile. "I guess I cleared out the guest room in the cabin a bit prematurely."

My pulse began to race—not at the imminent danger of the weather, but at the possibility of being holed up with Redford. Even if we weren't in the same bed, it smacked of familiarity, of intimacy.

And if we *were* in the same bed—

I massaged my temples and puffed out my cheeks in a long exhale—under no circumstances would we be in the same bed.

Then, somewhere from the depths of my brain, in a dark corner that remembered the time in Vegas, an idea formed and an inner voice gave it life: *This is your chance...spend the night with Redford...get it out of your system...it can't be as good as you remember...then you'll know that Redford isn't the fantasy man you've built him up to be in your mind...you can marry Barry with a clear heart, if not a clear conscience...*

The thought circled in my head until I was sure I had ruts worn into my brain. Suddenly I realized that everyone was looking at me, and for one mortifying moment, I thought I'd spoken aloud. Then I realized that we were back at Kenzie and Sam's. Good grief, how long had I been zoned out?

Kenzie touched my arm. "Redford said it was up to you. Can you take a day of vacation tomorrow and spend the night here?"

Darkness had fallen quickly and ice coated the truck windows, except for the windshield. Freezing rain pinged on the glass. My watch read 6:30 p.m. It would be a treacherous drive back to Manhattan. But from Redford's solemn expression in the rearview mirror, I knew if I wanted to go, he would deliver me home safely, even if it took all night to get there.

Preserving my chastity, however, didn't seem worth risking both our lives for. Not simply to make a point. And not simply to remove temptation from my path.

I wet my lips. "I can take a day of vacation tomorrow." Although, ironically, it might mean one less day I could take for my honeymoon.

"Whew, that's a relief," Kenzie said.

I caught Redford's gaze in the mirror, and there was something burning in his eyes, but I can't say it was relief. Hope? I pressed my lips together, wondering if I'd made a decision that I'd regret in the morning…if not before.

"Brrr, let's get inside and warm up," Kenzie said, then grinned. "And I think the men should fix chili for dinner."

Sam frowned over the front seat. "I thought spicy foods made you nauseous."

"Not today," she sang. "I'm craving peppers."

Sam looked at Redford. "Looks like we have kitchen duty."

Redford nodded. "Fair enough."

"Everyone head for the back door," Kenzie said. "We can shed wet clothes in the mudroom."

We sprinted through the icy rain, me slipping and sliding my way toward the house. Redford grabbed my hand and kept me upright. We were both laughing by the time we reached the back door. When we bounded into the mudroom, I didn't want to let go. Redford gave my hand a final squeeze, then we peeled off our wet jackets and boots in silence as Kenzie chattered on about the weather.

Dinner was fun, like a commercial about friends. Kenzie put on some music. The guys donned aprons and made chili and drank beer while Kenzie and I sat at the breakfast bar with our own drinks—beer for me, soda for her—and teased them. Redford seemed comfortable helping out in the kitchen. He and Sam even bantered about what secret ingredient made the best chili. I don't know why it surprised me that Redford could look sexy in a chef's apron, but it did. I sat at the bar and watched him move and interact with my friends as if he'd known them all of his life.

Sam and Kenzie asked him about the Corps, about Kentucky and about his family stables. I hung on every word. It was my chance to know the answers to all the questions I'd wanted to ask since he'd arrived, but had been afraid of delving into too deeply.

Redford talked about his career as a Marine with pride and fondness for the men and women he'd served with. But he said he was happy to be retired from the military at an age when he could still pursue another career. When he talked about Kentucky and his family stables, his voice took on an unmistakable warmth. It was clear he loved the place, and the horse business.

And it was clear to me that the woman in his life would have to do the same.

"So you're going back as soon as the IRS audit is over?" Kenzie asked Redford.

He glanced at me before he answered her. "That's the plan."

"Well, you don't have to worry about the audit," Kenzie said. "Denise is a money genius. She saved me and Sam thousands this year on our taxes."

Redford looked back to me and grinned. "I could sure use a money genius to help me grow the stables, if you can give me a referral."

I squirmed on my bar stool. "I'll give you the name of someone local that my firm has worked with."

"That'd be great," he said easily, lifting his beer bottle, but maintaining eye contact while he drank.

"Soup's on," Sam announced. "Or rather... chili's on."

We moved to the table and Redford held out my chair. I sat slowly, ultra-aware of his closeness crowding me as he scooted me in. The food was good, but my appetite was nil as I watched the clock move toward bedtime. I felt the pressure of a decision encroaching—I suspected that Redford would not turn me away from his bed.

I slanted a glance in his direction under my lashes.

On the other hand, maybe he had tired of my uncertainty and had decided not to get in the middle of my life.

"Oh," Kenzie said suddenly, covering her mouth. "I don't...feel...so well. Excuse me."

She fled in the direction of the bathroom, and Sam went after her.

I winced at Redford and he looked sympathetic. "Must be rough."

"Yeah, she looked green."

"No, I mean on Sam."

I gave him a light punch in the shoulder, which he tried to dodge. Then I pushed to my feet to clear the table. He stood to help, gathering bottles and glasses.

"I'm sorry, Denise."

I looked up, surprised. "About what?"

"About convincing you to come with me today. Now we're stuck here and you have to miss work tomorrow.... I know you have better things to do."

I loaded the dishwasher with our bowls and utensils. "It was my decision to come, Redford." I turned to look at him, dead-on. "And it was my decision to stay."

He dropped a glass, but caught it before it hit the floor. Then he looked at me, his expression cautious.

"Denise, I can stay here and bunk down on the couch or floor." A smile curved his mouth. "With the dogs."

Chivalrous to a fault. It was crazy, but I wanted to be close to him tonight, even if nothing happened between us. I moistened my lips. "That seems silly when there are two beds in the apartment."

Desire flickered in his dark eyes before he glanced away. When he looked back, he seemed calm…or resolute. "Okay."

"Sorry, folks," Sam announced, walking back into the kitchen. "Looks like Kenzie is out for the night."

"Is she going to be okay?" I asked.

"Oh, sure. I knew she'd regret the chili, but you can't tell that woman anything. I'll walk you to the clinic and get you settled in."

He produced a stack of clothes. "These should help tide you over for tonight. There's a washer and dryer in the apartment, plus a television and a phone if you need to make calls. Lots of hot water for a shower." He caught himself. "Or two." Then he burst out whistling, presumably to keep from putting his foot in his mouth.

My skin felt prickly on the short walk to the clinic, and it wasn't the rain because it had stopped. Everything—every blade of grass, every twig—was coated with a layer of ice. The yard looked like a winter wonderland, glistening like diamonds beneath the dusk-to-dawn light. The ground crunched beneath our feet, but water dripped from the utility lines—a good sign that the temperature was rising above freezing and we'd be able to leave in the morning.

But frankly, I could barely think past tonight.

Sam unlocked the door of the clinic and led us

through a lobby, down a long hall past an office and an examination room, and up a flight of stairs.

"This is where I lived while I built the cabin," he explained, opening a door and flipping a light on inside.

And where Kenzie had stayed when she'd visited Sam to write the article, I recalled.

The suite was spacious, with a combination bedroom/living room/kitchen area containing two twin beds—that seemed to scream at me—an overstuffed couch and chair situated around a television, and an efficiency-size kitchen. A separate bathroom contained a washer/dryer closet and was stocked with toiletries.

Sam nodded to one long window facing the cabin. "It'll be warmer if you keep the curtains closed," he said, then he coughed into his hand and strode back to the doorway. "Call us if you need anything."

My feet itched with the sudden urge to run past him and back to the cabin. I could bunk down on one of their couches, if the dogs were willing to share. My knees were literally trembling. I was in a full sweat.

"Thank you, Sam," Redford said, then glanced in my direction, his eyebrow raised slightly. He was offering me an out. No doubt my nerves were palpable. I took in his face and the body that could turn me on with a twitch—and I panicked.

"Sam!" I cried.

Sam turned back. "Yeah, Denise?"

There are a few defining moments in every person's life, when one simple decision can change the person they are, and the person they become. I knew in my heart of hearts, this was one of those moments.

"Thanks," I said, managing a smile, "for your hospitality."

"No problem. See you two in the morning."

The door closed, and I felt rooted to the floor.

Redford removed his coat, hung his black hat on the post of one of the beds and jammed his big hands on his hips…waiting. Waiting for a sign, either way. Morning was hours and hours away. How would we spend those hours?

"Denise," he said finally, his voice low and hoarse. "I'm tired of beating around the bush here."

(It was, admittedly, a fitting sexual interpretation of the saying.) My heart thudded in my chest in anticipation of his next words.

"I want you in my bed tonight, but the choice is entirely yours."

Desire flooded my body, rushing through my veins, awakening every nerve ending. The silence stretched between us for long seconds, while my mind raced with uncertainty. "I…" I swallowed and tried again, not entirely sure what words might tumble out of my mouth. "I…excuse me."

I escaped to the bathroom, closed the door behind me and leaned against it with a long exhale. I was steamy from wearing my fringe suede coat, which was still damp. I shrugged out of my coat, but the weight wasn't lifted from my shoulders. I stared at myself in the mirror, touched my skin, my hair, concrete things that defined me, things I knew to be true because I saw them in the mirror every day. But what about the things I couldn't see? What about those deep, dark desires that lurked in my heart? Those things defined me, too, whether I liked it or not.

I didn't like it, knowing that my body could override my reason. But I moistened my lips with my tongue and acknowledged how much I wanted Redford, how much I wanted to share his bed tonight. Worse, I *needed* to do this.

With shaking hands, I slipped my engagement ring from my finger and set it on the vanity, then opened the door, inhaled deeply and walked out to the bedroom.

16

REDFORD'S BACK was to me when I emerged from the bathroom, and when he turned, I was afraid I would lose my nerve. But when I saw his handsome face, his powerfully built body, his questioning eyes, my hunger for him exploded, and I rushed into his arms.

He caught me up against him, practically lifting me off the ground as he kissed me deeply, crushing me in his embrace. Our meeting was feverish, our breathing ragged, our hands rushed as we tore at each other's clothes. His shirt fell away, then his T-shirt, my sweater, shirt and jeans. I smoothed my hands up the wide expanse of his chest, the dark crisp hairs tickling my palms. His was a working man's body—corded with muscle, lean and tan. I closed my eyes, reveling in the smooth skin of his back, the indention of his spine, the tapering of his waist. Dark hair converged on the flat planes of his stomach into a line that disappeared into the waist of his jeans that, without his belt, barely hung on his hips, revealing the elastic waistband of his white boxers.

Experiencing the textures of his body, combined with his exploration of mine, made me breathless. He cupped my breasts through my flimsy bra, teasing the budded nipples. I don't have a model body, but my breasts are my one asset. Did he remember how much I loved him touching them?

Yes, I decided when he unhooked my bra and dropped to his knees to kiss and lick each pink peak thoroughly, dragging his teeth across the sensitive skin, sending instant moisture to wet my thin panties. I cried out, my hands kneading his neck, my knees buckling. I fell forward and he picked me up, then carried me to one of the beds, settling me on the edge and rolling my panties down the length of my legs.

He spread my knees and knelt to rain kisses up my inner thighs, moving back and forth, nipping at my skin. I leaned back on my elbows because in addition to the unbelievable sparkles of pleasure of having his mouth on me, in addition to the almost unbearable anticipation of having his tongue *inside* me, I took great pleasure in watching Redford enjoy the act of making love to me with his mouth. When he reached the culmination of his journey, his warm tongue flicked against my wet folds and our moans melded. Seeing his dark head between my thighs was incredibly erotic.

When he plunged his tongue inside me, my body jerked in response to the icy fire racing through my muscles. After teasing me mercilessly, he found my sensual switch and worked it with his tongue until I clenched my fists in the bedspread, murmuring his name, begging for release. He moaned against my clit to escalate the vibrations, launching me to an orgasm so powerful, that even in the throes of the intense spasms, the possibility of a health implication crossed my mind—a burst vein, a permanent muscle contraction, a heart attack.

But happily, I lived to reach for his waistband and unzip his jeans, feeling another surge of desire when I freed his enormous erection. He groaned, then sucked in a sharp breath when I pushed down his soft cotton boxers to cradle his sex in my hands.

I had hinted—okay, *bragged*—to my friends at Redford's massive size. I had dreamed of his nude body countless times, had conjured up his image for dozens of erotic sessions alone and—I'm not proud to admit—when in bed with other men. But when I saw and felt his rigid, straining shaft, I was awed all over again…thick and long, with an enormous tip, already shiny with pre-come. I dipped my head for a taste, but Redford stopped me with a groan.

"Don't think I don't want you to," he gasped. "But I'm so hot for you right now, I won't last two seconds. And I want to be inside you…the first time."

A pang of longing struck me low and hard. I nodded my agreement, then almost panicked. "Do you have protection?"

He grinned sheepishly. "At the risk of seeming presumptuous, I came prepared."

At the moment, I didn't care about his motivation

for bringing condoms, I was just weak with relief that he'd brought them. He retrieved one from his wallet, then handed it to me. With him standing in front of me seated on the edge of the bed, I rolled it on carefully, conscious of his size and our safety. Then reached down to caress his velvety sack and the sensitive ridge beneath—things I'd never done to any other man. He clenched my shoulders in a long moan, then urged me back on the bed. He followed me, stretching out on top of me, bracing himself with his arms. The sensation of full-body contact with him almost overwhelmed me—and I knew there was so much more to come.

He kissed me hard, slanting his mouth over mine, delving his tongue deep, sharing my essence with me. He captured my hands, entwining our fingers, and pinned them to the bed over my head. Our bodies were slick with perspiration, and the musk of his maleness only fueled my desire. "Now, Redford…now."

He shifted his hips, easing his erection between my thighs. His jaw was clenched with restraint as he found my entrance and pushed in slowly, one breathtaking inch at a time, until he was fully sheathed in my body. It was an amazing feeling, to be so filled, for every centimeter of my slick channel to be stimulated at once. I squeezed his fingers between mine and contracted my inner muscles around him.

"Oh, Denise," he groaned. "Oh, God, that feels… soooo…good."

He flexed his hips, making tiny thrusts that prodded an untapped spot deep inside me. Almost immediately, the waves of a powerful orgasm began to build, radiating from my womb. I flailed as the tension in my body mounted. His thrusts intensified—longer, deeper, faster. Our moans mingled as the sensations ratcheted higher. I climaxed in a sudden explosion of color and light, and sank my teeth into his shoulder to stifle my cries. His shuddering release came a split second after mine, his face contorted in pleasure-pain, my name on his lips.

Our "little death" coincided exactly with the death of the twin bed. One lower corner fell to the floor, giving us a good bounce on the box springs, then the post fell over with a thud.

We collapsed into each other laughing, our skin flushed and hot to the touch and wet with exertion. "Looks like we'll be sleeping in the other bed," he muttered.

Then he rolled me over on top of him and exhaled noisily. "That," he murmured, "was amazing."

I sighed against his chest, feeling languid and blissful, my body still pulsing from the pleasure he'd given me. "I have a confession to make."

He tensed. "What?"

"I almost got off while I was riding that horse today."

Two seconds of dead silence was split open by his howl of laughter.

I swatted at his chest. "It's not that funny."

"Yes, it is," he said, whooping. "No wonder you wanted to get down from there so fast."

"It's your fault."

"How?"

"You goaded me into riding that beast."

He emitted a low growl. "If I'd known what was going on up there, I would've made old Reggie gallop."

"Gee, thanks for not making me feel like an idiot."

He laughed. "Don't be so hard on yourself. I've heard of it happening before."

"You have?"

"Well, only with extraordinarily horny women."

"Oh, you!" I pushed up to move away, but he captured my wrist.

"Where do you think you're going?"

"To take a shower."

"Not without me, you're not."

Warmth filtered through my chest as he pushed to his feet and pulled me into the bathroom. He closed the door and pinned me against the door. "But first, I have to do something that I've been dying to do since I got here."

Full of female pride, I grinned. "I thought we just did that."

He laughed. "Yes, but there's one more thing."

He reached behind my neck and gently, ever so gently, he released my hair from its clasp and pushed his hands into it, pulling it forward around my shoulders. "Beautiful," he breathed.

I couldn't speak. The feelings welling up in my

chest… I didn't even want to think about what they might mean.

He kissed me lightly. "You like the water hot, don't you?"

I nodded, inordinately pleased he remembered.

While he turned on the water and adjusted the temperature, I leaned against the vanity, enjoying the view of his lean backside and powerful hamstrings. And the treasure on the other side…*sigh*. Lust pumped through my body with such force that I pressed a fist to my mouth to regain control. This man brought out the worst in me.

Out of the corner of my eye, I caught sight of my engagement ring on the vanity where I'd left it. With much effort, I pushed down the spike of guilt, and when Redford turned around, I reached out and flipped off the light.

A few seconds later his chuckle reverberated in the tiled room. "It's a little late for shyness, don't you think, Denise?"

Seizing a deliciously wicked opportunity, I pushed off the vanity, felt my way over to him and pressed my breasts into his warm back. "I thought we could take a shower in the dark."

He gave a low laugh of compliance and we climbed under the spray together.

When one sense is taken away, the other senses truly do become more keen. With the door closed, the windowless room was completely dark, and suddenly, I could feel the smooth surface of the tub beneath my feet, the softness of the country water splashing over my face, the callused tips of Redford's hands caressing my bottom.

I wrapped my arms around his waist and flicked my tongue over his nipples, reveling in the saltiness of his skin. I felt around the wall until I found a soft loofah and what felt like a new bar of soap. I lathered the loofah and scrubbed Redford's back in large, massaging circles, applying as much pressure as I could.

"Ooh, that's great," he moaned.

The acoustics in our little cocoon were wonderful, magnifying our noises. Methodically, I worked the loofah over his shoulders and down his arms, then down to his lower back and hips. I turned him around slowly and massaged the lather onto his chest, ignoring for the time being his erection prodding my stomach. He submitted to my ministrations, murmuring approval as I moved across his stomach and hip bones, then moved down to his thighs. I knelt to better feel my way down the fronts of his legs, then handed him the loofah and the soap. Still kneeling, I gently washed his cock with my hands, massaging and stroking him clean. Then I took the velvety tip into my mouth, eliciting a gasp from Redford. The water spilled over my hair and face as I pleasured him with my mouth, taking in as much of his length as I could accommodate, stroking the base of him with my fingers.

With a guttural groan, Redford stopped me, lifted me to my feet and whispered, "Your turn." He moved behind me and began to massage my neck and shoulders. I sighed in appreciation, planting my hands against the shower wall, allowing the spray to wash over my face. While he moved the loofah over my back, he slid his hand around to massage my breasts. It was ecstasy, feeling so many sensations and textures at once—and knowing that with Redford, the best was yet to come.

He worked the loofah down my back and over my hips, while sliding his other hand down my stomach and into the curls between my thighs. "Mmm, ohhh, yesssss."

"You like?" he whispered.

"Umm-hmm."

He slipped a finger inside me from behind. "You like?" he whispered.

"Ummm-hmmm." I contracted around him, and he pressed forward. The man knew how to push my button, from both sides. I could feel another orgasm coming on and gave in to it, brought to higher heights with every stroke at his urging in my ear. When one wave subsided, another crashed through my body, vibrating me down to my bones. At last, when I was too weak to stand, Redford supported me with one hand and turned off the shower with the other.

Unfortunately, I slipped and threw him off balance, too. I could feel us going down and grabbed for the shower curtain, which came crashing down with us, but helped to break our fall.

"Are you okay?" he asked.

"Fine," I moaned. "You?"

"Yeah, I think so."

I started giggling. "So much for showering in the dark."

We both laughed until we were limp, then wrapped towels around ourselves and went back to the other room, where we rubbed each other down.

Of course, the rubbing led to other touching, and the touching lead to kissing, and the kissing led to us concluding that both the crippled bed and the other twin bed were simply too small.

"We can push them together," I suggested, and Redford agreed. But when they were about two feet apart, his eyes lit up.

"What?" I asked.

He moved to stand between the beds, then urged me up, to straddle the beds—to straddle him. I grinned, then looped my arms around his neck and whispered naughty things in his ear until his erection was so stiff, I could have impaled myself on him. Instead, I leveraged myself on the two beds and lowered myself on him bit by thrilling bit as he nuzzled my breasts.

The position was mind-blowing, matching up our boy and girl parts perfectly, allowing Redford to reach my highest secret places, and providing enough frontal friction that another orgasm for me was only a matter of time. Our hands were free to roam, and best of all: we could look into each other's eyes.

Redford had the sexiest eyes—endlessly deep and

expressive. I could tell every time he reached a new pleasure plateau. When my body began to tremble with the onset of a powerful climax, he curled his hand around the nape of my neck and brought my face up to his.

"I want to see you come," he said. "I want to see your face, see how I make you feel."

His words sent me soaring over the edge, my already sensitized erogenous zones screaming with release. I clung to him while spasms racked my body. He uttered a long, quaking groan and picked me up, climaxing with my arms and legs wrapped around him like a vise. It was a religious experience.

When our bodies quieted, we found that we had somehow traveled several feet away from the bed. He looked for a place to lower me, and we almost made it to the couch. My dismount was wobbly and I hooked a floor lamp on my way down, sending it crashing to the floor, crushing the shade and shattering the bulb.

We were trashing Kenzie and Sam's place…but I knew if anyone would understand, they would.

We decided to sleep where we fell, on the couch. My body was fatigued beyond words, but my mind wouldn't shut down so easily. I lay with my head on Redford's chest and listened as his heart quieted, then fell into a steady sleep rhythm. Slowly, like a leaky dyke, my troubles seeped through the sex-haze I had immersed myself in for the past couple of hours, until I was saturated in shame.

What had I done? Had sex with a man I had no intention of having a relationship with—and every indication that he felt the same. Hadn't he thanked me for filing the annulment papers? For the second time, we had been brought together on a whim, enjoyed each other's bodies and would separate.

Except he would go back to the life he'd planned for himself without breaking stride, while the life that I'd planned for myself—with Barry—had been compromised. What was I thinking? I had a *ring*. And I had a wedding dress, assuming Cindy managed to outbid SYLVIESMOM. Barry was in L.A., slaving away to build his career, to make a better life for both of us, and I was…here.

Naked with the man I'd married, then annulled myself from. Naked with my biggest mistake. Again.

A shiver passed over my body, the chill in the room seeking out the moist, naughty parts of me that still sang from Redford's touch. Unable to lie still any longer, I eased off the couch to make my way toward the bathroom. A few steps later, something sliced into the bottom of my foot, sending fire shooting up my leg. I cried out, and Redford was awake and on his feet before I could take another step.

"What happened?" he said, alarm in his voice.

I limped toward the bathroom. "I stepped on glass from the lightbulb…be careful."

He skirted the broken glass and followed me. "Let me take a look at it."

"No, that's okay," I said, fighting back tears…as

much for the pain radiating in my foot as for the situation I'd landed myself in. "Just clean up the glass."

In the bathroom, I swept aside the torn shower curtain and broken rod and lowered myself to the edge of the tub. The amount of blood staining the white tile floor was distressing, but when I stuck my foot under cold running water, I was relieved to discover it was actually a small wound. Still, my eyes overflowed and I was shaking. My engagement ring glittered from the vanity. I reached over and picked it up, then slid it onto my finger, my tears coming in earnest now.

"Are you okay?" Redford said from the doorway.

I looked up, then hastily brushed at my cheeks and nodded. "It's not as bad as it looks." I pulled the shower curtain over me—it was much too late for modestly, but still.

"Let me take a look," he said gently. "To make sure the glass is out."

I yielded, lifting my foot and swiveling. He cradled my foot in his big hand, then pinched open the cut. I flinched.

"Sorry," he said, then patted my foot. "But it looks clean. Let me see if I can find a bandage. I'm sure Sam has plenty of supplies around." He rummaged in the vanity, then removed a bottle of peroxide and a box of adhesive bandages.

I was still while he dressed the wound, my throat and chest tight. He occasionally glanced to my left hand, at the ring, but he didn't say anything.

"Does it hurt?" he asked finally.

I wiped at more tears, but shook my head. I couldn't tell him why I was crying. I wasn't even sure myself.

He made a rueful noise. "It will in the morning."

I swallowed in resignation.

I was pretty sure that everything would be hurting in the morning.

17

KENZIE OPENED the back door when I knocked the next morning. "Good morning."

"Good morning," I said with as much nonchalance as I could muster considering every muscle in my body screamed with pain.

Her smile was questioning, but she simply sipped from her coffee cup while I followed her into the kitchen.

"You're limping," she said, pointing.

I stacked the unused clothes that Sam had loaned us on the table and lowered myself onto a bar stool. "Um, we had a little accident last night."

"We?" she asked.

I squirmed. "I hope the furnishings in the apartment weren't family heirlooms."

Her eyes widened. "Did you set a fire, too?"

"No, thank God. But one of the beds is broken, the shower curtain is torn and the curtain rod snapped… and the floor lamp is history. Oh, and there are a few, um, bloodstains on the carpet."

She frowned. "What?" Then she gave a dismissive wave. "Don't worry about the furniture, it's all secondhand. But what on earth did you two do over there?"

My face flamed. "I'd rather not talk about it."

She handed me a mug of coffee and smirked. "Is he as big as you remember?"

I took a deep drink. "Yes."

She gasped, her eyes dancing, until she spotted my engagement ring. "You're still wearing your ring?"

I shifted on the stool. "I took it off...*during*. Now things are...back to normal."

She looked worried. "So that's it, then. This thing with Redford was just a fling?"

"Right. It was always just sex between me and Redford. This was...my last hurrah before settling down."

"So he goes back to Kentucky—"

"And I stay in New York, where I belong," I finished.

Footsteps sounded in the mudroom, ending our conversation. Redford stuck his head in the kitchen. "Sorry, I knocked."

I busied myself drinking from my cup. Mine and Redford's conversation this morning had been brief and stilted. Worse, I could barely look at him without wanting to go at it again. I was pathetic.

"We don't stand on ceremony here, Redford," Kenzie said. "Come on in. Coffee?"

He wore his hat and coat, and his cheeks were red from the cold. "Sounds good." He glanced at me, his expression unreadable. "I started the truck to warm it up. Looks like the roads will be fine for the drive back."

"Good." I had called my office from the clinic and told them I wouldn't be in today.

Kenzie handed Redford a cup of coffee and he thanked her. "Sam's truck is gone. Has he left for the day?"

Kenzie nodded. "He asked me to give you his regrets. He got a call about an expectant cow mom in distress on a farm across the county." She grinned. "I figure if I get as big as a cow with this baby, he'll feel right at home."

"Are you feeling better this morning?" I asked, standing.

"Much."

"Are you coming back to the city this week?"

She sighed. "I hope so. I have to admit, I'm getting cabin fever on this mountain, especially since it's too cold to go outside. I miss the city. And you girls."

I gave her a hug. "Call me when you get back and we'll have lunch."

"You bet," she said. "Redford, it was a pleasure meeting you."

He nodded and thanked her for the hospitality. "Good luck with the baby." He smiled. "And with the foal."

She followed us to the door. "Good luck to you guys tomorrow on the audit."

I closed my eyes briefly—one more thing to dread.

The drive back to the city was, shall I say, *loooooong*. If we exchanged ten words, it was a lot. We listened to music and I plowed through the rest of the tax documents. But even though we didn't talk, Redford's body communicated with mine, sending out vibes that kept my senses on edge. Scenes from the previous night kept flashing into my mind. By the time we began to see signs for the city limits, I was almost frantic to be away from him.

"I left some cash in the apartment to cover the damages," he said suddenly.

"Oh…that was good of you."

"How's your foot?"

It throbbed. "It's okay, just a little sore."

He rolled his shoulders. "I'm sore all over."

I averted my gaze to my hands…and my ring.

He made a rueful noise in his throat. "I have the distinct feeling that you have regrets about last night."

I exhaled slowly and looked out the window. "Don't we all have regrets about things in our lives?"

"Absolutely. Vegas, for instance."

My chest tightened. "Right. Vegas." At least we agreed on one thing.

I was never so happy to see my apartment building. Redford pulled in to a rare empty parking space in front, then reached across the seat and picked up my hand. The gesture was unexpected, and sent my pulse spiking.

He rubbed his fingers across my palm. "Denise, I'm sorry about last night." He glanced up with a wry smile. "I feel like I'm always saying I'm sorry."

I swallowed hard. "Redford, you don't have to

apologize. You gave me a choice, and I made my decision. I went to you with my eyes wide open." I just hadn't realized my heart had been ajar, too.

He looked thoughtful and kept stroking my palm, sending little shivers up my arm. "It wasn't fair of me to put you in that position." He turned my hand over and fingered my engagement ring. "I know you feel guilty about what we did. I feel as if I've stormed through your life…again…and messed up your plans."

I didn't say anything, especially since I could barely speak when he touched me like that. He was trying to apologize for last night, and heaven help me, all I could think about was him kissing me again.

And suddenly, he *was* kissing me. First tenderly, then hungrily. We devoured each other, our tongues parlaying, our lips sliding, our teeth clicking. He hauled me across the seat into his lap and I ran my hands over his chest, his arms, drove my fingers into his hair.

"We could do it right here," he murmured raggedly, unbuttoning the top button of my blouse.

A memory chord vibrated…the very words I'd said to Barry, tempting him to do something naughty…

But when Redford stroked my nipple, I was willing to do anything he asked.

I loved him, I realized with a burst of adrenaline. *I loved this man.*

I returned his kiss like a starved woman, our hands roving, hunting for buttons, snaps.

A sharp rap on the window startled me—and Redford. My first thought was that it was the police and we were about to be booked for public indecency. But when I saw the astonished face of the person on the sidewalk, my stomach bottomed out.

"Mom?" I whispered.

"Mom?" Redford said, his voice panicked. "That woman is your mother?"

"And that man is my father," I murmured, utterly and completely horrified to see them staring in at us. Although, in fairness, they looked equally horrified. I slid off Redford's lap, straightening my clothes, gasping for air. "Omigod, omigod, omigod. Redford, when I get out, just drive away."

He frowned. "I'm not going to drive away like some teenage kid. I'm going to introduce myself to your father."

I was starting to hyperventilate. "I don't think that's a good idea."

"We've done a lot of things this weekend that weren't particularly bright. Come on."

There was no time to calm myself. I opened the truck door and climbed down, my heart jumping in my chest at the sight of my parents standing there, the epitome of upper-middle-classdom in their prim winter resort wear, surrounded by suitcases, looking shell-shocked.

"Mom…Dad…what a surprise."

My mother drew herself up. "That's obvious, dear."

"We tried to call you," my dad piped up, "but you

weren't answering your cell phone, or your phone at work. We thought we'd take our chances and see if you were home."

"I th-thought you were in *England*."

"The weather was miserable, so we decided to cut our trip short and stop here on our way home to congratulate you—" her eyes cut to Redford suspiciously "—on your engagement."

I wanted to evaporate. After a few seconds of gluey silence, I cleared my throat. "Um, Gayle and Harrison Cooke, this is Redford DeMoss."

Redford removed his hat and shook their hands. "How do you do, ma'am, sir?"

"And how do you know our Denise?" my mother asked sharply.

Oh...my...God.

Redford turned to me, his mouth slack with surprise. "Ma'am, I'll let Denise explain it." Then he put his hat back on his head. "After I leave you folks to enjoy your reunion."

Without being asked, he picked up the suitcases and carried them to the landing, then came back and tipped his hat. "Ma'am...sir...Denise." He looked at me, his eyes hard. "I'll see you tomorrow morning?"

The audit...of course. "I...I'll meet you there."

He nodded curtly, then climbed into his truck and drove away. My heart caved in when I saw him glance in the rearview mirror, then look away. Watching him leave was jarring to my senses. But I would have to get used to it.

I turned and gave my folks the best smile I could manage under the circumstances. "We need to talk."

My mother gave me a disapproving look. "I believe so."

I couldn't even bring myself to look at my poor dad—no doubt to his great relief. As we entered my apartment, I experienced age regression. By the time we had deposited their suitcases in a corner of the living room, I felt about twelve years old. The day of reckoning had arrived—the day my parents discovered that little Denise, squeaky-clean honor student who never caused them a day of trouble, wasn't perfect after all. Not even close. I thought I might be sick.

We had barely removed our coats before my mother crossed her arms and demanded, "Denise, *who* was that man you were *kissing* on the street?"

I turned to look at them and sighed. "Please sit down."

They sat on my couch and looked at me expectantly.

I took a deep breath and on the exhale said, "Redford and I were…married."

My mother clutched her chest. *"What? When?"*

"Three years ago."

She shrieked and grabbed my father's arm. "You're *married,* and you didn't even tell us?"

"No," I said, holding up my hand. "We *were* married. For six weeks. I had the marriage annulled."

My father looked completely lost. "Is that legal?"

"Yes. It means our marriage never happened."

He lifted his hands. "Who is this man and how did you meet him?"

Another deep breath. "I was in Vegas for the holidays. He was a Marine, on leave from the Gulf. That's where we met and…were married."

"In *Vegas?*" My mother looked horrified. "Harrison, it's our fault. That's the year we went on the Bahamas golf trip with the Sutherlands. If we'd stayed home, Denise would have been with us and this would never have happened." She teared up. "I didn't want to go on that trip—it was your idea—and just look what happened!"

Dad handed her his handkerchief. I pinched the bridge of my nose.

"Oh, Denise," she cried, "tell me the wedding at least took place in a church, not in one of those tacky chapels."

I winced. "It was in a tacky chapel." I cleared my throat—in for a penny, in for a pound. "Actually, in the drive-through."

My mother looked faint. "Harrison, get my heart pills."

My dad dutifully reached for Mom's purse and rummaged through the various prescriptions before handing her a bottle.

"Did that man take advantage of you?" he demanded. His face turned red. "Were you…with child?"

This was going well.

"No, Dad, no. Redford was…is a complete gentleman." I thought of the scene they'd witnessed outside and swallowed hard. "Ninety-nine percent of the time. We got married on the spur of the moment and when I came back to New York and he went back to the Gulf, we realized we'd made a mistake. That's all."

"That's all?" my mother asked. "Denise, marriage isn't something to take lightly."

I balked. "I know that. I'm not proud of what I did, which is why I didn't tell you."

"I don't understand," my dad said. "If you had the marriage annulled, then what is that man doing here?"

"He had to come to New York because our joint tax return is being audited by the IRS. We have an interview in the morning."

Now my dad looked truly horrified. "The IRS can ruin your life."

My mother's head bobbed. "Do you remember the McGoverns? Their 1040 form went astray and they lost their house. The IRS came and threw all their things out in the yard for anyone to take. Miriam lost her mother's silver—she said the mailman took it."

I rolled my eyes. "Mom, the IRS doesn't take that kind of action simply because a 1040 form wasn't filed. Besides, ours is just a routine audit." I hoped.

"Where does this young man live?" my dad wanted to know.

"Kentucky. He's retired from the Marines and works in his family stables."

My mother frowned. "He's a stable boy?"

"Um, no. They run a horse breeding business."

She made a face. (My utterance of the word "breeding" was as close to a "sex talk" as my mother and I had ever gotten.)

"So when did you and Barry break up?" she asked.

I swallowed. "We didn't."

Her gaze flew to my finger and she gasped, temporarily diverted. "Your ring is gorgeous!" She reached for my hand and scrutinized the diamond. "Oh, my, it looks flawless."

"It is."

She glanced up, then her eyes narrowed. "Where is Barry?"

"In L.A."

"So you're kissing this Redmon fellow in the street while your fiancé is out of town?"

"His name is Redford." And I was guilty of so much more than kissing.

"Your father and I raised you better than that, Denise."

I squirmed. "I'm sorry you and Dad had to see that. It…just happened…and it was a mistake."

She frowned. "Well, considering that ring on your finger, I hope it doesn't happen again. Why aren't you at work today?"

I didn't have time to think of a lie. "I went with Redford to upstate New York yesterday to look at a stud horse, and the weather was too bad for us to return last night."

My mother's eyebrows shot up and I didn't want

to know what was going through her mind. A lump formed in my throat and I felt very, very dirty.

My dad stood abruptly. "Gayle, we'd better go. Denise has a lot on her mind right now. Honey, we'll call you in a few days."

He gathered their coats and suitcases and shepherded my mother toward the door. But at the last minute, she turned back and wagged her finger at me. "Denise, a wise person learns from their mistakes."

KENZIE GASPED. "No, they didn't."

"Yes," I said into the phone miserably. "They did."

"Oh, my God, you were making out in his truck? In broad daylight?"

I closed my eyes. "Yes, but we weren't naked… yet." Thank goodness for small miracles.

"Well, what did you tell your parents?"

I sighed. "The truth."

"What did they say?"

I teared up. "They were shocked. My mother said that they raised me better than that, and then they left." I sniffed. "I can't imagine what they think of me."

Kenzie made a sympathetic noise. "They probably think that you're human, and that everyone makes mistakes. Give them some time to come around. Besides, Denise, you're an adult."

I pressed my lips together. "Which means I can be deceitful or even immoral without being accountable?"

"Of course not. But you have to decide for yourself what's right and what's wrong for *you*. You're the one who has to live with your mistakes."

"But my mistakes affect other people's lives, too."

"So explain to your mom that this thing between you and Redford was just a blip. That you were having cold feet after Barry proposed."

My throat ached from the lump that formed there. "Except I'm starting to think that it wasn't a blip... for me."

She gasped. "Are you in love with him again?"

"Maybe...yes."

"And what are you going to do about it?"

"Nothing. Kenzie, Redford *thanked* me for filing for the annulment, said it had allowed us to get on with our lives."

"So what about last night?"

I gave a little laugh. "Obviously, we're still attracted to each other. But sex is the only thing Redford and I have in common."

"It's about the only thing that Sam and I had in common."

"And look—" I stopped and bit my tongue.

"And look, what?" Kenzie asked lightly. "Look at how my life has changed?"

"Yes," I said finally.

"Hmm, let's see—before I met Sam I worked eighty hours a week and had no social life. Now I get to do the job I enjoy at a sane pace, and I have a husband who loves me and his baby in my belly." She sighed. "Denise, yes, my life has changed, and I couldn't be happier. I'm not saying that the way I did it would work for everyone, but sometimes you have to be willing to take a risk...like you did in Vegas."

I frowned. "But that was a disaster."

"Only because you came back and allowed everyone to convince you that it was a crazy thing to do."

"But it *was* a crazy thing to do."

"So? Just because it was crazy, doesn't mean it was a mistake."

I was quiet, digesting her words. "I guess I need more order in my life than most people. As much as I care about Redford, I just feel so...*reckless* when I'm around him. I can't live like that, Kenzie."

She sighed. "Then it sounds as if you've made the right decision to write this off as a fling and go on with your life."

I murmured my agreement, but I didn't feel as good as I'd hoped to feel.

"So, where is Redford tonight?"

"At his hotel, I assume. The scene with my parents caught him off guard, but he handled it well. Shook my father's hand and looked him in the eye before he left."

"Hmm...not easy to do after you've been caught with your pants down."

I sniffed. *"Tell me."*

"So he left?"

"He said he wanted to give us privacy. Basically, he was giving me an out if I wanted to lie to my parents. Again."

"Very chivalrous of him."

"Yes." Redford was nothing if not noble, which is why he would have stayed in a quickie Vegas marriage, even after he had realized his mistake. "Anyway, I'll see him tomorrow at the audit, and that will be the end of it."

Kenzie made a doubtful noise. "If you say so. Let me know how the audit goes."

I hung up the phone, leaden with despair. I found the plane tickets to Vegas I had bought as a Valentine's Day surprise for Barry and wavered. Maybe Barry and I simply didn't have enough fun together. Maybe I wasn't being fair. Then I stared at my laboratory-engineered-diamond engagement ring until my vision blurred. On top of everything else, the money already spent on our relationship was giving me an ulcer. And second thoughts.

With my heart pounding in my ears, I picked up the handset and dialed Barry's cell phone.

18

A SMALL PART OF ME hoped this was one of those times that Barry wouldn't answer his phone.

"Hello?" he answered on the first ring.

Apparently, I was not to be let off the hook so easily. I pressed my lips together to fight back tears.

"Hello?" he repeated, sounding tired.

"Hi," I croaked. "It's me…Denise."

"Oh, hi. I left you a couple of messages today at work."

"Um…I wound up taking the day off."

"Are you ill?"

Mentally, yes. "I'm fine, just needed to catch up on some things."

"I talked to Ellen this morning. She said she ran into you Saturday night at a Broadway show, that you were with some gay guy?"

I closed my eyes. "Um, yes…he's a…friend of mine."

"And she said the two of you are getting together tomorrow afternoon to talk business."

"That's right."

"Have you already thought of what you're going to do with your big bonus? I was thinking maybe we could take a trip."

I clenched my jaw.

"Are you there?"

"Yeah, I'm here."

"You don't sound well."

"Barry, I can't marry you." I winced, wishing I hadn't just blurted it out like that, but I couldn't take it back now.

"What?" he said, sounding floored. Then he laughed. "Denise...what are you saying?"

I sighed and summoned strength—I didn't want to hurt him. "I'm saying that I can't marry you, Barry. I'm sorry, but I don't love you...enough."

After a few seconds of silence, he scoffed. "You don't love me *enough?* You either love someone or you don't, Denise."

I swallowed. "All right then...I don't love you. I don't want to marry you."

"You don't want to marry me?"

"That's right."

He scoffed, making blustery noises. "I don't believe this. If you didn't want to get married, then what's with the wedding dress?"

I blinked. "How did you know about the wedding dress?"

"I saw it hanging in your closet the night I was looking for my toiletry bag."

And he had proposed the following night. I

brought my fist to my mouth as a horrible suspicion bloomed in my mind. "Are you saying you proposed because you saw the wedding dress in my closet?"

"Well…yeah. I mean, that's one big hell of a hint, don't you think?"

Humiliation rolled over me in waves. I sat down hard in a chair. "So…you really don't want to get married, either?"

"Well, I'm crazy about you, Denise, and we don't argue, and we have so much in common…I thought maybe it was time to just bite the bullet."

Bite the bullet. Barry was comparing marriage to me with sticking a gun in his mouth.

I was numb. My mouth opened and closed, but I couldn't seem to form words. Finally I managed, "Barry, I don't believe either one of us is ready to make that kind of commitment to each other."

He sighed. "Denise, I'm swamped right now. Can we talk about this later?"

"No. I don't think we should see each other anymore."

He scoffed. "Just like that? No explanation, nothing?"

"I'm sorry, Barry…I can't explain it to myself. Just know that this has nothing to do with you. It's me."

"You're making a mistake, Denise."

His words sent a chill through me. Maybe I was… maybe my life was just one long series of mistakes and missed opportunities.

"I'll send the ring to your office," I said in a

choked voice. (I hoped he could get a refund.) "I'm truly sorry, Barry."

He made some disbelieving noises, all understandable—I was in a state of disbelief myself.

"Speaking of the office," he said bitterly, "don't be surprised if our breakup affects Ellen's decision to do business with Trayser Brothers."

I couldn't blame him for being angry. "I'll understand if she changes her mind. Goodbye, Barry."

I hung up the phone, took off the man-made diamond ring and cried. Sobbed. Really boo-hooed. (I never cried...*ever.*) Over losing my friendship with Barry, losing my heart to Redford, and losing my mind over love in general.

And I was in love with Redford again. Or had I never really fallen out of love with him?

In a torturous mood, I walked over to the cigar box of keepsakes and opened the lid, assailed by bittersweet recollections. I sat on the floor cross-legged and removed each item, turned it over, rubbed it between my palms, wringing the memories out of each memento in an effort to conjure up my state of mind at the time. I closed my eyes, tried to push everything else out of my mind, trying to remember with all five senses.

I had been so...*happy* with Redford. Blissfully so...childlike. To the point that I thought it couldn't possibly last...it had to be a mistake. And it was. My judgment where relationships were concerned was officially abysmal.

My mother's parting words came back to me. *A wise person learns from their mistakes.*

Not me. I'd spent the last three years kicking myself for being stupid enough to marry Redford, only to turn around and almost make another mistake by marrying Barry. When I thought of how close I'd come to marrying a man who had proposed because of a lousy dress, I was nauseous.

The ringing phone roused me from my bout of self-loathing. I wiped my eyes and cleared my throat, then answered the phone, wondering which person I didn't want to talk to could be calling. Mother? Barry? Redford?

"Hi, it's me!" Cindy sang into the phone. "He called again!"

"Who?"

"Jim—the guy from my Positive Thinking class. Just now! We talked for almost an hour on the phone, and he asked me out again. Oh, Denise, I have such a good feeling about this guy!"

Her announcement roused me from my melancholy mood, and I smiled. "That's wonderful, Cindy. At least we know the man has good taste. And who knows—maybe he's *the one*."

She sighed. "Oh, I hope so. Denise, it sounds crazy, but I think I'm half in love with him already."

"Easy, girl," I said with a little laugh. But I knew just how she felt.

"Oh, gracious, I almost forgot the reason I really

called! I won the auction—you can keep your wedding gown!"

I dropped back into the chair, caught between laughing and crying. I'd forgotten all about the auction. I'd set this entire mess into motion when I'd made the mistake of buying that stupid wedding dress. Now after having Cindy bid like a madwoman to win it back, I had it.

Plus one fabulous gown—*minus* one fiancé.

My life was just too sad for words.

_19_

I WAS A NERVOUS WRECK when I walked into the IRS office Tuesday morning at the appointed time. I'd gotten no sleep to speak of, tossing and turning and soaking my pillow. I was racked with guilt over the way I'd behaved with Redford, and what I'd sacrificed—my relationship with Barry, my self-integrity. Even my parents knew that I had betrayed my fiancé with another man. That fact alone was enough to launch me into therapy.

But the basic truth was that my fixation on Redford simply wasn't healthy. Both times he'd rolled through my life, he'd left a wake of destruction. I didn't even want to think about how long it would take me to get over him this time.

I straightened my shoulders, focusing on my goal to get through the audit. I'd worn my most stylish suit in anticipation of meeting with Ellen Brant later; but sensible shoes since I was still hobbling from my foot injury. And after much self-debate, I'd also decided to wear Barry's ring to the interview...I didn't want its absence to trigger any questions from Redford.

Not that I thought he'd notice, but still.

As I shifted the box of tax papers, my mind clicked ahead to the possible costly outcomes. Since I no longer had an "in" with Ellen Brant, I couldn't count on the bonus for her account. If the IRS levied stiff penalties and interest for my mistakes, I'd have to sell my…what?

My wedding gown? The wedding band that Redford had given me? I could have a "has been" bridal yard sale.

And what if Redford had to pay a huge sum? What if it jeopardized the cash flow of his family business?

More than the audit itself, I was dreading seeing him this morning. Dreading the visceral response to him I knew was virtually irrepressible. A physical reminder that I couldn't trust my own judgment when I was around him.

I was well on my way to developing a migraine when I was shown to a small office containing a long utilitarian table, a few uncomfortable chairs and a wall bookshelf of imposing tax tomes—just in case they had to whip out a revenue code to prove their point, I assumed.

"Someone will be right with you," the woman threatened.

I set the box on the table and walked over to the window, parting the miniblinds with my fingers. It was the kind of cold, blustery day that made people hurry—trotting along, bundled in their coats and scarves, heads down. Redford stood out even more than usual as he walked toward the building, his stride long and precise, his duster coat flapping, a briefcase in his hand, his hat planted on his head, his chin level.

My thighs quickened. Even from this distance, he could affect me. I stepped back, and the blinds snapped closed. I chewed my last remaining fingernail down to the nub, my nerves ratcheting higher as each minute on the clock ticked by.

When the door opened suddenly, I was so startled I nearly cried out. Redford walked in and nodded to me, his face passive. "Good morning."

"Good m-morning," I stammered.

He set the saddle-tan briefcase on the table and shrugged out of his coat, then removed his hat. He wore dark jeans, a white dress shirt, and a gray sport coat. He looked so handsome, my heart ached.

"How was your visit with your folks?"

I wet my lips. "I told them everything, Redford. About the wedding and the annulment."

He pursed his mouth. "They must have been shocked, hearing it for the first time."

I nodded, clasping my hands together. "They were disappointed. I was raised very conservatively. It's not the sort of thing they expected out of me." I gave an embarrassed little laugh. "They think I'm Miss Perfect."

He shifted from foot to foot. "I'm sorry to be the cause of blowing their perception of you."

"I apologized for them seeing us…together. I

explained that it…just happened and that it was a mistake."

He glanced at my left hand. "I hope it didn't spoil their celebration of your engagement."

"No," I murmured. "They were…understanding."

His expression was unreadable. "Good."

The door burst open, admitting a stern-faced man holding a thick folder. He eyed us over half-glasses. "Are you Mr. and Mrs. DeMoss?"

I blinked.

"Formerly," Redford said, straightening. "I'm Redford DeMoss, and this is Denise Cooke."

"Adam Helmut. I'll be performing the audit." The man shook Redford's hand, then mine. His fingers were cold and stiff. "Have a seat."

Redford and I sat in adjacent chairs. When I crossed my legs, I accidentally brushed his leg. I jerked back and Redford looked at me, his eyes mocking. I knew what was going through his mind—Sunday night I had welcomed him deep into my body, and today I could barely touch him.

Mr. Helmut pulled out our tax form and reviewed a colored sheet of what looked like handwritten notes. After verifying our social security numbers and the tax year in question, he ticked through personal data and made more notes on the sheet.

"When and where were you married?"

I cited the date, then felt my cheeks grow hot. "At the Taking Care of Business wedding chapel in Las Vegas."

He looked up, then back to the sheet, writing.

"And when did you divorce?"

"The marriage was annulled," Redford said in a low tone.

"Ah. In what calendar year?"

"The following year."

The man nodded as if to say that he'd expected as much. "Do you have the annulment papers with you?"

With a start, I realized I'd left them tucked into my silly cigar box. "I didn't bring them."

Redford reached for his briefcase. "I brought a copy."

My heart thumped against my breastbone as the man so clinically examined the papers that had expunged our marriage, then made a check on his notes. "So the return in question is the only year the two of you filed jointly?"

"That's correct," I said.

"Have either of you remarried?"

"No," we said in unison.

He looked up, then down again. "Mr. DeMoss, you were a sergeant in the U.S. Marines?"

"First Sergeant—yes, sir."

"And what was your pay grade?"

"E-8."

The man seemed impressed. "Career man?"

Redford nodded. "I retired last year."

Helmut turned to me and verified my employment at the time and my address, which was the address on the form, then pulled out a calculator and announced, "Okay, let's get down to it. Did you bring copies of your original source documents?"

"I have them," I said, nervously pulling the box of papers close to me. When I transferred the stack to the table, the books I'd bought on Thoroughbreds and the Marine Corps and logistics were in the bottom of the box. My cheeks warmed to see my newlywed eagerness revealed. Redford glanced at them and a wrinkle formed between his eyebrows, but he didn't say anything.

For the next two hours, the auditor painstakingly reviewed every figure on every line, questioning every number, recalculating the entire return. My anxiety grew as we moved toward the schedule of deductions for my home office.

"Ms. Cooke, you were at the time establishing a home-based financial business?"

I nodded. "But since then, I've taken a job with Trayser Brothers. Most of my clients followed me there."

He pursed his mouth. "Trayser Brothers…impressive. Well, let's take a look at the receipts for these business expenses, shall we?"

My stomach churned, but I pulled out the documents. One by one, we went over the figures and I tried to defend the expenses for which I didn't have receipts. He frowned occasionally and made notes on the colored sheet of paper. The more marks he made, the more worried I became.

"Excuse me for a few minutes," he said abruptly, then left with our form and his calculator.

When the door closed, Redford turned to me. "How do you think it's going?"

"Hard to tell," I said, touching my temples. But I had a vision of Mr. Helmut gathering troops—a director or someone with police authority—to lower the boom.

"Redford," I said in a choked voice. "I...might have...fudged a little on the deductions I took."

One eyebrow went up. "You? Miss Perfect cheated on her taxes?"

I frowned. "Shh! This room might be bugged."

He laughed, seemingly unfazed by my concern, then gave me a pointed look. "Relax, Denise. Your secrets—all of them—are safe with me."

I flinched. He was telling me that he knew the real me, the me that I kept hidden from everyone around me. Only he saw past the facade of Denise Cooke, neat freak, compulsive saver, reserved investment broker. He saw the woman who could bend the rules, and occasionally break them. The woman who threw caution to the wind and reason out the window.

What he didn't realize was that he was the only person who saw it, because he was the only person who could bring out that wayward side of me. Strangely, relief sliced through me because I realized that when Redford left, he would take my dirty little secrets with him. And as long as I stayed away from him, I'd eventually be back to normal. And once this audit was finished, we'd never see each other again.

The door swung open and Mr. Helmut came in, followed, as I had feared, by another well-dressed man with impressive-looking identification cards on lanyards around his neck.

"Mr. and Mrs. DeMoss?"

"Formerly," we said in unison.

"I'm Stuart Stanley, the director for this field office. Mr. Helmut has just informed me of some discrepancies on your tax form."

My stomach pitched.

"There are *quite* a few deductions that are being disallowed."

My intestines cramped.

"But apparently, you weren't given the extra income credit allowed for military personnel overseas, during the time for which you filed."

My eyes widened. "I wasn't aware of an extra income credit."

The director smiled. "You wouldn't have been. The original tax relief bill for soldiers was so riddled with problems that some people were actually penalized for their status. When the tax code was revamped, the government mandated that the IRS review each tax form and apply the credit were applicable. It seems that yours, Mr. DeMoss, was overlooked."

He extended his hand. "Our sincere apologies. The credit will more than offset the disallowed deductions. We'll process an amended form immediately, but by our estimation, you'll be receiving a small refund."

I was stunned. And weak with relief. I looked at

Redford and he looked amused. "So are we finished here?" he asked the men.

"Yes," the director said. "Thank you very much for coming in today. The receptionist will sign you out."

When the door closed behind them, I looked at Redford and he laughed.

"Looks like one mistake cancelled out the other."

"Yes," I said, looking at him, my heart twisting. "If only all of life were that way."

He stared into my eyes and moistened his lips. "Denise…"

"What?" My heart thudded in my ears.

He picked up my left hand. "Don't marry this guy unless you really love him."

I swallowed. "You're a good one to be handing out marital advice, Redford."

"I just don't want to see you make another mistake."

Anger suffused my chest. "And what do you care?"

His dark eyes looked pained. "I love you, Denise."

His words sent a tremor through my heart, but in the back of my mind, I kept reminding myself that our reunion had been unplanned. Redford could have looked me up when he lived in Albany and hadn't. Wasn't that proof enough that his interest in me was fleeting and based on proximity…on sex?

"Don't say that," I said, shaking my head. "I don't want to hear it."

"I know you don't," he said, his voice low. "I heard what you told Kenzie yesterday morning. That Sunday night was just a fling, that it always had been just sex between the two of us."

I inhaled a sharp breath, but didn't deny what I'd said.

"Maybe it was only sex to you," he said. "But I'm not going to leave without telling you that Sunday night meant something to me."

I panicked and looked away. He was doing it again—mistaking sex for love. And I was dangerously close to falling for it again. "Sunday night... shouldn't have happened, Redford."

His jaw hardened. "Just like our marriage shouldn't have happened?"

My pulse clicked higher and I looked at him. "That's right."

"Well, maybe we should just call an attorney and draw up papers to have our night of great sex annulled!"

My heart shivered. Our relationship always came back to sex. I started gathering up my things. "I have to be somewhere. Goodbye, Redford."

He was silent, then after several long seconds, he said, "Goodbye, Denise."

I didn't look up as he left the room, not until after the door closed. My throat and chest strained to hold back the river of tears. It was for the best, I kept telling myself.

I love you, Denise.

And how long would that have lasted? Another six weeks, until we realized that we were too different to make a life together? I needed more than a few impulsive words to hang the rest of my life on.

I moved my papers haphazardly back to the box,

barely able to focus through my tears. I blinked rapidly to diminish the moisture and my gaze landed on the open file at the end of the table. The top of the colored sheet of paper read, *Reason for audit: Anonymous informant alleged improprieties.*

I frowned. Informant? Someone had accused us of *cheating* on our taxes? Growing more indignant by the minute, my mind sorted through the possibilities. A disgruntled client of mine? A competitor? A vindictive girlfriend of Redford's?

I scoured the paper and next to the word "informant" was a phone number, an area code that I didn't recognize, but that wasn't saying much. Overcome with curiosity, I wrote down the number, then shoved it in my wallet and left the building. I forced my mind to think about my appointment with Ellen Brant. There would be plenty of time this evening to cry over Redford DeMoss.

And tomorrow.

And the next day.

My nerves were still clacking as I climbed on a bus to take me back into the city. Thoroughly miserable, I dropped into a seat, pulled out my cell phone and called Ellen's number. If she were going to cancel our appointment because of my split with Barry, I wanted to know before I made the trip to her office.

"Ellen Brant."

"Ellen, this is Denise DeMoss."

"Pardon me?"

Appalled, I realized my gaffe. "I mean, this is Denise Cooke." Where was my head? "I just wanted to make sure we were still on for this afternoon."

"I spoke with Barry this morning, Denise. He says the two of you aren't seeing each other anymore."

"That's right," I said, swallowing hard. "I broke off our engagement. And I understand if that makes you uneasy to have me handling your investments."

"No, dear. Barry is a wonderfully talented man who will go far, but I have to admit I didn't detect any chemistry between the two of you."

I blinked. "Oh?"

"I rather thought the two of you reminded me of brother and sister."

I winced. "You did?"

She gave a little laugh. "To be honest, there was more chemistry between you and that yummy gay friend of yours."

I closed my eyes, but forced a laugh from my throat. "So I'll see you this afternoon?"

"Absolutely. And don't worry, Denise. You'll find love again. I intend to."

She hung up and I stared at my phone, astonished. Then, clicking with curiosity—and anger—I pulled out the piece of paper on which I'd written the number for the "informant" and dialed.

After four rings, I was ready to hang up, but then a voice sounded on the other end.

"Hello?"

I squinted, certain my ears were playing tricks on me. *"Redford?"*

20

"DENISE." REDFORD SIGHED. "I'm busted, aren't I?"

My mouth worked up and down. "Redford, what is going on? Are you on a cell phone?"

"Yep."

"I thought you said you didn't have one."

"I was afraid you'd somehow get this number from the IRS. You did, didn't you?"

"I saw the number on our file before I left," I said, my mind whirling. "What's this all about? *You* called and reported us for cheating on our taxes?"

"Yes, I did."

I touched my temple, incredulous. *"Why?"*

"Because I wanted to see you again. I know it was a dumb long shot, but I had to try."

I gasped. "You were in Albany for over a year and you didn't call, but you do this?"

"I can't explain it," he said. "I wanted to call you a hundred times—you were so close I could feel you. But I was afraid…ashamed. I felt terrible about what I'd put you through three years ago. I wasn't about to call you before my time in the service was up, before I could offer you some semblance of a normal life."

I slumped back in my seat, limp with shock.

"Denise, I thought this audit would be a chance to see how you were doing, and if there was a chance that you still cared about me…that you ever cared about me…with no pressure." He cleared his throat. "Please forgive me. Good luck with your wedding. I hope you're happy with your new husband."

I started shaking…just my hands at first, then my leg started jumping, then my entire body was vibrating with revelation. Redford *loved* me. Had planned this entire thing to give us a second chance, with no pressure on me. Just another happenstance meeting, like before, to see if the magic was still there.

And it had been. My heart vaulted in my chest. I suddenly understood why Kenzie had been happy to change her life, why Sam had been happy to change his. Because anywhere together was better than anywhere apart. I would follow this man to Kentucky or Timbuktu. We'd already wasted three years.

"Redford, you made a big mistake."

"I know."

"You see, I'm *not* engaged anymore."

After a few seconds of silence, he said, "You're not?"

"No. I broke off the engagement last night."

"But you were still wearing your ring today."

"I didn't want you to know what I had done, to know that I'd done it because…I love you. I love you,

Redford. I've never gotten over you, never stopped hoping you would…come for me."

"Let me make sure I got this straight," he said, his voice thick. "You no longer have a fiancé?"

"No," I said, my heart leaping with joy. "But I still have the wedding band you gave me, a great dress and two tickets to Vegas."

Then I had that bottomless feeling that I'd been too bold, too presumptuous.

"I'm turning around," he said, his voice breaking.

My eyes welled with tears and I smiled into the phone. "How are we going to make this work?"

"How do you feel about Albany?"

"Albany?"

"I've been asked by the government to consult part-time at the Marine base."

"But what about your family business?"

"My father will be disappointed, but it's more important that I be close to you." He laughed. "Besides, I'd still have time to look after a couple of horses of my own…if that would be okay with you."

I blinked tears down my cheeks. "Albany sounds…close. And good."

"We'll make it work, Denise. I promise you, after finding you again, I'm never going to let you go."

I was crying for real now. And I never cried…*ever.* "I'll be waiting at my apartment. Drive safely."

"I love you."

"I love you, too." I disconnected the call, feeling light-headed. In the space of a few minutes, my life had changed. No…my life had changed three years ago when I'd first met Redford.

I had so much to do! I suddenly remembered that I needed to call Ellen Brant and reschedule. I punched in her number, so excited I could barely see.

"Ellen Brant."

"Ellen, this is Denise Cooke again. I'm sorry, but I'm going to have to reschedule our appointment this afternoon."

"Oh? Is everything okay?"

"More than okay," I said. "I'm going to Vegas to get married."

"I thought you and Barry broke up."

"We did. I'm marrying the man I was with Saturday night."

She made a little noise in her throat. "Denise, I know you're on the rebound, but don't you think you're making a big mistake?"

"Maybe," I said happily. "And it won't be my first…but it *will* be my favorite."

Epilogue

LIFE DOESN'T always turn out the way you think it's going to, but it somehow always turns out the way it's supposed to. Redford and I flew to Vegas, (I am now a member of the mile-high club…er, twice) and were joined by my parents who, after the initial shock wore off, were very happy for me. Since Redford was making an honest woman out of me, my parents seemed willing to forget about the entire "making out in public" scene and welcomed him as my husband-to-be. In fact, he and my dad actually hit it off. (Who knew my dad had worked at a horse racetrack when he was young?)

Redford's parents flew out from Kentucky and brought his dress uniform and his grandmother's diamond ring, which was flawed (and perfect). The DeMosses were delightful people who jelled with my parents amazingly well and immediately treated me like part of the family.

Cindy canceled her date with Jim from her Positive Thinking class in order to be my maid of honor—is that a friend, or what? But imagine our surprise when Redford's buddy Jim, who flew out to be his best man, turned out to be *Cindy's* Jim! They are a darling couple, I have to admit. And judging from the way Jim looks at Cindy when she enters a room, I'd say that wedding bells are in the cards.

And *my* wedding…ah, my second wedding was everything I dreamed it would be because I was marrying my first husband! We went back to the Taking Care of Business wedding chapel—it just seemed right—but were married inside this time. I was dazzling in my bargain gown, and Redford was gorgeous in his dress blues. When I looked down the aisle, and saw his face shining with love and desire for me, my heart was so full I thought it might burst. When we slid our wedding bands on each other's fingers, they were the perfect symbols of our love coming full circle.

Isn't life grand? Even the bloopers, the blunders and the slipups. Because if you never make a mistake, it means you're not living life to its fullest.

My mother once said that a wise person learns from their mistakes. I agree…but that includes knowing which mistakes are worth repeating.

* * * * *

We hope you enjoyed
My Favourite Mistake *by Stephanie Bond.*

*Now turn the page to reveal some hot tips on
how to make your own Valentine's evening one
to remember and then flip the book to read
another scorching romance.*

Are you a chocolate lover?

Try WALDORF CHOCOLATE FONDUE a true chocolate decadence

While many couples choose to dine out on Valentine's Day, one of the most romantic things you can do for your sweetheart is to prepare an elegant meal – right in the comfort of your own home.

M&B asked John Doherty, executive chef at the Waldorf-Astoria Hotel in New York City, for his recipe for seduction – the famous Waldorf Chocolate Fondue…

WALDORF CHOCOLATE FONDUE
Serves 6-8

2 cups water
1/2 cup corn syrup*
1 cup sugar
8oz dark bitter chocolate, chopped
1 pound cake*
2-3 cups assorted berries
2 cups pineapple
1/2 cup peanut brittle

*UK readers can try golden syrup and Madeira cake

Bring water, syrup and sugar to boil in a medium-size pot. Turn off the heat and add the chopped chocolate. Strain and pour into fondue pot. Cut cake and fruit into cubes and I-inch pieces. Place fondue pot in the centre of a serving plate, arrange cake, fruit and peanut brittle around pot. Serve with forks.

An Invitation for Love

Seductive Tips

Find a special way to invite your guy into your M&B moment. Letting him know you're looking for a little romance will help put his mind on the same page as yours. In fact, if you do it right, he won't be able to stop thinking about you till he sees you again!

You could send him a long-stemmed rose tied to an invitation that leaves a lot up to the imagination.

♥

Autograph a favourite photo of you and tape it on the appointed day in his day planner. Block out the hours he'll be spending with you.

♥

Send him a local map and put an X on the place you want him to meet you. Write: "I'm lost without you. Come and find me. Tonight at eight." Use magazine cutouts and photographs to paste images of romance and the two of you all over the map.

♥

Send him something personal that he'll recognise as yours to his office. Write: "If found, please return. Owner offers reward to anyone returning item by 7.30 on Saturday night."
Don't sign the card.

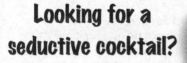

Looking for a seductive cocktail?

Try Ero-Desiac – a dazzling martini

With its warm apricot walls yet cool atmosphere, Verlaine is quickly becoming one of New York's hottest nightspots. Verlaine created a light, subtle yet seductive martini for us: the Ero-Desiac. Sake warms the heart and soul, while jasmine and passion fruit ignite the senses…

The Ero-Desiac

Combine vodka, sake, passion fruit puree and jasmine tea. Mix and shake. Strain into a martini glass, then rest pomegranate syrup on the edge of the martini glass and drizzle the syrup down the inside of the glass.

M&B on location

Whatever your dream date location, pick a setting and a time that won't be interrupted by your daily responsibilities. This is a special time together. Here are a few hopelessly romantic settings to inspire you – they might as well be ripped right out of an M&B novel!

Bad weather can be so good.

Take a walk together after a fresh snowfall or when it's just stopped raining. Pick a snowball (or a puddle) fight and see how long it takes to get each other soaked to the bone. Then enjoy drying off in front of a fire, or perhaps surrounded by lots and lots of candles, with yummy hot chocolate to warm things up.

Candlelight dinner for two…in the bedroom.

Romantic music and candles will instantly transform the place you sleep into a cosy little love nest, perfect for nibbling. Why not lay down a blanket and open a picnic basket at the foot of your bed? Or set a beautiful table with your finest dishes and glowing candles to set the mood. Either way, a little bubbly and lots of light finger foods will make this a meal to remember.

A wild and crazy week night.

Do something unpredictable…on a week night straight from work. Go to an art opening, a sports game, the local playhouse, a book signing by an author or a jazz club – anything but the usual blockbuster movie. There's something romantic about being a little wild and crazy – or at least out of the ordinary – that will bring out the flirt in both of you. And you won't be able to resist thinking about each other in anticipation of your hot date…or telling everyone the day after.

We hope you enjoyed Valentine Vendetta
by Sharon Kendrick.

*Now turn the page to reveal some hot tips
on how to make your own Valentine's evening
one to remember and then flip the book to
read another scorching romance.*

Two Sizzling Affairs

Valentine
FANTASIES

My Favourite Mistake by Stephanie Bond

When Denise Cooke married Redford DeMoss in a chapel in Vegas, she knew it was a mistake. So, despite an *incredible* honeymoon, she filed for divorce. Little did she realise that Redford would turn out to be her true Valentine…

&

Valentine Vendetta by Sharon Kendrick

Fran was out for revenge against devastatingly attractive Sam Lockhart – the man who'd broken her best friend's heart. But as Fran worked with Sam on his charity ball, Fran's new Valentine wish was to have Sam all to herself!

Read one novel then flip the book and read the other.

And don't miss our romantic, hot tips for your own Valentine's Evening!

Sharon Kendrick was born in West London, England and has had heaps of jobs, which include photography, nursing, driving an ambulance across the Australian desert and cooking her way round Europe in a converted double-decker bus! Without a doubt, writing is the best job she's ever had, and when she's not dreaming up new heroes (some of which are based on her doctor husband) she like cooking, reading, theatre, listening to American West Coast music and talking to her two children, Celia and Patrick.

Valentine FANTASIES

STEPHANIE BOND &
SHARON KENDRICK

*All the characters in this book have no existence outside the
imagination of the author, and have no relation whatsoever to anyone
bearing the same name or names. They are not even distantly inspired
by any individual known or unknown to the author, and all the
incidents are pure invention.*

*First published in Great Britain 2006
by Harlequin Mills & Boon Limited, Eton House,
18-24 Paradise Road, Richmond, Surrey TW9 1SR*

VALENTINE FANTASIES © by Harlequin Books SA 2006

My Favourite Mistake and *Valentine Vendetta* were first published
by Harlequin Mills & Boon Limited in separate, single volumes.

My Favourite Mistake © Stephanie Bond 2005
Valentine Vendetta © Sharon Kendrick 1999

ISBN 0 263 84981 3

109-0206

*Printed and bound in Spain
by Litografía Rosés S.A., Barcelona*

VALENTINE
VENDETTA

SHARON
KENDRICK

To the only other literary agent as gorgeous as
Sam Lockhart, the inestimable and inspirational
Giles Gordon.

CHAPTER ONE

'FRAN—I'm at my wit's end! She seems to be having some kind of mid-life crisis!'

'But she's only twenty-six,' said Fran.

'Exactly!'

The memory of that phone call still burned in Fran's ears. A dramatic phone call, from a woman not given to dramatization.

'Just go and see her, would you, Fran?' Rosie's mother had pleaded. 'Something has happened to upset her and I can't get any sense out of her. But I suppose you girls don't tell your mothers anything.'

'So you've no idea what's wrong?' Fran had probed, thinking that it was rather flattering to be called a girl at the ripe old age of twenty-six!

'I think it has to do with some man—'

'Oh,' said Fran drily. 'The usual story.'

'And that life isn't worth living any more.'

'She said *what*?' That had been the statement which had brought Fran up short and had her booking the next London-bound flight out of Dublin. Not that she believed for a minute that Rosie would do anything *stupid*—but she was normally such a happy-go-lucky person. For her mother to be this worried, things must be bad.

Now she could see for herself that they were worse than bad.

She had found Rosie curled up like a baby on the sofa of one very cold flat. And the conversation had gone round and round in a loop, consisting of Rosie saying,

'Oh, Fran. Fran! *Fran!*' Followed by a renewed bout of shuddering tears.

'Ssssh, now. It's all right.' Fran squeezed her friend's shoulder tightly as the tears came thick and fast. 'Why don't you take a deep breath, calm down and tell me what's wrong.'

Rosie made a sound like a cat who was trying to swallow a mouse in one. 'C-c-can't!' she shuddered.

'Off the top of my head, I'd say it's a man?' said Fran, thinking that it might be wise not to mention the worried phone call. Not just yet.

Rosie nodded.

'So tell me about him.'

'He's….he's…*oh!*'

'He's what?' prompted Fran softly.

'He's a bastard—and I still love him!'

Fran nodded. So. As she had thought. The usual story. She'd heard women pour the same sorry tale out countless times before and the more cruel the man, the more they seemed to love him. She wondered if some women were so lacking in self-esteem that they chose someone who would walk all over them. But she wouldn't have put *Rosie* in that category. 'Oh, I see.'

'No, you don't, Fran!' Rosie shook her head in frustration. 'You say you do but you don't! How could anyone see? You just sit there with that seen-it-all-before look on your face—'

'I've never seen *you* like this before,' Fran disagreed immediately. 'And I've known you most of your life! And before you insult me much more, Rosie Nichols— I might just remind you that I've flown over at top speed from Dublin, in answer to an urgent request from your mother that I find out exactly what's wrong with you.'

'My mother asked you to come?'

'She wasn't interfering, if that's what you're thinking. She was just worried, and wanted me to see how you were.'

Rosie looked at her defiantly. 'So now you know.'

Fran shook her head. 'Oh, no,' she corrected grimly. 'I haven't even started yet! All I know is that I walk into your flat which looks as though a major war has broken out—to find you sitting in a pathetic heap looking gaunt and tear-stained—sobbing bitterly about some mystery man whose name you can't bring yourself to utter—'

'Sam,' sniffed Rosie. 'His name is Sam.'

'Sam!' echoed Fran with a ghost of a smile. 'That's Sam whose paternity you questioned just a minute ago, is it? And does this Sam have a surname?'

'It's Lockhart.' Rosie looked at her expectantly. 'Sam Lockhart.'

'Sam Lockhart.' Fran considered this. 'Cute name. Catchy.'

'You haven't heard of him?'

'No. Should I have done?'

'Maybe not. But he's rich and gorgeous and those kind of attributes tend to get you known—especially among women.'

'Tell me more.'

Rosie shrugged her shoulders morosely. 'He's a literary agent. The best. They say if Sam takes you on, you're almost certain to end up living in tax-exile! He's got an instinctive nose for a best seller!'

Fran tried not to look too disapproving. 'And I suppose he's married?'

'*Married?* You're kidding!' Rosie shook her head so that wild curls spilled untidily around her face. 'What do you take me for?'

Fran breathed a sigh of relief. 'Well, he's not *completely* bad, then,' she said. 'Married men who play away from home are the worst. And *I* should know!' She flicked Rosie another look. 'Has he ever been married?'

Rosie shook her head. 'No, he's single. Still single,' she added, and stared down at her chewed fingernails as tears began to splash uninhibitedly onto her hands.

Fran gave Rosie's shoulder another squeeze. 'Want to tell me all about it?'

'I guess,' said Rosie listlessly.

'How long since you've eaten?'

Rosie shrugged. 'I had coffee for breakfast—but there's nothing much in the flat.'

Resisting the urge to remark that judging by the general air of neglect any food would probably carry a health warning, Fran shook her head. 'Don't be silly,' she said gently. 'I'm taking you out for dinner.'

Rosie momentarily brightened until she caught sight of herself in the mirror. 'But I can't go out looking like this!'

'Too right—you can't,' agreed Fran calmly. 'So go and do something to your hair, slap on some warpaint and for goodness sake, *lose* those hideous baggy trousers!'

An hour later, they were installed in a booth at 'Jacko's!'—a restaurant/bar which had just opened up on the water's edge at one of London's less fashionable riverside locations. It had the indefinable buzz of success about it. Fran smiled up at the waitress whose skirt barely covered her underwear and ordered two alien-sounding cocktails from the menu.

She stared across the table at Rosie whom she had known since they were both fat-faced three-year-olds

toddling into school on their first day at Nursery, where
Rosie had demonstrated her ability for attracting trouble
by losing her teddy bear down the side of a bookcase.
And Fran had slipped her small hand in and retrieved it.

It had set a pattern for their school years. Rosie got
herself into a scrape and Fran got her out of it! Since
Fran had moved to Dublin five years ago, their paths
rarely crossed, but after a few minutes back in her old
friend's company, Fran felt as if they'd never been apart.

Well, maybe not quite.

Rosie seemed terribly distracted, jumpy even—but
maybe in the circumstances that was understandable. Her
face looked harder, too. But Fran told herself that people
changed—she had changed herself. She had had to. That
was all part of life's rich tapestry. Or so they said....

'Now tell me,' she said firmly. 'Just who Sam
Lockhart *is*—and why you've fallen in love with him.'

'Oh, everyone falls in love with him!' Rosie gave a
gloomy shrug. 'You can't help yourself.'

'Then it's a pity *I* can't meet him,' observed Fran.
'Since that sounds like the sort of challenge it would
give me great pleasure to resist!'

'I'd like to see you try!'

Fran liberated a smooth strand of hair which had
somehow become all twisted up in the string of pearls
she wore and fixed her friend with a stern expression.
'In my earlier life as an agony aunt on a well-known
Dublin radio station,' she said, 'I soon learnt that the
easiest way to forget a man is to start thinking of him
as a mere mortal and not as a god. Debunk the myth,
that's what I say!'

Rosie screwed her nose up. 'Come again?'

'Stop making everything about him seem so wonderful and extraordinary—'

'But it is!'

Fran shook her head. 'That's the wrong way to look at it. Try concentrating on all the *bad* things about him instead!'

'Like what?'

'Well, I don't know the man, so I can't really help you with that. But instead of describing him as, say, utterly unobtainable, tell yourself that he's arrogant and distant and nobody in their right mind would want to live with him! Right?'

'Er, right,' said Rosie doubtfully.

Fran winced as a silver beaker of what looked and smelt like cough medicine was placed in front of her. She took a tentative sip through the straw and nearly shot off the edge of her seat before a dreamy kind of lethargy began to melt her bones. Still, some light an-aesthetic might be just what Rosie needed.

'Drink up,' she instructed and leaned forward eagerly as she began to slide the drink across the table towards Rosie. 'And tell me what happened. Like—where did you meet him?'

Rosie took a quick slug of the cocktail. 'Remember when I did that stint as a secretary for Gordon-Browne—that big firm of literary agents? Well, Sam was their star player and we got kind of, you know…involved.'

Fran nodded, thinking how unusually coy Rosie sounded. 'So how long did it last?'

'Er, not as long as I would have liked.'

'And when did it end?'

'Oh, ages ago now,' gulped Rosie vaguely. 'Months and months. Longer, even. Over two years,' she admitted at last.

'Two *years*?' Fran blinked. 'But surely you should be getting over it by now?'

'Why?' Rosie sniffed. 'How long did it take you to get over the breakup of your marriage to Sholto?'

'Oh, no.' Fran shook her head. 'We're here to talk about you, not me. Surely you haven't been like this since it ended?'

Rosie shook her head. 'No, of course I haven't—but my life has never been the same since Sam. He brought me bad luck. I haven't been able to settle into another job *or* another relationship. And now I've heard....' Her voice tailed off into silence.

Fran hoped to high heaven that this man Sam hadn't done something like announcing his engagement to someone else. That would be hard. Though maybe a brutal demonstration of his love for someone else might be just the cure that Rosie actually needed. 'Heard what?' she asked.

'He's planning to throw a ball. Which is *totally* out of character!'

Which immediately told Fran that he must be rich. And well connected. 'And?'

'It's a Valentine's Day Ball. And I want to be invited,' said Rosie fiercely.

'Well, you might be. Don't you think?'

'No, I don't. But I would, wouldn't I—if *you* were organizing it! You'd make sure of that!' Rosie's eyes took on a hopeful gleam.

Fran shook her head as she saw which way the conversation was heading. 'Oh, no!'

'Fran, it's your job! That's what you do for a living, you plan people's parties for them.'

'Yes, you're right, I do. But it's also my livelihood, Rosie, and I have my reputation to think of. Huge, high-profile society balls aren't really my thing. And I don't just go around using these events to settle grudges for

friends—however much I love them. Staging some kind of Valentine vendetta! Which I presume is what you want me to do. Or is it just an invitation you're after? You want to dress to kill and then knock his socks off, is that it?'

'Maybe.'

Fran gave a wistful smile. 'It won't work, you know. It never does. If this man Sam has fallen out of love with you—then nothing you can say or do will bring him back. Nothing,' she emphasised flatly. 'That's life, I'm afraid.'

Rosie bit down on her lip. 'But he never *was* in love with me.'

'Oh. Oh, I see.' Fran's eyes softened. 'Well, in that case I'm very sorry, hon,' she said gently. 'What can I say?'

Rosie took a mouthful of Fran's discarded cocktail, then looked up, her eyes two fierce burning stars in her face. 'I was just another virgin for Sam to seduce,' she said dully. 'To pick up and discard once he'd had what he wanted!'

Something primitive cracked like an old bone inside Fran's head. She remembered their schoolgirl dreams about men and rice and white dresses and knew she should not be shocked at what Rosie had just told her— certainly not in this day and age, and yet she *was* shocked. Deeply. 'He took your virginity?' she said slowly. 'Did he *know*?'

'Yes, of course he knew.' Rosie gave a cynical laugh. 'I saved it, Fran. I saved my virginity for the man I loved.'

But he didn't love you back, Fran thought, flexing her hands on the table, unconsciously mirroring the move- ment of a fat, ginger cat who lay sprawled across one

corner of the bar. 'And in spite of not loving you—he took the most precious thing you had to offer?'

'That's right,' sniffed Rosie. 'And I wasn't the only one!'

'You mean there were *others*?'

'Hundreds!'

'Hundreds?'

'Well, tens anyway. Loads!' Rosie spat the word out. 'Women who adored him. Women he didn't give tuppence for! Women who were all too easy to trick into his bed!'

'You're kidding!'

'I wish I was!'

Fran stared down at the silver gleam of the high-tech table, and thought of rich Sam Lockhart luring decent, hard-working girls like Rosie into his bed. A powerful man abusing that power to seduce innocent young women.

When she eventually lifted her golden-brown head to meet her friend's eyes, her own were deadly serious. She remembered the scrapes that Rosie had managed to land herself in at school, scrapes that Fran had somehow always got her out of. But this was different. Was it her place to help, even if she could?

'What do you want me to do?' she asked at last.

Rosie didn't even have to think about it. 'Nothing too major,' she shrugged. 'I'm not asking you to break any laws for me, Fran.'

'What then?'

'Just pay him back.'

CHAPTER TWO

FRAN'S fingers hovered uncertainly over the push-button telephone and she smiled at the irony of her situation. She was actually shaking. *Shaking.* She who was frightened of no man or no thing, was trembling like a schoolgirl at the thought of ringing Sam Lockhart.

Five minutes earlier she had already tapped the numbers out before hanging up immediately in a panic. Then thought how absolutely stupid *that* was! What if he had one of those sophisticated telephones which told him exactly who had called? He was probably used to lovesick women dialling the number and then changing their minds and hanging up. Did she want to arouse his suspicions by doing the same?

She punched the numbers out again, and listened to the ringing tone, certain that some minion would answer his mobile phone for him.

'Hel-lo?' The deep, velvety voice ringing down the line was as unexpected as it was irresistible. It *had* to be him—minions didn't sound like sex gods—and Fran had to frown with concentration to keep her voice steady.

'Sam Lockhart?' she said.

'Speaking.'

She drew a deep breath. 'Mr. Lockhart, you don't know me—'

'Not unless you decide to tell me your name, I don't,' he agreed softly.

Mistake number one. Ring someone up to try and

drum up their business, and then manage to sound as unprofessional as possible! 'It's Fran,' she said quickly. 'Fran Fisher.'

She could practically hear his mind flipping through its backlog of female names and coming up with a definite blank. But he was either too polite or too cautious to say so. Maybe he thought she was another in the long line of willing virgins offering herself up for pleasurable sacrifice!

'Are you a writer?' he asked in the wary and weary tone of someone who got more than their fair share of calls from would-be authors.

'No, I'm not.'

A sigh of relief. 'Thank God for that!' A note of caution returned to the deep voice. 'So what exactly can I do for you, Fran Fisher?'

'Actually, it's more a case of what I can do for you, Mr. Lockhart.'

'Oh?'

In that one word Fran heard resignation—as if he was gearing himself up to withstand a crude attempt at flirtation. Which, according to Rosie—was an occupational hazard when you happened to be Sam Lockhart.

And which meant there was nothing to be gained by playing for time. That would irritate a man like this, not intrigue him. She tried her most businesslike approach. 'Mr. Lockhart, I understand you're planning to hold a ball on Valentine's Day—'

'Are you a journalist?' he snapped.

'No, I'm not!'

'Who are you, then?'

'I told you—'

'I don't need you to tell me your name again! I've never met you before, have I?'

Well, it had taken him long enough to decide *that* and he still didn't sound one hundred per cent certain! She wondered how he would react if she adopted a sultry accent and purred, 'Are you sure?' 'No,' she said stiffly 'You've never met me.'

'Yet you know the number of my mobile?'

She was tempted to mention that he was stating the obvious, but resisted. 'Yes.'

'How?'

'Er, your agency gave me the number.'

'Well, they shouldn't have!' he snapped. 'Certainly not to a complete stranger!' There was silence down the line for a moment. 'You've never met me and you're not a writer,' he mused. 'So what exactly *is* your angle Fran Fisher?'

If it hadn't been for Rosie she probably would have hung up on him there and then. How absolutely ridiculous he sounded! Quizzing her as though she were some sort of second-rate spy and he the valuable prize within her sights! 'My "angle",' she said sweetly, 'is that I'm a professional party-planner—'

'But unsuccessful?' he suggested drawlingly.

'On the contrary!' she defended. 'I'm extremely successful!'

'So successful, in fact,' he continued, 'that you need to spend your time making cold calls to strangers in order to drum up a little business? I thought that your line of work relied solely on word-of-mouth recommendation?'

'Yes, of course it does! *Normally…*' She pulled a hideous face as she imagined him standing in the room with her. She *wanted* to dislike him, for Rosie's sake—and the way he was speaking to her meant that she didn't have to try very hard. But her dilemma lay in disliking

him *too* much. Because if that happened, it would undoubtedly show in her attitude towards him, and then he certainly wouldn't give her the job! 'But I have to help things on their way. I've been working in Ireland, you see—'

He sounded weary. Like a man used to being bombarded with ambition. 'And now you want to break into the market over here?'

'Er...yes,' she stumbled, caught off guard. No need to tell him that this was going to be a one-off! 'Yes, I do. Actually, I'm quite well-known in Dublin. Ask anyone. And I've organised lots of fund-raisers—'

'Have you really?' he questioned, clearly not believing a word she said.

Fran bristled. 'I expect that if I mentioned some of my clients, their names would be instantly recognizable—even to you, Mr. Lockhart,' she told him stiffly.

'For example?' he shot back.

'I did some corporate work for the Irish Film Festival a couple of years ago, and on the back of that I got quite a few private functions. Cormack Casey, the screenwriter—he recommended me—'

'Cormack?' he interrupted, in surprise. 'You know him?'

'Well, not *intimately*,' she said, then wished she hadn't because it was obvious from the faint and disapproving intake of breath that he had misinterpreted her words. 'I organised the catering for the baptism of his first child.'

'Did you indeed?' asked Sam, in surprise. He'd been invited to that very same baptism, but a book tour in the States by one of his best-selling authors had put paid to that. 'And if I rang Cormack—he'd vouch for you, would he?'

'I certainly hope so. Triss—that's his wife—'

'I know who Triss is. I've known Cormack for years.'

'Oh. Well, she told me they'd be happy to help with references.' Fran suspected that the handsome Irish writer and his model wife had felt sorry for her. At the time she had been thinking about filing for a divorce from Sholto, and the baptism had been the only joyous thing in her life. She had poured her heart and soul into making the party match the moving ceremony of baptism, and she had been inundated with work ever since....

'Did she?' Sam Lockhart sounded impressed.

Fran cleared her throat, sensing that this was just the right time to appeal to his greed. 'The thing is, Mr. Lockhart—if you hire me to organise your ball for you, then I guarantee we will raise more money than you ever dreamed of.'

'That's fighting talk,' Sam commented drily, then added, 'Who told you about it, by the way?'

'You mean the ball?'

'No, Man landing on the moon!' he drawled sarcastically. 'Yes, of course I mean the ball!'

This might have been tricky if she hadn't anticipated the question. But Rosie had said that he was vain enough and realistic enough to know that everyone in his circle and beyond, would be clamouring for an invitation.

'Oh, no one in particular,' she said vaguely. 'You know what it's like. People talk. Particularly before an event has been organised—it gives them a certain cachet if they know about a highly desirable party before it's officially been advertised.' She drew a deep breath and added shamelessly, 'And believe me, Mr. Lockhart—from what I understand—this is going to be the hottest ticket in town.'

'I hope so,' he said thoughtfully. 'Well, I already have someone in mind for the job, I'm afraid. Several women have already offered—'

She could imagine! 'Amateurs?' asked Fran sharply. 'Or professionals?'

'Well, all of them have organised similar functions before—'

'You know exactly where you are with a professional,' put in Fran smoothly.

'Really?' He sounded unconvinced.

It was time for a little feminine desperation. To see whether a breathy, heartfelt plea would get through to the man Rosie had described as a 'virile robot.' 'Won't you at least *see* me, Mr. Lockhart?' she questioned.

'I'm a busy man.'

'Well, of course you are!' She used the soothing tone of a children's nanny, then added a little flattery for good measure. 'Successful men always are. But could you forgive yourself if your hectic schedule meant that your ball didn't fulfill all your expectations, simply because you wouldn't make time to see me?'

He actually laughed at this—a bubbling, honeyed chuckle—and it was such a warm and sexy sound that Fran found herself gripping the receiver as though it might fly out of her fingers.

'Determination is a quality I admire almost as much as self-belief,' he mused. 'Provided it is backed up by talent—'

'Oh, it is!'

There was a pause. 'Very well, Miss Fisher—I'll give you exactly ten minutes to convince me that I'd be a fool not to employ you.'

Thank God! 'You won't regret it, Mr. Lockhart,' she enthused, hoping that her voice carried no trace of in-

sincerity. 'Tell me where and tell me when and I'll be there!'

'Okay. How about this afternoon?'

'You mean *today*?'

'Well, I certainly don't mean tomorrow,' he purred. 'I'm flying to Europe with one of my authors later on this evening. I can see you at home—briefly—before I leave.'

He managed to make it sound as though he was making an appointment for her at the dentist—and come to think of it, her adrenalin levels were as high as they might have been if he *were* a dentist! 'In London?' she guessed hopefully, since Rosie had already informed her that he had a flat in town and a house somewhere in the country.

'No, in Cambridge,' he stated.

'Cambridge,' she repeated faintly, her heart sinking as she thought of travelling to the flat, ploughed fields of the fens on a filthy cold November afternoon. Maybe on a fool's mission.

'Is getting to Cambridge going to be a problem for you, Miss Fisher?' he questioned. 'It's hardly on the other side of the world, you know!'

Rule number one: a party-planner must be prepared for any eventuality! 'Problem? None whatsoever!' she lied cheerfully. 'Just give me a few easy-to-understand directions and I'll be there in time for tea!'

'I can hardly wait,' he said, and Fran could have sworn that he was *laughing* at her.

The light was already fading from the sky when the train pulled into Eversford station and the bleak, unwelcoming platform made Fran feel as though she was on the film-set of an old-fashioned murder mystery.

She knotted her scarf tightly around her neck and looked around. Sam Lockhart had told her where she could get a cab and she walked out of the station into the dreary afternoon, where a fine mist of grey rain clogged the air and slicked onto the roofs of the cars like grease.

There was no one else in the queue and the driver looked at her with interest as she told him the name of the house.

'Sam Lockhart's place,' he commented, as he switched on his meter and pulled out of the station forecourt.

'You know it?'

'Should do. He brings us plenty of work. Thought that's where you'd be headed,' he said, smiling.

Fran, who was hunting around in her handbag for a mirror, paused, mid-search. 'Oh?' She smiled back. 'Can you guess where all your passengers are headed, then?'

'No. Just his.' The driver stopped at some red lights and grinned at her in his rear mirror. 'If it's someone glamorous getting off the London train, then the odds are that she wants to go out to Sam Lockhart's place!'

Fran bristled as the driver's giveaway remark reminded her why she was here in the first place. Poor Rosie! 'Oh?' She thought how indignant she sounded! 'He has a whole stream of women arriving here, does he?'

The driver shook his head hastily. 'Oh, no! Never more than one at a time!' he joked. 'And we only notice because nothing much happens around here. It's a pretty isolated place.'

'So I see.' Fran looked out of the window as the buildings and lights of the town began to get more sparse and the landscape began to acquire the vast, untouched emp-

tiness of perfectly flat countryside. It could have been boring, but she thought that it had a stark, distinctive beauty all of its own. Even so, its very bleakness did not fit in with her idea of where a sex god would live. Why had he chosen to settle out here, she wondered, when he could be raving it up in London? 'Is it very far?'

'Another couple of miles,' he answered, slowing the car right down as the lane narrowed. 'Writer, are you?'

'Not me, I'm afraid!' she told him cheerfully, and picked up her hand mirror to see what sort of face Sam Lockhart would be greeted by.

Unexciting was the word which immediately sprang to mind.

Her skin looked too pale, but then it always did—and the green-gold eyes could have done with a little more mascara to make the best of them. But apart from the fact that she had left in a hurry, Fran had deliberately played safe, unwilling to look as though she'd spent hours in front of the mirror in an effort to impress Sam Lockhart. Apart from the fact that it just wasn't her style—sex gods were used to women slapping on the entire contents of their make-up bags. She knew that from living with her husband. So she would be different. Because there was one other thing she knew about that particular breed of man…they were easily bored and something different always intrigued them.

So she had contented herself with a slick of nude lipstick which simply looked like she had been licking her lips. Just enough make-up to look as though she wasn't wearing any at all—but only a woman would be able to tell that!

'Here we are!' said the driver. The car slowed down and began indicating right as a high, dark hedge began to loom up beside them. Before her stretched a long

drive which curved off unexpectedly to the left, and impulse made her lean over to tap the driver on the shoulder.

'Would you mind stopping here?' she asked.

'It's a long drive.'

'I can see that. I don't mind walking. In fact I'd rather walk. I just want to get the...*feel*...of the place first.' That first gut reaction to someone's home was invaluable. Houses and owners taken unawares told you volumes about what they were *really* like—and the better you knew a client, the better you would be able to judge the perfect party for their particular needs. A car drawing up outside would alert Sam Lockhart to her arrival and that would not do. She wanted to see the face of the seducer taken off guard.

Ignoring the driver's curious expression, she paid her fare and gave him a healthy tip.

'Thanks very much, Miss. Will you be wanting to go back to the station...tonight?' He put the question so delicately that Fran might have laughed if she weren't feeling so indignant on Rosie's behalf. What was Lockhart running here, for goodness' sake? A harem?

'Yes, I will,' she answered crisply. 'But I don't know what time that will be—so if you'd give me one of your cards I'll ring.'

She waited until the red tail-lights of the car had retreated before setting off up the wide path, her sensible brown leather boots sending little shoals of gravel spraying in her wake.

The grounds—they were much too extensive to be called a garden—wore the muddy, leafless brown of a winter coat, but the sparse flower-beds were curved and beautifully shaped, and the trees had been imaginatively planted to stand dramatically against the huge, bare sky.

The house was old. A beautifully proportioned white-washed villa which was perfect in its simplicity.

And it looked deserted.

Moving quietly, Fran crept forward to peer into one of the leaded windows at the front of the house, and nearly died with shock when she saw a man sitting in there, before the golden flicker of a log fire. A dark, denim-clad figure sprawled in a comfortable-looking armchair, his long legs stretched in front of him as he read from what looked like a manuscript.

She came to within nose-pressing distance of the window and her movement must have caught his attention, for he looked up from his reading and his dark-featured face registered no emotion whatsoever at seeing her standing there. Not surprise or fright or irritation. Not even a mild curiosity.

Then he pointed a rather dismissive finger in the direction of the front of the house and mimed, 'the door's open.'

And started reading again!

How very *rude*, she thought! Especially when she'd travelled all this way to see him! Fran crunched her way over to the front door, pushed it open and stepped inside, narrowing her eyes with surprise as she looked around.

It wasn't what she had expected.

On the wooden floor lay mud-covered wellington boots, a gardening catalogue, a pair of secateurs and a battered old panama hat. Waterproof coats and jackets were heaped on the coat stand and a variety of different coloured umbrellas stood in an untidy stack behind the front door. The walls were deep and scarlet and womb-like and welcoming.

So where were the wall-to-wall mirrors and the

shaggy fur rugs where he made lots of love to lots of different women?

It felt like coming home, she thought, with an unwelcome jolt. And it *shouldn't*, she told herself fiercely. This was the house of the man who was responsible for Rosie's heartache—not the house of her dreams!

She turned and walked along a narrow corridor which led to the study and stood framed in the doorway with the light behind her.

He looked up, all unshaven and ruffled, as if he'd just got out of bed. Or hadn't been to bed. 'Hi,' he said, and yawned. 'You must be Fran Fisher.'

His eyes were the most incredible shade of deep blue, she noticed—night-dark and piercing and remarkable enough to eclipse even the rugged symmetry of his face. With the jeans went untidy, slightly too-long hair, making him more rock-star than literary agent.

Yes, Fran thought, her heart pounding like a mad thing. No wonder Rosie had fallen so badly. He looked *exactly* like a sex god! 'And you must be Sam Lockhart,' she gulped.

He shot a brief glance at his wristwatch and she found herself thinking that she had never seen a man so at ease in his own skin as this one.

'Yeah,' he drawled. 'That's me!'

'Nice of you to come to the door and meet me!'

'If you can't manage to navigate your way from the front door to the study, then I think you're in the wrong job, honey.' He yawned again. 'Come in and sit down.'

Fran gazed around the room. 'Where?'

Sam conceded that she did have a point. Just about every available surface was given over to manuscripts of varying thicknesses. Some had even overflowed from his desk to form small paper towers on the Persian rug.

'Don't you ever clear up after you?' she asked, before she had time to think about whether or not it was a wise question.

'If you tidy manuscripts away, you lose them,' he shrugged, as he rescued the telephone from underneath a shoal of papers. 'At least if they're staring you in the face you can't hide away from the fact that you need to get around to reading them sometime!'

The blue eyes glanced rather absently around the study. 'Though maybe it *is* a little cluttered in here. The sitting room is just along there.' He pointed towards a low door at the far end of the room. 'Why don't you trot along and wait for me in there. Make yourself comfortable. I'm expecting a call any minute, but I shan't be long.'

'Please don't rush on my account,' she gritted, irritated at being told to trot along—as if she was some kind of pit-pony!

This drew a sardonic smile. 'Don't worry, I won't.'

The first thing Fran decided when she walked into Sam Lockhart's sitting room, was that there was no woman living in the house with him—or if there was, then she must be a very passive and insipid woman because the place had masculinity stamped indelibly all over it. Deep, bold colours and substantial furniture.

Fran was used to being in strangers' houses; it was part of her job. She knew how much a home environment could tell you about a person, and over the years she had become an expert at reading the signs of domestic bliss.

Or turmoil.

The room had all the untidy informality of truly bachelor territory. For a start he seemed to be incapable of throwing away a single newspaper—since she could see

Sunday supplements dating back from the previous month, and beyond. And there were enough books heaped on a low table and on the floor surrounding it for him to consider opening his own personal library! She crouched briefly to scan some of the titles and was alarmed to see that they shared some of the same taste in authors. Disturbing.

She rose to her feet and carried on looking. There were no photos scattered anywhere, but that didn't really surprise her. Women were the ones who put photos in a room—reminders of great family occasions like engagements and weddings and christenings. Which were also a mark of possession and ownership—marks that men seemed to need less than woman.

She picked up a beautifully worked tapestry cushion which was lying on the chair, and was so busy examining it that she didn't hear him come into the room. It was only when she turned around to find herself being studied intently by a pair of dark-blue eyes that Fran realised he was standing watching her.

Still holding onto the cushion, she blinked. As well as taking the phone call, he must have washed his face and swiftly shaved the blue-black blur of shadow away from the square chin. And run a comb through the dark tangle of his hair. He had put a dark sweater on too, and the soft navy cashmere clung to the definition of broad shoulders.

Suddenly, his blue eyes looked even bluer, so that their soft brilliance seemed to cut right through you, like a sword. Oh, my goodness, she thought weakly, he really *is* gorgeous. Fran clutched the cushion against her chest, like a breastplate, and saw him frown.

'Planning to take that home with you?' he queried softly.

Fran stared down at the cushion in her hands. On one side the single word Sam was embroidered, in a heart-shaped frame made of tiny scarlet flowers. On the other side was an intricately crafted message which said, A love given can never be taken away.

'This is beautiful,' she said politely, wondering who the maker of the cushion was. Someone who obviously adored him. 'Absolutely beautiful.'

So why did his face close up so that it looked all shuttered and cold?

'Yes,' he said repressively. 'It is.'

Part of her job was asking questions; making connections. If she saw something she liked she tried to find out where it came from, because you never knew when you might want one just like it. 'Do you mind me asking where you got it from?'

His eyes narrowed and Fran was surprised by the sudden appearance of pain which briefly hardened their appearance from blue to bruise. So he could be hurt, could he?

'Yes, I do mind! I told you that I had a plane to catch,' he said coldly. 'Yet you seem to want to spend what little time we have discussing soft furnishings.'

Feeling slightly fazed at the criticism, Fran quickly put the cushion back down on the sofa and looked at him expectantly. 'Sorry about that,' she said lightly. 'Force of habit.'

He didn't even acknowledge the apology. 'Why don't we just get down to business.'

Standing there, with her sheepskin coat making her feel distinctly overdressed, Fran felt hot and out-of-place and very slightly foolish. He could have done with a crash course in common courtesy, she thought. 'Mind if I take my coat off first?'

'Feel free.'

She noticed that he didn't attempt to help her remove the heavy, fur-lined garment and was irritated with herself for even caring. He was a future client—hopefully—not somebody she would be taking home to meet her mother!

She draped the coat over the arm of a chair and stood in front of him, feeling slightly awkward, and not in the least bit confident. So now what did she do? She found herself wondering what was going on behind those dark eyes of his. And what he saw when he looked at her in that curiously intent way of his.

Her clothes were practical and comfortable, in that order—it went with the job. Very short skirts which meant you couldn't bend over without inhibition were out. So were spindly and unsafe heels designed to make legs look longer. But although Fran was a little curvier than she would have ideally liked, she was also tall enough to carry off most clothes with style. Today, her brown woollen skirt skimmed her leather-booted ankles and the warm, cream sweater cleverly concealed the thermal vest which lay beneath.

She glanced at him to see if there was any kind of reaction to her appearance, but Sam Lockhart's expression remained as enigmatic as the Mona Lisa. Now why did that bother her? Because the arch-philanderer didn't think she warranted a second look? For heaven's sake, woman, she told herself—you're here to avenge some broken hearts—not join their ranks!

'So are you going to sit down?' he murmured. 'I'd prefer to stretch my legs before my flight, but there's no reason why the interview should be uncomfortable for you, is there?'

'Er, no, I'll stay standing,' she stumbled. 'W-what interview?'

'The interview which helps me decide whether to give you the job or not.' A mocking look. 'What else did you think this was going to be? A tea party? I have to decide whether I want you to work for me and you have to decide whether or not you could bear to.' Another mocking look. 'Or did you think the job would be yours the moment I stared into those great big golden-green eyes of yours?'

Fran blinked with astonishment. So, beneath that cool exterior he *had* been noticing the way she looked! 'No, of course I didn't!' she retorted, feeling slightly reassured that he had started to flirt with her. It kind of reinforced what Rosie had told her to expect. 'I'm a professional through and through and I'd *never* use sex appeal to sell myself!'

'Not consciously, perhaps?' he challenged softly. 'But most women use their sex quite ruthlessly—in my experience.'

'And that's extensive, is it?' she challenged in return.

'That depends on your definition of extensive,' came the silky reply. 'But I would advise against making assumptions like that about a man you've only just met.'

There was nothing to be gained by irritating him, and clearly she *was* irritating him. Very much. 'Sorry,' she backtracked hastily.

'So can I see your portfolio?' he asked.

'My…portfolio?'

'You do *have* a portfolio showing me examples of your work?'

'Of course I do,' she said. She just hadn't been planning on using it… 'But unfortunately I had to leave it with a client in Ireland. Anyway, word-of-mouth is the

best recommendation—and the only way you can assess my work is to speak to some of the people who've hired me in the past.'

'I already did.'

She shouldn't have been surprised. But she was. 'Who?'

'Cormack Casey. His was the only name you gave me. Fortunately he's the kind of man I trust.'

Fran blinked. On the phone he had said that he knew Cormack, but the warmth in his voice suggested a deeper relationship than mere acquaintanceship. 'You mean you're friends?'

'Yes, we are. What's the matter?' He raised his eyebrows. 'You sound surprised?'

Well, she was. Because Cormack, for all his good looks and sex appeal, was fiercely loyal to his wife, Triss. A one-woman man. A man with morals. So how come he was matey with the arch-heartbreaker Sam Lockhart?

'What did Cormack tell you about me?'

'That you were good.' There was a pause. 'Very good.'

'Now *you* sound surprised!' she observed.

He shrugged. 'People who are good don't usually have to go out looking for business. Not in your line of work. Cormack was a little taken aback when I told him you'd rung me. In fact, he found it difficult to believe.'

Fran felt the first prickle of apprehension. 'D-did he?'

'Mmmm. He said it was completely out of character. Said you were cool and sought-after and he couldn't imagine *you* ever *touting for trade*.' He emphasised the words with a brief, black-hearted smile.

It was an offensive way to put it and Fran prayed that she wouldn't start blushing. And not to be disconcerted

by the intense question in those blue eyes. Maybe no
looking at him was the only way to guarantee that.

'So why start now?' he mused.

'Well, I've been working in Ireland,' she defended
swallowing down her anxiety. 'No one knows me here
in England—and I needed to do something. Something
big to get me established over here.'

'And working for me will do that?'

She met his gaze reluctantly, feeling the erratic pumping of her heart in response. Did he have this effect on
anyone with two X chromosomes in their body, she
wondered? 'You know it will,' she answered bluntly.

There was a brief hooding of his eyes as he nodded
as if acknowledging her honesty. If only he knew, Fran
thought, with the slightest shimmer of guilt. Until she
remembered Rosie's tear-stained face. And her damning
list of just how many hearts he had broken along the
way. Sam Lockhart deserved everything he was about to
get! That is, if she got the job....

'So my Valentine ball will put you firmly on the
map?' he observed.

Fran nodded.

'That's what I can do for you,' he mused, and his
voice was a soft caress which whispered temptingly at
her senses. 'Which leaves me wondering what I'll get
from you in return?'

It was blatant. Flagrant. Outrageous. Fran's hand hovered above and then clutched onto her pearl necklace,
her fingers sliding over the slippery surface of the
lustrous jewels. Rosie had said he was rampant—but she
had been expecting a little more finesse than *that*.
'*W-what* exactly did you have in mind?' she demanded
hoarsely.

He frowned, and his gaze seemed to scorch her skin

as he searched her face. He seemed to be keeping a straight face with some difficulty as he observed her reaction. 'This is purely a business transaction, Miss Fisher,' he reminded her wryly. 'Not a sexual one.'

Fran's face went scarlet. 'I wasn't suggesting for a moment—'

'Oh, yes, you were,' he contradicted softly. 'It was written all over your face. And your body.' His voice lowered. 'I'm flattered.'

'Well, don't be!' she snapped. 'Maybe I *did* jump to the wrong conclusion, but women have to be on their guard against innuendo. Against men coming on strong.'

'Yes, I can imagine that you must keep coming up against that kind of thing,' he commented innocently.

Fran looked at him suspiciously. Was he making fun of her? 'Perhaps we should talk about the ball now,' she said primly.

He gave a wolfish smile, aware that he was finding this verbal skirmish *extremely stimulating* indeed. 'But that's exactly what I've been trying to do for the last five minutes. You *do* dither, don't you, Miss Fisher?'

'Not normally, no—it must be the effect you're having on me!' Fran took a deep breath as she forced herself to ignore his sarcasm and to inject her voice with enthusiasm. 'Anyway, Valentine's Day is such a *fantastic* date for any kind of party!' she began breezily. 'It gives us so much *scope* for decorations!'

'Such as?'

'Oh, you know.... Hearts! Flowers! Love! Romance!'

'Aren't you forgetting originality?' he put in, his face deadpan.

Now he *was* making fun of her. Fran frowned, forgetting Rosie, forgetting everything except doing what she was good at. And she was very good at pitching for

a job....'Mr. Lockhart—' She gave him a patient look. 'Valentine's Day is just like Christmas—'

'It is?'

'It certainly is. As a traditional celebration—people expect certain customs to be adhered to.'

'They do?'

'Of course they do!' she enthused, really warming to her subject now. 'Its rituals comfort and reassure—because people don't always want to be surprised, you know. They want the predictable—'

'How very boring,' he murmured.

Fran cleared her throat. That sizzling little glance of his was annoyingly distracting. 'Wrong!' she smiled. 'I can assure you that while what I am suggesting may not exactly be ground-breaking stuff—'

'Mmmm?'

'It most certainly will not be *boring*! You will have the very best food and wines and the most wonderful music—all served up in a setting which will quite simply take your breath away!'

His eyes rested on her thoughtfully for a moment or two, before shooting another glance at his watch. 'Right. Well, thank you very much for your time, Miss Fisher.'

Fran stared at him in astonishment. Surely that wasn't *it*? Yes, he'd said ten minutes, but he'd barely let her talk for more than thirty seconds! She glanced at her own watch. No. A man of his word. It had been ten minutes exactly. 'You mean, that's it?'

'I'm afraid so. You see, it really *is* time that I was leaving for the airport. I can drop you off at the station on the way if you like.'

The words were as dismissive as the way he said them. So that was that. No job. No pay-back. She'd let Rosie down, but even worse, she'd let herself down, by

stupidly jumping to the conclusion that he had been coming on to her. That was why he wasn't going to give her the job. Acting naive and gauche round a man like this, as though she was still wet around the ears. Instead of a woman who had single-handedly built up a thriving business for herself out of the ruins of her failed marriage.

'No, I'll take a cab.'

'Sure? It'll be quicker by car.' The lazy smile grew wider. 'Or don't you trust yourself to be alone in the car with me?'

Huh! She might be leaving without the job. She might have travelled halfway across the country on one of the filthiest days of the year. But there was no need for her to leave with him thinking that she was some kind of emotional *hysteric*. She had underestimated Sam Lockhart and her rather dizzy reaction to him, and for that she had paid the price. It was time to withdraw in a cool and dignified manner.

'Don't be absurd, Mr. Lockhart,' she said, forcing a cool smile. 'I'd love a lift. Just as long as it isn't out of your way?'

'No, not at all. Come on.'

He paused only to pick up a compact-looking brief-case in the hall and to engage in a complex locking-system for the front door. 'The car's out in the garage at the back,' he said.

His long legs covered the ground at twice the pace she was used to, but she managed to keep up with him on their way to the stable-block which had been converted to house a clutch of cars. But Sam Lockhart was obviously not a man who collected wealthy toys—for there was only one vehicle sitting there. Fran had expected something predictable—the rich man's phallic

substitute of a long, low car in screaming scarlet or devilish black.

Instead she saw a mud-splattered four-wheel drive
which had golf clubs and a tennis racket companionably
jumbled around a tartan picnic rug in the back, along
with a muddle of magazines and discarded sweet wrap-
pers. An empty water bottle lay next to a pair of battered
old running shoes. A large brown envelope marked
Sam—*Urgent!* lay on the passenger seat.

This was the car of an action-packed life, whose
owner had neither the time nor the inclination to vacuum
the carpet, thought Fran. It did *not* look like the car of
a playboy, she thought with mild confusion.

He saw her expression of surprise. 'Excuse the state
of the car.'

'No, I like it,' she said, without thinking. 'Honestly.
It's homely.'

He smiled. 'Mmmm. Messy might be more accurate,'
he murmured. He moved the envelope, threw his suitcase
in the back and waited until Fran had strapped herself
in before starting the engine.

His driving surprised her, too. That did not fit with
the rich-man stereotype, either. No roar of accelerator or
screech of brakes. His driving was safe, not showy—just
like the car. Bizarrely, Fran even felt herself relaxing,
until she reminded herself just who was next to her, and
sat bolt upright to stare fixedly out of the window.

But he didn't seem to notice her frozen posture, just
switched on the radio and listened to the news channel.
He didn't speak during the entire journey to the station
and neither did Fran. She couldn't think of a thing to
say. Well, she could. But something simpered on the
lines of, 'I hope you didn't get the wrong idea about me
earlier' would damn her even further in his eyes, and

she wasn't prepared to do that. Not even for Rosie. But more especially for herself. Because for some unfathomable reason, she would rather have made a fool of herself in front of anyone than in front of Sam Lockhart.

She was desperate for the journey to end, yet her heart sank with disappointment as the car bumped across the station forecourt. I won't ever see him again, she thought, wondering why it should matter.

'Thanks for the lift.' She owed him the brief glance, the polite smile, but was totally unprepared for the watchfulness in his blue eyes.

'I don't have your card,' he said.

'My card?' she repeated stupidly.

'Your business card.'

She scarcely dared hope why he wanted it, just fumbled around in her handbag until she found one. 'Here.'

He glanced at it. 'This is a Dublin code.'

'Well, there's my mobile number,' she pointed. 'You can always reach me on that.'

'When are you going back to Ireland?'

'I'm…not sure.' She hadn't decided, because her decision was based on whether he gave her the job or not. Somehow she doubted it—but she certainly wouldn't find out by trying to read his mind. She tried not to sound either too nervous or too tentative. 'Am I still in the running for the job, then?'

'No.' There was a pause as the word dropped like a guillotine, severing all her hopes. Poor Rosie, she thought fleetingly, until she realised that he was speaking again, but so quietly that she had to strain her ears to hear.

'The job is yours.'

'Pardon?'

'The job is yours,' he repeated, eyes gleaming as he

enjoyed her startled reaction. 'That is, if you still want it?'

'Er, yes. I still want it,' she answered, wondering why victory—and such unexpected victory—should taste so hollow. But she had to know. 'But why? I mean, why are you offering it to me?'

He frowned. 'I wouldn't have thought that it was particularly good psychology to sound so incredulous if someone offers you the job.' His eyes narrowed critically. 'It might even make *some* people reconsider.'

'Well, I certainly didn't give the best interview of my life,' she told him candidly.

'No, you didn't,' he agreed. 'But Cormack said you were the best—'

She gave a slow flush of pleasure. 'Did he?'

'Yeah, he did. And he's the kind of man whose opinion people listen to—me included.'

'And that's why you're offering me the job—because of Cormack's say-so?'

'Partly. But also because you're a fresh face on the scene, and fresh faces bring enthusiasm. I've never hosted a ball before, and I want it to work.' His blue eyes gleamed with a hard determination. 'Really work.'

Suddenly all her old fervour was back. The ball *would* be a success. She would make sure of that. Rosie's payback was merely an offshoot—an insignificant little offshoot. A lesson he needed to learn which would probably benefit him in the end! And who knew, maybe one day he might even be grateful to her! 'Oh, it'll work, all right—I can guarantee you that, Mr. Lockhart,' she breathed.

'Sam,' he corrected.

'Sam,' Fran repeated obediently. It felt so right to say

his name. Too right. Like having one long lean leg mere inches away from hers felt right, too.

Not since Sholto had she been so tuned in to a man's presence. Only this seemed all wrong. This wasn't just a knockout individual with searing blue eyes and a body which had been constructed in the dream-factory. This was the man who had robbed her best friend of her innocence.

So why did she find herself wanting to curl up like a kitten in his lap, instead of lashing out at him with her claws?

'I'll be out of the country all week,' he told her. 'I'll ring you when I get back and we'll arrange a meet in London to discuss details and budget, that kind of thing. Okay with you?'

'Sure,' she nodded, and was just reaching over to unlock the car door when he suddenly leaned over and caught hold of her left hand and turned it over to study it closely.

'No marks, I see,' he observed, tracing her bare ring finger with the pad of his thumb.

All she could feel was the rough warmth of his skin and the shock of the unexpected contact made every sane thought trickle out of her mind. 'I b-beg your pardon?'

'Marks. From your wedding ring.'

'Who told you I was married? Cormack?'

The blaze from his eyes was like a searchlight. 'Yeah. Who else? You don't wear the fact tattooed on your forehead, that's for sure!'

Fran shifted awkwardly on her seat. 'Well, that's past tense. I'm divorced now.'

'So I understand. There's a lot of it around,' he drawled. 'But even so...' He let his thumb trickle slowly around the base of her finger in a gesture which to Fran

seemed both highly suggestive and highly erotic and she shivered despite the warmth of the car. 'Wedding rings always leave their mark—one way or the other.'

This was getting too close for comfort. Fran tore her hand away from his and pushed open the car door, her breath coming hot and thick in her throat. 'I'll see you when you get back from Europe,' she croaked.

CHAPTER THREE

FRAN rang the doorbell and moments later a blurry-eyed Rosie peered out from behind the safety chain.

'Wassa time?' she mumbled.

Fran frowned and stared at her friend in horror and amazement. 'Five o'clock. Rosie, have you been drinking?'

Rosie swallowed back a hiccup and then beamed. 'I jus'…jus' ha' a small one. I was nervous, see. Knowing that you were meeting Sam.' Her eyes focussed at last. 'Did you? Meet him?'

'I did.'

'And?'

Fran shivered. It had been a long and boring journey back on the train which had stopped at about a hundred stations between Eversford and London. She was cold and she was tired and frankly, not at all sure that she was doing the right thing in trying to teach Rosie's ex-lover a lesson. From her brief meeting with him, he had not seemed the ideal candidate to have the wool pulled over his eyes. She was going to have to be very careful.…

'Rosie, do we have to *have* this conversation on the doorstep?'

'Oh! Sorry! Come in!' Rosie unhooked the chain and Fran followed her into the flat which seemed to have had nothing done to it in the way of housework since she had been there the day before yesterday. She wrinkled her nose. How *stale* it smelt.

Rosie turned to her eagerly. 'So! Did you get the job?'

Again, Fran felt the oddest shiver of apprehension. 'Yes, I did.'

'Oh, joy of joys!' gurgled Rosie. 'Well done! Let's go and have a drink to celebrate!'

'Haven't you had enough?'

Rosie looked at her sharply. 'Maybe I have,' she shrugged. 'But that doesn't stop you, does it?'

'No, I'm fine. I had tea on the train. I just want to take the weight off my feet.'

Fran waited until they were both settled in the sitting room where dirty cups and glasses littered the coffee table, before she said anything.

'The place could do with a bit of a clean-up, you know, Rosie.'

Rosie pulled a face. 'Bet you didn't say that to Sam! He's nearly as untidy as me! God, I used to despair of the way he dropped his shirts on the bedroom floor!'

It was a statement which told how intimate they had been, and Fran clenched her teeth as she tried to block out the image of Sam Lockhart peeling the clothes from that impressive body of his. Surely she wasn't *jealous*? Not of Rosie? But maybe it was that which made her plump for a home truth rather than sparing Rosie's feelings any longer. 'He may be untidy,' she agreed sternly. 'But at least his house is clean.'

Rosie, who was in the process of rubbing her finger at a sticky brown ring left by a sherry glass, looked up abruptly. 'Are you saying my flat is dirty?'

'I'm saying it could do with an airing,' said Fran diplomatically. 'And a bit of a blitz.'

Rosie nodded with the distracted air of someone who wasn't really listening. 'Tell me what Sam said first. Tell me what you thought of him.'

Fran chose her next words even more carefully. 'He's certainly very good-looking. I can see why you fell for him.'

Rosie squinted. 'C'mon, Fran. You can do better than that. What did you *really* think of him?'

Tricky. 'Well, he wasn't what I was expecting,' she said slowly.

'Mmmm? What were you expecting then?'

Fran wriggled her shoulders as she tried to put it into words. 'The way you described him, I thought he'd be kind of...*obvious*. You know. Mr. Smarm. But he wasn't. He was...' Now she really couldn't go on. Being honest was one thing, but not if it had the effect of wounding the very person you were supposed to be helping. And if Fran told Rosie the truth—that she had been more attracted to him than any man since Sholto—then wouldn't that make *her* look foolish? And an appalling judge of character?

'Sexy?' enquired Rosie.

Fran winced. It would not have been her first word of choice. 'I suppose so.'

'That's because he is. Very. Fran, I didn't have any real experience of men before I met Sam—but believe me when I tell you that he is just *dynamite* in bed—'

'Rosie! I don't want to know!'

'Why not?'

'Because other people's sex lives should remain private, that's why!' Except that she wasn't being completely truthful. It was more that she couldn't *bear* to think of Sam Lockhart being intimate with anyone—and the reasons for that were confusing the hell out of her. 'Change the subject, Rosie!' she growled. 'Or I'll wash my hands of the whole idea!'

'Okay, okay—keep your hair on!' Rosie slanted her a

glance from beneath the heavy fringe which flopped into her eyes. 'So what's happening about the ball?'

'He's ringing me when he gets back from Europe. That's when we'll discuss all the details. You know, the budget, the venue—' she yawned. 'That kind of thing.'

'And the guest list?'

'That's right. Most of the planning I can organise by phone from Dublin, but I'm going to need a temporary base in London.'

'Stay here with me!' said Rosie impulsively.

Fran shook her head. She suspected that a few years down the line, sharing a flat might test their friendship to breaking point. 'How can I, Rosie?' she asked gently. '*You* live here. And Sam knows you live here, doesn't he? I know it's unlikely, but imagine if he saw me coming out of your flat. It would rather give the game away, wouldn't it? No, I'll ring my mother up—she's got loads of rich friends and relatives. One of them might just be planning a winter holiday in the sun. I could do with a few weeks off—and I'm the world's best house-sitter!'

She studied the finger that Sam had so softly circled, and swallowed. 'You know, maybe this is the opportunity I need to make the break and get out of Ireland—'

'I thought you loved it!'

'I do. Just that Dublin is such a small city—'

'And you keep running into Sholto and his new girl-friend, I suppose?'

Fran forced a smile. 'Something like that.' She stood up decisively. 'Got any bleach?'

'*Bleach?*' Rosie blinked. 'You aren't planning to go blond, are you?' she asked in horror.

Fran's smile widened of its own accord. 'Not *that* kind

of bleach, stupid! I meant the kind that cleans floors!'

'Oh, *that*!' said Rosie gloomily, and went off to find some.

By the time Sam Lockhart rang her a week later, Fran had established a London base she could use whenever she needed. One of her mother's many cousins was visiting her daughter in Australia for the winter, leaving a high-ceilinged flat vacant in Hampstead village—in a road which was apparently a burglar's paradise.

'She'd be delighted to have you keeping your eye on the place,' Fran's mother had said. 'But I'd like to see you myself, darling. When are you coming up to Scotland?'

Fran prodded a neglected-looking plant which was badly in need of a gallon or two of water, and frowned. 'I promise I'll be there for Christmas.'

'What—not until then?'

'Mum, it's only weeks away.' Fran kept her voice patient.

'Is Rosie any better?'

'A bit. Still misses this man Sam Lockhart.'

'Didn't that all finish ages ago?'

'Uh-huh. I guess some broken hearts just take longer to heal than others.' But Fran deliberately omitted to mention the fact that Sam was one of her new clients. The information would be bound to set her mother thinking, and for some strange reason Fran was convinced that she would try to talk her out of getting involved in some kind of vendetta.

There was a long and loaded pause followed by a question which was studiedly casual. 'So how's Sholto?'

The pause from Fran's end was equally loaded. 'How should I know, Mum? I don't have anything to do with

Sholto anymore. Why would I, when we're divorced now? Apparently, he's got a new girlfriend—'

'Well, *that* doesn't surprise me—'

'Er, yes. Listen, Mum, I have to go now.' And Fran abruptly ended the conversation.

It was funny. When people heard that you were divorcing, or divorced, they always asked whether you had any children. And when Fran said that no, they didn't, the response was always the same. 'Oh, *that's* all right, then.' As though a marriage didn't matter if there weren't any offspring involved.

But it *did* matter. Divorce left a stubborn stain behind which you could never quite shift. And it affected people's attitudes towards you. Fran could read it in her mother's disappointed voice. She had read it the other day in Sam's rather disdainful reaction. What had he said? 'There's a lot of it around.' As though it was some kind of nasty infectious disease! And he was right. The world was full of divorced people, and however amicable the agreement, it marked you out like a leper....

Fran's mobile phone shrilled into life early one morning, exactly a week after Sam Lockhart had dropped her off at the train station.

The deep voice was instantly recognizable—it was just that Fran, emerging from a restless night's sleep, was not at her sharpest. She had spent the previous evening at the cinema with Rosie, who had insisted they leave halfway through the film, because apparently the leading actor in it had reminded her of Sam. Fran hadn't been able to see it herself. True, he had Sam's startling blue eyes, but not their intensity, and the face had been much softer....

So the two of them had gone to eat an indulgent supper instead, which had ended up with Rosie drinking far

too much and sobbing into her bread and butter pudding that her life was a vacuum, and it was all Sam's fault. Listening to a different version of the same story Fran felt as though she was on a fast train to nowhere....

Fran opened bleary eyes and picked up the phone. 'Hel-lo?' she yawned sleepily.

'It's Sam Lockhart.'

She sat bolt upright in bed. 'Oh, my goodness!'

'Sam Lockhart,' he repeated impatiently.

'Yes, I know it is! I heard you the first time.'

'Then you should try improving your telephone technique,' he said caustically. 'I'm back in England for a few days. Can you meet for lunch?'

'When?'

'Well, I was thinking of today,' he responded.

'Nice of you to give me so much notice.' Again!

'So you're busy today, are you?'

'Actually, no, as it happens—I'm not.'

'Are you trying to make a point?' he drawled.

Fran bit back the sarcastic comment which was looming temptingly on the tip of her tongue. No need to make him more grouchy than he already sounded. She made her voice saccharin-sweet instead. 'No point at all! Where shall we meet?'

'How about Green's? Do you know where that is?'

'Of course I do!'

'Good. I'll see you in there at one,' he said, and rang off.

Green's restaurant was situated in the middle of the Strand and famous for being famous, with branches in Paris, New York and Milan. It also prided itself on being impossible to get a reservation unless you were 'somebody' and Fran wondered if that was why Sam Lockhart had chosen it. To rub in just how important he was.

By the time she walked into the restaurant at just after one, it was nearly full and Sam was seated at a table towards the back of the room, which commanded a fine view of everything, but was well enough away from the general hubbub to provide privacy. Good table, she noted automatically.

He had been studying the menu but looked up almost as though he had sensed her approaching, his blue eyes briefly flicking over her, as though he was scanning a menu. And Fran felt a distinct disappointment. Because yes, if she was being truthful she *had* dressed to impress—and surely the way she looked deserved a bit more than that dismissive glance?

The mirrors lining the walls threw back her reflection. A caramel dress in softest cashmere, which clung to her curves and brought out the honey-gold in her hair. And high suede boots in glowing cinnamon, which had cost her more than a week's salary! Her hair was pinned into a casual chignon which had actually required a good deal of attention. She knew she looked polished and professional, but obviously not in the least bit sexy—not judging from that noncommittal response. But then, looking sexy was the last thing she was aiming for.

Wasn't it?

'Hello, Fran,' he said slowly, wondering if she *ever* looked unruffled.

'Hello, Sam.'

'Please sit down.'

'Thanks.' She slid down onto the chair opposite him, wondering if the deep blue of his suit had been chosen specifically to emphasise the dazzling colour of his eyes.

'Let's order straight away, shall we?' he suggested, with a swift smile. 'Then we can get down to business without interruption.'

'Okay with me.' She found herself nodding like an obedient dog, trying to look interested in the menu, when food was the last thing on her mind. She had never felt less like eating, and she wondered why. Guilt, perhaps? That she was here on false pretences? That she should find deceit so deliciously easy?

'What will you have?'

'Er, chef's salad followed by er, chicken, please.' She smiled rather weakly up at the waiter.

'Not hungry?'

'Not particularly.'

His mouth curved as he glanced at the lush lines of her body. 'And yet you look like a woman who enjoys her food,' he observed.

'Not when I'm working,' she lied. Normally she had no problem polishing off the most carbohydrate-filled concoction on the menu! But there was something unsettling about that bright gaze. She wasn't sure that her hands were completely steady, and the last thing she wanted was to send pasta flying all over her lap! Or to bite into a roast potato and have grease splatter all over her chin!

Once the waiter had taken their orders and poured water and gone away, Fran found herself growing restless under that keen stare.

'Everything okay?' he asked, wondering if she was *always* this jumpy.

'Oh, yes! Everything's fine!' She pointed to the briefcase by her feet. 'Um—I've had some of my presscuttings faxed over from Dublin—which I thought you might like to see.'

His brow creased into a faint frown. 'Why?'

'Well, last week you mentioned that I had nothing to show you—'

'I doubt that I would have put it *quite* as inelegantly as that,' he objected, raising his eyebrows by a fraction, so that the crease in his brow deepened to a furrow.

Fran flushed. 'You know what I mean.'

'Yes, I know what you mean, but it's a little late in the day for references, surely? Especially since I've already given you the job.' His eyes glimmered. 'And am unlikely to change my mind about *that*. Unless you start committing unforgivable acts. Like wasting my time,' he finished deliberately. 'Again.'

Fran maintained a pleasant smile with the ease born of years of dealing with difficult clients and she could see that Sam was going to take first prize for being difficult. 'My time is as precious as yours, Mr. Lockhart—'

'I told you to call me *Sam*!' he grumbled.

'Okay. Then let's get on with discussing your needs, shall we, *Sam*?'

Sam was relieved that the waiter chose precisely that moment to deposit two plates of salad in front of them. Why, he wondered, did everything she say come out sounding like a sexy invitation? Especially when she definitely *wasn't* flirting. In fact, he'd go so far as to say that she was deliberately trying to avoid the instant physical attraction which had mushroomed between them at their first meeting.

Maybe that was why. He was so used to women coming on to him that it was novel, if somewhat confusing, when a member of the opposite sex kept sending out signals he simply couldn't recognise.... One minute she was hot, hot, *hot*. The next she was running scared.

He sat back in his chair and smiled. 'Okay. What exactly do you need to know?'

For one bizarre moment, she felt like asking him whether he had ever really been in love? Or whether

women were just sport to him. Like some men hunted foxes, did he hunt women before moving in for the kill and then moving on?

Fran fished a notebook and pencil from her shoulder bag. 'Right. How many guests?'

'About a hundred and fifty. Strictly by invitation only.'

'Well, that goes without saying.'

'And definitely no gatecrashers,' he growled.

This bald statement gave Fran the first glimmering of an idea. 'Oh? Are you expecting any?'

'Maybe. You know what it's like. Think you can cope with them?' He seemed to relax and actually grinned at this point, and suddenly Fran understood exactly why Rosie didn't seem able to get him out of her system. Even after two years. He wasn't just gorgeous, she thought despairingly—he was absolutely *irresistible*!

'Yes, of course I can. Trust me.' Oh, heck! Her tongue had very nearly tripped over those lying words. Guiltily, she sipped at the water in front of her. 'Any ideas about the venue?'

'At my house in Cambridge,' he said immediately. 'I was thinking of a marquee in the garden.' He fixed her with a quizzical look. 'Though I guess it might be too cold to party in a tent in February?'

Fran shook her head. 'Not at all. They can make marquees as warm and as comfortable as palaces these days.'

'Can they now?' he teased.

'Um, yes.' Fran rapidly sipped some more water, wishing that he wouldn't look at her like that. Her cheeks felt so *hot*. 'But London would be a much better place to hold it, especially if you have people flying in from other countries to attend.'

Sam's mouth flattened. 'No way. If people can afford the air fare to travel to a ball, then they can afford the connection from London to Cambridge! And a hotel for the night.'

Fran flapped her notebook in front of her face, wishing that she had worn something cooler than the woollen dress. Did all women get hot and bothered around him?

'You're looking a little flustered,' he told her softly.

'I'm hot!'

'Yes,' he murmured as he allowed his gaze to drift over her flushed cheeks. 'So I see.'

His smile was so devastating that Fran felt quite faint. She drew an unnecessary question mark in the margin of her notebook and kept her voice efficient. 'We haven't discussed the proceeds,' she said.

'So let's discuss them now.'

'Er, have you decided whether you're going to donate the profits to charity?'

'As opposed to donating them to my Swiss bank account, you mean?' he asked drily. 'Actually, yes—I have. Every penny will go to the cardiology ward of the local Children's hospital.'

'Very admirable,' she said carefully. 'And, of course, paediatrics is always a very popular choice of charity.'

He narrowed his eyes. 'Why do I get the distinct impression that you're shocked?'

No, not shocked. Surprised. Because surely the type of man who ruthlessly treated women as sex objects wouldn't really be bothered about the plight of sick children? 'Why would I be shocked?'

'You think I've chosen a worthy cause just so it reflects well on me?'

'Now you're sounding paranoid!' she said nervously.

'I'm pretty good at picking up signals. And I'm get-

ing a heavy sense of disapproval being directed across he table towards me at the moment.' He gave a bland, questioning smile as he poured himself a glass of wine. 'I just haven't worked out why.'

'Rubbish!' said Fran, as fervently as her conscience would allow her.

'Is it?' His eyes glittered. 'Anyway,' he put the glass back down on the table, 'I want as many doctors and nurses there as possible.'

Fran glanced down at the green leaves of rocolla which glistened unappetizingly on the plate in front of her. When she looked up again it was to still see those perceptive eyes fixed frowningly on her.

'Something wrong?' he enquired.

Fran shrugged, uncomfortable with her own thoughts. 'Well, doctors and nurses in England don't earn very much—'

'Don't I know it,' he agreed grimly.

Fran felt even more perplexed. The arch-heartbreaker was not supposed to feel sympathy for poorly paid employees of the service industry! Unless he was one of those men who was able to successfully compartmentalise his life. Just because he had an uncontrollable libido didn't mean that he couldn't have a soft heart, did it! Fran drew another question mark. 'But that means we'll have to keep ticket prices artificially low if they're to be able to afford it, doesn't it?'

He shook his dark head. 'On the contrary. Hospital staff will get subsidised tickets. Only the rich will pay more!'

'Gosh,' breathed Fran as the waiter took her salad plate away and replaced it with a perfectly poached chicken breast. 'You're a real little Robin Hood, aren't you?'

He raised his eyebrows. 'Now you *do* sound shocked!'

'Not many people care about financial inequality as much as you seem to!'

Sam frowned, his mind buzzing with all the mixed messages he seemed to be getting from her. He found himself wondering if she was always this prickly. And the prickliness intrigued him....

'Well, a variety of incomes guarantees a more lively mix, doesn't it?' he reasoned. 'And if you get the rich together—they seem to do nothing but compare incomes and complain about the service!'

Fran laughed nervously. Okay, so it appeared that he had something resembling a social conscience, too. Any minute now he would sprout a halo! 'How about colours for the marquee? Any preferences?'

'Nope.'

'Any specific food requests?'

'Nope.' He shrugged the broad shoulders and gave her a lazy, glimmering smile. 'That's what I'm paying you for, honey.'

'And my b-budget?' she questioned, her heart slamming against her ribcage.

He mentioned a sum and sizzled her a questioning look. 'How does that sound?'

Astute man. Fran nodded. 'You've pitched it just right. Unlimited budgets inevitably mean waste—and a limited budget always shows.' She looked at him curiously. 'What made you decide to throw this ball in the first place?'

'You mean I don't seem the type?'

'No, you don't.' People who threw balls tended *not* to be bookish recluses. And even Rosie had said it was completely out of character.

He shrugged. 'I met one of the local heart surgeons

at a party, and he told me that they could do so much more if they had more funds.'

'And so you decided to raise some? Just like that?'

'Just like that,' he echoed softly.

'Oh,' she said quietly.

'Oh!' he teased, and picked up a chip with his fingers. 'So that's the ball out of the way. Now what shall we talk about?'

She sawed mechanically at a piece of chicken. 'Pass.'

Sam leaned back in his chair and studied her, wondering what her hair would look like loose and falling all over her shoulders. 'You know, you're nothing like I imagined you would be,' he said slowly.

The feeling was mutual. 'And what were you expecting?'

'I thought that a party-planner would be outrageously glamorous—'

'Thanks very much!'

'The kind of person who looked like she partied non-stop herself.'

'And I don't?'

He shook his head. 'No, you don't.' She looked remote. Untouchable. The last type of woman you could imagine captured in the throes of passion on a very large bed. And consequently, the very person you wanted on that bed.... 'You look like you go to bed all clean, in a starched nightdress, with your teeth all brushed and minty,' he said huskily.

His voice stilled her, while his expression dealt a velvet blow to her heart. Something glowing crept inside her, touching a part of her she had thought Sholto had killed off forever. Oh, Lord—why hadn't Rosie warned her that she would be in danger of falling for him herself? Actually, when she thought about it—Rosie *had*

warned her. She had just thought she would be immune to it.

Sitting in this gorgeous restaurant it was all too easy to be beguiled by that lazy charm. To forget that he had used it ruthlessly and manipulatively. 'Is that supposed to be a compliment?'

'If you like. Is it true?'

Fran gave a ghost of a laugh. 'I have absolutely no intention of telling you what I wear to bed!'

Her unwillingness to open up intrigued him, too. Most women told you their life story at the drop of a hat. 'Did you really use to work for a radio station?'

'Who told you that?'

'Cormack.' He smiled, as though he found it terribly amusing. 'He said you'd been an agony aunt for a while.'

'I'm afraid he's right,' she answered, wondering just *when* they had had this discussion about her. And why.

'Unusual kind of job.' He narrowed his eyes. 'How did you get into that?'

'In a very roundabout way. I was living in London at the time and working in a big department store.'

'Boring job?'

'Very. I used to play netball with the girls every Thursday night, and afterwards we all used to go to the pub for a drink. One night we met a load of guys who were over on holiday from Ireland. One of them started telling me all his problems—'

'Was that your ex-husband?' he asked suddenly.

Fran nodded. Clever of him. 'Yes. He was working part-time at the radio station in Dublin.'

'So let me guess—you gave him all the right answers and sorted his whole life out for him and he fell in love with you?'

Fran shook her head. 'Not quite. That's what you *don't* do. You direct, not dictate. People are supposed to choose their own solution to a problem.'

'And did he choose the right one?'

Fran remembered back. 'Yes, I guess he did,' she said slowly. Sholto had been unable to decide whether to follow his father into the family banking business, or to follow his heart and become a full-time disc jockey instead. She had asked him which was more important to him—his parents' approval, or his own sense of worth. Afterwards he had told her that in that one moment he had known that he wanted to marry her. And that had frightened her—to think that love could strike so randomly, so indiscriminately and so unsuitably...

'It's a nice story,' he said unexpectedly.

His crinkly-eyed comment threw her, made her feel even more of a fraud than she already felt. 'It had a nice beginning,' she told him quietly. 'It was just the ending which came unstuck.'

'Yes,' he said thoughtfully.

'When did you speak to Cormack?'

'After you came to see me.' No point lying about it, or being coy. She had aroused his interest, and he couldn't for the life of him work out why.

'What else did he tell you about me?'

He placed his hand on his heart, oath-style. 'I cannot betray a confidence, ma'am!'

She ran her fingertip over the rim of her wineglass, realizing that she knew very little about *him*—other than what Rosie had told her—and most of that had been about Rosie herself. 'How about you?' she asked coolly. 'Do you have any significant other in your life?'

'Why, will it cramp your style?' he teased.

She treated the remark with the scorn it deserved, by ignoring it. 'Have you?'

'Not at the moment.'

'But there must have been someone?'

His look was faintly incredulous. 'Of course there has—I'm thirty-two years of age, Fran! Surely you didn't imagine that I'd never had a serious relationship before? Do I look like some kind of loser?'

No, he didn't. Fran pushed her barely touched chicken away from her, something niggling at her consciousness. He had a way of answering questions which didn't add up with her image of him as serial seducer. 'I'm sure you've had loads of women,' she said lightly.

Sam frowned. 'No, not loads. Loads makes me sound indiscriminate—and I'm just the opposite.' His eyes glinted mockingly in her direction. '*Very* discriminate.'

'I'm sure you are,' she said politely.

Aware of the frosty vibes icing their way towards him, Sam wondered why he was getting the feeling that she was holding something back. 'So what do I need to do between now and the ball?'

She was aware of the sudden edge to his voice, and wondered if she was coming over as judgmental. She beamed him a megawatt smile. 'Just sign the cheques, Sam,' she replied, making every effort to sound her normal enthusiastic self and not a person in serious doubt of her own judgement. 'And turn up in your best bib and tucker on Valentine's Day!'

CHAPTER FOUR

FRAN stepped back to inspect the marquee and sighed with a kind of guilty pleasure. It looked magnificent—there was no other word to describe it.

The place was a riot of crimson and satin—red-swathed tables decked with hearts and flowers. Crimson roses adorned every available surface and romantic garlands of dark-green ivy seductively snaked their way up the pillars.

Was it too much, she wondered, narrowing her eyes and trying to view the decor with impartiality. No. It was perfect. The sumptuous interior did her justice. And she was glad that she had followed her instincts and opted for the traditional. After all, not providing red hearts and references to love on Valentine's Day would be a little like inviting guests for Christmas lunch and offering no tree or turkey! People would feel cheated!

There were three hours to go until the first guests were due to arrive, and so far—Fran superstitiously touched the wood of a chair back—everything was going according to schedule.

A delicious menu was in the process of being prepared by four chefs in the service tent adjoining the marquee. Hordes of waitresses were sorting out place-names, polishing wine-glasses and putting the final finishing touches to the tables. Soon the band would arrive. Almost every invitation had been accepted with the kind of disbelieving gratitude which might have been ex-

pected of a royal summons. And there were a few surprises in store....

Fran swallowed down her irrational fears. She had persuaded Rosie that less was more. That there was no need to overdose on the revenge bit. And that Mr. Sam Lockhart needed nothing more than a gentle rebuke to make him rethink the way he treated his women. A wry reminder of just how many notches he had managed to accumulate on his belt. That was all....

She nervously smoothed her hands down the bodice of the scarlet ball gown she had hired for the evening, then wished she hadn't. Her hands were all clammy and sweaty and it was more than just the usual pre-party nerves. To be honest, she would be glad when the evening was over. It had been hanging over her for weeks now with all the allure of an execution.

Still, Rosie had been pacified with her plan.

The DJ would play the record which Sam seduced all his women by. And one by one, some of those women would appear from the shadows and ask him to dance. Simple, effective and not *too* inflammatory. She hoped.

More importantly, Rosie had promised Fran that after tonight, whatever the outcome, she would get on with her life. Start living in the present instead of a bitter past or a wistful future. And cut down on the drinking.

'Hello, Fran,' said a soft, deep voice behind her, and as she whirled round to see Sam standing there, she gave a start of pleasure. They hadn't met since last month, for what was supposed to be a brief get-together. But he had taken her for an old-fashioned afternoon tea in an equally old-fashioned London hotel, and it had somehow gone on much longer than she had planned.

It had been the perfect antidote to the January blues—with scones and cream and outrageously fattening cakes

and Fran had savoured the afternoon and his company with a guilty pleasure.

And they spoke on the phone most weeks. He had an easy and familiar way of talking to her which made her feel that they were old friends from way-back, rather than new and temporary colleagues. Dangerous.

'Sam!' She looked up into his eyes and found that she couldn't disguise her delight in seeing him. Now why this overwhelming feeling of pleased recognition towards a man she was supposed to dislike, and had met on precisely three occasions?

And why was he wearing *jeans*, for heaven's sake? And not just any old jeans, either—these ones looked like denim-coloured skin—the way they clung to those magnificent thighs and buttocks. Fran Fisher! she thought despairingly. What on earth are you *thinking* of?

'Why aren't you dressed, Sam?' she demanded.

A smile played at the corners of his mouth. He was surprisingly pleased to see her. But then she hadn't done what he had expected she would do. Plagued him with phone call after phone call. Invented all kinds of spurious reasons why she needed to meet with him. After a lifetime of women pursuing him, it was rather a relief to find one who didn't. For the first time in longer than he cared to remember *he* had been the one making the phone calls!

He stared down at the faded denim and the crumpled blue linen shirt he wore. 'It's true I look a little rumpled,' he admitted, with another lazy smile. 'But I'm not indecent, am I, honey?'

Fran blanched at the sexy undertone to his voice. Good! she thought. Make some more outrageous remarks like that! Remind me why I'm here. Reinforce that manipulative sex-appeal of yours so I don't get af-

fected by that occasional glimpse of little boy lost in those big blue eyes of yours. 'I meant,' she said stiffly, 'you aren't dressed for dinner. And time is getting on!' She gave a repressive glare at her watch.

'Rubbish! We've got hours to go yet.'

'Three, to be precise. And there's still lots to do.'

'Well, while we're on the subject of clothes,' his eyes skimmed over the scarlet gown, pupils darkening into jet— 'aren't you a little…um…overdressed for last-minute checking?'

Maybe she was, but she had good reason to be. Sam had offered her the use of his house to get changed, and she had deliberately chosen to change early. Because the last thing she had wanted was to risk running into him outside the bathroom.…

The red dress she had hired was in richest velvet with a tight, boned bodice. From the waist, the material flared out over a stiffened petticoat, falling in great swathes of intense, glowing colour which brushed the ground as she walked.

Only her shoulders were bare—with lots of gold-flecked flesh on show. And she had been persuaded by the hire-shop to wear a strapless bra which pushed her breasts together, giving her an impressive cleavage which spilled over the top of her gown like overfilled ice-cream cornets.

It wasn't a colour or a style she would normally have come within six feet of, but the woman in the hire-shop had told her that it was perfect. 'You don't like it?' she asked him uncertainly.

He gave a small, disappointed laugh, thinking that women had a very devious way of inviting compliments. 'That wasn't what I said at all and you're smart enough to know it. If you're really interested—you look exactly

like the heroine of an old-fashioned bodice-ripper. Or at least, you would if you let your hair down.' He gave her a questioning look and resisted the urge to run his tongue over his lips. 'Are you going to?'

'Since I have no desire to look like the front cover of a lurid book—no, I'm not!'

'Pity,' he said softly. There was a pause. The pulse in his temple begin to accelerate as he thought of how she *could* answer his next question. 'And what exactly are you planning to do between now and the start of the ball, Fran?'

Something in his eyes was making the tips of her breasts push hard and uncomfortably against the tight bodice. 'Oh, you know—'

'No, I don't. Tell me.'

She felt the breath begin to catch in the back of her throat and threaten to choke her. 'L-last minute checking.'

His eyes flickered over the straining swell of the bodice. 'Won't you be a little...' he paused, and his voice deepened imperceptibly. 'Hot?'

She felt her body reacting to the sensuality in his voice, even as her mind rebelled against it. This was how she had got into trouble last time. With Sholto. She had fallen for a lazy smile and an abundance of sex appeal. Silver eyes and a silver tongue. And just look where that had led her.... She fixed him with the kind of prim smile which an elderly schoolteacher might give to an unruly young pupil.

'Oh, no!' She shook her sleek, coiffeured head and not a strand moved. 'The temperature in the marquee is maintained at a steady degree throughout the evening— thermostatically controlled, of course! Right now it is comfortable, but it will obviously be lowered when the

place starts to fill up,' she added helpfully. 'So none o
your guests will get overheated, if that's what you'r
worried about, Sam.'

'That wasn't what I meant.' He gave a faint, perplexe
smile.

She knew that, but sometimes playing the innocen
was safer. 'I'm sorry.' Her voice was bright and inter
ested as she gave him a brisk, professional smile. 'Wha
exactly *did* you mean?'

'It doesn't matter,' he growled.

'Well, if you're sure…?'

'Yeah. I'm sure.' Oh, that prissy way she had of talk
ing could be incredibly erotic, thought Sam achingly
'Everything looks pretty-near perfect to me,' he mur
mured, finding that he couldn't tear his eyes away from
the creamy expanse of her shoulders. There was some
thing almost unbearably erotic about the contrast be
tween the white-gold flesh and the glowing scarlet of he
dress. Why didn't she dress in colours like that more
often, he wondered? Instead of those drab, dreary shade
she always seemed to wear. 'Just perfect,' he finishe
slowly.

'Why, thank you, Sam!'

'So why don't we go into the house and have a quie
glass of champagne before everyone arrives?'

She couldn't deny that she was tempted. Who
wouldn't be tempted, for goodness' sake, when he had
the knack of making a simple request to have a drink
sound like an invitation to commit some kind of glorious
and unforgettable sin?

She shook her head. 'I'd better take it easy. I have to
drive back to London later and I'm not really used to
the hire-car.'

'You don't have to drive anywhere,' he said tightly.

'There are four spare bedrooms in my house, all at your disposal. I can't understand why you won't stay.'

'I told you—I never stay over if it's just a one-off, like a ball. It's different if it's a house-party.' Which wasn't strictly true, of course. She *might* have stayed—and in fact she was going to have to come back tomorrow anyway. And it wasn't that she didn't trust him—that was the crazy part. She did—deep down inside, where it mattered. In spite of what Rosie had said. But she didn't know how angry he would be with her after the ball, or with Rosie. Or with the others. Whether he would accept the fairly innocent piece of revenge with good grace and a shrug of the shoulders. Or whether he would rage round the place like a rampaging bull!

After a lot of thought, she had decided not to risk it. Much safer to drive back and finish the clearing up tomorrow—once Sam had had the chance to see the funny side of things! 'Honestly, Sam,' she smiled. 'It's very sweet of you, but I won't.'

'How about a coffee, then?'

Oh, but he was testing her resolve! 'I really don't have time—and even if I did,' she let an apologetic note creep into her voice, 'it's a rule of mine never to fraternise with clients. You know? It sort of blurs the boundaries of the working relationship, particularly in this kind of business. And that makes for complications. I'm sure you'll understand, Sam.'

Sam couldn't remember having been snubbed so effectively for years. If ever. He felt a potent mixture of fury and frustration, and a sneaking kind of admiration....

'Forgive me,' he said faintly. 'I had no idea that I was stepping into the realms of the unacceptable. Maybe you're right. Champagne might blur my senses. And I

have the feeling I'll need all my faculties about me to-night.' He gave a wicked and unrepentant grin as he saw her cheeks grow hot, enjoying the old-fashioned display of embarrassment. 'I think I'll go and relax in a hot tub.'

And with that teasing glitter lurking in the depths of his eyes, he turned away, leaving Fran staring after him wishing that she could rewrite the entire conversation and sneak off into the house with him. So much for being a strong woman!

Outside, waiters were scurrying in and out of the attached service tent where all the food was being prepared. Fran went and checked that the portable loos were up to scratch and on her way back into the marquee, looked up at the sky.

It was a clear, starry night—thank heavens. February was always a dodgy, unpredictable month where the weather was concerned. Rain was always a disaster. Hairdos got ruined. High-heeled shoes became stuck in rivers of mud. And female guests spent the whole evening with their teeth chattering. But rain on Valentine's Day was even more of a calamity—romance did not go hand-in-hand with the drowned rat look!

It seemed only minutes after Sam had left to take a bath that the string quartet arrived. The four musicians had been booked to play throughout the meal and afterwards there was going to be a disco, when the floor would be cleared for dancing. Fran organised a tray of coffee and cake, and left them to tune up while she swished round the room in her flowing red dress, nervously straightening a glass here, a napkin there.

She swallowed down the lump of anxiety which seemed to have taken up permanent residence in the back of her throat as she looked at all the place-names.

Unsurprisingly, Rosie had not been on Sam's guest

list. And neither had the names of the other women he had so cruelly dumped. Yet the list had been so varied and so balanced. There were authors, actors, doctors, secretaries, cleaners and even a used-car salesman! Fran had been reluctantly impressed.

'Well, hello, again, Little-Miss-Industrious.'

Fran looked up and found herself opening her mouth with instinctive pleasure as she saw just what Sam Lockhart had managed to do to a dinner jacket.

'Managing to keep yourself busy?' he murmured.

'Uh-huh. There's always something to do—if you look hard enough,' she gulped, wondering if he realised that he looked like the subject of a professional make-over.

But all men looked good in a dinner jacket, she reasoned. There was something about the colour and cut which slimmed them down, while the bow-tie made them look just old-fashioned elegant. But Sam needed no slimming down, or making elegant. What the jacket did for *him* was to emphasise the breadth of his shoulders, the length of his long, long legs and the darkness of the hair he had managed to tame into something resembling neatness.

But not quite. There was still something of the maverick about Sam Lockhart, something which no amount of grooming and expensive clothing could hide....

'Y-you've changed,' she said stupidly.

'Mmmm.' His blue eyes feasted themselves upon her bare shoulders again. What a pity she was working....

'But you haven't, I'm pleased to see.'

'No.'

'You should wear red more often,' he murmured.

Fran shot a desperate glance at her watch. 'They'll be here soon. The guests. In fact, oh, *look*—' and she felt

almost dizzy with relief as she saw a couple standing at the entrance to the marquee, looking around them slightly uncertainly. 'Here are your first arrivals!'

'So they are.' Sam shot her a slightly bemused glance. 'You know, you're like a cat on hot bricks tonight, Fran,' he murmured, before lifting his hand in welcome. 'Do you always get this nervous before an event?'

If she told him no, he might justifiably wonder why. 'Of course I do!' she retorted. 'Nerves means that the adrenalin is pumping—which means that you're giving your best.'

'You mean this is the best you can do?' he teased, but before she could think of a reply, he was calling 'Monica!' and 'Nick!' to the first couple.

Fran was pleased to escape. The clammy feeling in her hands had increased, so that her palms felt slick and oily with moisture as the place began to fill up.

She drank a glass of water thirstily. Her task was almost over. Her duties nearly complete. Thank God. It was her responsibility to see that the evening ran smoothly—to remain visible and yet discreet. She was dressed as a guest, and yet she had not been invited. Her job was to remain in the background in case Sam wanted her. Her official role as spectre at the feast....

The meal passed in a blur. Fran watched the waitresses move around the tables like well-schooled puppets, smoothly replacing course after course. Most of the women simply picked at their food, which presumably was how they maintained their slender figures.

Fran's biggest anxiety had been about Sam's choice of partner. What if he had invited a simply lovely girl who would not only see the host get his rightful comeuppance, but who might be desperately hurt and upset in the process? She didn't want to think about it.

But to her surprise, Sam was partner-less. The woman seated at his side this evening was his secretary, Maria— a fine-looking woman, it was true. But Fran doubted whether even Sam would be having an affair with a woman nearly twice his age!

He had actually invited Fran to join him on his table— a mixture of the great and the good and several dignitaries from the local children's hospital. But she had turned him down flat and Sam wasn't used to being turned down.

'Why not?' he demanded.

'Because I'm *working*!' Fran had explained. 'If anything goes wrong—and by the law of averages it will, believe me—I'll have to keep jumping up and down to sort it out. Not very discreet in front of all your worthy and famous friends!'

Sam curved a reluctant smile. What she said made perfect sense. It was just that women tended to break rules where he was concerned and he found himself wanting this woman to do the same.

'And does your professionalism rule out a dance with your client?' he demanded.

Fran shrugged, her heart thundering, the voice of her conscience telling her that she really ought to say no. She ignored it. 'My professionalism says I'll consider it,' she answered lightly, thinking of at least twenty reasons why not. 'If you ask me later.'

Their eyes locked. He wondered if she had invented the phrase hard-to-get. 'Oh, don't worry, I will.'

So Fran ate her dinner on the hoof—bobbing in and out of the service tent, grabbing an oyster here and a succulent lump of lobster there. She admired the perfect strawberry-heart desserts, with the clever little chocolate curls made to look like arrows. Perfect Valentine fare.

'How's it going?' she asked one of the chefs, as they were preparing to decant the strong coffee into jugs.

'Like a dream,' he said, smiling. 'But that might have something to do with the amount of champagne they've put away. Funny, isn't it, that people drink the stuff like it's going out of fashion on Valentine's Day.'

'Well, it *is* supposed to be the stuff of romance,' shrugged Fran.

'If it's drunk in those quantities, it isn't!' remarked the chef raucously. 'In fact, it tends to have a very unromantic effect!'

But Fran had noticed that Sam himself had remained moderate all evening, for he had none of the bright, flushed bonhomie produced by too much booze. Nor the smug righteousness of the abstainer, either.

She went back inside the marquee to find the tables being cleared, the string quartet bowing out after their second encore, and the man running the discotheque putting on the first dance number. Several couples rose to their feet and began to jig around rather self-consciously on the wooden dance floor.

Fran glanced at her watch. Just over an hour to go…

A shadow as dark as her fears loomed over her. 'Such a *troubled* face,' observed a deep, familiar voice. 'Is something wrong, Fran?'

'No! And I wish you wouldn't keep creeping up on me like that!' she said crossly.

He stared down at her consideringly. 'I could say that I wish you wouldn't keep jumping six feet into the air every time I approach you.'

Tension made her tactless. 'I'm surprised you're not used to having that effect on women!'

'How the hell would you know what effect I have on women?'

'Well, you're a good-looking man,' she said hastily, backtracking like mad.

'Now why does that sound more like an insult than a compliment?' he wondered aloud.

'I wouldn't want you getting a swollen head,' she told him sweetly.

'A swollen *what*?' came the innocent retort.

To her fury, Fran blushed and no words would come. No appropriate words, in any case.

'Oh, dear,' he murmured. 'You're determined to get hold of the wrong end of the stick tonight, aren't you, honey?'

'Stop it!'

'I wasn't aware that I was doing anything—other than trying to have a conversation with you. Any innuendo is entirely accidental. But that seems to be the effect you have on *me*.'

'Is that supposed to be a compliment?'

He shook his head. 'It was simply the truth. But since we seem unable to have a conversation without one of us inadvertently insulting the other—maybe you'd better come and dance with me instead,' he suggested gently.

'I can't!'

'Oh? Another rule?' he mocked. 'From the book of party dos and don'ts you wrote yourself?'

Fran studied the scarlet suede shoe which matched her dress perfectly. 'Something like that.'

'Well, let's break it, then. I hate rules.' He very gently put the tips of his fingers to her chin and tilted it upwards, not letting go, so that she was trapped by the blazing light of his eyes. Couldn't look away, even if she had wanted to.

'Come on, honey,' he murmured. 'Dance with me?'

He made it sound like a question, but of course it

wasn't. It was a beautifully-couched velvet command. He knew that and she knew that. And it would be impossible for her to turn him down without making a scene.

'The raffle,' whispered Fran frantically.

He frowned. 'What about the raffle?'

'This is the last chance for people to buy their tickets!' she babbled, lifting her hand triumphantly from the voluminous folds of her skirt and producing a book of tokens she was clutching. She waved them in front of him like a ticket tout, producing her most winning smile. 'I've sold hundreds already, and now that people have a few drinks under their belts, they'll dig even deeper into their pockets! First prize a luxury weekend in Paris!' she recited. 'Second prize a—'

'Okay, okay. I get the general idea,' he drawled, wondering if for the first time in his life she genuinely *didn't* want to know. But Sam was astute enough in the ways of human nature to know that whatever Fran Fisher felt for him it was definitely not indifference. It was… something…

He shook his head. Something he couldn't quite fathom. Not when she was this close. He let her go with a gracious shrug.

'How about after the raffle?'

Fran nodded, feeling like a born-again virgin! 'Ask me again.'

'I will.' Sam moved away, feeling curiously relieved. A dance in his current state would probably be the worst idea in the world right now. Resistance and refusal was more stimulating than he would have ever imagined and he would hate her to see the physical effect it was having on him.

Fran had never worked so hard to sell tickets, going

from table to table with her brightest smile, her most appealing eyes. Several men, too busy ogling her cleavage to pay attention, bought lavish amounts of tokens.

Slowly sipping from a glass of mineral water, Sam silently watched her progress from the opposite side of the room. She seemed distracted as well as committed, and genuinely oblivious to some of the more lecherous attentions she was being subjected to. He put the glass down and began to tap an impatient little beat on the linen-covered table, itching to haul some of those crass perverts out of their seats and throw them out of the marquee.

Some of them were old enough to be her father! Men he knew and usually respected. Made foolish and indiscreet by the ill-judged consumption of alcohol and the sight of a beautiful, unaccompanied woman.

But she was like a flower, he thought, flitting around in that bright, extravagant dress, her skin milky-pale in contrast. White and red. Innocence and experience. The drumming of his fingertips became insistent, matched only by a relentless pulse beating at his throat.

She was beckoning to him now, and he stood up stiffly to draw the raffle, moving towards her like a sailor to his siren. And suddenly, the world telescoped as she invaded his senses. All he was aware of was her standing close beside him, darting him those oddly shy little looks, her cheeks and her neck all flushed, like a woman in the aftermath of orgasm....

He was barely aware of presenting the prizes, of the sloppy kiss aimed at his mouth by one grateful female winner. By instinct he quickly turned so that kiss misfired and fell unwanted on his cheek, and all he could think of was how he wanted to explore the rose-red pet-

als of Fran's soft lips. First the ones on her face, and then…and then….

He shook his head, like a man waking from a coma. He felt drugged or drunk, and yet he had barely touched a drop of alcohol all evening.

Without giving her a chance to say no, he reached out his hand in full view of everyone, taking her fingers within his grasp. He dipped his head so that he was close enough to speak without anyone else hearing. 'Now?'

To Fran, the word he chose sounded unbearably intimate. She knew she should refuse him, but she couldn't. And not just because to do so would have been unforgivably rude. But because she wanted to feel his arms around her. Just this once.

'Okay,' she nodded.

Maybe this, she thought despairingly as he led her onto the dance floor, was how Rosie had been with him. Powerless in the face of this much charm. Who *could* resist him?

He put a hand on each side of her waist, marvelling at the swell of her hips as they curved downwards in a soft arc. He pulled her a little closer and felt her shiver in response, and triumph coursed around his veins like lifeblood.

In his youth, egged on by hormones and predatory women, Sam had quietly engaged in the silent lovemaking which was considered perfectly normal on the dance floor. The instinctive thrust of the hips to show how hard he was. The cradling of soft flesh against hard male contours. Breath hot against long perfumed necks, while breasts would be crushed tantalizingly against the muscled wall of his chest.

But this dance was exceedingly proper. Hell, it was

proper! He was using the kind of touch he might employ if he was dancing with an elderly and shockable maiden.

And it was the most erotic experience of his life so far!

He had to do something—and not the thing which was uppermost in his mind. Much more of this slow enchantment and he would be dragging her off somewhere like a caveman!

He needed to talk to her, to do something to take his mind off how much he wanted her. 'So do you enjoy your work, Fran?' he attempted conversationally, thinking how bland he sounded!

Fran blinked as the words broke in to the slow flush of pleasure she was feeling. She struggled to concentrate. To resist the desire to unbutton the buttons of his jacket and to rest her head tenderly against his silk-covered chest. 'I suppose I do. But it's just a job—like any other job.'

'And what does that mean?' he wondered. 'Is that a yes, or a no?'

'Well, every job has its good side—'

'And what's yours? Apart from the obvious advantage of dancing with men like me!'

Fran's mouth twitched in response. 'Well, everything pales into insignificance next to *that*! But I like the freedom, I guess. I don't have to get up at seven o'clock every morning and put on a suit.'

The thought of her wearing some constricting little suit, with stockings and high-heeled shiny shoes, made the roof of Sam's mouth dry out. 'Yes, that's true,' he said evenly. 'And I suppose there's the inevitable bonus of going to lots of parties!'

She shook her head, her hair brushing silkily against his neck. 'Not really. Once you've done that a few times,

you get it out of your system,' said Fran fervently. 'And believe me—parties and balls can become pretty boring after a while.'

'Well, thanks very much,' he said drily.

'Oh, not *this* one!' she corrected hurriedly, and then wondered if that sounded too gushing. Or too honest. She thought about the real reason why the last word she would have used to describe this night was boring, and blushed with guilt.

He saw the rise in colour which stained her neck, and an extraordinary sense of protectiveness washed over him. Sweet. He wasn't used to women blushing in his arms. 'You don't have to worry about saying what you mean, Fran,' he said gently. 'I'm not in the least bit offended.'

Fran stiffened. Oh, Lord! Any minute now and he would be! Why was he being so sweet to her? Why couldn't he do or say something outrageously sexist which would make her recoil? 'Good!' she said evenly.

He felt her grow rigid within his embrace, and frowned. Most women would have been gently parting their legs for him by now, waiting for the symbolic and proprietorial thrust of his thigh between theirs. The question silently asked and silently answered. Sam gave a grim smile and began to rub his thumb absently at the small of her back, feeling the pad brush against the scarlet bow which sat above the curve of her bottom.

The tiny movement was dissolving all her defences in a way which was totally alien to her, and Fran suddenly understood exactly *why* Rosie was overreacting. Just think of the effect he was having on *her*—still defensive and smarting from the failure of her marriage—after a few brief meetings and one innocent little dance. What on earth would it be like if he'd taken her out and show-

ered her with attention? Kissed her? Made love to her? Fran shivered.

She turned her face up to look at him for one last time before the joke was played, her lips parting before she could stop them.

He couldn't resist. Couldn't. Just bent his head and brushed his lips against the shimmering bow of hers. Her eyes were open and so were his, hers so big and so dark that they looked like jet rimmed with a thin band of glittering green-gold.

He gave a lazy smile as he felt her mouth tremble beneath his. 'Mmmm,' he murmured softly. 'Want to lose the crowd? Find somewhere more private?'

It was probably the most innocent request he had ever made and yet Fran jerked back as if he'd asked her to peel her dress off in public. She gazed up at him, startled and shivering. 'Sam?'

Sam frowned. 'What's the matter, honey? Are you cold?' His voice was full of concern and he found that he wanted to rip the jacket from his back to cover those bare, creamy shoulders.

'No.' Just terrified. Because at that very moment Fran saw a frilly white handkerchief appearing round the tented flap which marked the entrance to the marquee.

It was the signal she had been waiting for. And dreading.

She moved her hand from where it had been splayed over Sam's chest and rested it lightly on his shoulder instead, so that she could see her watch.

Fran swallowed. It was time.

Sam felt her move. He was restless himself. The meadow-sweet scent of her hair and the rich feel of the velvet against his skin was unbearably stimulating to the

senses. 'Want to sit this next one out?' he questioned huskily. 'Or dance on?'

'I think I've had enough dancing,' she told him truthfully. Much more of this and she would be blurting out what she had done.

'Me, too. You're a very distracting partner.' He cupped her chin in his hand, mimicking the gesture of earlier. His eyes crinkled as he smiled. 'At the risk of sounding terribly corny—do you want to save the last dance for me?'

'There must be someone else you'd rather dance with,' she said lightly.

'Nope.'

Their eyes were on a collision course and Fran couldn't have looked away, not if the world was tumbling about her ears around her. Come to think of it— in a few short minutes it might be doing exactly that!

'Fran, Fran, Fran,' he murmured. 'I'm blinded by the green-gold dazzle of your eyes but you still haven't given me your answer.'

'If you still want to dance with me later, then I will,' she hedged, knowing that the request would never be made.

She broke away from him and headed off in the direction of the white handkerchief, stepping outside into the crisp February air, her eyes adjusting to the darkness.

'Pssst! Fran!'

Fran turned round in the direction of the voice and she caught a glimmer of gold, heard a stifled giggle. Five women, all in evening dress, stood huddled beneath the shadows of a nearby tree like a coven of witches.

Only *five*? Rosie had implied that she would be bringing at least double that number.

Swallowing down her regrets, Fran carefully picked

her way over the foot-flattened grass towards them. Rosie was in the middle, wearing white, with most of her thighs on show and an air of suppressed excitement fizzing off her like electricity. The other four women were oddly disappointing. And not at all what she had been expecting. Over-perfumed and overmade-up, they looked cheap and out of place, like Christmas decorations brought out in the middle of summer.

And the last kind of women that she could imagine Sam seducing.

'Everything set?' Rosie whispered agitatedly.

Fran nodded gloomily. 'The song you requested will be played in five minutes' time.'

'Good!' Rosie gestured to the shivering bevy of women grouped behind her. 'Want me to introduce you?'

Fran shook her head. 'No, thanks. No offence, but I don't think I'm going to strike up any lasting friendships with any of you.'

'Is he in there?' whispered one of the women.

'Ask her,' answered a redhead in a silver jump suit, who pointed a talon-like fingernail at Fran. 'You were just dancing with him, weren't you? We all saw you smooching!'

Fran felt the accusation gathering up like a storm cloud as she faced five mutinous faces. 'I was *not* smooching!'

'No?' asked another spikily. 'We actually *saw* him kiss you, so I'd like to know what else you'd call it! Did you like the way it felt to have his arms around you, Fran?'

'He asked me to dance,' Fran said, realizing just how passive she sounded. 'What else could I do?'

A skinny brunette with bony shoulders narrowed her

eyes. 'Just be glad we're here,' she said huskily. 'And that we're saving you from certain heartbreak.'

Fran shook her head. 'I don't think I need rescuing.'

'You're trying to tell us that you *wouldn't* have ended the evening in bed with Sam?'

Fran shuddered with distaste and looked down at her watch, dreading what was about to happen next and yet longing for it to all be over. 'Your time has come ladies,' she said, forcing a smile. 'Over to you.'

Afterwards, Fran tried to convince herself that it wasn't as bad as people subsequently made out. That it just happened to be bad luck that the floor had completely cleared as the evocative song began its first, sultry notes.

Sam was sitting chatting to a man at his table when Rosie appeared from nowhere and walked up with a dramatic kind of swagger to ask him to dance.

Fran saw him give a brief, perplexed look, as though he didn't quite recognise her. As if she was the last person in the world he had expected to appear. Which she probably was. But he appeared to hesitate only momentarily, shrugging his shoulders with a gracious smile as he rose to his feet to dance with her.

Maybe that would have been enough.

Maybe.

But one by one the four other women appeared from the shadows, each dressed up to the nines, glittering smiles pinned like tinsel to their shiny lips.

They surrounded the dancing couple, like wild animals circling just before the kill, and when Rosie moved away from him, another was ready to move into her place in Sam's arms.

Fran started to feel nervous. People must have sensed

that something out-of-the-ordinary was happening, because an odd, watchful silence had fallen over the guests.

And then Fran knew that she was in trouble, because Rosie had started staggering over to the discotheque, and had plucked the microphone out of the startled DJ's hand.

'Good evening, everyone! You have been watching,' she said, with the false, toothy smile of the professional television presenter, 'your host—the luscious Mr. Sam Lockhart—get his comeuppance at last!' She gave him a glassy stare. 'Because you can't just take a woman's virginity and dump her the following morning, and expect to get away with it, can you, *honey*?'

The deathly silence briefly rose into a murmur of confused question.

Rosie held up her hand for silence. 'This is to show you, ladies and gentlemen—' she hiccuped loudly and then gave an apologetic smile. 'But especially all you *gentlemen* out there—that if you trample all over a woman's heart and emotions as Sam has done—then you can expect to get paid back in full! We could have done a lot worse, but we decided that public humiliation was the best form of revenge for this particular snake!'

This part was totally unscripted! Fran shrank behind one of the ivy-covered pillars, hardly daring to breathe, wondering just how on earth he would react.

But Sam was nothing if not unexpected. His broad-shouldered shrug was more rueful than wrathful. Every eye in the place was on him as he lightly shook his silver-dressed partner away from him as if she were no more than a troublesome fly, and strolled across the dance floor to take the microphone from Rosie, who was beginning to look out of her depth.

'Ladies and gentlemen,' he said smiling, and Fran

could have heard a pin drop. 'I shall not attempt to defend myself, other than to say that it appears I have loved not wisely but too well!' There was laughter around the room at this, particularly from the men. 'However, the unexpected...' he shot a brief, hard glance around the marquee as if searching for someone, and Fran froze from her sanctuary behind the pillar. Had he *seen* her?

'The unexpected arrival,' he continued, 'of these very glamorous ladies shall not be in vain. Be sure of that,' he finished, on a note of soft threat. 'Very sure.'

There was a buzz of excited chatter, but his face grew serious as he looked around the attentive marquee. 'Tonight we are here not simply to have a good time, but to help with the enormous costs of running the cardio-thoracic unit of our local paediatric hospital. Several of the surgeons and nurses from that unit are here with us tonight, and I know that you will join me in wishing them well.'

He smiled again as the involuntary applause subsided. 'Each of these ladies will dance with whoever asks them. But at a cost. A generous cost.' His eyes glittered as they scrutinised the audience. 'And I'm here to take your offers. So who will open the bidding for the gorgeous creature in the gold-spangled dress?'

There was a roar of approval and excitement as three scarlet-faced men leapt to their feet, waving wads of money.

But Fran didn't care what happened next. The ball had been a stupendous success—anyone could see that—and from the clamour around the marquee it was going from strength to strength. She would forgo being paid. Forgo anything. All she knew was that there was no way she was going to be able to face Sam Lockhart. Not tonight. Maybe not ever.

Stealthily grabbing her bag and the satin-lined scarlet wrap which she had hired to match her ball gown, she crept out of the marquee and round to the side of the service tent, standing as still as a statue while she waited to see whether he had followed her.

But he hadn't.

She picked up her skirts and began to run through the darkened garden towards the designated car-park, her breath puffing like clouds of smoke on the chill night air.

At Sam's insistence, she had left a holdall with warm clothes inside the house. He had told her she should get changed before driving back to London, but she wasn't risking going into the house to get them. What if Sam came looking, and what if he *found* her? What then?

Hands shaking with fear, she located her car, slithered into the front seat and started the engine. And only when she was moving did she expel a long, frozen breath of fear as she bumped her way across the cold, quiet lawn.

CHAPTER FIVE

FRAN focussed then refocussed her eyes, glancing down at the fax which had just come spilling angrily off her machine.

Another one!

And this one hadn't even bothered to *attempt* to sound polite! Her eyes flicked over it. Drone, drone, drone... and then the explanatory and telling phrase, 'we are sure you will understand our reluctance to continue with our agreement under the circumstances. Discretion is the by-word for a small, family business such as ours and any bad publicity—'

Fran gave a howl of rage before crumpling it into a tiny ball and hurling it to the opposite side of the room where it bounced off the wall and joined two others on the carpet.

Why hadn't she *thought* of this? Why hadn't she even *considered* that organizing a stupid stunt like the one she had allowed Rosie and her cronies to play on Sam would be bound to misfire on her, and her alone?

Fran thought back to that awful night—was it only eight short days and not a lifetime since it had happened?—when she had sped back to London in a mud-spattered evening dress, ruining it in the process and incurring not just the wrath of the hire-shop, but a huge bill into the bargain.

She had taken the first available flight over to Ireland, and gone straight away to see her friends Fergal and Patsy, who lived halfway up the side of a mountain in

County Sligo. She had told them the whole story of the ball, and instead of looking outraged, they had simply laughed.

'Sure, and wasn't it just a bit of fun?' Patsy had giggled.

'Maybe,' said Fran hopefully, wondering why she didn't find their words more reassuring.

Of course Patsy and Fergal had not seen that frosty gaze as Sam's eyes had swept around the marquee like an ice-axe—searching for *her*, no doubt. Oh, *why* had she cowered behind the pillar, instead of meeting that accusing stare head-on? She could even have gone one step further and joined Rosie and the others, had the courage of *their* convictions and told him that he was a no-good rat.

Except that the image of Sam as a no-good rat was one which was stubbornly refusing to be real any more. From the first time she'd met him it had been an image which had never seemed to fit.

Fran had gone back to her own flat, expecting to find that he had sent her some kind of furious communication. By fax. Or phone. Or e-mail. Or solicitor's letter...

But there was nothing. Not from Sam. Zilch. Just the faxes telling her that as a party-planner, her days were numbered.

Fran sighed. She may not have heard anything from the man who had the most right to be angry, but she had heard plenty from other people. The newspapers which had come flooding through her letter-box in the days following the incident, for a start.

It had made a very readable little piece on a quiet weekday morning, when there was no real news around. Mirroring the theme of a film which had been popular

at the end of the previous year, the column had inspired a whole clutch of 'revenge' articles.

Arguments then raged across the features pages of the tabloid press for days. Did Sam Deserve It? screamed one. While another carried a photograph of Rosie drinking a glass of champagne and lying on a chaise-longue in a too-low dress, proclaiming 'I Still Love the Bastard!'

Fran looked at the photograph closely. For all the dramatic headlines Rosie looked as if she was enjoying every minute of it, judging by the picture. It looked like her broken heart was intact once more. Fran sighed.

Outside the streets of Dublin buzzed with life, while inside Fran felt as empty as a biscuit tin, with a feeling of loneliness she couldn't quite shake off. Not surprising, really. No work to keep her occupied—and not a lot of any in the immediate future, either. Not until all this fuss had died down, that was for sure.

No relationship, either, of course. Mustn't forget that. Funny how it had never seemed to bother her before. In fact, she had sworn herself off men when her marriage had collapsed. The slow, nagging pain of a divorce seemed to pervade every aspect of your life and Fran had decided that it was better to steer clear of men, than risk them messing up your life for her.

So what was different now?

Because one man had stirred her emotions up? And because that man would never look at her with anything but disdain ever again?

The doorbell buzzed and Fran pulled a face, tempted to ignore it. Who could it be, other than the bearer of yet more bad tidings? Another letter terminating a contract, perhaps. Or a panicky pronouncement from her neurotic landlord, maybe. Asking her how she was in-

tending to pay her rent when everyone in the city knew that she wasn't working and wasn't likely to in the foreseeable future.

The doorbell buzzed again.

'*All right!* I'm coming!' she called crossly, tightly knotting the belt of her gold kimono.

She didn't use the peephole, or the chain—but maybe that was because Dublin had always felt so utterly safe to her ever since she had first gone to live there. She pulled the door open and there stood Sam blocking out just about every bit of available light. But then, he was a big man.

Fran blinked uneasily. 'Sam,' she said cautiously.

'Yeah,' he said quietly. 'Sam. The man himself.'

Fran gulped. Yes, indeed.

As usual, he was dressed in denim—the jeans and jacket a bright, familiar blue. Underneath the jacket he wore a dark, roll-neck sweater which looked very soft. Unlike his eyes which were hard and bright. They looked like eyes which meant trouble, and Fran wished that she had enough guts to tell him to go away and then to shut the door in his face.

She saw that he was carrying the overnight bag she had left behind and when he noticed her looking at it, he dropped it unceremoniously at her feet.

'You left in such a *hurry*,' he emphasised sarcastically, 'that you forgot to take this.'

She pushed it against the wall with her bare foot. 'Er, thanks.'

'Well, Fran,' he said silkily, and she was appalled to discover how pleased she was to hear that honey-sweet voice. 'Aren't you going to invite me inside?'

Was he angry with her? It was impossible to work out from the look on his face just what he was feeling inside.

Still. He didn't *seem* too hostile.

His eyes flicked from the topknot of her hair, down over the clinging gold satin of the embroidered kimono to where her bare toes clutched the mat, like a swimmer about to dive. 'Or were you still in bed?' he drawled.

'No, I've been awake for hours.'

He pursed his lips into a mocking kiss-shape. 'But one doesn't necessarily rule out the other, does it?'

The Sam she had known would not have spoken to her with that curling distaste. If she had thought he wasn't angry, then she had misjudged the situation badly. Because he was. Not a shouting, screaming, banging-on-the-wall kind of angry, no. More a quietly bubbling rage which had a dangerous intensity all of its own.

Better to placate him than to antagonise him with a smart answer, surely? Fran tried a smile. It felt like a stranger to her face. But then, she hadn't exactly had a whole heap to smile about lately. 'You'd better come in! I…er…wasn't expecting you.'

'Weren't you?' he murmured, but there was an acid tinge to his words. 'Did you think I was just some poor punter you'd mucked around and made a fool of, and that I would quietly creep off into a corner, never to be heard of again? If so, then you underestimated me, Fran. Badly.'

She tried to imagine him creeping anywhere. It was a ludicrous idea! Fran shook her head, trying to appear calm, but it wasn't easy. She'd forgotten just what physical presence he had. And she felt especially vulnerable in this clinging kimono. She shook her head. 'I thought nothing of the sort! I meant that I wasn't expecting you to turn up on my doorstep at eight o'clock on a Tuesday morning. Especially not after all this time.'

'What—eight days?' he mocked. 'I decided to wait

until my anger had subsided a little.' He paused, and the look in his blue eyes was positively steely. 'I've always found that decisions made in the heat of temper are often the ones you most regret. I also wanted to be sure you would be in. That's why I didn't choose Monday—a notoriously unpredictable time to catch someone in—'

She stared at him uncomprehendingly. 'Why?'

'In case you'd been lucky, and scored at the weekend,' he elaborated. 'Although, maybe that's presumptuous of me—maybe I've disturbed a little early-morning lovemaking? Have you left some poor unfortunate high and dry in your bed panting for more?' His navy eyes peered over her shoulder in the direction of the half-open bedroom door. 'If so, I can always come back later?'

She knew then that she was trapped. There was no way on earth she was going to get out of this meeting. She had better just grit her teeth and bear it.

Wishing that she had gone with her initial reaction of shutting the door in his face, Fran stepped aside to let him pass, and her feelings of nervousness increased as she pushed the front door closed behind him. Should she excuse herself now and go and get dressed in something more substantial?

He hadn't waited to be invited in. Had just marched into her sitting room as if he were a regular visitor and was now standing in the middle of the room, completely dwarfing the place with his tall, denim-blue frame, his black hair looking tousled as it curled around his collar. He was squinting his eyes half-shut as he looked out of the window to where the Liffey was a faint, grey dazzle in the distance.

He turned around as she came in and she wondered could he see the faint shadows beneath her eyes? With

so much leisure time on her hands just lately, she shouldn't have been tired. But tired she was.

'So,' she began cautiously, not daring to offer him a drink, because that really *would* be too hypocritical. 'You'd better get it over with, and say what you came for, Sam.'

As he turned, his fingers briefly skated over a large, round pebble she had found on the beach at nearby Dalkey and had brought home and polished.

'Please don't play dumb with me, Fran. It insults my intelligence.' He gave the glimmer of a smile. Only it didn't look the kind of smile you made when you found something funny. And his voice sounded different, too. Cold. Pithy.

'Sam, I—'

But he cut across her words as brutally as a scythe cutting through long grass. 'I realise now that my first instinct not to trust you was the correct one. You didn't just *hear* about the job, did you, Fran? It was a set-up.'

Fran opened her mouth to deny it and then closed it again. 'Yes.'

'Masterminded by a woman who isn't mature enough to know that rejection is part and parcel of most adult relationships! Particularly ones—' But he shook his head as he halted himself mid-flow, and walked back over to the window instead.

God, how cynical he sounded! 'I've known Rosie for years!' she defended. 'And I've never seen her in such a state over a man!'

'Is it my fault that women find me so irresistible?' he questioned, and Fran could have cheerfully punched him for his arrogance.

'No, but there are ways of dumping them which are

ot guaranteed to break their hearts as you seem to have done!'

He turned around. 'Not if they don't want to hear what you're saying,' he contradicted softly.

Accusation burned in her eyes. 'Well, maybe Rosie took it so badly because it wasn't just her heart you stole!'

There was a long, loaded silence. 'What else did I steal, Fran?' he asked eventually. 'Her sense of proportion? Her powers of reasoning?'

'You know damned well what else!'

'Tell me!' he challenged, and met her accusing stare, head on. 'Go on! Say it out loud!'

She drew in a deep, shuddering, indignant breath. 'Rosie was a virgin before she met you!'

There was a long, odd silence. 'Oh, I see,' he said, nodding his head slowly. '*Now* I understand.'

'So you're not denying it?'

'That I was her first lover?' His mouth flattened as he shook his head. 'No, I'm not denying it. How could I, when it's true?'

Funny that it should hurt so much to hear him admit it. 'Well, at least that's one thing sorted out,' she said flatly.

'I'm just rather surprised that she told you about it, that's all.'

'Really?'

His eyes were piercing. 'Well, do *you* talk about your sex life with your friends?'

'No. Of course I don't.' Not that she had a sex life to talk about, of course.

'So you see me as some barbaric despoiler, do you, Fran? Plundering the treasures of innocent young women? Taking their virtue and then discarding them

afterwards, like a piece of garbage? Positively medie
val,' he mused.

Put like that, it *did* sound a little far-fetched. 'I didn'
say that—'

'No. But that's what you meant.' His eyes bored into
her. 'Or maybe you think I raped Rosie?'

'*No!*' She stared at him in horror.

Her vehemence was reassuring. 'Well, then—the log
ical conclusion to what you're suggesting is that because
we had sex, then we should have got married. I don'
think people travel down that particular road any more
Fran.' He saw the frozen expression on her face and his
eyes widened in fascinated astonishment. 'I don't believe
it,' he said softly. '*You* did just that! That's why you go
married, isn't it? Because he took your virginity?'

'That's none of your damn business!'

'No, maybe it isn't.' But her face told him that his
guess was accurate enough. 'What *is* my business
though, is how you and that pathetic pack of women
attempted to sabotage a charity ball!'

Fran awkwardly rubbed her bare toes over the carpet
'Look, Sam, it was just a case of five women playing a
little joke—'

'A *little joke*?' he choked incredulously. 'Really?
Making me out to be a serial seducer in front of friends
and colleagues whose opinion I value? Forgive me if I
don't share your sense of humour!'

'Rosie is a friend whose opinion I value!'

'But you didn't bother to check your facts, did you?
What *did* she tell you, by the way?'

Fran's cheeks went the colour of brick. 'The same as
she said at the ball—'

'Oh, you mean that charming announcement of being
deflowered and dumped?'

'Which was unplanned, by the way—'

'Was it really?' he questioned witheringly. 'Sure you hadn't been rehearsing it together for days?'

'No! I had no idea that she was going to say that!'

'But you believed everything she told you, didn't you?'

'I've known her since we were at school together. Of course I believed her!' Her eyes flashed. 'Okay then, Sam—why don't you give me *your* version of what happened?'

He shook his head and gave a shudder of disgust. 'I wouldn't dream of talking about what I did with an ex-lover to a third party!'

Fran's heart plummeted. 'But you're not denying what she said? That you took her virginity?'

'No,' he breathed reluctantly. 'Those facts concerning Rosie are unfortunately true.'

Disappointment lanced at her skin like a million pin-pricks. 'And she had four other women to back her up, all with virtually the same tale to tell!'

Now anger turned to disbelief. 'You think I took the virginity of all *five* of them?' he queried incredulously.

'I only know about Rosie!' she snapped. 'I didn't ask for a blow-by-blow account of just how far you went with the others—and will you stop smirking like that!'

'You have an unfortunate way of phrasing yourself,' he said drily.

'Well, whatever happened, you certainly made them angry enough to want to get their own back,' hissed Fran. 'Or are you saying that they *all* made up their stories?'

'I'm saying that they have pretty fertile imaginations! Or have you never heard the expression "Hell hath no fury like a woman scorned!"?'

'What? A couple of scorned women I could believe! But five against one? At *least*! Oh, come on, Sam! The odds are pretty stacked against you!'

'Hell,' he murmured savagely. 'You really enjoy believing the very worst about men, don't you, Fran? Did your marriage do that to you? Did you decide to despise all men because one of them had let you down?'

Fran looked at him. 'Why don't you just tell me what happened?'

'I didn't lay a finger on any of the other four!' he told her softly. 'Did they *look* like the kind of women I'd be intimate with?'

She owed it to him to be one hundred per cent truthful here. 'Well, er, no. They didn't.'

'Even though they virtually offered themselves to me on a plate! Shall I tell you what really happened, Fran? Shall I?'

Fran nodded uncertainly.

'They all worked at Gordon-Browne when I was there—and they made no secret of the fact that they all found me sexually desirable.'

Which she could understand.

'Let me tell you—it was like having a permanently dark, dank cloud in the building with their dreary attempts at non-stop flirtation! They used to come on to me like second-rate hookers!'

'Then why didn't you have them sacked?'

'Because sacking four women would have been more hassle than it was worth! Imagine having to endure an unfair dismissal tribunal! Imagine all the publicity they would stir up by going to the *newspapers*,' he glowered pointedly. 'And by that time I had decided to go freelance anyway so it wasn't going to be my problem any more. Besides, there was an exquisite kind of irony

about telling them I was leaving and to see their hard, desperate little faces as they realised they would never see me again!'

Fran bit her lip as she realised that his version made far more sense. She believed him, that was the trouble. Every single word. Once she had seen the four women for herself, she had never really been able to imagine him being intimate with *any* of them. They simply weren't in the same league as Sam.

He narrowed his eyes at her. 'So why did you do it, Fran? I thought we got along fine together. Why think so badly of me? Why try and make a fool of me?'

Did he have a better nature to appeal to? 'Look,' she sighed and held up her hands in defence. 'It was a joke which—I agree—got out of hand. But it ended up doing you a favour, didn't it? *I'm* the one who looks like they're going to lose out. The bidding—which you began—raised an enormous amount of money for the hospital. No one thinks any the worse of *you*—'

'Other than my reputation as a stud being enhanced, you mean?'

'Okay, you may get a few offers!' she quipped recklessly. 'So what? You're now in the position of being able to pick and choose from any opportunities which may come your way as a result!'

Sam could never remember feeling quite so angry in his entire life. 'So you're completely unrepentant?'

She saw from the furious glitter in his eyes that she may have gone one step too far. 'Not completely, no,' she admitted. 'I certainly wouldn't do anything like that again!'

'Well, hallelujah!' he murmured.

There was a pause.

'So if that's everything?' she said warily.

Sam almost laughed. 'Everything? Honey, I haven't even begun!'

'But there's nothing you can do about it, is there?' Fran had started to feel nervous. 'Not now!'

He felt like a courtroom lawyer, all the facts at his fingertips, moving in for the kill.... 'Are you quite sure about that, Fran? When you failed to fulfil your contractual obligations to me?'

'How?' Fran shook her head and frowned. 'You mean letting Rosie—?'

'No.' He met her eyes. 'Let's forget the cabaret for a moment. Even though the rest of the world doesn't seem to want to. I was actually referring to your desertion—'

'Desertion?'

'Uh-huh. You were contracted to stay to the end of the ball, and to help clear the place up. But, like Cinderella—you slipped away as the clock chimed twelve.'

'So sue me!'

His eyes gleamed. When she straightened her shoulders like that, her breasts looked like two luscious missiles pointing straight at him.... He swallowed. 'Pretty foolish to issue a challenge like that.'

'Or courageous? To stand up to a man who makes veiled threats.'

'You think I wouldn't follow through?'

'Who knows? Why don't you just do it, instead of hinting at it!' she said, daring him.

'Oh, Fran, how I'm tempted,' he laughed softly, feeling himself momentarily harden as she made the provocative challenge. He ruthlessly pushed the erotic thoughts away. 'But quite frankly, I wouldn't bother suing you. I mean, it would be a complete waste of my time.'

Something in his voice put her senses on full alert. 'Oh?'

'Well, it's no secret that your business—if you can still call it that—is in danger of going down the pan. People don't like bad publicity. Clients have been pulling out of deals like rats leaving a sinking ship, haven't they?'

Pointless to tell a lie. He had obviously checked his facts. 'A few.'

'And your profession is the kind that stands or falls on its reputation, isn't it, honey?'

She felt an infuriating prickle of excitement when he called her that, even if the endearment was more snarled than whispered. But she shouldn't be surprised, not really. After all, Sam Lockhart's indisputable sex appeal was the reason she had gone charging to Rosie's rescue in the first place.

'Can't you see the writing on the wall?' he mocked.

'Get to the point, will you!'

'Okay.' Sam narrowed his eyes. 'Suppose I *did* sue you—it would be bye-bye to your business, wouldn't it?'

'Maybe it would! But it wouldn't be the end of the world. Not to me. Your threats don't frighten me, you see, Sam. No one has died. No one is ill. And I'm very adaptable.'

'I'm sure you are.' A pulse began to flicker in his cheek as he let his gaze drift slowly over her. He had wanted her to beg him, to plead with him, but her determination surprised him and intrigued him. Made the fight more equal. And the victory all the sweeter.

She had succeeded in making a fool of him, but more than that, had made him doubt his critical judgment. He had trusted her, warmed to her. For a man unaccustomed to giving either, it had been a shock to have them torn

up and thrown back in his face. A unfamiliar anger had burned deep inside him, and he had forced himself to sit tight for days and consider his options. And not to take any action until he was in full control of his emotions.

Well, now he was.

'I'm sure you're many things,' he murmured, thinking how unworldly she looked, with her scrubbed face and clear eyes. It could be so misleading, a face devoid of make-up.... Only the sun-gold satin straining over the swell of her breasts and her hips reminded him of the siren's body beneath, and suddenly he wanted to possess that body. Possess it and ride it to glorious fulfillment.

She saw the blatantly sexual way he was looking at her, and felt her body begin to stir in response. Of course, if she had been expecting him she might have worn something a little more concealing. A satin robe with just a pair of pants underneath was provocative at the best of times. And no one in their right mind could describe this meeting as the best of *anything*.

She raised her eyebrows at him. 'So is that it? Have you said everything you came to say? You've tried to frighten me into fearing for my livelihood—and this, I guess is where you storm out again—to put the word around that I'm finished. The unforgiving victor, with just the sound of my desolate sobs shuddering in the background?'

Sam smiled. So she was a feisty adversary as well as being an extremely sexy one, was she?

'And what if I were to do the very opposite?' he questioned smoothly. 'To prove to you what a wonderful human being I am, and that Rosie and her rather pitiful acolytes were at best deluding themselves, and at worst...seriously deluding you.'

'And how do you propose to do that? By having a personality transplant?'

For a person being offered what appeared to be a reprieve, she was bloody ungrateful! Sam felt an overpowering need to crush that indomitable spirit beneath his lips, and then to fill her so utterly that she would never again feel satisfied in the arms of another man. That would be both his revenge and gift to her....

'No, by spending a couple of days with me.'

Fran's heart clenched. 'Doing what?'

'What you do best. I want you to organise a small party for me.'

'You *are* kidding?'

'No, I'm not. I have no complaints about your organizational skills, Fran. Quite the opposite, in fact. The proceeds from the ball exceeded all expectations—the hospital went crazy with thanks. Several jaded socialites told me it was the very best party they had been to in ages—praise indeed. Particularly for the floor show.' His gaze was steady. Steady enough to notice that a pulse was flickering hectically at the base of her throat. And he wondered if that meant what it usually meant.... 'You're very good at what you do, Fran.'

She screwed her eyes up at him suspiciously. 'But won't people think it very strange for me to be working for you after all the adverse publicity? Won't they wonder why you're even giving me house-room?'

'No.' He shook his head. 'People will see us working....' he chose the next word with great care. He wanted to say 'intimately,' but that might frighten her off. '*Closely* together, and they will dismiss all the stories as rubbish.'

'And what if I say no?'

'Then I could make life very difficult for you.'

He said it almost pleasantly, Fran thought—and that made the simple statement all the more unsettling. She didn't doubt that he could make big trouble for her if he wanted to. And right now he looked powerful enough for anything.... 'What kind of party?'

His eyes betrayed no triumph—no emotion whatsoever. 'My mother will be travelling up from Cornwall, with my sisters. It's her birthday and I'd like to host a surprise dinner for her. Nothing big. Or fancy.'

'Your *mother*?'

'Well, I do have one. Don't you?' He gave a bitter laugh. 'It was the existence of my father which Rosie brought into question in that appalling newspaper article, and I'm afraid that once again, she got it wrong. He *is* dead—but he was very happily married to my mother for many years.' His mouth twisted. 'Sorry if that doesn't fit the stereotype either!'

'I wasn't the one who called you a bastard!' Fran protested.

'No, but you thought it, didn't you?'

She looked at him steadily. 'Are we going to spend the whole time raking up the fact that you think you've been misjudged by me, Sam?'

'No, I guess you're right. There's no point.' He controlled his temper with an almighty effort. 'My mother is going to be seventy. And I want to make sure she has a wonderful birthday. You can do that for me, can't you, Fran?'

'Well, I can,' she told him. 'But if she's seen the newspaper reports, then she may not be very happy about having me anywhere within a ten-mile radius!'

'My mother is an unusual woman. And never predictable,' he said, a trace of wry humour lightening his eyes. 'According to the sister who sent her Rosie's ar-

ticle, she burst out laughing when she read the piece and
said that she never thought she'd see the day when I'd
eat humble pie.'

'I can imagine.'

He ran the flat of his hand down over one hard, den-
imed thigh and Fran followed the movement with an
unstoppable fascination.

'And that's where you come in, honey. Your presence
will prove to her that you were mistaken about me. And
that as far as I'm concerned—humble pie is a dish that's
never been on the menu.'

CHAPTER SIX

SAM scowled as he waited for the connection to be made. It was hard enough trying to get hold of Cormack in normal circumstances, and these were definitely not normal circumstances.

Cormack hated telephones with a passion, often furtively disconnecting them and not bothering to inform anyone that he had done so. Like Triss, his wife. Or Sam, his agent.

Sam yawned. It was wonderful representing one of cinematography's most talented scriptwriters—just that he wished that Cormack would occasionally live his life by the same rules as other, lesser mortals. But the fact that Triss was newly pregnant with their second baby made the volatile Irishman even more erratic.

There was a click. 'Hello?' came a wary American accent and Sam almost burst out laughing. Until he remembered why he was ringing Cormack in the first place.

'Stop trying to disguise your voice, Cormack!'

The American drawl deepened. 'Excuse me?'

'It's me, Sam!'

'Well, why the hell didn't you say so?' roared Cormack. 'How the hell are you, man?'

Sam had a few things he wanted to get off his chest to the man who over the last few years had become a close friend, but he needed to check that Cormack's life was running smoothly before he unburdened himself. 'Tell me first, how's Triss?'

The Irish voice softened into a purr. 'Beautiful. Glowing like a jewel. And hardly showing at all. Just the tiniest swell around her belly, but she won't rest enough. I can see that I'm going to have to chain her to the sofa!'

'Or the bed?' suggested Sam.

Cormack laughed. 'Well, that too!'

'And Conor?'

The deep, Belfast accent became as soft as a pussycat's. 'The most incredible child ever to be born! As handsome as the day is long, and my heart's needle!'

Fairly safe to say, then, that Cormack's life was millpond smooth.

Sam opened his mouth and just lost it.

'That Fran Fisher—' he began menacingly.

Cormack interrupted with a whistle. 'Gorgeous, isn't she? In that very English way. Cool and collected. Never a hair out of place. The sort of woman where you wonder what goes on beneath the surface. You know, if I weren't a happily married man—'

'Cormack! You aren't listening! The woman is a conniving, manipulating, out-and-out—'

'Well, women are sometimes,' said Cormack indulgently. 'It's the way they're made!'

'Bitch!' Sam finished violently.

There was a stunned silence. And when he spoke again, Cormack's voice was positively frosty.

'Did you have something in particular you wanted to say to me, Sam?'

'Don't freeze me out, Cormack!'

'Then don't call a woman I like and respect names like that!'

Sam drew a deep breath. 'Well, *I* liked her, too!' he

stormed. 'I liked her a lot! Until she lied and cheated and tried to make a fool of me!'

'How?'

'*How?* Cormack don't you ever read the papers?'

'Never!' came the smug reply. 'What happened?'

Sam sighed. 'It would take more time and more energy than I have to explain. Remember that ball you couldn't come to because you were working?'

'Don't blame me for that, Sam—you missed Conor's baptism for exactly the same reasons!'

'I'm not blaming *you*! I'm blaming *her*! She set me up! She made me look a fool! And suffice to say that I'm mad. No, I'm not just mad—I want to get even!'

Cormack sucked in a long breath. 'Listen, man, the revenge thing never gets you anywhere. Ask my wife. If Fran has hurt you and got under your skin, then my advice to you is either to forget her—'

'Or?'

'Or marry her.'

'Or make her want me so bad that she can't forget *me*,' said Sam softly.

There was a long pause. 'Hell, Sam, what did she *do* to you?'

'She took from me something very precious, something that I didn't think existed any more,' said Sam grimly as he remembered the mushy way he'd felt when he danced with her. Feelings he had never imagined he would have for a woman again. 'And then destroyed it as surely as if she'd smashed it underneath the heel of her boot!'

'If you're thinking about revenge, I'm telling you again not to bother. There are more civilised ways to resolve things,' advised Cormack, in the tone of a man

who knew what he was talking about. 'And trying to get our own back always misfires on you.'

'That's just what Fran Fisher is about to find out!' said Sam grimly.

'Sam?' Cormack chided. 'You're talking in riddles now! What are you planning to do?'

'She thinks I'm such a bastard!' Sam growled. 'Well, I'll give her something to really get her teeth into!' He shuddered involuntarily as he realised that the threat could feel exquisitely sensual.

'How?'

'I'm going to spend a night having sex with her!' Sam vowed. 'The most wonderful sex she'll ever have experienced in her life!' he added, knowing instinctively that it would be mutual.

'And then?'

There was a long pause before Sam spoke. 'And then...nothing. Just something to remember me by.'

Cormack sounded worried now. 'Listen, why don't you forget all that, and come out here for a holiday? Take your mind off things. We'd love to see you—Triss, specially. And Conor wouldn't object to being spoiled rotten, I'm sure!'

'Maybe I will,' said Sam, looking at the calendar with a gleam of anticipation in his dark-blue eyes. 'But not until after my mother's birthday.'

CHAPTER SEVEN

FRAN spent the next couple of days trying to contact Rosie and getting precisely nowhere. She wanted to know which story was true. Had Rosie's four colleagues made Sam's life a misery? Or vice versa? Except that she had a strong gut feeling which story would hold up.

But the message on Rosie's answerphone said she was out of town, and even her mother couldn't help.

'I'm sorry, Frances, dear,' she said down the phone. 'But she's gone off on holiday without telling me exactly where she's going. Most inconsiderate of her, especially when you think of everything that's happened in the last couple of weeks!'

'Yes,' said Fran glumly.

'But she seems to be much happier in herself, thank goodness. And she seems to be over that wretched man Sam, at long last!'

Fran glowered at her reflection in the mirror. 'Er, yes, I expect she is. She didn't happen to mention who she was going on holiday with?'

'Well, that *is* the interesting part! Did you see the first article that was printed in the newspaper, the one all about her and Sam?'

'I certainly did!' said Fran vehemently.

'I didn't really approve of the language she used, I must say, but she *did* look lovely lying on the sofa in that dress, didn't she, dear?'

Fran winced. How blinding mother-love could be sometimes! 'Mmmm!' she said encouragingly.

'Well, apparently the piece inspired a *huge* mailbag, and now the newspaper has flown her off to some secret destination, promising to find her a man as gorgeous as Sam Lockhart, only one who treats her properly this time. This I *would* like to see! I do hope she behaves herself, Fran,' she added worriedly. 'She's been drinking far more than is good for her just lately—and I actually thought that he looked terribly nice, this Sam Lockhart. Well, as much as I could make out from the snatched photograph I saw! He appears to have been scowling at the photographer. I can see exactly why she fell for him.'

'Er, yes.' Fran wondered whether that had been before or after he had threatened to land the photographer with a punch, as had been gleefully reported. Sam Lockhart was in terrible danger of becoming a minor celebrity, she thought with a sinking feeling of guilt.

'So when are you coming over to England next, dear?'

'I'm—' Oh, it would be much too complicated to tell Rosie's mother that she was calling from Eversford Station, having flown in from Dublin that morning. And even longer to explain why she was waiting for Sam to pick her up and take her to his house to start planning his mother's seventieth birthday party! 'I'm in a bit of a rush now! Can you tell Rosie that I'll call again, and that I need to *speak* to her! She can get me anytime on my mobile!'

She cut the connection just in time to see a mud-splattered four-wheel drive nosing its way into the station forecourt. No need to ask who was driving *that*! Fran felt the automatic clenching of her heart as she saw the rugged profile of the man behind the wheel. The dark hair which kissed the collar of the leather jacket.

He glanced across, saw her, and gave a grim kind of smile.

Fran walked over to his car just as he climbed out o the driver's seat, managing to turn a few heads as he di so, even though he was wearing nothing more sensa tional than faded denims and a beaten-up flying jacke But he *did* look remarkable and the casual clothes di nothing to conceal his raw sex appeal.

His hair was windswept and his eyes sapphire-dark and Fran remembered the feel of his arms around he waist as they had danced, his lazy suggestion that the should find somewhere private, and wondered what i would be like to go to bed with a man like San Lockhart.

She felt like an explorer entering uncharted territory 'Hello, Sam,' she said quietly.

'Hi.' He kept his voice noncommittal, but he wishe she wouldn't look at him with that solemn expression o expectation. He stared at her. In the cold, bright light o an early spring day he was discovering that it was goin to be difficult to sustain the great rage he had felt whil talking to Cormack. After all, she was here, wasn't she Now it was all up to him....

'Good flight?'

Fran shook her head. 'A bit bumpy.'

'Pick up your connection okay?'

She nodded.

He wasn't sure that he liked her quiet and complian like this. Looking like she was about to have her teeth pulled. He jerked his head in the direction of the station café. 'Do you want to get a coffee in there? Can't guar antee the quality, but it'll warm you up.'

She was more than a little surprised. After severa sleepless nights dreading this confrontation, she had been expecting growled commands, not consideration 'No, I'll be fine. We might as well get going.'

'Okay,' he nodded, silently observing her through the lush, dark curtain of his lashes, as he put her one small bag in the back.

Again, he was slightly perplexed at what she was wearing. Apart from that night at the ball—when she had been dressed to kill, and more—she was obviously a woman who believed that less was more.

She wore camel-coloured trousers which were casual, but definitely not jeans. He suspected that she would consider jeans unprofessional when she was working. And a big, creamy roll-neck sweater underneath a workaday brown jacket. He wondered who had advised her to wear those neutral colours so that she merged into the background. Big mistake. She had looked utterly sensational in that scarlet ball gown. Maybe it was deliberate. Maybe she liked resembling the wallpaper. Blending in safely.

He looked at her white face and felt another irritating stab of concern. 'We'll drive with the window open. You look like you could do with some fresh air.'

'Why are you being so nice to me?' she demanded suspiciously.

'Because it makes sense.' He clipped the words out, allowing the mantle of hostility to settle around his shoulders with relief. 'You're here to work, aren't you? I need to keep you relatively happy, since I don't want you simmering away with resentment and glaring at everyone, just as we start singing ''Happy Birthday'' to my mother!'

She felt oddly disappointed, but didn't show it as she slithered into the vehicle. 'I would never be so unprofessional!'

He shot her a look as he climbed in beside her. 'But you think that arranging an ambush of embittered

women falls into the category of professional behaviour?'

She didn't answer, but began edging away from him a little instead, thinking that if his legs weren't quite so long and so lean, then she might be able to tear her eyes away from them!

He knew exactly what was going on in her mind. She was as aware of him as he was of her! It was written on every delicious pore in her body which those boring and staid clothes couldn't quite disguise.

'Do you often have to go and stay in people's homes like this?' he questioned, unprepared for the slicing sensation of jealousy at the thought of her alone in a house with some of the men of *his* acquaintance.

'I do if it's a proper house party involving several meals, and it's out in the middle of nowhere like this.'

He frowned. 'Isn't it strangely…intimate, staying with people you hardly know?'

She wondered if he had used the word just to embarrass her. 'No more intimate than groups of work colleagues who go away on conferences and stay in the same hotel and eat breakfast together, surely? It's just a job,' she told him, though that was not strictly true in this particular instance. This time it *did* feel strange. Not like work at all. And it was in grave danger of becoming—to use *his* word—intimate.

He drove out of the station and shot her a sideways glance. 'So. Pleased to be back in England?'

Fran almost smiled. Almost. 'I'll leave that to your imagination.'

'You'd rather be somewhere else?'

Anywhere! 'A beach in Tobago would do,' she said drily. 'But—'

'Beggars can't be choosers, right?'

'Right.' She found the sight of those long legs utterly distracting. Best to sidetrack her thoughts. She glanced curiously out of the window at the flat, empty landscape whizzing by. 'Why choose to live in such an out-of-the-way place?'

Sam changed gear. 'Well, I like the country and I need the isolation. Space and peace and quiet. These days I only go to London when it's absolutely necessary. Most people seem to labour under the misconception that literary agents spend their whole lives swanning around the world in the lap of luxury and pulling off film deals, when they're not lurching from boozy party to boozy party, that is.' He shot her a swift glance. 'What do you think I spend most of my time doing?'

Having sex, she wondered wildly, going hot with just the thought of it. 'Er—reading?'

'*Exactly!*' he enthused, pleased by her perception. Women were notoriously hopeless at understanding his job. He threw her another glance and saw that she was blushing. 'Why have your cheeks gone all blotchy, Fran?' he asked, with cruel candour. 'Surely you don't find the idea of books sexually exciting?'

'Well, some, of course,' she parried. 'Don't you?'

'Oh, yes,' he said softly, thinking that this visit was getting more interesting by the second. '*Ve-ry* exciting. Maybe we should compare choices some time? We could even have a private reading of erotic literature while you're here, what do you say?'

She suspected that he could make a train timetable sound erotic, if he read it aloud! 'I doubt there will be the time for literary analysis,' she said crushingly. 'So why don't you stop wasting time and tell me about the sort of party you want for your mother instead.'

He threw her an innocent look. 'But I thought that

was your department? To advise me. You had very de
inite ideas about the Valentine Ball, as I recall.'

'Balls are different—you can generalise.' She swe
on, unwilling to dwell on an evening which still had tl
power to make her feel uncomfortable. 'Birthday parti
have to be tailored to the person they're for. So you'
have to tell me something about your mother.'

He slowed down as they reached some traffic light
'Well, she's quite a lady,' he said, smiling.

The trouble was that the longer she spent with hir
the harder it was to stay indignant. And harder still
accept that this was the man who had—by his own ad
mission—robbed her friend of her virginity on a on
night stand. Yet a man who described his mother in suc
a fond way was the kind of man you couldn't hel
warming to. If he had raved on and on about her, sh
might have thought that he was a 'Mummy's Boy' an
if he'd expressed nothing but dislike she would have ha
him down as cold and unfeeling. He'd managed to gaug
it just right.

'Go on,' prompted Fran.

He turned up the narrow lane which led to his hous
'She was an actress—in fact, she still is. She does tl
odd voice-over and the occasional television comme
cial.'

'Would I have heard of her?'

'I don't know. You might. Her stage name was Hele
Hart and she used to work in children's television in tl
very early days—'

'Helen *Hart*!' Fran's face broke into a smile as sh
remembered tumbles of curls and a mobile mouth whic
could contort itself into all kinds of funny expression
Helen Hart was Sam's mother! 'Gosh! Didn't she use
to be Rolly the rag doll on "Tea-Time for Tots"?'

Sam grinned. 'Aren't you a little too young to remember that?'

'Of course I am!' she said severely. 'But it's a television classic! They're always showing those old black-and-white clips, and most people know Rolly's special tune, even if they weren't born when she used to sing it!' Her voice began to bubble over with enthusiasm. 'And, of course, she *must* have a birthday cake with Rolly on the top—no question.'

He thought how infectious her smile could be. 'I don't see how. They probably wouldn't be able to produce it at the local bakers—not unless you drew them a picture,' he said gently. 'It was so long ago.'

'You're probably right.' Fran smoothed back her already smooth hair. 'So I'll just have to make it myself, won't I? When is she arriving?'

'Tomorrow afternoon.'

'It'll be tight—but I'll manage it.'

The car was crunching up the drive towards his front door now and Fran felt fear and excitement all mingled up with this odd sense of her body feeling like it belonged to someone else.

Her clothes, which were good-quality clothes she had worn and felt comfortable in many times before, suddenly seemed all *wrong*. He looked so casual, and she looked so uptight.

She felt like a rat in a trap with the constricting roll-neck sweater enveloping her face like a ruff and the camel trousers all scratchy against her legs. Her face was still flushed and hot and her hair felt too-tight in its restricting pins. She found her fingers were itching to creep up and loosen them, and yank them out so that the glossy, golden-brown waves fell in a liberated cascade all the way down past her shoulders.

'Here we are!' Sam stopped the car and saw her ros
cheeks and her frowning profile and wondered why sh
was so uptight. Was it because she could feel the sexua
tension closing in on them like a storm brewing, th
same as he could?

Bizarrely, he found himself asking, 'Do you alway
wear your hair up?'

Fran turned round, vexed by a question which some
how managed to sound as personal as if he'd just aske
her whether she always wore a bra! 'Why?' she ques
tioned acidly. 'Does it bother you?'

Crazily, he wanted to tell her that, yes—it bothere
him a great deal. That he would never know a ful
night's sleep until he had seen and felt the silk of tha
hair lying all over his bare chest. He swallowed dow
the desire and tried to make the subject sound scientific
'It would just be interesting to see what it looks lik
down.'

She didn't need his opinion. So why did she suddenl
find herself seeking it? Her fingertips tentatively touche
one of the restraining hairpins. 'You don't like it?'

'Not much.'

'Well, go on, then. You can't just make a statemen
like that without clarifying it! Why not? Does it mak
my nose look big? My chin look wobbly?'

He shook his head. 'Nope. It just suggests characte
traits which I don't find particularly attractive in i
woman.'

Don't ask him any more, Fran. Just don't *ask*, she tol
herself sternly! 'Such as?'

He seemed as reluctant to answer as she had been t
ask. 'Oh, you know. Neatness, inflexibility, uptightness.
He withdrew the key from the ignition, and shrugged. '
guess that's why it's so provocative when a woman un

pins her hair. It symbolises the removal of all inhibitions—' Sam cleared his throat, unable to believe what was happening to him! Much more of this and he would be incapable of getting out of the car without her seeing just how aroused he was. And wouldn't that just support Rosie's poisonous prejudices? The stud with nothing but sex on his mind! 'Let's go inside, shall we,' he suggested throatily as he reached over for her bag. 'And I'll show you to your room.'

Fran fumbled for the car door handle to follow him inside the house, trying to ignore what he had said, and the way he had said it. She wasn't stupid. And to ignore that a strong, sexual attraction existed between them would be extremely stupid indeed. Perhaps it was a good thing that his mother was arriving tomorrow! Mothers made naturally good chaperones!

The bedroom he showed her to was low and cottagey. In fact, the door frame was so low that she had to stoop her head when she went in.

It was also downstairs.

Sam saw her quickly hidden look of surprise as he threw the door open. 'Thought you'd want to be near the kitchen,' he explained.

Which was true. Unfortunately, it also created an unflattering image of herself bustling around the stove, her sleeves rolled up and smudges of flour on her cheeks! 'Oh,' she said faintly. 'Well, yes. I suppose that does make sense.'

He frowned. He had thought she would want to be as far away as possible from him. He had certainly considered it sensible to have her on a completely different floor. He didn't want her to be on her guard, wary and defensive.

'I'm putting my mother in the biggest guest bedroom

and my sisters will each have one of the others. That just leaves mine—' It took all the will-power he possessed not to give her the smoky smile which was threatening to play on his lips. 'And it seemed pretty pointless for me to move out of my bed, just for a couple of nights, don't you think?'

He said no more but the unspoken statement hovered as clearly on the air as if he had shouted the words out loud. That she had a choice where she slept....

It was a pretty room. Plain and simply furnished, it was painted white with dark-wood furniture. Several framed samplers decorated the walls and a beautiful burst of embroidered sunflowers hung over the bed itself.

Fran began to unpack her few clothes and to slide her underwear neatly into one of the drawers of the dresser. Just what was the matter with her? She was here because she owed him. And he wanted to show her—apparently—that he did *not* have his brains situated in his groin. So why did everything they were saying to one another sound as though they couldn't wait to leap into bed and start tearing at each other's clothes? Was that what people called animal attraction? Was this what he and Rosie had felt for one another? How it had all started?

While Fran unpacked, Sam clattered around in the kitchen making tea, mightily relieved when the telephone rang and he could focus his mind on something other than wondering whether her underwear was as uptight and starchy as her outerwear....

'Hello?' he barked.

'Hello, Sam?' came an exaggerated stage whisper. 'Is that you?'

It was Maddy, his youngest sister. An actress like her mother, and scattier even than her mother—which was

saying something. Never was a person more aptly named than Madelaine Lockhart, he thought with slightly grim indulgence. 'Of course it's me! I live here, don't I? Who else would you expect to answer the phone?'

Maddy dropped her voice so that it was almost unintelligible. 'Mmmm Nggg Mummm,' she muttered.

Sam frowned at the phone. 'Is Mum there with you? In the room?'

'No!'

'Then stop talking in that incomprehensible voice! What's up?'

'Nothing's up! Just tell me where we're meeting for this birthday dinner which you've been so bloody evasive about!'

'I had to organise the...er...catering,' he said, sounding even more evasive. 'And we're not meeting anywhere. We're eating here. The dinner's going to be held here.'

'At your *home*?' screeched Maddy in disbelief. 'You mean, *not* in a restaurant?'

'What's wrong with that? Dining at home gives you more privacy and flexibility than a restaurant.'

'Don't be so flippant, Sam! That's not what I'm talking about! You can't even boil an egg—you know you can't! How you've lived on your own for so long, I simply *don't* know!'

'I eat simple food. Anyway, I can't help it,' he said, realizing that it was true. 'Suddenly I *feel* flippant!'

'What *is* the matter with you lately?' demanded Maddy. 'From being the personification of I-Want-To-Be-Alone, you start throwing your house open on every available opportunity!'

'A small birthday dinner for my mother,' he corrected

modestly. 'Hardly takes me into the league of big-time entertaining!'

'What about this famous Valentine Ball? The one that made all the papers and which my friends all read about! This from a man who shuns personal publicity! And I notice that neither of your two beloved sisters were invited!'

'Do you and Merry invite me to every social function which *you* have?' he asked reasonably.

'No! Because we got fed up with you persistently refusing to come! So what *has* happened to turn you from hermit to socialite overnight?'

'It isn't as simple as that—'

'I'll bet it isn't!' said Maddy. 'It must be a woman!'

'You couldn't be more wrong.'

'I'll bet it is!'

'Maddy—' he said warningly. 'What did you ring up about?'

'I want to know do we dress Mum up before we leave? Or should she pack her diamanté in her suitcase? What do we tell her?'

'Tell her that I'm cooking dinner for her.'

'And are you? Really?'

'Yeah. I am,' he said, suddenly smiling as he put the phone down.

Standing in the doorway, Fran cleared her throat to let him know she was there. She had removed the heavy donkey-brown jacket and redone her hair so that not a strand stood out from the gleaming topknot. Sam thought she looked as though she was about to take dictation.

'*You're* cooking dinner?' she asked. 'Not me?'

Sam stirred the tea and turned round. She'd obviously heard his conversation. He frowned, thinking that she looked sort of *right* standing in the doorway, for all that

her outfit made her look so prim. It had something to do with the pink cheeks, the bright eyes. Curves in all the right places. Oh, he was going to enjoy taking her to bed....

'It would certainly make the birthday a surprise if I could,' he admitted, trying to calm down his lust.

'Can you cook?'

'Not so's you'd notice. But I presume you can?'

'Big presumption to make, Sam! You should have checked first. Some party-planners can't make a phone call without delegating the task of dialling the number to someone else! It isn't part of the job description, you know!'

He ignored all that. 'But you can?'

'Actually, yes, I can.'

'Then you could tell me how to cook the meal—'

'*And* make the birthday cake, organise breakfast kedgeree, set the table and organise the flowers? Perhaps you could provide me with some brightly-coloured balls and I can juggle at the same time!'

'I can't see you'd find that a problem,' he murmured, watching her breasts move as she waved her arms around like that.

'Flattery won't work, Sam.' Fran glanced down at her watch. 'But I presume you've bought most of the ingredients?' She gave him a questioning look.

'Ah!' He shrugged his shoulders. 'Now who is making assumptions? Maybe we'd better skip the tea and go shopping.'

'I've got a better idea—let's drink the tea and *then* go shopping!'

Sam poured them each a cup and wondered if he was turning into some sort of masochist. He found he actually liked it when she spoke to him like that. It certainly

made a change. He wasn't being arrogant—merely accepting what was true—that most women seemed to develop a severe case of hero worship whenever he was around. And someone who worshipped you could never be your equal....

Shaking off her objections, he found himself helping her into her ugly brown jacket, aware of the faint scent of flowers from her hair which drifted into his nostrils and which stubbornly refused to leave them for the rest of the day.

CHAPTER EIGHT

THE fluorescent lighting hurt her eyes and the tinny piped Muzak assaulted her ears. Fran felt like she had just landed on an alien planet.

'What *is* the matter with you?' Sam felt compelled to ask, though he guessed it was a pretty crazy question. She doesn't want to be here, he told himself. That's all.

But her answer surprised him.

'I'm just not used to going round the supermarket with anyone.' Particularly someone who had insisted on pushing the trolley for her and who saw fit to walk at least three feet behind her, so that every time she picked up a carton of cream, or a packet of butter, she had to wait for him to catch her up. 'Can't you walk a little faster?'

Well, he could. But from where he was standing—or walking—he could take advantage of the magnificent sight of her bottom, pertly swaying from side to side as she walked down each aisle consulting her list. Maybe those slim-cut trousers *could* be sexy, after all! They certainly gave a tantalizing glimpse of each buttock as she moved.

It was most peculiar. In his mind he had done nothing but demonise her ever since the Valentine ball. And that in itself had bothered him. She had been like a stubborn little itch beneath his skin that wouldn't go away—and he badly wanted her to go away.

He had also thought that once he had succeeded in luring her back—so to speak—he would soon get her out of his system. So how come he was tamely trotting

around a supermarket behind her, thinking about her delicious bottom? A pulse begin to hammer at his temple. This wasn't how he had planned to do things. Not at all. What on earth had made him offer to *cook*, for a start?

'If *I* were cooking this meal, then the shopping wouldn't be a problem,' said Fran slightly peevishly, as she realised that the store was fresh out of basil. 'What on earth possessed *you* to offer, I just don't know!' She frowned. 'And why are you staring at me like that, Sam?'

'Because—' Hell, he had forgotten how incredibly provocative it could be to have a woman echo your thoughts like that. 'Because I was thinking *exactly* the same thing myself!' he said, with a certain sense of wonder.

Fran willed herself not to warm to that indulgent little dip to his voice. 'Well, that's hardly an earth-shattering conclusion,' she told him repressively. 'Since we're both relative strangers walking around a shop together buying ingredients for a meal, it would be pretty odd if we weren't thinking about who was going to cook it, wouldn't it?'

Sam felt oddly deflated. He was used to women seizing on the odd complimentary crumb he threw them— grabbing at them with the dedication of vultures picking over a carcass! Had he expected her to be immensely grateful that he was employing her again, so grateful that she would just fall to her.... He glared at a defenceless head of celery as the erotic image dissolved, and just hoped he hadn't sent his blood pressure rocketing up too much in the process.

'Why *are* you cooking it?' persisted Fran, mainly because he had looked almost hurt when she had snapped at him just then. And she had found herself stupidly

wanting to ruffle that thick, dark hair and tell him everything was going to be all right. How dumb could you get?

'Because I can't think of anything which will give my mother a bigger surprise,' he admitted. 'And because she's reached that stage in her life where nothing really surprises her any more. She's eaten at some of the best restaurants in the world. So it has to be good.'

'Well, you can't really go wrong with simple, fresh ingredients,' said Fran. 'Here!' And she threw a pack of almonds in his direction.

He caught it, placed it carefully in the trolley, then carried on pushing. 'So didn't you ever go shopping with your husband?' he asked casually, and wondered if he was going *completely* mad. He, who usually ran to the opposite ends of the globe once relationships started entering the realms of the personal, now found himself avidly interested to learn about her marriage!

Fran frowned, tempted to tell him to mind his own business.

Sam noticed the frown and picked up a newspaper and pretended to scan the front page. 'Of course, if it still *hurts* to talk about it—'

'Not at all,' she said stiffly, wondering if he had deliberately goaded her into being on the defensive.

'He didn't like shopping? Or he didn't eat?'

'Of course he ate!' Fran sighed. 'Sholto was a DJ—'

'He played records?'

She giggled in spite of herself. She had once naively said the same thing! 'They don't actually *do* that any more, Sam. It's all computerised, digital. It is on the radio, anyway.'

There was a pause.

'Go on, then,' he said.

'Go on, what?'

'Tell me more. About Sholto.'

She stared at him incredulously. 'Tell you about my ex-husband? Why ever would I do that?'

Anger came back like a gritty balm to rub over his skin. He held onto it with an odd sense of relief. 'It might even things up between us,' he grated. 'You seem to know a hell of a lot about *me*—while I know practically nothing about *you*.'

She supposed that he did have a point. And what harm could it do? After all, they were going to have to talk about *something*. 'Well, Sholto became quite famous in Dublin. It's a small city and the entertainment industry is correspondingly small. He hated going to the shops because lots of fifteen-year-old girls would come rushing up to him waving their autograph books. And occasionally some even more intimate items of clothing.' She shrugged awkwardly.

'So…?' He looked at her unapologetically. 'What happened? Why did you split up? Did your hours clash? Or did you just find that you were incompatible?'

Fran nearly hurled the pineapple she was holding, at his head. And yet, *why* did she never talk about it? Because she felt ashamed? Wasn't it more shameful to keep it all bottled up inside her like some dark, guilty secret—especially when she felt she didn't have anything to be guilty about.…

'You're a very nosy man!' she complained.

'No, just interested.' His voice was a velvet snare. 'Go on, Fran, you know you're dying to tell me.'

Fran shot him a frustrated look. What a persuasive individual he could be! Was this how he had got Rosie into bed? And how best to describe her ex-husband without sounding like a Grade I bitch?

'Sholto was a big fish in a little pond,' she told him. 'Who happened to be amazingly good-looking and could charm the birds off the trees. Which he did. Frequently. The human variety, I mean.' She glared at him, just daring him to ask her any more. 'There! Does that tell you everything you wanted to know about the reasons for my divorce, Sam?'

It certainly made the picture a little clearer. She had married a philanderer, and the betrayal must have been even worse because he strongly suspected she had been a virgin when they married. Was that why she had so blindly gone along with everything which Rosie had told her, he wondered?

'I guess it does,' he said thoughtfully.

Fran felt curiously exposed. 'And what about you?' she questioned, more ferociously than she had intended.

'Me?' he asked blandly. 'What do you want to know about me?'

'Having quizzed me all about mine, how about telling me something about *your* love life?'

He savoured the moment in the over-held look they shared. But now, he reasoned, was *not* the moment to tell her about Megan. 'I thought you knew everything there was to know on the subject,' he said smoothly, picking up a huge box of Belgian chocolates. 'Shall we buy some of these, too?'

She swallowed down her indignation. She certainly wasn't going to *beg* him to tell her! 'Yes, let's!' she agreed, looking at the size of the box he had chosen with undisguised greed. 'I'm a bit of a chocoholic, on the quiet!'

Which, presumably, was why she had that refreshingly shapely body, thought Sam as he followed her towards the cheese counter—though, of course, he

wouldn't dream of telling her that. Women were notoriously touchy about being told that they had healthy curves!

With all the shopping bought and loaded into the Range Rover, they headed back to the house and Fran had a distinct holiday feeling. Invigorated. Uplifted. Almost relaxed.

She shouldn't be feeling like this, she reminded herself. She was supposed to be here on sufferance—not enjoying herself!

'Now what?' asked Sam, as they carried the last few carrier bags into the big, warm kitchen.

'Now you unpack the shopping,' she told him sweetly. 'So that I can see where everything goes.'

The rest of the day was spent as congenially as it was possible to spend time with a man who essentially hated your guts, Fran decided. And there was a strange irony in her being able to give him step-by-step instructions on how to make beef bourgignon, and him almost meekly following them while she made his mother's birthday cake!

Fuelled by cups of tea and the occasional biscuit, the only interruptions they had were several frantic phone calls from one of his more talented but neurotic authors, whose new book was about to go up for auction. They worked side by side in the kitchen until nearly eight o'clock that evening, by which time the room was filled with the most wonderful smells imaginable.

'That's it!' Fran wiped the back of her hand over her forehead, leaving a splodge of flour behind. 'We can't do any more until tomorrow.'

'Right.' He was itching to brush the flour away, but he held back. Her proximity all afternoon had been spellbinding, and his body was in such a high state of desire

that he didn't feel safe going anywhere near her. Something to douse this unbearable sense of need was what was called for. 'I think I'll take a shower now and then maybe ring out for some Chinese food? That's if you eat takeaways,' he looked at her, a question in his eyes. 'Or maybe you'd prefer to cook something yourself.'

'Or maybe not!' said Fran with a grimace. 'Actually, I *love* Chinese.'

'Yeah.' He couldn't stop himself. He reached his hand forward. 'There.' A fingertip brushed against her cheek and came away caked in flour. 'You've covered yourself in cake-mix.'

The feather-light touch felt like something much more sensual than the simple removal of flour. Fran saw the darkening of his eyes, felt the prickle of her body in response to it—and the danger which hummed in the air around them. She licked her lips. 'Do you....uh...just have the one shower?'

'No,' he said huskily, silently cursing the architect who had recommended the second bathroom. Though what was he expecting—that she would take all her clothes off and offer to share with him? Oh, yes please, he thought longingly. 'My room has an en suite. Feel free to use the one on the ground floor.'

'Thanks.' Fran maintained her composed smile until she was standing safely beneath the punishing jets of the shower, praying that the force of the water beating against her skin would rid her of some of her demons. Demons which took the shape of Sam as phantom-lover—and this in spite of everything she knew about him!

Back in her room and wrapped in a huge, fluffy towel, Fran opened the wardrobe door and surveyed the few

clothes she'd brought with her. They were the normal selection she would take to a job like this, but to her dissatisfied eye they seemed lamentably few.

In the end, she put on the same camel trousers that she'd arrived in, but teamed them with a silky-looking gold shirt rather than the cream sweater. The house was well heated and she always seemed plenty warm enough whenever Sam was around!

She was just brushing her wet hair when there was a rap on the door, and when she opened it Sam was there, a printed menu in his hand, a look of query on his face.

'I'll order now, shall I—' He broke off in midsentence, and frowned. She looked...

Fran frowned back. 'What is it?'

'Your hair.'

She touched a wet strand as if she were touching a talisman. 'What's wrong with it?'

'It's loose,' he murmured, aware that his voice sounded slightly dazed. As if she were the only woman in the history of the world to have worn her hair wet and loose down her back! Yet the effect it had on her face was simply stunning—softening it, making her eyes look like bright green-gold beacons.

She deftly twisted a rope of hair between her fingers. 'I'm about to put it up.'

'No, don't.'

Fran looked at him. *'Don't?'*

'You look more relaxed that way.'

'Precisely,' she smiled repressively, then glanced down at the menu he was holding. Perhaps food would take her mind off the fact that he had left the three top buttons of his shirt undone and that the moisture from the shower was making his skin gleam like a precious metal. 'I like just about everything on the menu,' she

told him briskly. 'So you can order for me, can't you, Sam?'

If any other woman had asked that question, he would have adopted a look of jaded cynicism. It would have seemed overly cute. Too dependent. Too girly-girly. But then, any other woman would have asked him in a simpering way which usually meant that they wanted you. Fran didn't. So was that because she just didn't simper? Or because she just really didn't want him?

'I think I can just about manage that,' he said drily, thinking that a drive to the Chinese restaurant might also ease the ache in his groin.

Fran was in the sitting room when he arrived back, bearing all the different foil containers. He dipped his head as he entered the low room to find that she had lit the fire and warmed plates and brought trays in for them to eat in front of the roaring logs. She had also, he was immensely disappointed to discover, put her hair back up in a constricting topknot so that once more she looked remote and untouchable.

'Okay to eat in here?' she asked him. 'The dining room seemed a little cold, and a little formal and I thought it was best not to use it before your mother arrives.'

'In here is perfect. Did you read my mind?'

'No, I'm just feeling tired and lazy!'

'Me, too.' He had been dreading sitting facing her across a dining table with candlelight creating intimacy and making his blood sing with desire.

They ate prawns and chicken and rice and noodles, with cold wine to drink. Afterwards, Fran sat eating a fig and picking at a small bunch of white grapes, aware that he was watching her. And liking him watching her.

She knew what was happening. She was falling for

him big time. And he was about the most unsuitable candidate she could have picked, bearing in mind the circumstances which had brought her here. He had said that he wanted to prove he was a good guy at heart, and he seemed to be succeeding. With honours! Oh, hell, she thought, why did life have to be so damned complicated?

Sam drank more than he would usually have done, but then he reasoned that he would need some kind of sleeping aid tonight. He noticed that Fran was nearly matching him glass for glass, too.

'Shall I open another bottle?' he asked.

She was tempted. Then shook her head. 'Better not,' she said. 'I don't want to greet your mother with an almighty hangover.' Which was not the real reason at all. She was starting to feel woozy and pretty sure that if she had much more, then she might relax a little too much and find herself swaying in the direction of his arms!

She watched him lick a trickle of grape juice away from where it had made his lips all sticky. Just watching him eat was like a lesson in sensuality, with those long fingers pulling the succulent fruits from their stem. Popping them whole in his mouth. White teeth biting into firm, juicy flesh. How was he managing to cast this powerful spell over her?

She sat up straight and shifted her bottom back a bit. What would she be doing if she *didn't* find him the most attractive man she'd ever met? Talking! She cleared her throat, like an amateur about to make an after-dinner speech. 'So what made you decide to become a literary agent?' she asked him.

Sam gave a wry smile, recognizing immediately the reasoning behind the sudden change of tone. 'Because I love writing, I guess.'

'So why—?'

'Didn't I become a writer?' He resisted the desire to peel her a grape, and popped another in his own mouth instead. 'Well, I did. I wrote six novels—'

'*Six?*' she squeaked. 'And were they published?'

'Ouch!' He pulled a face. 'I'm used to adulation, not realism,' he told her drily. 'And yes, they were published—all six of them.'

'So what happened, did no one want to buy them?'

'Ouch again! You know how to hit a man where it hurts, don't you, Fran? Yes, some people wanted to buy them, and some even did! But not as many as I would have liked. I think I recognised that my books were *okay* rather than unputdownable! And rather than spend the rest of my life doing something at which I would only ever be mediocre, I decided to put my objective eye to good use. So I fought for authors whose work I *did* believe in. With some success,' he finished, not at all modestly.

Fran thought of the piles of manuscripts she had seen lying around his study. It would take a pretty long time to wade through all of *those*! 'It must be hard work?'

'Well, it's not like working down the mines.'

'And lonely?' she asked suddenly.

'Yeah. Pretty much.' He began to stack the empty cartons on the tray. 'But that's the kind of life I like.'

'And what about children?' she asked suddenly.

He hid his surprise. 'What about them?'

'Don't you want to have any...of your own?'

His eyes narrowed. 'Why Fran,' he asked softly. 'Is that a proposition?'

Which had the undesired effect of making her scramble to her feet. And taking her provocative body away

from where it was sending his pulses soaring, and off to bed instead.

Sam sighed.

Alone.

CHAPTER NINE

SAM'S mother arrived at three the following afternoon, accompanied by her two daughters, when the taxi carrying them roared to an abrupt halt outside the front door, sending gravel cascading everywhere.

Fran stood watching in the hall as Sam pulled open the front door, just in time to see the car execute a screeching three-point turn, and he wondered if the driver was a frustrated rally-driver, or merely had a death-wish!

A glamorous redhead wearing a floppy velvet hat was leaning out of the back window. 'Hello, Sam, darling! Aren't you going to give your baby sister a kiss?'

Sam glared at the taxi driver. 'Weren't you driving a little fast!'

'Sorry, guv,' shrugged the driver, with an expressive jerk of his head in the direction of the seat next to him.

'I told him to,' came an amused voice from the passenger seat. 'It was a condition of my giving him a tip, to wipe that furious look off your face, Sam Lockhart!'

Sam pretended to glower in through the window at his mother, and then his face broke out into the most uninhibited smile that Fran had ever seen. Standing unseen in the shadows of the hallway, she felt her heart beating erratically.

'Mother!' he reprimanded sternly. 'You're nothing but a speed freak!'

The redhead was clambering out, displaying show-stoppingly long legs. 'I actually offered to drive us my-

self instead of catching the train—stop looking so hor
rified, Sam! But they refused to insure me without me
having to practically take out a second mortgage—'

'Thank God,' breathed Sam, in a heartfelt voice.

'And just because I'm an actress, *honestly*! Why is the
world so prejudiced against actresses?'

'I used to have the same trouble myself,' said Mrs
Lockhart with an indulgent smile at her daughter. 'They
see us as flighty and undependable! Now come and help
me out of the car, Sam!'

Sam shot her a rueful expression as he gently helped
her out of the car. 'Forgive me for not offering,' he
remarked. 'But I have to tread on eggshells where you're
concerned. Once you berated me for hours for treating
you like an invalid!'

'Oh, I was years younger then!' dismissed Mrs
Lockhart airily.

'Just two as I recall,' he answered drily.

'That's absolute rubbish, Sam!'

From her hidden vantage point, Fran was able to get
a good look at Sam's family.

His mother was still—even at the age of seventy—a
remarkably striking presence. Almost as tall as Sam, her
finely-boned face was surrounded by iron-grey hair
which still fell in the mass of curls for which she had
been known in her heyday. She had all the bearing and
natural grace of an actress, and it was easy to recognize
the television star she had once been.

Madelaine and Meredith, known affectionately—'but
not *always* affectionately' as Sam had remarked ear
lier—as Maddy and Merry, were as different as chalk
and cheese.

The redhead in the floppy hat was Maddy, the actress
pin-thin and tall like her mother, wearing exquisitely em

roidered clothes of clashing colours and lots of velvet
and lace.

Merry, on the other hand, was dark like Sam, with
fierce navy eyes and a sensual mouth which smiled more
easily than her brother's did. A scientist by profession,
she was a quiet woman, who was frighteningly clever,
according to Sam.

Mrs. Lockhart was flapping one heavily-bangled hand
impatiently. 'Now just where *is* this girl?'

Sam frowned. 'Girl? What girl?'

'Maddy says you've been acting very strangely and it
must be due to a woman!'

Sam shot an acid glance in the direction of his
younger sister who gave a smug grin in response. 'Well,
Maddy—as usual, I'm afraid!—is engaging her mouth
before she uses her brain! The only woman here is Fran
Fisher, and she was hired to organize this birthday dinner
for you.'

Fran thought it might be diplomatic to slip back into
the shadows at this point.

'But Maddy also said that *you* were cooking!' said
Mrs. Lockhart, looking at her son in confusion. 'So what
will this Fran Fisher actually be doing?'

Fran reappeared at the door. 'I'll be setting the table,
pouring the drinks and doing the clearing up,' she
smiled. 'I'm Fran, by the way.'

'So Sam's playing wifey and you're playing husband?' said Maddy, looking directly at Fran with a
twitch of her wide lips. 'How very cosy!'

'Shut up, Maddy!' warned Sam. 'And Fran's actually
being too modest. She's made a birthday cake and has
been teaching me how to cook—'

'Even cosier!' gurgled Maddy gleefully.

'Shut up, Maddy!' said Meredith softly.

Sam narrowed his eyes. 'Fran, come and say hello to my mother and sisters.'

He watched with some amusement as the women all began to size one another up while they shook hands.

'Why don't I take your coats?' asked Fran. 'And you can all go in and sit by the fire while I prepare tea. Oh, and very many happy returns, Mrs. Lockhart!'

'Why, thank you, my dear!'

Soon they were all settled in the sitting room, and when Fran walked in carrying a loaded tray, she found them looking the picture of contentment. Mrs. Lockhart was sitting in the stiff-backed chair by the window, leaning forward so that Sam could place a cushion at the small of her back. Merry was reading the newspaper while pretending not to, and Maddy was stretched out like a cat in front of the fire, peeling an orange she had plucked from the fruit bowl and negligently throwing segment after segment into her wide mouth.

They all looked up as Fran put the tray down.

'Milk or lemon?' she recited. 'And there are scones, fruit cake—'

Sam was suddenly by her side. 'Sit down, Fran,' he instructed. 'I'll pour.'

'So you're playing Mummy as well as wifey, are you Sam?'

'Shut up, Maddy!'

Mrs. Lockhart accepted a cup of tea from her son and frowned at Fran. 'Aren't you the girl who arranged for a lot of Sam's ex-girlfriends to come and embarrass him at some dance or other?'

Maddy snorted with laughter, Merry merely raised her eyebrows while Fran flushed a bright and unbecoming red. Only Sam looked unabashed.

'It wasn't Fran's idea—'

She didn't want him leaping to her defence like that, particularly not when she didn't deserve it. 'But I allowed it to happen,' she said stiltedly. 'It was a joke that Rosie wanted to play on Sam—'

'Is this the same Rosie who was always writing you those letters?' quizzed Mrs. Lockhart.

Fran stared at Sam. 'What letters?'

He gave a dismissive shrug. 'I never discuss past affairs in detail. I already told you that, Fran.'

'I brought him up to be a gentleman!' said Mrs. Lockhart proudly. 'Just like his dear father!'

Fran stood up, feeling more confused by the second. She didn't need Mrs. Lockhart to tell her what she already knew. And her instincts told her that Sam was trustworthy, dependable and true. She knew that something didn't add up, but what? Had Rosie told her the whole story? Or just been selective in the telling of it? 'I'll go and make some more tea,' she said, glad to be able to escape from the curious eyes.

'Then you can show us to our bedrooms and we can go and unpack,' said Maddy, giving her brother an innocent smile. 'Are you and Fran sharing, Sam?'

'Just the cooking,' he said lightly.

In a way, it was easier having a house full of guests than being on her own with him, Fran decided. There were no loaded silences, no tense feelings as the bedrooms seemed to scream out their close proximity.

Sam came into the walk-in larder just as she was putting the finishing touches to the birthday cake. She had chosen to ice it there because it was cooler and out of the way. She didn't want to get underneath Sam's feet while he was cooking, and, to be perfectly honest, she found him too distracting to have around the kitchen!

He leaned over her shoulder to look as she piped last curl of hair with the icing nozzle.

'Heck!' he breathed admiringly. 'That's absolutel, *brilliant*!'

'I can only see the mistakes,' she said gloomily.

'Like what?'

'Well, the hair should be a bit more russet than or ange, don't you think? But that's the best mix of colou, I can manage.'

'You're a bit of a perfectionist, aren't you?' he teased

'I…' She looked up at him with reluctant pleasure He was smiling, and so was she, and their eyes ha, locked in such a shining moment that if it had bee, anyone else, in any other circumstances, then she migh have actively considered the unthinkable. That she foun, another man attractive enough to want to make love wit, him. Something she would have recoiled from, straigh after her divorce. 'Yes, I am,' she agreed evenly. 'An, speaking of which—did you put the potatoes in the over to bake?'

As a defuser of desire it was more effective than , cold shower, thought Sam, as he clenched his jaw, an, nodded. Oh, not the question itself, but the way in whicl she asked it. The world seemed to be turning in on itsel, as, for the first time in his life, Sam was discovering tha, his inbuilt sex appeal which over the years had cause, him more trouble than not, was simply not working. An, ironically, that made his hunger all the sharper.

'Yes,' he retorted. 'And before you ask—the casserol, is bubbling, the vegetables are prepared. The appetize, is ready and I've just taken the dessert out of the refrig erator! Anything else you'd like to know?'

'That's very good, Sam,' she said demurely. 'Ho,

bout the cheese? That needs to sit at room temperature,
o—'

'It is!' he snarled.

Fran gave him a thoughtful look. Had everything in
is charmed life always gone exactly the way he wanted
, she wondered? 'Do you think your sister likes me?'
he asked suddenly.

'Which one?'

'Maddy, of course—'

'Why?'

Fran shrugged. 'Well, she keeps making comments
hich are designed to embarrass me.'

'You've only blushed once!'

'So does she?'

'What?'

'Like me?'

Sam sighed. 'I expect so. Maddy's an actress. She
bserves human behaviour, and sometimes the best way
f doing that is to provoke a reaction—that's all she's
p to.'

'Well, I wish she wouldn't.'

He gave her a considering look. 'Want me to have a
ord with her?'

Fran shook her head. 'Good grief, no! I don't want to
e typecast as some kind of wimp who needs a man to
peak up for me!' She glanced down at her watch and
rimaced. 'And just look at the time! Is the shower free
et, do you know?'

He didn't miss a beat. 'Merry's in there at the moment
think,' he said steadily. 'But you're very welcome to
se mine.'

'How very kind of you.' Fran kept her face neutral.
But I think I'll wait.'

He didn't press it. He might just be tempted to offer

to scrub her back for her. Not, he decided, with an al
most masochistic kind of pleasure, that he thought for
moment she would do anything other than look at hir
with that cool, school-mistressy air of hers.

And decline.

'She shouldn't be long.'

'Thanks.'

Fran showered and dressed in record time, and wa
just piling her hair on top of her head, when there wa
a tap on the door. 'Come in,' she said rather inaudibly
since she had two hairpins in the side of her mouth.

It was Maddy, dressed entirely in green suede. An
somehow Fran wasn't surprised to see her.

'Sit down,' she gestured indistinctly.

'Thanks,' said Maddy, and raking her long finger
through the whorls of her glossy red hair, she plonke
herself down on the bed.

Fran speared the last two pins into her hair and turne
round. 'Yes, Maddy?' she said pleasantly.

'Do you always wear your hair up?' asked Maddy.

Fran smiled.

'What's so funny?'

'Just that your brother asked me exactly the sam
question. Yes, I do.'

'Why?'

'Because it's neat, and tidy. And often I'm workin
with food, and clients don't like to see someone wit
their hair all falling into the crème caramel!'

'And because it's controlled?' hazarded Maddy. 'An
that's the image you like to project of yourself?'

Fran felt slightly irritated at this instant character as
sessment from someone who barely knew her, but sh
didn't show it. And mainly because she suspected tha
like her brother before her, Maddy had hit on a funda

mental truth about her character. 'Perhaps it is,' she agreed, and looked at her expectantly. 'I'm due in the kitchen about ten minutes ago, so you'd better say what it is you want to say.'

'It's about Sam, actually.'

'I rather thought it might be.'

'Are you…'

Maddy paused delicately, but Fran was damned if she was going to help her out. If you wanted to be audacious with someone you had barely met, then you shouldn't expect favours!

'Am I what?' she asked.

'Are you having a relationship with my brother?'

'No, I'm not.'

'But you'd like to?'

Fran sighed. 'Some people might find your line of questioning intrusive, Maddy—for all that he's your brother. Is there a reason for it?'

Maddy fingered the patchwork coverlet on the bed. 'I just don't want to see him get hurt.'

Fran's first reaction was to laugh aloud. But she didn't. 'Sam's a big boy now,' she said, almost gently. 'Who can take care of himself.'

Maddy nodded. 'I'm not talking about that woman Rosie—'

'Before you say anything else I'd better tell you that she's my friend,' warned Fran.

Maddy shrugged. 'Maybe she is. Anyway, she's got nothing to do with it.'

Resisting the urge to mention the time again, Fran sat down on the chair next to the dressing table and sat facing Maddy. 'What are you trying to say?'

'Just that Sam was hurt once. Badly. And I think it's made him wary of women ever since—'

'We've all been hurt, Maddy,' Fran pointed out. 'I've been through a divorce myself.'

Maddy shook her head. 'At least you went through the marriage bit and all the passion that went with it. Okay—so if it burnt itself out, it burnt itself out. Sam never got that far.' She bit her lip. 'He was engaged...didn't you know?'

Fran felt as though a chasm was yawning open at her feet. And she felt like someone forced to look down into it. Someone who was terrified of heights... 'No,' she whispered. 'No, I didn't know that. What happened?'

'She *died*!' Maddy looked up then, defiant tears burning bright in her eyes. 'We all loved her, and then she died. Sam nursed her almost to the end. She was lovely. Absolutely lovely. Accomplished. Perfect for Sam. Even when she was ill she used to sew things, embroider things. She gave them all to Sam.' She pointed to the sunflower tapestry which hung over the bed. 'She made that.'

'It's beautiful.' Fran remembered the cushion she had picked up on her very first visit here. The bruised look of pain in his eyes. So *that* was why he lived this lonely, bookish life—because he had never got over the woman who had died. It was like being given a piece of something corrosive to eat just after a huge meal, but Fran kept her face carefully composed. 'I've seen other things that she's done,' she said quietly, feeling glad she had sat down. She suspected her knees might have buckled if she had stayed standing, and yet the information distressed her far more than it had any right to. 'Why are you telling me all this, Maddy?'

'Because he likes you—'

'I don't think so!'

'Yes, he does. I can see it in his eyes! He's different

with you. There's something about the way he looks at you.'

Fran gave a smile which was almost wistful. 'Believe me when I tell you that you're mistaking affection for good old-fashioned lust. I think he finds me sexually attractive, and I think that what adds to the attraction is the fact that I'm not all over him like a rash. Which is what he's used to.'

'He can't help the effect that *he* has on women! It isn't contrived, you know, it's inbuilt. And he doesn't deserve what that woman—your friend—has been saying about him!' said Maddy bitterly. 'It makes him out to be something he's not!'

'I don't know about that. All I do know are that the facts about Rosie and Sam are indisputable—Sam admitted that himself,' said Fran steadily. 'But what I let happen at the ball shouldn't have happened. I can see that now. It started out as a simple prank—so I thought—and then it just gathered momentum, like a rain running down the side of a mountain. But people will forget, they always do. And Sam will forget, too.'

'Yes, he will. So I can't understand why you're still here,' said Maddy.

And neither, to be perfectly honest, could Fran. The story about showing her that he was a good guy at heart didn't quite ring true. I mean, why *bother*, she thought? Surely hers was the last opinion he valued.

'After the Valentine ball, I owed him,' she told Maddy. 'It's a simple repayment of a debt, that's all.'

But Fran found that she had to pay attention not to ogle Sam as she and Maddy went along to join the others in the sitting room. But while she saw him in a new light, learning about his fiancée made her feel even more confused. Maybe that was the reason he was considered

cold and indifferent—because, at heart—he *was* cold and indifferent. And the reason for that could be that the only woman he had ever loved had been cruelly and prematurely taken away from him. Some people never got over something like that.

But she put it out of her mind in order to concentrate on the birthday dinner. They started with champagne when they not only toasted Helen, but Sam's late father and Fran felt her eyes growing stupidly bright as she sipped from the crystal flute Sam had filled for her.

'What's the matter, dear?' asked Mrs. Lockhart softly who had noticed.

Sam had also noticed. 'I think Fran's father died last year,' he said, meeting her eyes. 'This reminds her, that's all.'

Fran was touched that he had remembered, and grateful when he created a diversion by opening another bottle of champagne which had been made in the year of his mother's birth.

He also insisted that she sit down and join them for the meal.

'Oh, Sam, I *can't*!'

'Oh, Fran, you *can*!'

'It's supposed to be a family occasion—'

'It's also supposed to be a celebration! At least having you there will stop the evening degenerating into a predictable cycle of sibling arguments! And besides, what else are you supposed to do—sit out in the scullery, like Cinderella?'

'But you haven't got a scullery!'

'Well, then, that decides it! You *must* sit with us.'

She giggled. Had the champagne made her feel this light-hearted?

The meal went perfectly, except for the carrots being

very slightly underdone, but as Fran pointed out these days it was considered trendy to serve them almost raw!

The pièce de résistance was the birthday cake itself, and Helen Lockhart got quite teary-eyed when Sam carried it through, this time, on Fran's insistence.

'But it looks just *like* me!' cried Mrs. Lockhart, in delight, and then shrugged. 'Or rather, me as I *used* to look.'

'You still look pretty good to me!' said Sam gallantly and they all clinked their glasses together.

It was midnight when Helen Lockhart and her daughters went off to bed, leaving Sam to help Fran to clear away. When she straightened up from stacking the dishwasher, it was to find him standing on the other side of the kitchen, staring at her intently.

'You're very quiet,' he remarked.

'It's been a long day.' But she had been thinking about the fiancée who had died. The woman who had lovingly embroidered the cushion and the sunflowers. It was a harsh thing to have happened to him. What would he say if she asked him about it?

He nodded. 'A very long day,' he echoed, still watching her, almost obsessively. There was something different about her tonight. Some extra dimension to her. Something in her eyes he had not seen there before. A strand of hair had escaped from the tight topknot, and had floated down to dangle around the long, pure line of her neck, destroying the ordered symmetry of her hair. He longed to reach out and stroke it away. 'Go to bed, Fran,' he told her softly. 'I'll finish up in here.'

She looked up at him, unable to hold back any longer. 'Why didn't you tell me that you had a fiancée?'

He stilled. 'Who told you about my fiancée?' he asked eventually.

'That doesn't answer my question.'

'Maddy, I suppose?'

'Does it matter who told me?'

'Very loyal of you, Fran,' he observed wryly. 'I suppose it doesn't, no.'

'You never talk about it?'

'No, not really. I don't see the point most of the time.'

'Too painful?'

He nodded. 'Something like that.' But he saw in her eyes something more than the snooping kind of curiosity, which was what he normally encountered. He sighed. 'The pain has mostly gone now—the not telling bit is habit more than anything.'

'I wasn't planning on asking you any more questions—'

'I know you weren't. And that's probably why I'm talking to you about it.' He flicked her an astute look. 'Though maybe you don't want to hear?'

On a slightly-deranged emotional level, no, she most definitely *didn't* want to hear. But the wise and mature woman she wanted to be, knew that she *had* to hear. 'Yes, of course I do.' Fran dried her hands on a tea-towel and waited while he finished putting knives in one of the drawers.

'We first met at university when I was in my final year and Megan in her first. So long ago now,' he murmured as he looked back on the galloping years with a kind of disbelief. 'We had a brief fling at my graduation party, and then I left for London and I didn't see her for a long time after that.'

Fran nodded as she recognized the bond of young, shared passion. Powerful stuff.

'Megan came to my office to see me because she'd written a book, and knew that I was working for Gordon-

Browne. She brought the manuscript across to me, and I promised that I'd have a look at it for her.'

'And was it any good?'

Sam's laugh was tinged with sadness. 'The book was rubbish,' he said brutally. 'And when I told her so, she had the most terrible tantrum I'd ever seen. And after that, she decided to fall in love with me.'

'You make it sound like a clinical decision—'

'Maybe it was.' He shrugged.

'And one that you had no part in,' observed Fran, in surprise.

'Sometimes it *is* a bit like that, don't you agree?'

'Maybe,' said Fran thoughtfully, remembering how at first Sholto had felt secure in the stability she had provided for him. The same stability which had made him feel caged once passion had burnt itself out.

'I think my refusal to compromise my standards, by taking Megan's work on simply because I knew her, really appealed to her. She saw me as strong and unbendable.'

'And aren't you?'

He gave the glimmer of a smile. 'Not always, no. But we always give our lovers the qualities we want them to have.'

'Maybe we do,' she said thoughtfully.

'Didn't you do that with Sholto?'

'I'm not sure. What attracted me to Sholto was that he *needed* me. He was so wild, so artistic, so gorgeous, and yet he was attracted to mousy old me.'

'I think you're putting yourself down unnecessarily,' he said drily.

'Maybe I am,' she agreed. 'He was also the kind of person who was ruled by his emotions rather than common sense.'

'The opposite to you, in fact?' he hazarded.

'In a way, yes, I suppose he was. And all the very things which first attracted me to him and him to me— were ultimately the things which drove us apart.'

'I thought it was his infidelity which did that?'

Fran nodded. 'But he was only able to be successful with women *because* he was so sensual and so in touch with his emotions.'

Sam shook his head. 'I don't rate unfaithfulness as being successful with women, quite the opposite, I'd say. And if he was so in touch with his feelings, then why the hell didn't he consider that he was hurting *yours*?'

Fran smiled at the passionate defence, and thought that he had very cleverly turned the conversation away from him. And Megan.

'So when did Megan get ill?'

Sam grimaced. 'We'd been together about six months, just got engaged, when she started feeling tired all the time. At first, we thought that she might be pregnant.' He paused as his mind took him back. The initial stunned excitement coupled with sheer panic that there might be a baby on the way. 'But she wasn't. I nagged her to see the doctor, and when eventually she did it was like one of those bad dreams you pray you're going to wake up from.' He paused again, but this time his face looked ravaged. 'She was twenty-four years old and they told her that she had less than a year to live.'

Unnoticed, Fran poured them both a brandy from a bottle which had been used to flambé the bananas, and handed him a glass.

He drained the drink in one swallow, without seeming to notice that he had done so. 'She had test after test. Drug after drug. But every time we tried a new treatment, it dragged her down more and more. In the end,

she refused everything except painkillers, she said that acceptance was an easier thing to live with, than false hope.'

'She sounds like a remarkable woman,' said Fran quietly.

He looked at her for a long moment. 'Yes. She was. Thank you.'

'For what?' she asked, surprised.

For being generous to a woman who had me when I think you want me for yourself, he nearly said. But he didn't. That might scare her away. And besides, he wasn't sure just how much she wanted him.

'For making my mother's birthday so successful. For being such a good listener. Shall I go on?'

'Oh, please *do*!' she said, laughing. 'You're doing wonders for my ego!'

While she was doing precisely nothing for his abnormally high levels of frustration! 'I don't know why I've unburdened my soul like this,' he confessed.

Fran smiled. 'Oh, that's easy. Because you needed to,' she said simply. 'You live in a world of fantasy, reading your manuscripts in your beautiful, isolated house. But you've got to let reality in sometimes, Sam. However harsh it may be.'

Much more of this level of understanding, and he would be straddling her over the kitchen chair! 'Just go to bed, Fran, honey,' he growled. 'Before I retract my offer of finishing the clearing up!'

She knew from the look on his eyes that to argue would be futile. She also knew that if he tried to kiss her, she would not protest.

But there was no kiss, and no protest and she was not the kind of woman to make the first move—even if he was the kind of man who wanted her to. Her bed awaited

her, chaste and undisturbed. She would spend eight hours in it alone, as she had done last night. And tomorrow she would go home.

She thought that the silence which stretched out between the two of them seemed like a bridge—the kind made of wooden slats which swayed precariously whenever the wind blew.

A bit like life, really.

'I'll say good-night then, Sam.'

He smiled. 'Good night, honey.'

CHAPTER TEN

UNSURPRISINGLY, Fran couldn't sleep, and after a while she gave up trying, climbing out of bed and wandering over to the window to see what the stars were doing. She drew back the curtains and looked out.

Outside, the moon looked like a giant satellite dish in the sky, milk-bright and gleaming. How dark the trees appeared against that ghostly light, she thought. How flat and silent the landscape. She leaned her hands on the window ledge, and wondered what Sam was doing.

Sam had been unable to sleep and was genuinely thirsty. At least that's what he kept telling himself. So naturally he needed to go downstairs to make himself a drink. He moved as silently as a shadow only because he didn't wish to wake his elderly mother. Or his two sisters. All of whom needed their sleep.

And the only reason he walked down the passageway which lay *away* from the kitchen was because he thought he heard a noise. He definitely heard a noise. A soft, swishing noise like the sound of a curtain being gently pulled. And how could he be called any kind of man unless he investigated noises coming from the direction of Fran's room?

But when he crept silently and barefooted along the polished boards to stand outside the partially open door, it was to find that his heart and his stomach seemed to have fused somewhere in the region of his mouth.

It was like one of those films they hardly ever made any more, when you just forgot everything—*every-*

151

thing—except the person standing right in front of you who had invaded every single one of your senses.

She was wearing a long, pale sort of nightgown, worn high to the neck, and long to the ground. The sleeves were long, too, and gathered at the wrists, and the tip of the gown brushed the floor. If the window had been open, the wind would have blown the garment away from her in a diaphanous cloud, so that she would have resembled the figurehead of a ship, looking out to sea.

But it was her hair which captured his imagination most. Loose. Free. Spilling down her back like warm honey. And he knew that it was loose for the rest of the night. His breath caught in a small, choking sound.

She heard him, and turned, too dreamy with the sight of him to act like she wasn't used to dark, ruffled men appearing at her door, wearing nothing but a pair of jeans. Her heart began to plummet out of control, but this sense of feeling that this was somehow *meant* to happen, made her voice sound oddly calm.

'Hello, Sam,' she said.

He shook his head, fruitlessly trying to break the spell of her enchantment. 'Surprised to see me?'

Her eyes were slitted. 'No.'

He smiled at her lack of pretence. 'Can't you sleep?'

'No.'

'Me neither.' His eyes gathered her in. 'I was right about the nightdress.'

She looked down at the ghostly gown. 'Yes, you were.'

They stood staring at each other across the room, like two people seeing each other for the first time.

Sam felt the blood which thundered inside his head. 'Fran—'

She opened her eyes a little wider. If only her limbs idn't feel so heavy, her body so lethargic. 'What is it?'

He meant to say, 'You look beautiful,' but it came ut as, 'I want to kiss you.'

It was so heartstoppingly simple and direct that the words made her shiver. She meant to say, 'Sam, maybe his isn't such a good idea'—but it came out as, 'I'm ot stopping you.'

He laughed then, but with pleasure, not triumph, push-ng the door quietly shut behind him as he began to walk owards her, to cup her face between his hands. 'You aven't asked me why I'm here,' he whispered provoc-tively.

'I thought you wanted to kiss me.'

'Yes. I do.' He paused deliberately. 'Among many ther things.'

In the half light she blushed. 'Are you trying to shock ne now?'

'No. I'm giving you the opportunity to kick me out.'

'And if I don't?'

'Then I'm going to spend the rest of the night making ove to you, honey.'

Her eyes were like saucers, dark with question. 'But vhat about the others?'

He stiffened and scowled. He had thought she had vorked through all that stuff about Rosie and the vul-ures. 'What others?' he growled.

'Your mother.' She could feel his breath warm on her ips. 'And sisters.'

'I'm not planning to make a noise,' he whispered. Are you?'

'No. *Oh!*' But it wasn't easy. Not easy at all. Not vhen he had started kissing her like that and running his ands down the sides of her nightgown, so that the fabric

clung to her body like skin. She wanted to gasp alou
with sheer pleasure, because where his hands led, hi
mouth followed, lips warm and soft and seeking as the
suckled her breast through the filmy material.

'Is that good?' he smiled against the damp fabric.

'Don't ask questions to which you already know th
answers!'

He tightened his arms around her waist and she shiv
ered involuntarily, because oh, she had missed the fee
of a man's arms around her like this.

He could hear the distracted quickening of he
breathing and made himself stop kissing her, smoothin
her hair down as he tenderly kissed the tip of her nose
and then each cheek. 'Much more of this and I'm goin
to push you up against the wall and do it right there
honey,' he groaned.

Fran was so turned on she could barely speak. 'So?

He laughed with anticipation, but shook his head. 'N
way! Not the first time. Bed,' he said firmly.

'Bed,' she echoed, her whispered word fierce wit
need. Yet for all her bravado, she felt terribly shy as sh
let him lead her to the tiny bed, and he gave an exag
gerated sound of horror as he stared down at it.

'Just a touch on the small size,' he observed ruefully
'Maybe we should creep upstairs and find somewher
more comfortable.'

'Like where?'

'Well, the other bedrooms are all taken.' There was
pause. 'That just leaves mine.'

Fran swallowed with nerves. She had never seen in
side his bedroom, and just the thought of it made he
wonder how many women had clambered willingly be
tween the sheets with him. She wondered if Rosie..

'No,' she swallowed, shaking her head so that she could shake the thoughts away. 'We might wake them.'

He saw the dark, scared look on her face, felt her tense beneath the arm he was holding her with and knew immediately what she was thinking. He turned her towards him and put both his hands on her shoulders.

'Now listen to me, Fran,' he said gently. 'And believe me when I tell you that there are no ghosts to lay in this house of mine. None. And I won't be any more specific than that. Do you understand what I'm saying to you? This is my sanctuary and my haven—'

She stared up at him, not quite believing what she thought he was telling her, hesitating over her words of reply. 'You're saying I'm the first woman you've ever brought here?'

'No, not the first. The only woman,' he corrected.

It was both a compliment and a declaration, so what jinx made her say, 'Except for Megan, of course.'

He shook his head. 'No, Megan never came here. I bought the house just after she—' He hesitated, the word still sounded faintly obscene on his lips. 'Died.'

There was a pause. Facts, however painful, could not just be brushed aside because you didn't want to face them. 'How long ago was that?'

'Nearly five years.'

'Oh, Sam,' Fran reached her hand up and gently grazed her finger along the faint stubble of his chin. 'Sam!'

It hit him hard—that tender touch, and this overwhelming need to possess her made him feel as vulnerable as a kitten. 'But Fran—' He forced himself to say the words which could deny him everything he wanted from her, and more.... 'If the thought of other women is always going to be there like a barrier between us,

then maybe it's best if I just go now. It's crazy to start something if it's only going to be ruined by the past.'

She thought of him leaving her now, like this, and knew it was a complete non-starter.

Because Sam seemed fastidious where sex was concerned. She believed that, deep in her heart, despite what Rosie had said. And the better she knew him, the more she grew to know his fundamental decency. It all boiled down to whether she was going to let the fact that he'd had a brief fling with her friend affect her whole life? She shook her head. 'No. You don't have to go anywhere, Sam.'

He looked deep into her eyes. 'No ghosts to come between us, then?'

She wound her arms around his neck shyly. 'None.'

He groaned with pleasure as he drew her down onto the bed, peeling the nightgown up over her body as though he were slowly removing the skin of some very exotic fruit. 'Shall we take this off?'

'I think we'd better,' she nodded, holding her arms up like a child being stripped out of wet clothes.

Sam, consumed by the urgent need to possess her, was also aware of an air of almost primitive hunger. It all seemed new, uncharted. As though he had never done this before.

He unzipped his jeans almost ruefully when he saw just how aroused he was. Saw her looking at him with a mixture of awe and excitement.

'You know, this first time may not last long,' he confessed, as he lowered his head to flick a pink tongue wetly over her nipple.

Fran gasped and closed her eyes as he began to nudge against her, not realizing that pleasure could be *this*

acute. 'Oh, I don't know,' she purred. 'One way or another, it's going to last all night.'

When Fran woke up in the morning he had gone. She lay naked and aching beneath the duvet for a moment while fractured memories of the night came flickering back into her mind, one by one.

They'd made love most of the night. She had a whole marriage to compare it with, yet it had been the best night of her life. So how guilty did *that* make her feel?

She looked for her nightgown which was lying in a heap on the carpet, and then at the clock. She sat bolt upright.

Ten o'clock!

And she was supposed to be cooking breakfast for Sam's mother and his two sisters before they caught the train home! She jumped out of bed, consoling herself with the thought that at least she had made the kedgeree the day before.

She risked a glance in the mirror and then wished she hadn't. Her rosy cheeks and sparkling eyes rather gave the game away. Well, she would just have to brazen it out. And that meant throwing her clothes on and acting like nothing had happened.

There was a sink in her room, and she made the best use of it that she could. The old-fashioned strip wash made her shiver, but she welcomed it. The goose-bumps brought her crashing back down to earth, and that was the place she badly needed to be if she wasn't going to give the game away to his mother, or his sisters.

She slipped into a pair of cream trousers and a simple cream sweater and walked barefooted towards the kitchen, to see if she could help.

Sam was standing by the Aga, frying bacon. Merry

was buttering bread and reading the newspaper, while Maddy was busy chopping a melon and adding it to a rainbow pile of fruit already heaped in a glass dish.

They all looked up as she came into the room, and she could hardly look Sam in the eye, she felt so self-conscious and so *obvious*!

'Good morning, Fran,' he said, with an innocent, sunny smile. 'Sleep well, did you?'

She might have glared if that wouldn't have given the game away. 'I was—er—a little bit restless,' she replied truthfully, feeling the world's worst fraud as she did so.

'I expect that's why you overslept!' observed Maddy, looking up from a decapitated kiwi fruit with a knowing smile. 'And can I just say that your hair looks much better all loose around your shoulders like that. Sam said you always wore it scraped up on top of your head.'

'Did he?' asked Fran, thinking that fantastic sex must have addled her brain completely—she *always* put her hair up!

'He certainly did!'

Now when had he said that, Fran wondered? And how on earth had the subject of her hair arisen during a conversation with his sister?

'Coffee?' asked Sam, giving her a crooked smile and a look in his eyes which said that he wished they could be alone.

'Please.' But Fran felt as though she had no right to be there. Redundant. The three of them looked like a unit, all busy working in harmony together. While she had been employed to cook the breakfast and had overslept like an adolescent! 'Don't worry, Sam, I'll get it.' She poured herself a large mugful. 'Where's your mother?'

'She'll be down in a minute,' he said, smiling.

'She overslept.' Maddy stared at her unblinkingly. Just like you.'

'Oh,' Fran swallowed nervously, wondering if she could get away with offering to walk to the village shop to buy milk. Anything to get away from this awful feeling of having been caught up to no good. 'Can I do anything to help?'

'What did you have in mind?' Sam shot her an amused look and Fran quickly discovered that it was easy to feel like a guilty teenager, even though you were a woman of almost twenty-seven!

And Sam wasn't exactly helping matters, she thought furiously! 'How about the rest of the breakfast,' she queried coolly. 'After all, I'm supposed to be the one doing the cooking!'

Merry looked up from the newspaper. 'Stop embarrassing the poor girl, Sam,' she said mildly. 'And concentrate on the bacon, instead—it's burning! Surprised you didn't notice, but I guess your mind was on other things, huh?'

He gave a yelp as he whipped the frying-pan away from the heat and Fran began to gather jams and marmalades and sauces and took them into the dining room, glad to get out of the room.

Breakfast was eventually served. Fran found the prospect of food curiously unattractive and Helen Lockhart yawned throughout the meal.

'Are you okay?' Sam asked his mother.

'I'm fine, Sam, *do* stop fussing! I'm not used to rich food and fine wines and very late nights, that's all.' She peered closely at him. 'Though, quite frankly, you don't look as though you've slept very much yourself!'

'No, you don't,' murmured Maddy mischievously. 'Why's that, Sam?'

'Oh, *do* shut up, Maddy,' he said indulgently, but h
was looking so pleased with himself that Fran shot hir
a warning look across the table, terrified that he migh
announce to his mother and sisters the exact reason fo
his lack of sleep!

'So what are your plans?' he asked his mother instea
and held Fran's glare with an I-can't-wait-to-be-on-my
own-with-you stare of his own.

'Well, I'm having dinner in London tonight wit
Maddy's new man,' said Mrs. Lockhart.

'A new man. Hmmm, you've kept that very quie
Madelaine Lockhart!' observed Sam. 'Is it serious?'

Maddy sighed and pushed away her half-eaten bow
of fruit. 'Yes,' she said, in a mock-tragic voice. 'I'r
afraid that it is.'

'Don't tell me,' commented Sam, with a cynicis
born of familiarity with his sister's chequered love lif
'It's another actor? Who has beautiful cheekbones, bu
no money? And bags of talent, just can't get a job?'

'No, that's just the trouble! He's not,' sighed Madd
again. 'He's…' she bit her lip before announcing mourr
fully, '…an investment banker!'

'A *banker*!'

Fran thought that Sam couldn't have sounded mo
astonished if his baby sister had suddenly announced sh
was marrying an alien who had just landed from Mars

Mrs. Lockhart was laughing now. 'I think it's an ex
quisite irony that my free-spirited and artistic daughte
who has spent most of her adult life talking about finan
cial inequality on the planet, should fall in love with
man I am reliably informed could pay off most of th
national debt!'

'So you're…er…leaving soon?' asked Sam.

'Why, yes, darling, we are,' said Maddy, determine

to get her own back. 'But just to be diplomatic, you could *try* wiping that great big grin off your face! Anyone would think you were *glad* to get rid of us!'

Fran rose hurriedly to her feet. 'Er...more tea, anyone?'

'I'd love some,' Mrs. Lockhart said, smiling.

Fran escaped into the kitchen and put the kettle on, and wasn't at all surprised when Sam came into the kitchen minutes later, with a very satisfied expression plastered to his face. He put his arms around her waist and then bent his head to kiss her softly on the lips.

'Hello, beautiful,' he smiled. 'I didn't get the chance to say that to you this morning, did I? In fact, I didn't get the chance to say *anything* to you this morning! Shall we start all over again?' And he kissed her again.

She allowed herself to sink into the kiss for precisely three seconds, then snatched her head away. 'No, don't,' she whispered. 'Someone might come in and see us.'

'Well, we're not exactly committing a major felony, are we?' he teased. 'We're just two consenting adults doing and enjoying what comes naturally.'

Which was not the most romantic way in the world he could have described it, Fran thought rather disappointedly. 'I just don't want them to guess that we—'

'I think we may be a little late for that, honey,' he interrupted ruefully.

'Why, have they actually *said* something?'

'Nope.'

'Well, neither did we, so—'

'We didn't need to say anything.' He tilted her chin with a finger and looked down at her thoughtfully. 'The chemistry between us was obvious enough, and you'd have to be lacking in any kind of intuition not to have

noticed it crackling around the breakfast table like electricity—'

'Which leaves them to draw only one conclusion!' Fran groaned.

'Which is?'

'That we spent the night together!'

He mimicked her wide-eyed look of horror. 'Oh, my goodness!'

'Sam, I'm serious!'

'And so am I, honey. So am I.' The chin-tilting finger became a chin-stroking finger. 'What we've done is nothing to be ashamed of, is it?'

'But won't your mother think—'

'My mother has spent most of her life as an actress—there isn't a lot she hasn't seen or heard of, you know. I'm thirty-two and you're what—'

'Nearly twenty-seven,' she answered, miserable that he didn't know. And that he should ask her a question like that at a time like this.

'Well, then. Of *course* nobody in their right mind would be shocked or surprised to learn that we're two sexually active—'

'Sam!' snapped Fran, furious at the unromantic way he was describing what she had considered the most perfect night of her life. 'Please don't say any more!'

He frowned. Usually he was good with words—brilliant with words, even. He had to soothe neurotic authors daily and spent hours bargaining with steely contract managers at publishing houses on behalf of his clients.

So why was he coming out with crass lines that even the most insensitive person would reject under the circumstances? Last night they had made love and today they badly needed to talk. He gave her chin a last, lingering touch and decided that this could wait until every-

one had gone. Until they had the house to themselves and weren't hampered by the prospect of an audience bursting in whenever they were trying to have a private conversation!

'I have to take them all to the station,' he told her softly. 'And then we'll have the place to ourselves. How about that?'

Fran nodded.

'Hey,' he said softly, but at that moment there was a clattering sound coming from the direction of the dining room and she quickly moved away from him.

'Oh, look—the kettle's boiling!' she said brightly.

Fran was glad to have the breakfast things to clear away—it gave her something to do while Mrs. Lockhart and her daughters were preparing to leave. And whatever Sam said the situation certainly *felt* delicate. His mother might be the most unshockable, liberated and tolerant septuagenarian on the planet but it didn't alter the fact that Fran didn't feel right about openly cavorting with her son.

Sam came into the kitchen just as she was finishing loading the dishwasher and resisted the urge to cup his palms around those delicious, high buttocks. He cleared his throat instead. 'We're going, Fran.'

'I'll come and say goodbye.'

Mrs. Lockhart kissed her on both cheeks. 'I hope we see you again, Fran,' she smiled.

Maddy, who was sporting yellow ribbons in among the russet curls, gave Fran a questioning look, full of mischief. 'I rather think we will, don't you?'

'Well, if ever you need an event planned, I'd be happy to organise it for you.' Fran returned the cheeky look

with a smile. 'Like a wedding or engagement party, for instance?'

Maddy went pink. 'We'll see.'

'Bye,' said Merry, giving Fran a quick, unexpected and very welcome hug. 'Look after my big brother for me.'

'He doesn't need any looking after,' answered Fran truthfully.

'Nonsense!' Mrs. Lockhart shook her head vehemently. 'All men need looking after!'

'Does the man in question get any say in all this?' asked Sam, with a grin. 'Because I have to say that I'm firmly on the side of my mother on this one!' He picked up his car keys from the hall table. 'Bye, Fran,' he said softly, his eyes luminous with promise. 'See you soon.'

'Bye,' she whispered back.

Fran stood on the doorway waving them off, and wondered just what would happen when Sam came home. Well, she had a pretty good idea of what might happen in the short-term, and she felt the slow unfurling of excitement as her mind painted erotic pictures inside her head.

But where did they go from here as a couple? He had made it clear that he wasn't promiscuous, but it would be wrong to read too much into *that*. And just because he had taken her to bed didn't mean that he was about to start proposing they move in together. Did it?

She calculated that it would take fifteen minutes to reach the station, and Sam would wait until he had seen them safely boarded on the train. Which probably left her with enough time for the bath she hadn't had time for this morning....

She was just unpacking bubble bath from her bag when there was a sudden loud ringing on the doorbell,

and Fran looked with surprise at her watch. Surely that couldn't be Sam back already? No, impossible. And anyway, Sam had a key.

She opened the door without using the peep-hole and was slightly startled to see an unfamiliar broad-shouldered figure standing on the step, his dark-featured face scowling and angry.

'Don't you women *ever* use a peep-hole for security reasons?' he stormed.

With the sound of the musical Irish voice came recognition. 'Cormack!' cried Fran delightedly. 'Cormack Casey—the world-famous Irish screenwriter—as I live and breathe! What on earth are you doing here at this time in the morning?'

Cormack looked strained, Fran thought, but then the last time she had seen him had been at his son's baptism, which she had arranged, when he hadn't appeared to have had a care in the world.

'Can I come in?' he asked.

'Of course you can come in! I'll even make you some coffee, if you're lucky! Or breakfast. Have you eaten?'

But Cormack shook his head. 'Not now. I need to talk to Sam. Is he here?'

'No, but he won't be long. He's taken his mother and sisters to the station. He should be back in, say, half an hour.'

The lines of tension round the Irishman's mouth seemed to ease. 'Helen and the girls have been staying here?'

'Just for the one night.'

He looked watchful again. 'And how long have you been here, Fran?'

Fran frowned. Something wasn't right. 'Just the two nights. Cormack, is something the matter?'

He was one of the most decisive men she had ever met and yet now his face seemed to be cast in an agony of uncertainty. 'I hope not,' he said obscurely.

And suddenly Fran was fed up with feeling as though a play was taking place, only none of the action seemed to involve her!

'Cormack,' she demanded. 'Do you mind telling me exactly why you're here? And please don't say that you're just passing, because this isn't the kind of place that *anyone* passes.' Let alone a man for whom fame was the natural consequence of his success as a Hollywood screenwriter.

'I'm about to write a novel,' he told her gruffly. 'Sam has been on at me to do it for years. I can't keep putting it off. I've decided to write it now and I want to discuss it with Sam first.'

There was something about the way he was stubbornly refusing to meet her eyes. Something about the uncomfortable set of his shoulders. For a fundamentally truthful man, it must have been very difficult for him to try and lie to protect his friend, thought Fran.

'That may be so. But that isn't why you're here, is it?' she questioned insistently.

Their eyes met.

'No,' he said at last.

'I think we'd better go and sit down, don't you?'

He followed her into the sitting room, shaking his head with the air of someone who had a heavy burden resting on his broad shoulders. 'Triss told me not to come,' he sighed heavily.

'Well, you clearly ignored your wife's advice,' said Triss sternly. 'And now you're here you'd better start explaining.'

He narrowed his eyes at her, as if trying to read her mind. 'How *is* Sam?'

If she hadn't spent most of the night with Sam exploring her body both inside and out then she might have been able to answer the question without blushing as deeply as she could ever remember.

'Oh, *hell*!' snarled Cormack, before she had even had a chance to answer. 'Hell!'

Fran stared at him in pink-cheeked confusion. 'Cormack? What on earth is the matter?'

'Time is,' he shrugged. 'I'm too late, I guess. You've already—'

She frowned as he bit his lip and seemed to change his mind about what he was going to say. 'Already what?'

'It doesn't matter.'

'Oh, I think it does—certainly to me. So what was it, Cormack? You know you're going to have to tell me.'

He ground the words out with difficulty. 'Have you...slept with him?'

She was too shocked to be offended by the question. 'I think you'd better explain yourself,' she said quietly.

He shook his head. 'Just forget I ever asked.'

But something in the almost *defeated* slump of his shoulders both alarmed and unsettled her. And made her determined to get to the bottom of what was making Cormack look so uncharacteristically troubled. 'I can't do that. Not now. You know I can't. You've opened up a can of worms, we can't just close it again.'

'Let's wait for Sam.'

'No, let's not.' She gazed at him steadily. 'I'm waiting, Cormack.'

'Yeah.' He shrugged, and tried to play it down. 'I was just a little bit worried about you, that's all—'

She narrowed her eyes suspiciously. 'You came all the way here from Ireland because you were worried about me—'

'No. I had business in London as well.'

'So would you mind letting me into the cause for your concern?'

'Listen, Fran,' he screwed his face up awkwardly. 'I like Sam—'

'No, Cormack!' she cut across him furiously. 'Stop telling me half of what I want to hear! I want the truth—plain and unvarnished—not all dressed up with praise for your friend!'

'Okay.' He ran his hand distractedly through the thick, black hair, making it even more untidy. 'He told me he was angry with you after the ball. Said you'd spoilt the evening, that's all.'

Fran nodded. Was *that* all? 'That's okay,' she said cautiously. 'I already knew that. Don't worry,' she said, and even managed a smile. 'I've let him rant on for a bit and get it out of his system. We've made it up.'

He looked at her closely with the seasoned eye of the man whose job it was to observe the behaviour of other human beings and the question seemed to come out all on its own. 'But that's not all you did, is it, Fran?'

Her feeling of relief evaporated as quickly as it had arrived. 'Are you asking me whether we had sex?'

Cormack was momentarily lost for words.

'Are you?'

'Er, yes—I suppose I am.'

'And why should it worry you so much if we did?'

He shook his head. 'It doesn't matter.'

Fran turned to him, her eyes full of distrust. 'Yes, it does. You know it does, so stop saying it doesn't! Tell me, Cormack. *Please.*' And then she aimed straight for

the jugular. 'I mean, who out of the two of us do you think needs protecting most? Me—or Sam?'

Cormack hesitated only for a moment. 'He told me that he intended to pay you back for trying to make a fool of him.'

'And how was he going to do that?'

He sighed. 'I kind of got the idea that he was going to exact a form of payment which might be a mutually enjoyable experience....' His voice tailed off rather helplessly.

She gazed at him. 'Do you mean what I think you mean, Cormack? Or are you going to spell it out for me?'

'I took it to mean that he meant making love to you, yes.'

Had it all been a charade then? The closeness and communication she had thought existed between her and Sam. Had the sweet words and tender caresses of the night been nothing more than a sham?

She shook her head and turned away from him, not wanting Cormack to be witness to the betrayal and hurt in her eyes all over again. He had witnessed it with Sholto and Sholto had been her husband. So how come this new hurt seemed to wound her as nothing had before?

She waited until she was sure the threat of tears was at bay. 'Can you give me a lift to the station?' she asked him. 'And please don't spin me a line about hadn't I better see Sam first!'

'Fran—'

'Either you will, in which case I'd like to leave right now. Or you won't, so I'd need to call a taxi. And I'd prefer not to do that!'

There was a short silence while Cormack seemed to

weigh up his options against her determination. 'I'll give you a lift,' he agreed, at last. 'If only to know that you've boarded the train safely. But leave Sam a note, Fran. Please.'

She was tempted to tell him that she was in no mood to make bargains. 'Why should I?'

'Because otherwise he'll worry and go chasing after you and presumably, that's not what you want.' His eyes gleamed with a question. 'Or is it?'

'It's the last thing on earth I want,' she lied, and picked up a pen as if it were a sword. Her hands were trembling so much that she could barely write. 'But don't worry, Cormack,' she vowed grimly. 'I'll leave him a note he'll never forget!'

CHAPTER ELEVEN

THIS time Fran didn't go half way up a mountain to stay with her friends—she flew straight back to Dublin and stayed in her flat and waited.

And carried on waiting.

Then she tried to tell herself that she wasn't waiting at all. But that anyone would expect Sam to come running, under the circumstances. Even though her note had told him never to darken her door again.

But he didn't.

Which left Fran with no option but to try to sort out the tatters of her career and ultimately, her life. When she had left Ireland, people had been cancelling assignments right, left and centre. Her savings weren't *huge*, and she fully expected to have to go trawling round the employment agencies, looking for secretarial work to tide her over.

But she quickly discovered that people had very short memories and that offers of work, if not exactly flooding in, had certainly started trickling in steadily enough to provide an income. A old friend of Cormack's wanted a twenty-first birthday party arranged for his daughter. Through that came the request to organise a corporate function.

Fran found that she had enough work to keep herself busy and occupied...but there was a great, yawning space where her heart should have been.

Several times she lifted the telephone to ring him, and each time she slammed the receiver down with deter-

mined resolution. She had spent most of her time with Sholto overlooking his various betrayals. If she had learnt one lesson from her broken marriage it was that she was *not* going to be a doormat.

It was on a Sunday morning when Fran was wakened from a heavy sleep by the loud shrilling of the doorbell. She looked at the bedside clock. It had taken her hours to drop off last night and the plus side of having no social life was that she had blissfully imagined being able to sleep until noon. Or beyond.

She groped her hand out for the sun-gold dressing gown and struggled into it just as the doorbell shrilled again, and when she opened the door, there stood Sam. She stood there just gaping at him, swamping down her instinctive feeling of pleasure at seeing him. And replacing it with one of righteous indignation.

'Yes, Sam?'

'Can I come in?'

'Last time you didn't bother asking.'

'That was then.' His mouth flattened at the corners. 'This is now.'

She thought fleetingly that he didn't sound in the least bit apologetic. She opened the door with a shrug. 'Feel free.'

His mouth flattened even more and Fran could have cursed herself for her rather unfortunate choice of words.

They stood in the hallway, facing one another like two boxers in the ring, wariness and suspicion on both their faces. But Fran noticed one emotion which was clearly etched on *his* features.

Fury.

She studied him as coolly as she knew how. 'Well?'

'Have you always had such a problem with communication?' he queried, in a voice which was even colder

than hers. 'Is that what helped your marriage to break
down?'

She stared at him, not quite understanding.

'So that whenever there's a problem in your life, you
bury your head in the sand—'

'I don't know what you're talking about!'

'By running away and refusing to discuss anything?
Is that what you used to do with Sholto?'

'You leave Sholto out of this!' she flared. 'He has
nothing to do with it!'

'Are you sure?' The blue eyes glittered. 'Aren't the
sins of the first husband being revisited on every man
who follows?'

She wasn't going to take this opportunity to point out
that he was the *only* man who had followed. 'No. You
have enough sins of your own, Sam.'

He seemed bemused. 'Then maybe you'd care to list
them. Who knows, it might save me a visit to the ana-
lyst!'

She willed her voice to stay steady, to present the facts
as clearly as she could, without resorting to hysteria.
Which is what she felt like doing. 'It's quite simple.'
She drew a deep breath. 'You were furious with me after
the Valentine ball, weren't you?'

'That's hardly a state secret, Fran! I came here to tell
you that myself if you remember!'

'And the deal was that I would come over to England
and organise your mother's birthday—to make up for
what happened?'

'That was the deal,' he agreed steadily.

'And for you to prove to me that I had fundamentally
misjudged you, and that deep down you were a wonderful human being.'

'Wonderful? Hmmm. Maybe.' His eyes challenged

her. 'The choice of adjective was yours, remember Fran.'

She shook her head. She wasn't going to let him flir with her. 'But the truth was a lot more sinister, wasn' it, Sam? In fact, you were so angry that you decided you were going to get rid of that rage in a *very basic way indeed.*'

He raised his brows. 'You mean by making love to you?'

Fran shook her head. 'Oh, please don't dress it up Certainly not for my sake! We had sex, Sam. *Sex! Sex* which you had planned. Cormack told me—'

'Cormack had no *right* to come to tell you—'

'He may not have had the *right*,' she echoed fiercely 'But I'm bloody glad that he did!'

'Words which I said to him, in confidence and *in anger*, in the heat of the moment,' he emphasised slowly 'And which were not intended for your ears. Ask your self honestly, Fran, about what happened between us tha night. It was good, wasn't it?'

She turned her head away.

'Very good?'

He caught her arm but she pushed him away.

'*Wasn't* it?'

'Yes,' she said at last, reluctantly.

'And did my actions seem like the actions of a mar motivated only by anger? Or revenge?'

No, they didn't, and that was what was confusing her 'Maybe you're good at faking it?' she suggested insult ingly.

Sam took a slow, deep inhalation of air through hi nostrils. 'I thought that was what women tended to do, he murmured.

'I meant faking affection, not orgasm!' she snapped

thinking that no woman would have to fake *anything* if they were in bed with a man like Sam. But she closed her mind to her thoughts. Too dangerous. 'You were as sweet as honey to me, Sam!' she accused. 'Luring me into your arms—'

'Don't make me out to be some sort of primitive caveman,' he said, in a weary voice. 'I got the distinct impression that you were in just the right mood to be lured.'

'That's not the point!'

'No? Then what exactly *is* your point?'

'Just that you're good at getting what you want. You wanted Rosie and you've had her—and now you've had me, too!' There was a long pause. 'Cold-bloodedly using a charm offensive to have your way with us! Just like she said!'

The pause which followed this statement was even longer.

'So you're not even going to deny it?' she questioned shrilly.

'No.'

Fran had expected emotion. A furious denial. The true story of how he had come to take Rosie's virginity. But there was nothing. Just a rather bland, disappointed look. As if he had reached the end of the line.

'Well, if that's what you really think about, then there's nothing more to be said. Is there?' He looked at her for a long, considering moment, and Fran wondered what he would have done if she had thrown herself into his arms and told him that they would forget everything which had happened in the past. And start anew.

Except that they couldn't. She knew they couldn't. The accusations lay like a great, gaping gulf between them.

'Goodbye, Fran,' he said quietly.

'Goodbye, Sam,' she answered, in a wooden voice, waiting until she could see his tall, black-haired figure striding off down the road before she allowed herself the luxury of dissolving into tears.

But the tears brought her no comfort, only the growing realization that she had made a huge mistake. She picked up the phone to try Rosie's number in London, but the line was busy.

She was standing staring out at the Dublin skyline, when the telephone started ringing and she snatched it up.

'Fran?'

Her heart sank with disappointment. No, not Sam at all. Better get used to it. 'Oh, it's you, Rosie. What do you want?'

'That's a *very* nice greeting for your oldest friend, isn't it? Especially as I know from pressing my callback button, that you've just been trying to ring me. Oh, the wonders of modern science!'

Fran didn't say anything, not right then. She needed to know the whole story about what had happened between Rosie and Sam, but she wasn't sure if she could bear to listen to it.

'Are you still there, Fran?'

'Yes. I'm still here.'

'Well, listen, I've got the *most* exciting news!'

Fran tried and failed to inject even one syllable with enthusiasm. 'Go on.'

'You know that the newspaper tried to find me my perfect man—well, they succeeded! And how! Fran, I'm *getting married*!'

There was a short pause while Fran digested this astonishing piece of news. 'But I thought...'

'What?'

'I thought you were still in love with Sam,' said Fran, from between gritted teeth.

'*Sam?*' Rosie chuckled. 'Oh, no! I *thought* I was, but I realise now that it was more a case of wounded pride, because he didn't want me the way I wanted him.' Her voice sobered suddenly. 'I suppose he told you what really happened between us?'

'Of course he didn't tell me!' said Fran icily. 'Even though I asked him, he wouldn't!'

Rosie sighed. 'That's par for the course. Loyal man. And it's been part of Sam's trouble all along. He's just too good for his own good!'

'Well, you've certainly changed your tune,' snapped Fran, thinking that there had been no mention of goodness when Rosie had first poured her heart out to her. She had had to find that out for herself... Her patience finally gave way. 'Listen, Rosie, why don't you tell me once and for all just what *did* happen between you and Sam? Only I want the truth this time.'

'What, *now*? On the telephone?'

'Unless you'd like to jump on a flight over to Dublin?'

There was a pause. 'I don't think you're going to like me very much....'

'Go on,' said Fran grimly.

'I was mad for him—we all were. But he just wasn't interested, not in me, or the others, not in anyone. He was still getting over Megan, you see. Er, you do know about his fiancée who died?'

'I do now!' said Fran furiously. 'It would have been a lot more helpful if I had known about her before, but of course it wasn't in your interests to tell me, was it, Rosie?'

'I'm sorry—'

'Just get on with the story!'

Rosie sounded even more shamefaced. 'Once I realised that he was immune to the normal feminine wiles, I decided to become his friend instead. I feel so bad about it now, Fran,' she moaned. 'The calculated, cold-blooded way I got him to rely on me as a good mate!'

Another pause.

'And?' asked Fran coldly.

'One night I got him drunk. Deliberately. Then I used every trick in the book to get him into bed. Oh, Fran, I'll never forget the look of disgust on his face the next morning. He couldn't even *remember* what had happened! I tried to get him out of my mind, but I just couldn't. And the trouble was that it was great sex, even though—'

'Please don't give me those kind of details!' shrieked Fran.

'My confidence was shot to pieces, my self-esteem at an all-time low. I felt that my life was suspended because I still wanted him so much. I just couldn't get him out of my system.' She sighed. 'The Valentine ball was my last-ditch attempt, but I knew it was hopeless, even before I saw him dancing with you. The others thought that he really liked you.'

'I actually think that he did,' said Fran sadly. 'But it's too late now.'

'Are you sure?'

Fran was not in the mood for telling Rosie that he had just left, uttering the most final-sounding goodbye she had ever heard in her life. Because she had chosen to listen to the story of a scorned woman, instead of what she knew in her heart to be true. 'Quite sure,' she said crisply.

'Fran, just let me tell you something else.'

'What?' Fran's voice was wary.

'You know he kissed you on the dance floor?'

'What about it?'

'Well, that was when I realised that there was no hope any more. And that's what made me so reckless, I think. You see, he never kissed me, Fran, not once. Even though I shared his bed for the night.'

Fran swallowed as her mind tried to work out the implications of this. No kissing. Sex without tenderness. The opposite of what she had shared with him. 'Listen, Rosie, I have to go—'

'But don't you want to hear about the man I'm going to marry?'

Perhaps she should have chosen just that moment to tell Rosie that she was probably the most insensitive person in the world, but Fran didn't have the heart. Surely one person who was hurting this badly was enough to be with?

'Not now,' she said. 'I have something l need to do.'

After she had put the phone down, she paced round the flat, trying to put herself in Sam's place. Would he have flown straight back to London? Or booked into a hotel? And if so, which hotel?

She ran over to her address book where she had all the hotels listed, and started with the best, hardly able to believe her luck when they informed her that yes, Mr. Lockhart had a reservation, and that yes, they would try to find him for her, but they thought that he might be in the process of checking out, if he hadn't already done so.

Well, she wasn't going to give him the opportunity.

'If you see him—tell him to wait!' Fran puffed.

She ran straight out of the flat and into the street where she hailed a taxi. The driver pulled over, giving

her a rather funny look and she wondered why until she realised that she was still in her gold-satin kimono! She looked down at it in horror for a moment, and then shrugged her shoulders. What the heck, she thought. This was Ireland, after all!

'Get me to the Sherbourne, quick!' she demanded. 'Break as many speed limits as you like, just don't hurt anyone on the way!'

'Right!' grinned the driver, who looked as though he had spent his entire life waiting for someone to say just that to him!

The Sherbourne was opulent and grand without being in the least bit stuffy, but even so Fran raised more than a few eyebrows as she rushed inside, tightening the gold-satin sash around her waist as she did so.

'Can I help you?' asked the receptionist, giving an almost imperceptible look of alarm in the direction of one of the burly doormen.

'I'd like to see Mr. Sam Lockhart,' said Fran. 'Please.'

'And is he expecting you?'

Fran indicated her rather unconventional attire. 'Well, hardly!'

The receptionist ran her eyes down a list in front of her. 'I think he may have already checked out—'

'So I have,' came a deep voice and Fran spun round to find a pair of sapphire eyes studying her with some bemusement.

'Sam!' she cried. 'Oh, Sam!'

The receptionist was now obviously sizing the two of them up and had decided there was no way that someone like Sam would wish to be bothered with someone like Fran.

'I'm sorry if you've been bothered, Mr. Lockhart,' she said, with a flash of her green eyes which was a little

it more familiar than it needed to be. She looked dis-
approvingly at Fran, who was hastily re-knotting the belt
n her kimono. 'I can arrange to have security come
nd—'

Sam shook his dark head. 'No, that's fine,' he smiled.
Miss Fisher and I will be sitting over there—' He ges-
ured with his head to where tables were grouped in the
gh-ceilinged foyer, where people had been drinking
orning coffee and sliding scrumptious cakes onto bone
hina plates, but were now momentarily distracted by
he sight of Fran. 'Perhaps you could arrange to have a
ray of tea sent over in a little while?'

'Certainly, sir.'

Fran felt his hand firmly grip her elbow and propel
er towards a vacant table. 'Come and sit down,' he
urmured. 'Or are you enjoying drawing this much at-
ention to yourself?'

All her courage seemed to have suddenly deserted her.
I must look a sight,' she muttered.

'A fairly distracting sight,' he agreed. 'Come on. That
able over in the corner is free, and it's right out of the
vay.'

She was glad to sink down in a chair, away from all
he curious faces. Then she forced herself to look into
he dark-blue eyes, expecting to find bitterness and re-
rimination there, but was astonished to find none. Just
hat wry, questioning look.

'You aren't angry with me any more?' she said.

'Should I be?' He settled back in the chair watchfully.
My anger is all spent, Fran. Interested is the word I
vould use to describe my reaction to seeing you here
ressed in that extraordinary outfit. No, scrub that.
. trigued.'

She took a deep breath. This wasn't going to be easy,

and neither was she expecting it to be easy. So it was important that she expressed herself in a way which made it clear that there could be no misunderstanding.

'I'm so sorry, Sam,' she said simply. 'Really, really sorry.'

If she had stood up and performed a slow and erotic striptease, Sam could not have been more surprised.

'*You're* sorry?' His eyes narrowed. 'Why?'

'For allowing myself to be drawn into this whole stupid saga—this childish quest for revenge, without bothering to find out whether it was justified.'

He digested this for a moment. 'And what's brought all this on?'

'Rosie rang me—' she bit her lip.

'And?'

'And told me the truth about your encounter with her—'

'The *whole* truth?' he frowned.

'Well, not all the gory details. She said she'd got you drunk.' She looked at him with a question in her eyes.

Sam sighed. He had tried to do the decent thing by not telling her what had really happened that night, but suddenly he realised that his well-meaning courtesy had been badly misplaced. Half-truths bred like bacteria in the fertile breeding ground of the imagination and he needed to exorcise the knock-on effects of the whole sorry incident before it did any more harm.

'She caught me at a vulnerable time,' he said slowly. 'It had been the second anniversary of Megan's death and I couldn't face the thought of going home to an empty flat. Rosie was working at Gordon-Browne with me, always the listener, always attentive. But she wasn't in-my-face, like the other four. She had become a friend. Or so I thought.'

'Yes. She said.'

'That night she insisted that I needed to get out more, said that she'd take me to a wine-bar she knew for a quick drink on the way home.'

Fran nodded.

'The quick drink turned into a long drink. A very long drink. I was already quite smashed when we got into a cab and headed for my flat. I should have eaten something and crashed out and woken up with an almighty headache, but I allowed Rosie to persuade me to drink some whisky.' His eyes were very blue and very troubled. 'I have only vague recollections of what happened during the night, but my memory of the morning is much clearer. Rosie told me that we'd made love during the night, and that she had been a virgin.' His mouth twisted with horror and pain.

'I'm not trying to absolve myself of all the blame— obviously there must have been a part of me that wanted it to happen, otherwise, I presume I wouldn't have been capable.'

'Don't!' she whispered.

'I have to, honey.' He swallowed down the self-disgust he felt. 'I tried to feel something for Rosie, but I simply couldn't. Then when she let slip that she had been determined to have me, and had manoeuvred me into that position...well, I found that I didn't even want to see her any more. From being a friend whom I relied on she became the symbol of a night when I felt I'd sunk so low, I wasn't sure I'd ever be able to rise to the surface again.'

'But you did,' she said softly.

Sam reeled, taken aback by her generosity. 'Yes, I did. But I also knew that I needed space. And solitude. After that night I decided that I was going to leave London

and leave Gordon-Browne, and work from home, and that's what I did. I said sorry and goodbye to Rosie, and that—I thought—was that. It was so long ago. I can't believe she let it fester all this time.'

Fran nodded. She suspected that Sam had little idea of his real impact on the opposite sex. She also suspected that Rosie had not exactly lived like a nun in the ensuing years. 'The most attractive thing in the world is often the thing you know you can't have.'

'You look pretty attractive to me right now,' he said softly, a question in his eyes.

She thought of what he'd said about her inability to communicate, and knew that his words had more than a grain of truth in them. 'Well, you can have me any time you want me,' she smiled softly. 'You know you can.'

He leaned across, took her hand in his and raised it to his mouth. 'Oh, Fran,' he said, and his breath felt warm and alive against her skin. 'Don't you realise that I've fallen hopelessly in love with you?'

'Oh, not *hopelessly*!' she flirted. 'Because I love you too.'

Sam felt a tug of desire so overwhelming that he felt dizzy with the anticipation of it. 'No, not hopelessly,' he murmured.

'Rosie also told me—'

He groaned. 'Oh, honey! Haven't we exhausted the subject of Rosie yet?'

'That she was getting married—'

'Well, that's nice,' he said evenly. 'In fact, that's *wonderful*—to use one of your favourite adjectives. I'm not really interested in the details—certainly not now—but we'll send them a wedding present that's simply—'

'Wonderful!' she giggled, but her eyes were wide with question. 'You aren't angry with her?'

Sam shrugged. 'What's the point? Anger is such a waste of time. And anyway, I've got the woman of my dreams.' His brows lifted in delicate query. 'At least, I *think* I have? But maybe we should go somewhere more private, and discuss the question in some detail?'

'But you've just checked out,' she objected.

'So I have.' Sam smiled, but there was hunger in his eyes as he held out a hand towards her. 'I guess that means we'd better jump in a cab and go straight back to your flat, hadn't we, honey?'

CHAPTER TWELVE

'TWINS,' said Sam slightly unsteadily. *'Twins!'*

'Well, don't sound so shocked, darling,' said Fran demurely. 'When a couple spends so much time making love without using any form of protection then a pregnancy is almost certainly on the cards, wouldn't you say?'

'But *twins*,' he said again, in a dazed voice. 'Fran, honey. Two of everything—two cots, two high chairs, two car-seats—'

'Two babies,' she reminded him.

'Are you scared?'

'Terrified. And I've never been happier!'

'Haven't you?'

She heard the faint trace of wistfulness in his voice, and knew what had caused it. In the two years since they had been married, their happiness rating seemed to have almost shot off the scale. Particularly since they had decided to make their main home on the coast, just outside Dublin, where the beautiful blue sweep of the bay lulled you into thinking you were in the Mediterranean.

'I've been so happy with you, and it just gets better and better,' she told him gently. 'And the babies will only add to that happiness.'

'I know they will.' He raised her hand to his mouth and pressed it against his lips. 'It's just that I've had you all to myself and I know that you're going to be the most fantastic mother in the world, and—'

'And what?' she prompted softly.

'I'm going to have to share you now.' He raised his dark brows. 'Is that a terrible thing to say?'

Fran grinned. 'No, it's a wonderful thing to say. It means that we communicate honestly with one another and that's more priceless than gold-dust. Besides, don't you think I've thought it, too?'

'Honestly?'

'Honestly! Don't you know that every single positive event has a negative aspect to it? Our babies are going to be the most wonderful babies ever to be born, but we'd be fools if we closed our minds to some of the things which happen when you have them.'

His eyes were tender. 'Such as?'

'Well, babies make you tired. And put you off sex—'

'Oh, really?' he teased softly.

'Well, I can't quite see that happening,' she admitted, and blushed.

'No.' He lifted her chin and looked at her with love. At the soft green sweater which made her eyes look like bay leaves, and the sexy white jeans she wore. Her hair hung shimmering almost to her waist.

Fran had recognised that she had evolved a style of dressing to balance her husband's theatrical image. Now she didn't have to do that any more. The sensible, neutral clothes had gone. She had thrown off the shackles of her former life, and she was free to just be Fran Lockhart.

'Twins!' he said again, only now the smile on his face had broken into an unfettered grin and he picked her up in his arms and began to kiss her over and over again, while outside the waves of the Irish sea lapped like music beneath them.